WINGS

OF

STONE

THE DRAGONS OF ASCAVAR, BOOK 1

J.D. MONROE

Mighty Fine Books, LLC

PO Box 956

Evans, GA 30809

Editing by Tera Cuskaden, Gayla Leath

Cover Design by Celtic Ruins Designs

Book Design by Jessica Hawke

ISBN: 978-1-944142-17-9

First Edition: February 2017

10 9 8 7 6 5 4 3 2 1

for the warrior hearts — stay fierce.

SPEAK THE LANGUAGE

The Dragons of Ascavar – the *Kadirai* – have their own language and customs. While all terms are explained in context, a reference is provided in the back of the book for your interest.

CHAPTER ONE

As the sun sank over the Nevada desert, the young dragon was troubled. By Tarek's watch, it had been nearly seven hours since the princess and her trio of guards had passed through the great portal below. Her royal entourage should have been back through the Gate and on their way home to Adamantine Rise long before now. Despite her guardians' assurances that their trip would be short and uneventful—as if they could control such things by mere willpower—there had been no sign of them.

Tarek twitched his powerful shoulders, itching to climb into the skies in search of the princess. But he could imagine the queen's reaction.

"Your duty is to protect the Gate, Tarek-ahn," she would say, strangely affectionate even with her icy, imperious demeanor. "Just as it is Surik's duty to protect my daughter. He and his men are capable."

And you are not, he added mentally. *Not anymore.* That was, of course, the implication. Wasn't that why he was here, in the parched orange desert of the human world, watching over a Gate that hadn't been breached in decades? His assignment was an insult gift-wrapped in pity from his queen, who likely felt some kind of moral obligation to keep him around without giving him any real responsibility. After all, look what had happened when he'd had a real duty.

Still, the princess was in the human realm now, which made her his responsibility, at least by proxy. And any of the Adamant Guard would be concerned if Princess Ashariah had been out of contact for this long.

Tarek turned from his vantage point atop the empty motel, boots scraping on the dry gravel scattered across the rooftop. After a moment's consideration, he tucked the long spyglass into his leather satchel and stepped onto the roof's ledge. Drawing on the ambient magic crackling in the air around him, he leaped from the third story and pulled the air in a dense cushion around his feet to protect his joints. He landed gracefully on the cracked asphalt below, then walked to the empty front office of the motel.

After entering the key code on the electronic lock, Tarek let himself into the glass-walled front office. At first glance, the Drakemont Inn looked like a normal human establishment, though quite rundown. The posters on the walls were sun-faded to indistinct pastels, advertising discounts that had ended a decade earlier. Sitting askance on the dusty reception counter was a hand-written sign that matched the intentionally misspelled marquee outside: *Under Rennovations: Open for Bizness This Winter.*

A few months ago, the signs had promised to be open by summer, and before that, in the spring. Needless to say, the Drakemont Inn had not been in business since the Stoneflight had it built nearly four decades ago, and it would continue to be under renovations for quite some time. The poor conditions and questionable grammar had their desired effect of turning away potential customers.

Behind the counter was a heavy wooden door carved with Kadirai runes. A round metal panel was mounted on the door, glowing faint purple as Tarek approached. When he pressed his palm to it, a warm current washed over his fingers and up his arm. As the spell recognized him, the panel flashed bright, and the door opened on its own.

Beyond this door was a short hallway. Straight ahead were a handful of small, austere rooms for the Gatekeepers who lived here in the human realm. A few steps past the door on the left side of the hallway was an open archway which led to a staircase that stopped abruptly at another warded door. Tarek unlocked the wards and entered the Gate chamber.

The Gate chamber was a huge room built from the silver-veined stone of Ascavar. A shimmering portal hung suspended within a tall stone arch in the center of the room. The portal reminded Tarek of water pouring over rock, with brilliant blue light shining through the translucent veil. The stone arch was engraved with glowing runes in the familiar angular script of the Kadirai.

Several long racks of wickedly sharp weapons hung on the wall on either side of the door. The adjacent wall held a carved stone shrine to the Skymother. A number of blue candles and curled paper strips with inscribed prayers were scattered across its surface. The far corner of the chamber was sectioned off with dark blue curtains mounted from the ceiling and held back by a golden cord. To call it a bedroom would have been a gross overstatement; beyond the curtains were two stiff cots where the Gatekeepers took turns getting a few hours' sleep while on watch.

Shazakh was technically on watch at the moment, standing in front of the Gate. But the younger dragon was more interested in whatever was on his smartphone than in watching the Gate. Human technology, at its distracting best. Tarek might have scolded him, if not for the fact that the princess and her guards were the first to pass through their Gate in months. Theoretically, it was ideal for their job to be slow and uneventful, but a dragon could only stay cooped up in the stone chamber for so long before getting stir-crazy. And worse, he'd called Shazakh back from leave after only a few hours off duty. When the princess wanted a break from her luxurious palace life, there was no asking the Gatekeepers if it was a convenient time to visit the human realm.

"Shazakh," Tarek said sharply. "I'm going to the skies."

The younger man looked up from the screen, his eyebrows raised. "For what?"

"The princess," he said. "She's been gone a long time."

"She's got guards," Shazakh said, wrinkling his nose.

Tarek narrowed his eyes. Shazakh had never served in Adamantine Rise. He'd been barely more than a fledgling when he was first posted on the home side of the Gate, fetching supplies from the city on a weekly basis for the Gatekeepers. After several years of cargo duty, he was promoted to guarding the Gate, but he had no sense of duty to the queen, who was an unseen face in another realm. As far as Tarek knew, Shazakh had never even drawn a sword against anyone other than a sparring partner.

"I fear something has happened," Tarek said. "I'm going to check on them." He crossed the room and snatched the phone from Shazakh's hand. The younger man scowled at him and reached for it. "Go through and tell Kaliyah you'll need backup until I return."

He sighed. "Can Kaz go? I'm exhausted."

"From what? You've been sitting down here all day," Tarek said.

Shazakh scowled at him. "Yes, because I have not slept since you called me back from my leave, after I was on duty for four days," he said. "Forgive my failings." His voice dripped with sarcasm.

Tarek narrowed his eyes and pulled his arm back as if to lob the phone through the portal.

"*Vazredakh!* I'll do it!"

"Watch your language," Tarek said. He tossed the phone high into the air. Perhaps it was childish, but he rather enjoyed the fright in Shazak's whiskey-colored eyes as he watched the phone fall. As the younger dragon fumbled for it, Tarek twisted the air around the phone to slow its fall, letting it land right in the younger man's palm. "I'll call if I see anything."

"Can't wait," Shazakh muttered.

Tarek ignored his churlish tone and left the chamber. As he walked, he peeled his shirt over his head, then knelt to tuck it into his satchel. After checking for his phone and the spyglass, he slung the bag over his shoulder and murmured, "*Barathi.*" At the magical command, the strap tightened across his chest, fitting snugly.

With preparations completed, Tarek walked out into the dying light of the evening sun. Raising his head to the sky, he felt for the subtle shift of air currents and the electric hum of magic in the air.

The hunt was on.

CHAPTER TWO

THE WOMAN IN THE BED looked nothing like her sister, but that was all Gabrielle Rojas could think of as she examined the unfortunate Jane Doe in room seven. Gabby's little sister, Anna, was thin with red hair, while her mystery patient was voluptuous with dark hair. Maybe it was all the times that Gabby had stood at the foot of Anna's bed, wondering what the hell was going to happen next. She'd seen her sister in almost every patient she'd ever cared for, from her first day of clinical rotations to her first day as a resident here at Reno General. Being in the hospital brought a certain helplessness and vulnerability, so she worked for each patient with the same ferocity she would have if it was Anna. Some people, like Jane Doe, didn't have anyone to fight for them, which left it up to Gabby.

Even under the bruising and cuts that marred her face, it was clear that the unidentified woman was beautiful. And while the nurses had placed her height at nearly five feet and eleven inches, her weight at nearly one eighty, she looked frail and tiny beneath the coiled mess of tubes and wires that lay across her.

The Jane Doe had been brought in that afternoon from just outside the city limits. No matter how much Gabby had used her signature 'Dr. Death Stare', as the night nurses called it, no one could give an explanation for her condition.

A few hours earlier, Gabby had committed the cardinal sin of ER work. While sipping her lukewarm coffee and enjoying a rare opportunity to sit down for longer than twelve seconds to complete paperwork, she'd remarked, "It sure is quiet today."

The intake nurse, Claire, had rolled her eyes, looked up from charting, and said dramatically, "Dr. Rojaaaaas," in her fake whine. "You just went and cursed us."

Nurses' superstitions had a whole bucket of truth in them. Barely ten minutes after Gabby had invoked the curse of the Q-word, they'd received the call to mobilize the trauma team. Ten minutes after that, the ambulance had arrived with her dark-haired mystery patient, and it had been a whirlwind of activity since then.

The young woman was naked as the day she was born, with deep lacerations and purple-black bruises covering most of her body. There were massive raw red patches on her back, her knees, and her palms. If she'd been found under different circumstances, Gabby would have suspected a motorcycle accident, judging by the road rash. But the EMTs swore up and down there'd been no vehicle nearby, and nothing to indicate there ever had been, like broken glass or skid marks.

Whatever it was, someone or something had seriously hurt the dark-haired beauty in room seven. The trauma team had conducted a CT scan, determined the extent of her internal injuries, and gotten the worst of her wounds cleaned and dressed to prevent infection.

Once Jane Doe was stable, Gabby and a female police officer had the grim job of an intimate exam. She collected the required evidence for a rape kit, cleaned under the woman's fingernails, collected samples of suspicious dark material around several cuts, and sent it with Officer Timmons. If someone, rather than a freak accident, was responsible for Jane Doe's condition, Gabby Rojas would see them strung up by their nuts. Both she and Officer Timmons had breathed a sigh of relief upon finding that there was no indication of sexual assault, which would have added a whole other level of nightmare to Jane Doe's situation.

Judging by the extent of her injuries, Gabby figured their Jane Doe had a good few weeks in the hospital. Though it wasn't life-threatening, she had broken several vertebrae that would eventually need stabilizing with metal pins. Once they found her family, they'd have to talk about transferring her to the wound and burn center in Las Vegas, because her skin had been ground away almost to the bone in places. Jane Doe was looking at grafts and eventually plastic surgery to minimize the scarring. She had a long road to recovery, and none of it pleasant. Once Gabby got confirmation that the team upstairs was ready, Jane Doe was headed for a room in the shock trauma unit.

"What happened to you?" Gabby murmured as she watched the young woman's chest rise and fall. The ventilator let out a rhythmic, mechanical hiss as it forced air into her lungs. The steady rhythm of the machine and the beeping monitors were strangely reassuring to Gabby. When alarms went off, throwing everything into chaos, that was a sign that things were unraveling. Steady rhythms meant everything was under control.

The only other blessing Gabby had noted was that despite her other significant injuries, Jane Doe hadn't suffered major head trauma. There was a small dark spot on the initial CT scans that she'd be keeping an eye on, but so far there were no signs of brain injury.

As if to punctuate her question, the woman gasped sharply. The heart monitor emitted a shrill alarm. The waveforms on the ventilator's monitor were all over the place. "Nurse!" Gabby called sharply, her own heart rate spiking in response. Gabby hurried to the young woman's side, pressed her fingers to the side of her throat and tilted her chin up to clear the airway. Reaching for the penlight hanging from her lanyard, Gabby pried open one of the woman's eyelids to check her responses. One eye was nearly swollen shut, with a deep cut through her eyebrow. Beneath the swollen, bruised lid was a brilliant blue eye.

Something jolted Gabby physically, as if someone grabbed her shoulders and shook her violently. Jane Doe's gaze locked on hers, pupils dilating almost to the edge of her pale blue irises. That didn't make sense. She was unconscious, with enough Fentanyl in her veins to keep her in a dreamy haze for hours.

Gabrielle froze, pinned like a butterfly in her penetrating stare. The shrill alarms faded to a distant hum. Suddenly the world went white, and she was falling, plummeting from on high like an angel falling from paradise. The sky was below her, then above her, then below her again, rotating around her in a mad whirl.

Her body pinwheeled through the air, freefalling toward the orange desert below. As she spun again, she saw a huge shadow hanging above her like a thunder cloud. But it was no cloud; the shadow was cast by a monstrous body with a serpentine neck ending in a horned head, a long lashing tail, and arched wings that spread wide to blot out the sun. Its body was silvery-white, and its eyes burned like dying stars. She felt the eyes on her, burning into her, like insects crawling into her veins and into her brain.

Then she was spinning again, and her foot caught on a rocky outcropping, sending an excruciating wrenching sensation from her ankle all the way up her spine. She stared down in horror at her twisted limb, but the shock of seeing a lavender-scaled, taloned foot instead of her familiar foot with pink toenails nearly drowned out the pain of the break.

As she fell, she crashed into rocks, claws scraping uselessly across outcroppings as momentum and gravity conspired to do the most damage possible. Her body scraped painfully across the uneven surface until she finally came to a halt.

Awareness came in explosive bursts. First a stretch of black and gray, then a flash into her body again. Everything hurt. She couldn't even lift a limb. Her eyes went to the sky, where the dragon's shadow still hung, its burning eyes on her. Something whispered in her ear, but the thundering sound of her own heart drowned it out. Then black. Then white. The unmistakable feeling of changing, of shrinking back in on herself. Then black. Deafening noise as a squalling horn brought her back. A kindly old face screaming "*oh my God John, oh my God.*"

"Dr. Rojas!"

Something shook her. Gabrielle snapped back to reality, her head spinning as she turned to see Suzanne, one of the trauma nurses holding her arm. "I, uh..."

"You took a little trip there," Suzanne said warily. "You okay?"

"I was checking her... I was..." Gabby said. She looked back to the Jane

Doe, pried up her eyelid again, but her pupil had contracted to normal size. As her heart slowed from its adrenaline-fueled sprint, she examined her own hand. Familiar golden skin, too-short nails. No scales. "I'm fine."

She was fine, but what about Jane Doe? Under the harsh glow of her penlight, something was strange. Gabby turned the light away to make sure it wasn't an illusion. The split in Jane Doe's eyebrow was closed, with puckered pink at its tapered edge on her forehead.

What the hell was going on?

There was a perfectly good explanation. Maybe she'd just seen all the blood and thought it was worse than it was.

Nope.

This was impossible. That cut had been all the way to the bone. Gabby had even made a note to the trauma team to get a plastic surgeon in to look at her face and get it stitched cleanly because of how bad it was.

But there had to be an explanation. There was always a medical explanation, even if she didn't know what it was yet. Gabby gestured to Suzanne. "I need those tests. Blood samples. Call the lab and tell them I need my blood typing now."

CHAPTER THREE

SOARING THROUGH A CLOUDLESS SKY, with the brilliant colors of sunset reflecting off his cobalt-colored wings, it was easy to see why the princess would enjoy an excursion into the human realm. From up high, the desert was a thousand shades of rich orange and red, amplified by the setting sun. But Tarek couldn't appreciate the beauty, not with the heavy burden of worry on his mind. His sharp eyes searched for signs of a struggle, for evidence of danger.

There!

He abruptly turned in a tight circle, beating his massive wings to hover as he grasped at the thin thread of magic. The Kadirai, the dragonkin of his home world, left tiny threads of magic in their wake, like the smoky white trails of the human world's airplanes. They were hard to detect, but learning to follow them had been part of his training to join the Adamant Guard.

The princess and her entourage had left a faint bronze trail made of interwoven threads. It glimmered in the air like molten metal stretched into thin filaments and gave off a faint scent, a pleasantly smoky and earthy smell. It was faint, dissipating even as he watched. It had been some time since Ashariah and her guards had passed this way.

Tarek extended his wings, reaching out with his mind to grab onto the air currents. Like all of the Kadirai, he was born with an elemental affinity; in his case, he was an air dragon, one who could harness the power of the wind. Pushing hard against the air, he propelled himself at breakneck speed through the skies. The red-orange of the desert blurred beneath him as he flew, following the thin bronze trail.

A dark splotch far below caught his attention, and he eased to a slower speed, turning in a wide spiral. The metallic scent that drifted up into his nostrils wasn't magic. It was blood. He descended, landing gracefully a few yards from the body.

As he got closer, he smelled the hint of death, a smell he knew too well from his years in the Adamant Guard. In his dragon form, his senses were enhanced beyond measure. Even with his incredible vision, he saw no movement and heard nothing but the faraway sound of road noise. The only thing he smelled was the unmistakable reek of death.

Tarek didn't believe in taking chances. Though it was exhausting to maintain his dragon form, he remained so as he approached the unmoving body. If it was Ashariah...he wouldn't be able to do this again. He could not look the queen in the eye and tell her that another of her brood was dead. He would put the blade through his own neck and spare her the shame.

The body on the ground was definitely male. Tarek felt a sense of relief mixed with guilt as he inspected the muscular frame. In death, the guardian's body had reverted to his human form. Blood pooled around the corpse and reflected the waning sunlight.

Tarek recognized the silvery-pale hair, matted to the older dragon's head with his own blood. It was Surik, who had been guarding the princess since she was barely more than a baby. He'd obviously fought to the end, holding onto his dragon form as long as possible. Though his body had shrunk and reverted to human shape, there were still glinting golden scales down his slashed back, and the hint of protruding spikes down his spine.

A jagged blade protruded from Surik's chest. Tarek moved closer.

"I am sorry, old friend," he said, his voice low and rumbling in his massive chest.

He reached out for the long dagger, his talons crossing and clacking against the metal. The pommel and guard were decorated in ornate, bejeweled carvings of flames. He squinted at the blade, trying to make out the thick-carved runes on the blade.

"*Anakh Mardahl*," he growled. For the lands of Iron. Those bastards. The inscription was the rallying cry of the Ironflight, a nation of dragons who were the long-time rival of Tarek's people, the Stoneflight. A tenuous peace had held between them for decades, but this was an act of war.

Jolted by adrenaline, Tarek snapped to attention. If Surik, one of the greatest warriors in Queen Halmerah's guard had been felled, then Ashariah and her remaining guards, both young and relatively new, faced a formidable foe. He wanted to believe that Dakhar and Halcin would see her home safely, but he would not hang Ashariah's fate on hope alone.

Tarek spared one final look at Surik. There were rituals to be conducted, pleas to the Skymother to take the fallen dragon to her honored halls. His ashes were to be taken home to Ascavar, where his body would return to the earth. But there was no time.

"I'm sorry," Tarek murmured. He maneuvered the incriminating dagger under the leather strap around his shoulder. Leaving the dead dragon behind, he took to the sky. He found Ashariah's trail once more, locking his attention onto the glimmering bronze particles.

Tarek hated being right, at least when it involved what his comrades called paranoia. He often suspected danger, but he was often wrong. But was it better to be wrong because everything was fine, or to be wrong and unprepared when everything had turned to chaos?

He flew faster, running through the scenarios in his mind. If the flame dragons of the Ironflight had attacked en masse, then the princess was surely dead. And they would be at war once again.

Tarek was struck by an image of Ashariah lying in the desert with a sword through her heart, wide blue eyes open and unseeing as they stared at him in silent accusation. It took his breath away, and he lost his focus on the trail for a moment.

You don't know yet, he reminded himself. He had to hope that she lived. Forcing down the dread twisting his guts into knots, he searched again for her trail and latched onto it like a drowning man with a life rope. The faint glimmer kept him moving, forcing his huge wings to move faster as he cut through the sky. The thread of magic drew him northwest, farther and farther from the Gate.

His entire body ached and burned with the effort of flying so fast, but he pressed forward. Reaching down into the spark of magic inside him, he manipulated the air around him to cut through the sky like an arrow from a bow.

The sun had just dipped below the horizon when a city came into sight. Neon lights threw a rainbow haze into the darkening sky, glowing against the dark backdrop of mountains.

Tarek changed tactics then, allowing his pace to slow as he wrapped the air around himself like a shimmering curtain. The mirage would hide his passage, preventing any inquisitive eyes from noticing him as he flew over the city.

Ashariah's trail was dense and strong as he approached the human development. The stronger it grew, the more crooked it grew. It was like she'd had difficulty flying, dipping low before recovering some speed for a few seconds. Then it plummeted and ended abruptly in a dark stretch of asphalt.

Tarek landed silently beside the road, following the tangled trail to its end a few feet off the roadside. Along the trail, his eyes found the bright glint of scales, the opalescent lavender of Ashariah's dragon form. The scent of blood was strong here, laced with the acrid smell of fear.

But with all the signs of her fall, there was no Ashariah. There were no footprints to indicate that she'd walked away, but there were tire treads in the soft dirt alongside the road.

Where was she?

Tarek was torn as he stood at the edge of the road. One way led back into the desert, while the other led into the city. Ashariah had been hurt somehow, likely by the Ironflight. Where were Dakhar and Halcin? He'd seen no sign of the other guards, which meant they'd either gone after Ashariah, been taken prisoner, or left for dead somewhere in the desert.

And what did the tire treads mean? Had the Ironflight resorted to human vehicles and technology? They might have driven her somewhere to hold her captive.

Reaching deep into his rapidly waning magic, Tarek called upon the air once more and tuned into his sense of smell. A thousand smells vied for his attention: the dry dust of the desert, a dozen brands of motor oil splattered and baked into the old asphalt, a sewage line a quarter mile away. Like a tiny thread in a tapestry, he found her smell; the smoky, earthy smell of her magic wrapped in the stink of fear and pain. He tugged it mentally, feeling it tug back and set him in the right direction.

With his eyes closed, he took a tentative step toward the scent. After another few steps, he peeked to see himself drawing nearer to the city. She'd gone that way, into the throng of humanity.

Ducking behind a rocky outcropping, Tarek released his hold on his dragon form. His bones ached, and his skin burned molten hot for an agonizing minute as he returned to his human form. It took longer than usual to catch his breath, thanks to his furious flight from the Gate.

The transformation left him naked as a babe, but the enchanted leather satchel was still hooked over his shoulder. The magic-enhanced strap had expanded to accommodate his large frame, while protecting the cargo inside the bag. The cool night air nipped at his bare skin, and he shivered as he took his stowed clothing from the satchel. He hurried to dress, leaning against the rock for balance as the dizzying rush of magic dissipated. With one shoe still half hanging off his foot, he broke into a brisk jog down the road toward town.

God, he hated being right.

CHAPTER FOUR

"THIS CAN'T BE RIGHT," Gabby said.

"You keep saying that," Suzanne said. "I'm just the messenger."

Gabby flipped the report over again. She'd been called back down to the ER to check out a kid who'd busted his head open trying to do skateboard tricks. After a dozen stitches and making him promise not to try any more half pipe or whatever crap he'd been doing, she'd sent him on his way with a note to miss school for a few days, much to his delight, and a brochure on concussion symptoms for his mother to watch. Upon returning to the trauma unit, Suzanne had handed over Jane Doe's bloodwork report.

Not found.

There was a yellow sticky note on top of the report with a handwritten note that said *bad sample–administer O- for now and get fresh sample ASAP.*

"Did you contaminate the sample?" Gabby asked.

Suzanne scowled in response. "You watched me do the draw, Dr. Rojas."

"You're sure you didn't get something in it?"

Suzanne planted her gloved hands on her broad hips. "How?"

Sassy attitude aside, she was right. Gabby had watched her unwrap a sterile syringe, connect it to one of Jane Doe's IVs, and draw a sample directly into the testing vial. There was no way to contaminate it.

"Okay, I believe you," Gabby said. Irritation flared in Suzanne's eyes.

The woman was an excellent nurse, but she had a Scottish temper and a stubborn streak almost as strong as Gabby's. It made her a good trauma nurse but they'd butted heads plenty of times. "Do another one."

"Doctor—"

"I'm not saying you did anything wrong," Gabby interrupted. "Maybe they spilled something or ran the machine wrong. Just do it, please. Do a fresh stick just in case so we know it's not on our end, okay?"

Suzanne sighed and walked back out of the room to get supplies to do another blood draw. Gabby turned back to inspect Jane Doe. She'd been out of the room for almost half an hour, but to look at the woman in the bed, it could have been days. Where her face had been nearly purple with bruises, some of the bruising had already spread and turned sickly greenish-yellow. The cut on her brow had healed completely, leaving a puckered pink scar. If not for the sudden break in her eyebrow, she'd never have known it was cut.

Jane Doe was not normal.

And she certainly hadn't forgotten the bizarre vision. It was probably the result of too many long shifts and too much coffee. Gabby's mother frequently warned her that all that caffeine would rot her brain and make her sick. Though Gabby was the only one of the Rojas family to go to medical school, she had to admit her mother might have a point. Sleep deprivation could cause hallucinations and other cognitive disturbances. And her vivid vision of dragons in the desert certainly qualified as a cognitive disturbance.

She'd been in the middle of tying off Cody Brown's stitches when she'd finally accepted that she'd hallucinated about being a dragon. Not just seeing one, but *being* a damn dragon, complete with wings and scales and claws.

What the hell was that all about? If she was going to have a daytime hallucination, her caffeine-saturated brain could have at least had the decency to give her a hot tub romp with the Chippendales or something else equally unbelievable as a dragon.

And as long as it had taken to wrap her brain around *dragon*, she still wasn't ready to acknowledge the part of her brain that whispered, *you know it wasn't a hallucination.* The vision didn't have the hazy, surreal feel of a dream. And it didn't slip through her fingers like sand when she thought about it, the way a fleeting hallucination would. It was solid and real, like a memory.

Which didn't make one bit of sense.

Gabby folded her arms, leaning against the counter as she watched Jane Doe. What the hell was she dealing with here? She'd always believed that there were scientific answers for everything. Even the most mysterious symptoms and illnesses had an explanation; it was simply a matter of putting the puzzle together correctly.

Some people did heal quicker than others. But no one went from bone-deep cut to completely healed in a few hours. Furthermore, every human in existence had one of four blood types. So what did that make Jane Doe?

It had to be a machine error, contamination in the sample, or maybe the technician simply made a mistake. There could have been any number of explanations. But if another came back with the same results...

"Oh wonderful," Suzanne said from outside. Gabby frowned and looked up to see the nurse standing at the door with a handsome man looming behind her. "Dr. Rojas, this is—"

"Derek," he said warmly. Well, he was a looker. Suzanne looked like she was ready to hump his leg if he held still for too long. Not that Gabby could blame her. Derek was tall and broad-shouldered, with smooth olive skin and thick dark hair that looked wind-blown in that perfectly sexy underwear model way. His body was concealed in a pair of dark jeans, a snug t-shirt, and a leather jacket, but the wiry tendons on his neck and veins on the backs of his hands told her he was shredded underneath his clothes. She could start an IV on that guy blind. That was, if she could quit staring into those amber eyes that felt like they were burning right through her skull. "I heard about your Jane Doe. I came to identify her."

"Isn't that wonderful?" Suzanne said. The dreamy tone in the nurse's voice jarred Gabby. Suzanne had been single a while, but he wasn't *that* sexy.

Okay, he really was, but being hot didn't mean he got to bypass security. And considering Jane Doe's condition, Gabby wasn't going to let some strange guy walk in and endanger her. For all she knew, he'd beaten her bloody and left her for dead, and now he was here to finish his work. Well, not on Dr. Rojas' watch. Jane Doe didn't have anyone else, so Gabby would protect her like she would have her own little sister. With rules and regulations first, and then with tooth and claw if she had to.

"Who are you?" Gabby said sharply.

Derek cocked his head. "I'm her fr—her brother."

"Which is it? Friend or brother?"

He looked confused as he extended his hand. "I'm sorry, we didn't meet properly. Thanks, Suzanne," he said. "We've got this." Suzanne smiled dreamily, then turned and walked back to the nurse's station without a second glance.

Okay, what the hell was going on? Suzanne had called for security once because a visitor left his backpack outside her station and she thought it might be a bomb.

Gabby stepped forward, regarding him warily as she put her body between him and Jane Doe. She didn't offer her hand, instead keeping her arms crossed over her chest. "Why don't we go talk outside at the nurse's station?" Out where there were other people, including a couple of armed police officers watching the attempted convenience store robber who'd managed to break his leg while robbing a gas station.

Her heart thumped, and she tried to keep from flinching as Derek took another step toward her. His hand brushed against her upper arm. Even through the dense fabric of her lab coat, she felt the burning warmth in his touch. It sent a shiver up her spine, which annoyed her to no end. She wasn't some silly girl who went all weak-kneed at the sight of an attractive man.

"Everything's fine," he said, locking his warm golden gaze on her. "This is my sister. And you don't have to worry about her now."

"What are you talking about?" There was something odd about his voice. It was sweet and warm, and she suddenly felt the warm rubbery sensation in her legs that usually came with too many glasses of white wine at happy hour. It wasn't just because he was attractive. He was doing something to her, like Jane Doe had done something to her.

His eyebrow perked. "Really, Dr....Rojas. You can release her to me." He pronounced her name wrong, pronouncing it like an English *j*. She was about to correct him, but his hand closed around her upper arm suddenly, his strong fingers digging into her bicep. "You can trust me." His amber eyes narrowed as he stared her down.

The rubbery sensation intensified, surging up through her chest and toward her head. She felt dizzy as she looked in his eyes, but his voice was far away, like someone trying to talk as she sank underwater.

He kept talking, but something far more interesting was happening. Behind the decidedly man-shaped frame, there was a shimmer in the air, like a mirage in the distance on a desert road. But the mirage had a definite shape; the shimmer was made of dark blue particles, and they hung in midair in the form of a great wingspan that filled the room. And his eyes were something to behold, glowing like the burning heart of a volcano.

Gabby reached back and put one hand on the plastic bed railing. She shook off Derek's grasp. The illusion broke, and he returned to normal. But in her mind's eye, she still saw the outstretched wings. Dragon wings. No way. "What the hell are you?"

His jaw dropped. He looked down like he was expecting to see something on his shirt, then back up at her. Then he looked over his shoulder, then back at her. "What do you mean?"

"Something insane is happening here," she said. "Start talking or I'm calling security."

CHAPTER FIVE

TAREK WINDSTRIKER HAD KNOWN FEAR in his life, having seen his life blood spilled on the ground around him before looking up at the wrong end of a dozen enemy swords. And on the day that those near-fatal wounds healed enough to allow him to stand before his queen and give his account of how he had failed to protect her eldest daughter from their enemies, he had known that fear once more. Having faced such things, he did not expect a mere human woman to bring him to his knees, at least metaphorically speaking.

But here he was.

There were not a dozen Ironflight warriors, ready to spit searing gouts of flame at him, standing between him and his princess. He was close enough to see the princess's delicate eyelashes fluttering. And the only thing standing between him and Ashariah was a human woman.

"Start talking, or I'm calling security," she ordered with the imperious confidence of a queen. If she was intimidated by him in the least, she didn't show it.

The nurse had given him no trouble. He'd shown her his ID—a well-made fake for a dragon with no records in the human world—and assured her that he was trustworthy. She'd obviously wanted more information, but a gentle push had convinced her it would be better for her to get back to work.

Thanks to the magic running in his veins, reinforced by the magic lingering in the air, he'd had no trouble persuading her.

So why was this—Gabrielle Rojas, by her name tag—resisting him so easily?

"Well?" she demanded. Her hand crept toward a plastic remote hanging on the edge of Ashariah's bed. There was a large red button on one end, and if the satellite TV he and Shazakh occasionally watched to pass the time was to be trusted, pushing that button would bring a world of trouble his way.

"Wait!" he said. It had to be because he was exhausted. A lengthy transformation, flying hundreds of miles in pursuit of Ashariah, and all of it when he was rather out of shape. That had to be it.

With his heart pounding, Tarek drew the magic of the air into himself, and reached for Gabrielle. She flinched, but he simply rested one hand on her cheek. Her dark eyes flitted to his hand as she gasped.

There was an instant moment of connection as their gazes locked. He felt the warm thrum of her life energy. His persuasive power was one that came to most of his kind as they reached maturity, though it only worked on humans. With his mind, he leaned in, pushing against her will. "You can trust me. You will release this young woman to me."

Her pupils dilated, spreading inky black all the way to the irises. But there was a resistance there, like pushing a blade through leathery hide. And he could not break through, no matter how hard he pushed. He gritted his teeth and pushed again.

Something hot and sharp lashed back at him, like a heated blade slashing his face. He recoiled, staring at her in shock. Instinctively, he reached up to check his face for blood.

With wide eyes, Gabrielle grabbed the button and pushed it. When Tarek started toward her, she planted her feet wide in front of Ashariah and threw one hand out in a *stop* motion. "Don't come any closer! Security!" she shouted.

It was absolutely inappropriate for the time and place, but there was something incredibly beautiful about Gabrielle.

"Is everything okay, Dr. Rojas?" a woman asked from behind him.

Tarek was stunned from his fixation on the woman and turned to see another woman in light blue hospital scrubs standing in the doorway with an armful of files. Her eyes were wide as she looked back and forth between Tarek and Gabrielle.

"Go call-" Gabrielle said.

"Everything's fine..." Tarek's sharp eyes searched the woman for a badge. "Carla! I am family. Dr. Rojas was just filling me in on what happened to my sister." He locked onto Carla's gaze. It took a few moments, but he found the connection to her will and pushed ever so gently.

Carla's eyes widened, and the worry that creased her features eased, smoothing into a serene expression. "Oh, how wonderful," she said, her voice lilting.

"What the hell are you doing? Carla, go call security," Gabrielle ordered.

Carla cocked her head, looking to Tarek for guidance. "Is everything all right here?"

"Carla!"

"Everything's fine," Tarek said. "You can go check on your other patients."

"I'll do that," Carla said. "I'm so glad someone is here for her."

And without so much as a glance back, Carla turned on her heel. The push only worked on humans, and then only if it was something they would be willing to do. He couldn't have forced Carla to kill Gabrielle, or to light the building on fire. But on some level, Carla did want to believe he was family, and that he was there to help. Gabrielle on the other hand...she either had some sort of natural resistance to him, or she was absolutely dead-set against releasing Ashariah into his custody.

Tarek spun around to see Gabrielle looking for more options. He was used to watching the enemy for the shifts in weight, the subtle hints at their next strike. So when Gabrielle took a tentative step toward the door, he was ready. With a graceful step and turn, he lightly kicked the door shut, then lunged forward to catch Gabrielle by the wrist. She struggled with him, with a great deal more strength than he expected from his first impression.

"Help!" The shrill voice startled him, and out of instinct, he clapped one hand over her mouth and pushed her backward until her hips bumped against the bed railing. Her eyes were wide and terrified, searching him for answers.

"I am not here to hurt you," he said in a calm, quiet voice. "And I know you don't understand, but I need to take this woman with me. It's part of my job to protect her."

"Mmph," Gabrielle said. She struggled against him, and he instinctively wrapped his arm around her, pressing her body tightly to his and trapping her arms.

She was pressed tight enough to him that he smelled the vanilla and coconut smell of shampoo from her hair and felt the smooth curve of her breasts against him. Never mind that she'd probably prefer to bite him over kiss him, but she was quite lovely, and with the spirit of a warrior at that. Her eyes were frightened, but they were not the frozen, helpless eyes of cornered prey. Her dark eyes were narrowed into a glare. There was no sign of resignation, but rather cool calculation that said he had better watch his back.

"Look, I know that this is all very strange to you, but I assure you that I will care for her and see that she makes it home safely," he said.

Gabrielle's brow furrowed, her nose wrinkling in a sneer. "Mrrph!"

What was he supposed to say? That she was fiercely protecting dragon royalty from her own guardian? The Kadirai had strict laws about maintaining secrecy when they visited the mundane world, so as not to encourage any would-be dragon slayers. Their law was *takara vhan*–keep the secret, at all costs. Normally it wasn't an issue, thanks to the ability to nudge humans into ignoring them, but that wasn't an option with Gabrielle for some inexplicable reason.

He had to do something. *Think, Tarek.*

Well, for starters, he could start thinking with his brain instead of the less intelligent parts of his anatomy. If Gabrielle were a man, then she'd already be unconscious on the ground. He couldn't bring himself to strike such a lovely face, but a carefully applied pressure on the side of her throat would leave her unconscious in a few seconds, with no ill effects.

"I'm terribly sorry," he said. Moving with the lightning-fast reflexes that had earned him his place on the Adamant Guard, he released Gabrielle long enough to spin her around roughly by the shoulders, then threw one muscular arm around her neck. She struggled in vain against him, with one hand clawing at his arm. Unfortunately for her, her warrior spirit did nothing against his size and strength.

Her other hand slammed down on the bed near Ashariah's. Her tanned fingers crawled over the princess's scraped, pale hand. Working carefully, the doctor disconnected a wire taped to her hand. Suddenly, a shrill alarm sounded.

The sound sent a chill down Tarek's spine. Gabrielle twitched against him, digging her other hand into his arm and pinching painfully through the leather jacket. Then she froze, her whole body tensing against him. A wave of electric heat slammed through her and into him, and he lost his grip on her temporarily as the energy stunned him.

Ashariah's pale hand gripped Gabrielle's wrist. Her blue eyes were open wide, staring into the distance. Overhead, a monitor showed a tiny heart symbol with a number that kept increasing. Tarek didn't know the first thing about human medicine, but with all the noise the machine was emitting, it couldn't be good.

"Tarek."

He froze. It was Gabrielle's voice, but she pronounced his name clearly, with the crisp consonants of his native tongue. And she hadn't said *Derek*, but his real name. "How do you know that name?"

"She showed me."

Chapter Six

THIS WAS SHAPING UP to be the strangest day of Gabrielle Rojas' career. First, a Jane Doe with freakishly fast healing had made her hallucinate. Then, a hot but creepy stranger had tried to sweet-talk his way into the room only to jump Gabby, but he'd been weirdly gentle, like he was trying to win a gold star for being a polite attacker. And to top it all off, she'd gotten weirdo vision number two, this one far more precise and continuous than the first.

This time she wasn't falling from the sky, but running through a huge garden of massive, colorful flowers twining around stone pillars that disappeared into the clouds. And she was definitely human, with smooth, tan skin and toes that ended in pale pink nails. She was a child, judging by her short legs and the way everything towered over her. Sapphire pants threaded with gold billowed around her legs as she ran. The grass was a strange turquoise hue, kissed by cold dew that tickled her muddy toes.

Peals of laughter echoed off the stone around her as she ran, listening for the footsteps of her pursuer. Suddenly, a male figure leaped out from behind a pillar, a familiar face with dark hair and warm amber eyes. His lips curled into a smile as he crouched low, then sprang at her. He grabbed her around the waist and spun her high overhead like she was no more than a feather.

She felt warm and safe. "Tarek!" she squealed in delight.

The man's face spread into a genuine smile as he pulled her back down and rested her on his hip. He wore a sleeveless leather tunic that showed off muscular arms that would have no trouble wielding the gleaming sword that hung in the sheath on his belt. As he carried her through the garden, bouncing lightly, he spoke in an unfamiliar language. It was harsh and precise, yet still strangely pleasant to the ear.

"*Kaare! Esa kuthra!*" he told her, pointing up to the open air above the garden. As she followed his gesture, she saw the massive scope of the garden. Rising in the distance were walls of dark gray stone, but the garden was open to the sky, with arches that met at a high point in the center. Circling overhead was a huge dragon, with the early morning light gleaming off its dark purple scales.

She felt a surge of warmth and affection, throwing out her hands in greeting to the familiar figure. "*Kuthra!*"

A shrill beeping blocked out whatever the handsome man said next. Like waking too soon from a dream, she tried to hold onto the dissolving threads of the vision, but she opened her eyes to the stark white and gray of a hospital room. "Tarek?" she said, the name unfamiliar on her tongue. He'd introduced himself as *Derek*, but this suited him.

"How do you know that name?"

"She showed me," Gabrielle murmured. He had all but released her, and she turned slowly, her back still pressed against the Jane Doe's bed as she looked up at him. His amber eyes were captivating, the rich color of clover honey.

"She showed you?" He looked as confused as she felt.

31

"Dr. Rojas?" Suzanne called from the doorway.

Gabby's heart leaped in her chest as Tarek moved aside to allow her a view of the doorway, where Suzanne stood with her hand halfway into a clean glove. Her plan to get help by setting off Jane Doe's heart monitor had worked as planned, but now she wasn't sure she needed the help. She wasn't sure what the hell was going on anymore.

Her cheeks flushed, like she'd been caught making out with a high school boyfriend. "Everything's fine," she said. "I bumped one of her monitors, nothing to worry about."

"Okay," Suzanne said. Her gaze tracked up to Derek—no, *Tarek,* Gabby mentally corrected—and regarded him suspiciously.

"Everything's fine, Suzanne," Tarek said, his voice mellow and resonant.

As before, Suzanne relaxed, and the tension flowed out of her face. "Okay," she said pleasantly. "I'll just get back to work."

"Will you close the door behind you? Please?" Tarek said politely.

"Of course, honey," Suzanne said with a broad smile. She left them, closing the door behind her.

"Okay, what did you do to her?" Gabby asked as he turned back to look at her.

"I can't really explain," he said with a pained expression.

He drew closer to Gabby, but it wasn't to touch her, which was a pity. Maybe it was the single life catching up with her, but for a split second she'd enjoyed the feel of his body, which was every bit as solid and warm as she'd guessed from her initial sizing up. Yes, she'd also been scared out of her damn mind, but that was beside the point.

Instead of pressing against her again, he stood next to her, his shoulder brushing hers as he leaned over Jane Doe. Gabby still didn't know what to make of the situation, but one thing was clear, even if it was completely absurd. Jane Doe had showed her something. As soon as she and Tarek had confronted one another, Jane Doe had reacted, like she was trying to reassure Gabby and let her know that Tarek was someone she knew and trusted.

No. That was insane.

Or was it?

"Can I approach without you attacking me?" Tarek asked.

"Me attacking you? You're the one who came in here acting sketchy," Gabby said. But she didn't move to block him. Instead, she watched as he gently leaned over the bed and brushed his fingers over Jane Doe's pale forehead. It wasn't the gentle caress of a lover, but the fierce concern of a brother or a parent. "Is she really your sister?"

"No," he said. "But I am obligated to protect her."

"What are you?"

"I don't know what you mean."

"I'm not stupid, so don't treat me like I am," Gabby said. "You're not...normal." He wasn't human. That's what she meant, but the scientific part of her couldn't quite say it, even as her mind babbled *dragon-dragon-dragon. Come on, you saw the wings yourself.*

There was a long quiet as he stared at her, his mouth half-open and his lips moving slightly as if he was trying out words and finding them lacking.

Gabby didn't know what she wanted him to say. *Yes, I'm an otherworldly creature and magic is totally a thing,* or *You've had a psychotic break and it's time for your meds.* Either way, this day had rocked her world and then some, and considering Tarek had yet to answer her question, it was probably about to get a whole lot weirder.

Gabby's heart thumped harder and harder as the silence stretched between them. The warm affection from Jane Doe's vision was evaporating as cold calculation took over. This was still a dangerous man, even if this woman trusted him.

She finally broke the silence. "Are you going to answer me? What is this? What are you?"

He flinched at the *what* and hesitated. "It would be better for you if you didn't know."

"Oh for God's sake, could you be more of a cliché? Don't give me that," she said. "That is literally never true."

Tarek frowned and leaned over Jane Doe again. His fingers lingered on one of the coils of IV tubing, one that pumped saline into her veins to keep her blood pressure up. "How badly is she hurt?"

"Nice subject change."

He turned to her, his eyes pinning her like a butterfly. "I need to know."

"She's hurt pretty bad," Gabby said. The rapid switch in his mood reminded her that only minutes ago he'd been ready to knock her out with a Special Ops-worthy sleeper hold and whisk Jane Doe right out of here.

"Clarify," he ordered.

"Extensive superficial injuries, bruising and cuts mostly. I'd think a motorcycle accident if I didn't know better. She's got a couple of vertebrae cracked, T8 and T9 specifically." He looked confused. She hesitated, then took a step toward him and pressed her fingers into the middle of his back. Even through the leather jacket, she could feel the dense muscle around his spine. Damn. Her cheeks flushed as she took a deep breath that smelled like well-oiled leather. *You're a freaking professional, Rojas, focus.* "Here. There doesn't appear to be any damage to the spinal cord, but I want to get a look in there with an MRI to be sure. Either way, I'd guess there's surgery in the future to stabilize the discs. Broken ribs, punctured lung, and virtually every joint in her right leg is shattered. Minimal head trauma, which is good."

Tarek let out a heavy sigh, then pinched the bridge of his nose like a massive headache had just hit him. He spoke quietly to Jane Doe, but Gabby couldn't make out the language.

"What is that?"

"What?"

"The language you're speaking."

"Spanish," he said automatically.

Was he even trying? She held up her name badge to his eye level. "Dr. Rojas," she said, rolling the *r* harder than her *abuela*. "You're gonna have to do better than that, *pendejo*."

"I don't have time for this, nonsense," he said. "I need to take her somewhere safe. She needs to go home."

"She's already somewhere safe," Gabby said. "And unless home is a well-equipped hospital, then absolutely not."

"She is my responsibility," Tarek said, his tone sharpening as he turned to face her. He was close enough that he had to look down to hold her gaze. "And I do not need your permission to take her."

His imperious tone struck an oft-abused nerve in Gabby. She squared her shoulders and glared up at him. "You're in my hospital, buddy. Maybe this hurts your whole *look at me, I'm the alpha male* persona, but you absolutely need my permission to take her out of here, and you're not getting it. And if it was your responsibility to protect her, then I wouldn't trust you with my houseplants."

His nostrils flared, and his eyes widened. But it wasn't anger that shadowed his features; it was something more like guilt or fear. The sudden shift made her feel strangely guilty. What soft place had she struck? Finally, he took a deep breath through gritted teeth and held it for several seconds before he spoke again. "This does not concern you. I appreciate your devotion to her care, but I will be taking her now."

"Over my dead body."

He paused. "Do not say such things. One might see them happen."

A chill of fear ran down her spine, but a rush of anger was close behind, like a spark igniting a trail of gasoline. "Did you really just threaten me?"

Tarek ignored her and walked to the other side of the bed. After inspecting the monitors briefly, he examined Jane Doe. Then he calmly unhooked one of the IV bags and laid it on the bed. Then the second.

"Stop! You don't know what you're doing," Gabby said. She hurried to stop him, but his hand closed around her wrist and held it easily away from the pole. When she tried to grab for his other hand, he caught her other wrist, pinning both wrists easily. He was crazy strong. He glared down at her.

"You are a most difficult person," he said. Like it was nothing, he grasped both of her wrists in one hand. She wasn't a petite thing, but her wrists were like twigs in his large hand.

"Imagine that, when you're trying to steal a critically injured patient," she spat. His hotness—which was considerable—didn't outweigh his psycho factor. She craned her neck to see the door, which was still closed thanks to Tarek's dreamy whammy on Suzanne. "Help! Anyone!" she shouted.

Tarek spun her around, pressing her to his chest as he covered her mouth with one hand, holding her wrists to her chest with the other. "Shh," he hissed, his lips brushing her ear.

Part of Gabby's rotations had been in a rough part of town, and her boyfriend at the time had insisted on self-defense classes. Fortunately, she'd always been a fast learner.

She threw her hips back, throwing Tarek into the plastic railing. Then she stomped down on his foot as hard as she could. He grunted, losing his hold on her long enough to let her wrench free. His hand tangled in the back of her coat, but she managed to lunge for the door and yank it open.

She stuck her head out and yelled, "Help!"

But the sight that awaited her was every bit as strange as the visions she'd had. Suzanne and Carla were sitting at the nurse's station with their heads slumped over folded arms, like they'd laid down for a nap right on top of their charts. Further down the narrow corridor, Dr. Martin lay on his back in the middle of the hallway, mouth open as he snored. Alarms blared from rooms on all sides, but there was no movement, no one responding.

What the hell?

On the opposite side of the square counter stood two strangers, seemingly the only conscious people on the floor. One was a woman with hair so pale it was nearly white, hanging in a long ponytail down her back. Her partner was a tall, broad-shouldered man with reddish-blonde hair pulled into a short ponytail. And they were both staring at her.

"There," the woman said pointing in her direction. Gabby's heart stopped dead in her chest as the white-haired woman lunged around the counter for her.

Something yanked her back by the collar. Her heart pounded as Tarek spun her around and kicked the door shut. Bending so that he was on eye level, he gripped her shoulders. "We don't have time for any more silliness," he said. "You must trust me."

Chapter Seven

Adrenaline surged through Tarek's veins. The spark of magic in his core crackled and burned as the dragon within stirred. There was a phantom twitch across his back, as if his wings were already bursting through the skin.

The two newcomers across the hall had to be Kadirai dragon-shifters like him. Their magic permeated the air, thick and electric.

Tarek was woefully underprepared. Teeth and claws were the only weapons he'd brought with him, and unless he transformed right here, he didn't even have that. He would definitely have the advantage of strength in his dragon form, but he'd be also be penned in with the low ceilings and narrow corridors. And that was assuming he survived the transformation without one of the newcomers taking advantage of his vulnerability while in transition.

No, he'd have to be clever and quick.

Tarek looked back at Gabrielle. She was frozen, staring at him with wide eyes. He could smell the fear on her. Guilt gripped him as he scanned her. He had no intention of saying so, but he'd sacrifice her in a second to rescue Ashariah. But the thought of seeing her come to harm twisted his guts into a knot. There was a warrior's soul in her, and he would not see her die if he could help it.

"Gabrielle," he said evenly as he backed up against the door to brace himself. She jumped at the sound of his voice. "Those people are here to hurt her. Probably to finish what they began. Do you want that to happen?"

She shook her head rapidly. "Of course not. Did they…" she took a shuddering breath. "Did they kill everyone?"

"I don't think so," Tarek said. "But they will kill her if they get in here. So I need you to unhook those things and help me get her out of here." The door shook at his back as something pounded against it. The jolt ran up his spine. The burning spark flared brighter as the dragon stirred, eager for the fight.

"I can't…we have to…she needs this," Gabrielle stammered. She made a sweeping gesture toward the machinery.

"Can she breathe on her own?"

Gabrielle looked at the machine. "It's only providing pressure support, but I'm not sure what will happen if we-"

"That doesn't mean anything to me," Tarek said. "She's not like you. She'll heal fast. And I trust you to take care of her." He'd intended to inspire confidence, but judging by the way her golden skin went ashen, it hadn't had the desired effect. "Get the bare essentials and be ready to move."

As he stood with his back to the door, it occurred to him that he did have a cell phone. He could call Shazakh and order him to come for backup, but even if the younger dragon flew at breakneck speed, it would take hours to get here.

The door jolted again. This time Tarek spun away from it. It had been years since he had worn the mantle of the Adamant Guard, but time had not dulled his instincts. His affection for Ashariah and his fleeting lust for the human woman evaporated like smoke in the face of cold, calculating duty. He yanked the door open to find the white-haired woman on the other side. Tarek snapped his elbow up and into her face. As she reeled, he planted his foot in her belly and sent her stumbling backward into the nurse's station.

Blood roared in his ears as he assessed the situation. Half a dozen humans lay prone, but he didn't smell death. The Ironflight intruders must have used an enchantment to lull them to sleep.

Someone seized Tarek's arm, planted a hand in his back, and hurled him bodily into the wall. As his face smashed painfully into the drywall, he squinted over his locked shoulder to see the red-haired man.

Tarek twisted against the arm bar, turning the joints in his arm nearly to a snapping point, and managed to grab the man's throat with his free hand. With Tarek's fingers digging into his delicate windpipe, the other man made an *urk* sound. His grip on Tarek's arm loosened.

Rage bubbled in Tarek's gut as he tackled the other man, wrapping his arms around his neck. With his hand tangled in the man's hair and pushing his head forward, he only had to apply enough force to snap the other man's neck. His primal instincts were clear. *Kill or be killed. Remove the threat.* He repositioned himself so he had more leverage to break through the spine.

Over the Ironflight male's shoulder, Tarek saw the white-haired woman finally regain her footing. Blood streamed from her nose, over her full lips and onto the white blouse she wore. Her hand came up with a gun. It wasn't like in the movies, though. She didn't demand her companion's release or make a pithy comment. She simply aimed and pulled the trigger. Thunder cracked, and white-hot pain ripped through his leg. There was another crack, and another lance of searing pain in his side.

Tarek grunted, his muscles seizing involuntarily at the pain. The other man shook him off and reached into his jacket. With no weapons and no room to transform, Tarek couldn't face off against two gun-wielding attackers. He was a warrior, but he wasn't bulletproof.

Instead of going after either of them, Tarek shoved the red-haired man into his partner and darted back into the hospital room. Gabrielle was standing over Ashariah, carefully laying the fluid-filled bags on the princess's chest. Her hands trembled as she disconnected a wire from a beeping monitor. "Shut up!" she told it. "I hear you, dammit."

"Is she ready?" Tarek said. The pain of the two bullets was catching up to him, throbbing in time with his racing heart. Wet heat streamed down his side. He shouldn't have hesitated when he saw the gun. He should have snapped the bastard's neck when he had the chance. *Stupid.*

"I guess. I mean, what the hell is happening?"

"No time," Tarek said. He limped past her, grabbed the metal pole with the beeping monitors, and swung it like a club into the plate glass window. The glass splintered away from the blow in a spiderweb pattern. Gabrielle shrieked in surprise, but she instinctively shielded Ashariah, spreading herself out and covering the princess's face. Tarek swung it again, and the glass exploded outward. Thank the Skymother that the emergency room was on the first floor. He dove outside onto the glass-littered sidewalk and released the tension that had been building, allowing the dragon to take over.

Finally.

CHAPTER EIGHT

UNTIL NOW, Gabby had never understood the fainting response in movies. Things had gotten progressively weirder, but she'd been able to process it until just now. Weird hallucinations, gun-toting attackers, fine. Hell, watching Tarek shatter the safety glass and jump out hadn't even fazed her. But when he threw his head back, his amber eyes burning with their own internal flame, and began to...change? That was about as much as she could take.

Her head pounded, and she felt like the ground dropped out from under her. It was only sheer stubbornness that kept her on her feet as she watched him transform.

Bluish-white light swirled around him. His handsome face seemed to split open as his skull elongated into the huge horned head of a dragon. His clothing ripped apart across his broadening frame, falling to the ground in shreds of leather and denim. He went from standing upright to crouching on all fours. Bone snapped and swelled. Through the veil of light, she could see his face contorted with agony. If she'd asked him about his pain level with her handy little chart, he'd be at a ten, no doubt. There was a sound like fabric snapping in the wind as broad wings unfurled from his back.

Jesus, Mary, and Joseph. What had she stumbled into?

"Here," Tarek said. His voice was a deep growl, a rich sound like a lion purring into a pipe organ. He was absolutely beautiful, like a sculpture come to life. His whole body was covered in jewel-like blue scales. Where his strong hands had been, there were now broad, razor-sharp claws at the end of muscular, scaled limbs. Running from the top of his head to the end of a long, swishing tail were spiked ridges.

Her gaze fell on his back left leg, which was punctured and oozing red. His blood was bright against the blue scales.

"Huh?"

"To me!" Tarek bellowed. His voice shook the remaining fragments of glass from the window frame. They fell tinkling to the ground.

The door to the hospital room flew open, revealing their two attackers. The woman was bloody-faced, and the man looked furious. The woman shouted something in a harsh language. Tarek roared back in response. The thunderous sound left Gabby's ears ringing.

The white-haired woman's eyes went wide as she took in the sight of the dragon at the window. Clearly, she hadn't been prepared for the whole dragon thing, either.

Tarek bellowed something else, but the words were buried in the rumbling growl. He reached one limb through the window and planted his claws on her shoulder.Her knees buckled under the weight. Her eyes widened at the sight of the sharp, black talon pressing hard into the white canvas of her coat. She started to protest, but as she looked up, his head poked through the window. His eyes glowed blue, and an icy wind whipped around her. Glass shattered, and thunder roared as machinery went flying. She squeezed her eyes shut as shards of glass from the broken window flew around her like jagged hail.

When the wind died down, Tarek set her back on her feet. She opened her eyes to see the room looking as if a tornado had blown through. But there was no sign of the white-haired woman or her companion. She turned to Tarek, who was making a strangely human *come here* gesture with one curved claw. He growled, then closed his eyes. When he spoke, his voice was still loud and deep, but clear. "Bring her."

She didn't question it, just kicked the locking mechanisms free on Jane Doe's bed and pushed her toward the window. Tarek moved his head, and then stuck in one big arm. He scooped Jane Doe off the bed, pressing her tight to his massive chest.

He backed away from the window. Gabrielle started to follow, but she realized he was unfurling his wings, ready to take to the sky. Without her.

She wasn't sure why, but it stung. This was utterly insane, but apparently it wasn't a fairytale. He wasn't going to sweep her off her feet and carry her away to something exciting.

"Where will you go?" she called out the window.

He growled again in response. "Can you help?"

She nodded. She didn't want trouble, but she wanted Jane Doe to be safe. And she sure didn't want to be here to take the brunt of their attackers' frustration when they recovered. And if she quit living in denial, then she could admit she wanted to see him again, if for no other reason than to find out what the hell was going on.

"I cannot carry you both," Tarek said. "Meet me?"

"Call me," Gabby said. How ridiculous was it to tell a dragon to call her?

She leaned toward the window and gestured to him. He came closer, and she grabbed the edge of Jane Doe's hospital gown. Taking a marker from her pocket, she scrawled her cell number on the hem of the gown. His head tilted as she wrote.

"You should leave," Tarek said. "They will harm you to get to me."

Gabby nodded. "Be careful."

He bowed his head to her. Even in the dragon form, his huge eyes were still that dark honey shade. They bored into her as he spoke, sending a thrill of heat down her spine. "I am grateful." There was something noble about him. Maybe it had been there all along, but she'd been distracted by the whole kidnapper vibe.

He turned in place, crouched, then launched himself into the sky with his powerful back legs. As he rose, his wings spread and caught the air. Then to her surprise, he faded, his form masked by a shimmering mirage. If she hadn't seen him go up, she'd never have known he was there. Her eyes followed the shimmering silhouette for several seconds, until she realized what was happening.

As he disappeared from sight, the magic of the moment evaporated. She slammed back to reality, where alarms were shrieking and her heart was pounding.

She had to go.

Gabby hurried to the door and peeked out. Both of their attackers lay on the ground. Propping herself up on one shaking arm, the woman patted the man's face, trying to wake him. Gabby took a tentative step out the door, but the movement caught the woman's eye. Her head snapped up, silver eyes narrowing as she got up to follow Gabby.

Oh hell. Her feet pounded on the linoleum, her ears ringing from the echoing alarms. *Please don't shoot me,* she prayed as she ran for the double doors that connected the unit to the rest of the hospital. Just inside the doors was a familiar red box. She looked over her shoulder, then yanked the fire alarm to bring security running.

Her mind raced, her heart thumping as she froze at the double doors. Her mind screamed, *run run run,* but her feet were rooted to the grungy tile. Alarms blared all around, each one the sound of a patient who was in peril with all of the staff apparently knocked unconscious or worse.

Gabby stole a glance over her shoulder. Now the man was on his feet. The pair split, one coming around the nurse's station from each direction. She bolted into the closest room. She yanked the door closed behind her, scanning the room with frantic eyes. The patient in the angled bed was a teenage girl named Laura who'd been in a three car collision. Her mother sat in a wooden chair, her head lolled back. Instinctively, Gabby ran to Laura's side and inspected the monitors.

Over her years of taking care of her chronically ill baby sister and years of residency, she'd learned how to default to cold, calculated logic. Panic had never once helped her sister Anna during an episode, and it would never help Gabby take care of a patient. Assess, plan, and execute.

She watched the monitors. Laura had sustained a head injury, and had a drain in her skull to relieve the intracranial pressure. The pressure was climbing to dangerous levels, and her blood pressure with it. Respiration was rapid, but oxygen saturation was fine. Her heart rate was climbing too, bouncing erratically. Even unconscious, her body registered pain and reacted to it. Gabby turned on her heel, focusing on each step ahead.

Glove up.

Turn off the alarm to give her some quiet.

Holy shit there are dragons.

Not now.

Adjust the valve to drain the accumulating fluid.

Something pounded against the door, rattling it in the frame. Gabby's heart skipped a beat, its rate accelerating to match Laura's. She sucked a deep breath through her nose, held it for a three count, and let it out.

Tweak the saline drip. Bolus of pain medication.

Another hard *bang* against the door.

As she watched the monitors, she peeled off one glove and reached into her pocket for her phone. She dialed 911 and waited, trying to stay calm. It sure was nice of Tarek to take off and leave her with his mess to deal with.

"911, what's your emergency?"

"I'm at Reno General. We have two shooters in the trauma unit," she said, trying to keep the creeping note of panic out of her voice.

"Okay ma'am, I want you to stay calm," the operator said. "The incident has already been called in, and we have the police headed your way. Are you all right?"

"I'm fine."

"Are you near the shooters?"

"They're outside the door," Gabby said.

"Okay," she said. "I want you to get somewhere safe if you can. Don't try to be a hero. Can you stay on the line with me?"

Gabby looked up at the monitors. The readout for the teenager's intracranial pressure was dropping steadily into the safe range. Her heart rate was normalizing, and her respiration slowed. Assess, decide, and execute. She had control over the situation.

The banging hadn't come for quite a while. With the alarms silenced, Gabby could hear the two talking outside. She didn't recognize the language, but she heard the woman say something emphatically. The man gave a short response, and then it was quiet.

"Ma'am?"

"Hold on," Gabby whispered. She crept closer to the door and pressed her ear toward the crack. From across the unit, she heard more alarms blaring. Frantic voices drew closer, and in the distance was the unmistakable sound of sirens. But she didn't hear the two attackers talking. Were they waiting right outside for her to let her guard down?

Someone knocked on the door. She jumped back and let out a shout of surprise.

"Reno Police," a voice said.

Gabby cracked the door to see a hint of a dark blue uniform. She opened it further, revealing a silver name plate. This time, she was happy to see the gun in the man's hand.

"Are you all right?"

"I need a drink," Gabby replied.

"Don't worry, we've got this under control," he said, but it didn't reassure her. She didn't know how to tell him that there were dragons in the sky, and that this was one scenario he definitely hadn't been trained for.

CHAPTER NINE

FLYING OVER THE NEON GLOW of Reno by night, Tarek was torn with indecision. Tactically speaking, the wisest course of action was to return to the Gate. But he was exhausted, and there was no way he could fly hundreds of miles with Ashariah as dead weight.

As if to remind him of his circumstances, Tarek's head spun, and he dropped into a sharp descent. He was dangerously weak, thanks to his quick pursuit across the desert and now the unwelcome presence of bullets buried in his flesh. If he was home in Adamantine Rise, he would heal quickly, but here in the human realm, he was bleeding and losing strength at an alarming rate.

Forcing his wings back, he righted his flight path and tightened his grip on Ashariah. The princess was breathing steadily, but he could hear the irregular hitch of her heartbeat. He suspected that the human medical treatment, though well-intended, had probably caused her some physical distress on top of her significant injuries.

We'll be home soon, Ashariah-tahn.

Tarek gritted his teeth and scanned the garish rainbow landscape. To his right was the glimmering streak of casinos that made up Reno's Strip. He definitely didn't need that kind of crowd. He wheeled around, looking toward the edge of the city. His gaze fell on the familiar green sign of a chain motel.

A few hours rest and recuperation would do him good, and at least ensure that he could make it back across the desert to the Gate, where he could pass Ashariah off into more capable hands.

Tarek slowly descended, using all his willpower to keep himself in flight while maintaining the mirage-like concealment around himself. His wing stroke faltered as he neared the ground, and he made an awkward landing in the open parking lot behind the hotel.

After a moment to catch his breath, he surveyed the parking lot. There were a handful of cars in the lot. Windows were illuminated in a haphazard pattern along the two levels of the motel. Tarek maintained his dragon form and followed his keen sense of smell toward one side of the L-shaped building. He smelled the scents of life—human sweat, someone having sex in the corner room, and greasy Chinese food a few doors down.

A room toward the corner was empty. He smelled only the fading scent of bleach and cleaning products. Keeping his illusion up, Tarek took a long jump across the lot, catching the air to lift him in a gentle arc.

He focused his energy on his hearing instead now, listening for signs of life. The amorous couple was definitely in the next room, and they were having a quite a time by the sound of it. The TV was on, playing a sports broadcast two doors down. Room 112 was empty and silent. Good.

Tarek shifted Ashariah into one arm, wrapped his claws around the handle and snapped it off easily. He bumped the door open, then laid Ashariah down as gently as possible in front of the door. After checking that no witnesses were around to see him, he wrapped his wings around himself and released his hold on the dragon. Heat burst through him as his bones broke and reshaped themselves.

When the pain of the transformation had passed, leaving him trembling on his knees on the concrete, he realized several things. His clothing was in shreds outside of Gabrielle's hospital. Without his magical illusion to conceal him, he was bare-assed to the whole world. The second realization came as the cold night air nipped at his bare skin. His back and leg felt like they were on fire. Adrenaline and flight had helped him ignore the two gunshot wounds, but now his body was catching up on lost time.

He knelt to pick up Ashariah and let out a groan of effort as he picked her up. The princess didn't stir as he hauled her into the empty room and deposited her on the bed. The bags of medicine and tubes were tangled in a knot on her stomach.

He slammed the door and leaned against it as he regarded the princess. She should have been clothed in finery and jewels instead of a wash-worn hospital gown. An unkind thought crossed his mind. *If I'd been protecting you, this wouldn't have happened.* But was that true? He'd done no better to protect her elder sister, so what made him think he could have fared better?

Along the hem of the faded gown was a series of numbers. He'd barely noticed in the tumult that Gabrielle had left her phone number. He didn't want to involve her more than he already had, but he could use the help. He had no clothes and no money. And judging by the bloody footprints he'd left heading into the room, he needed a doctor's attention.

He sighed in resignation and went to the phone.

CHAPTER TEN

SHE HAD TO CALL her mother and her sister. By the time Gabby merged onto the highway to get away from the insanity, the radio announcers had interrupted their usual commercial-free block with a report of an active shooter at Reno General. If Maria Rojas heard the news report, she'd turn from a staunch Roman Catholic to a worrying Jewish mother in a nanosecond.

Once the Reno police had declared the hospital situation contained, Gabby had been ushered off to a staff lounge to answer questions for a harried-looking investigator. She'd answered all his questions the best she could, except for the blown out windows and the conspicuously empty bed in room seven. When any of Detective Bennett's questions veered in that direction, she chalked it up to stress turning her memory to Swiss cheese. Still, it wouldn't be long before someone realized that their Jane Doe, the topic of much discussion around the hospital over the course of the day, had simply disappeared.

But for now, the chaos would keep everyone distracted. The police were sweeping the hospital for the shooters. Meanwhile, there were seven staff, four patients, and six visitors who'd been affected by an unknown substance. They'd all been admitted to be evaluated for poisons and other toxins. Emergency services was redirecting all but the most critical patients to other area hospitals while Reno General pulled nurses from around the hospital and brought in off-duty ER physicians to cover for the rest of the evening shift.

Once she'd given report to the frazzled staff who'd arrived in the middle of the chaos, Gabby collected her bag and hurried out of the hospital before someone started asking her more questions.

There was a part of her that felt guilty at bolting like she had, leaving her patients behind. She always worried when she left for the day. They were in the hands of capable doctors, many of whom had far more experience than Gabby. Still, there was a certain sense of reassurance about knowing that she was there to make the right decisions. She would worry about Laura, and whether the night nurses would carefully watch her pressure numbers for signs of trouble. She hadn't quite mastered the art of "turning it off" when she left the hospital like some of her colleagues.

But today, it was easier than it usually was. For one, barely an hour ago, she'd watched Tarek jump through a window and transform into an actual, honest-to-goodness dragon. Scales, wings, teeth and everything. And then he'd just taken to the sky and flown away like it was the most normal thing in the world.

Where had he flown off to? How was Jane Doe? Had she done the right thing in letting him take her? And who the hell was she kidding? If the guy could turn into a ten-foot tall dragon, who was *letting* him do anything?

And while she was on the topic of wonder, how long was it going to be until her nervous breakdown was complete? Because the day had been about as insane as it could possibly be. How exactly did one go back to normal after watching a human man turn into a dragon?

Her phone vibrated, then emitted a shrill ring. She activated the car's hands-free system. "Hello?"

There was a pause. "Gabrielle?"

The rich voice belonged to Tarek. Her heart fluttered as she pictured him holding the phone, his amber eyes serious. She mentally reprimanded herself. This was *not* an appropriate reaction to the situation, no matter how dreamy those eyes were. "Tarek?"

He sighed, audibly relieved. "Yes. I got her to a hotel. I don't like to ask for help, but I have to admit that I could use it, and you're the only person I can ask at the moment. Could I impose upon you?"

To her surprise, excitement bubbled up inside her. She knew she shouldn't want to get involved, but there was an undeniable magnetism that made her want to be close to him again. "What do you need?"

"Clothes," he said. "I sort of lost mine."

Oh my.

Nope. She was *not* going to imagine what he looked like naked, because there was no doubt that it was a sight to behold. Whoops. Too late. "Okay," she said, hoping her voice sounded normal. "Anything else?'

"I, um...well, I've been shot," he said matter-of-factly. "Twice."

"*Dios mio*," she muttered. "Where are you?"

Ten minutes later she made it through an unexpected snarl of late-night traffic and parked at the back of the Target shopping center. She sat in her parked car for a few minutes and stared at the glowing red bullseye as she asked herself, *what the hell are you doing?*

Was she really doing this? Was she really involving herself in this situation instead of chalking it up as the utter insanity that it was? If her mother knew that she was about to walk into a store and spend her hard-earned money on first aid and new clothes for a strange man who had split his open turning into a *dragon*—because God forbid she forget that part—then she would have a heart attack.

"Mom," Gabby murmured. She reached for the phone and found *Missed Call (3)* glaring across her screen. Shit. It must have come through while she was on the handsfree trying to tell Tarek how to keep Jane Doe stabilized and position her so her back and neck were protected. She thumbed past the notification and searched through her contacts until she landed on *Mom*. She stepped out of the car, relishing the cool night air on her face as the phone rang.

Her mother answered halfway through the first ring. "Jesus, Mary, and Joseph, Gabrielle, why didn't you answer when I called?" Her mother's voice was deep and smoky. Her English was precise, but heavily accented. "I saw the news and I ..."

"I'm fine, Mama," she said. She hated to lie but she knew she'd be on the phone for an hour giving her mother all the details if she told the truth. "I had already left work when it happened."

Her mother sighed heavily. "Thank the Lord," she said. "I was so worried. Anna and I watched it on the television and she said it was in your office."

My unit, she mentally corrected. "How is Anna? Can I talk to her?"

"She already fell asleep. Her new medicine makes her sleep a lot. She wanted me to wake her when I heard from you."

Anna's diagnosis of cystic fibrosis meant years of hospital visits, taking dozens of pills a day, scares with infections and the extreme precautions to avoid illness, all of which had taken a toll on their family. Their father had taken off when they were kids and had a new family down in Florida, which was a source of much bitterness for Gabby and her mother. As if she hadn't been dealt a tough enough hand, Anna's liver had begun to fail in the last few years, and she'd returned home to live with Mom while treating it.

Gabby knew better than anyone what Anna's prognosis was. She tried to keep things positive by bringing home news of research and experimental treatments that were improving outcomes for CF patients, but the fact was that Anna's life expectancy was drastically shortened, and at thirty-one, she was already on borrowed time. With the liver difficulties, her chances were poor, and she was a low priority for a transplant.

"Don't wake her," Gabby said. "I'll text her, and she can call me later if she wakes up. Are you doing okay?"

Her mother paused. "She is struggling. So am I. Are you still coming home to see us this weekend?"

"Of course," Gabby said. She glanced at her watch. It had already been twenty minutes since she'd spoken to Tarek. Time was of the essence in dealing with a gunshot wound. Then again, he wasn't exactly her average patient. If he'd managed to fly across town carrying an unconscious woman, he wasn't exactly going to die if she took another few minutes to chat. "Listen, Mama, I just wanted to tell you I was all right. But I have to go,

"Okay, *mija*. Get some sleep," she said. "You sound tired."

It wouldn't have mattered if she'd just woken from a full night's sleep; her mother would always think she sounded tired. And if she was at home, her mother wouldn't rest until Gabby had a plate of home cooked food in her hands and another covered in tinfoil to take home. "*Te quiero*," Gabby said.

"*Te quiero mucho*," her mother said.

Gabby let out a sigh as she hung up the call. Back into the fray.

CHAPTER ELEVEN

WHERE WAS SHE? Had she forgotten him? Tarek sat awkwardly in the lumpy chair across from Ashariah's bed staring at the phone. Now that the adrenaline of his transformation and flight had worn off, his back and leg throbbed, and he had a ferocious headache.

Furthermore, he was beginning to doubt his decision to take Ashariah away from the hospital. She was still breathing, but her usually golden skin was the dead white of the rough pillow under her head, and her chest movements were slow and shallow. A familiar dread washed over him as he contemplated standing before Halmerah to tell her that he had lost her only surviving child. His mouth went dry, his stomach tying in a tight knot.

But he'd had to do something, hadn't he? With the Ironflight on the attack, she wasn't safe in the care of the humans. He wasn't much of an improvement, but at least he knew what he was up against. Regardless of their numbers and advanced technology, the humans were no match for a full cadre of Ironflight dragons, who would burn the hospital down to charred rubble and slag metal just to be thorough.

His phone rattled noisily on the glass pane atop the nightstand. He jumped up, instantly regretting the motion as lightning struck from heel to hip in his wounded leg. Balancing instead on his good leg, he answered it. "Hello?"

"Um…Tarek? Where are you?" The sound of Gabrielle's voice, warm and inviting even as she questioned, sent a shiver down his spine. *Focus, Tarek.*

"Uh," he said. He gathered the small towel around his waist with one hand and hobbled to the door. He pulled it open and poked his head out to see Gabrielle standing on the opposite end of the parking lot. "Turn around."

She turned slowly. Her eyes widened when she noticed him waving at her. Her eyes raked over him for a moment before she snapped back to attention and hurried toward him. He ducked back into the room and held the door open for her.

He caught a hint of mint and the strong smell of coffee as she bustled in. She was still dressed in her pale blue hospital scrubs. She carried a bright pink gym bag over one shoulder, and held clusters of white shopping bags in either hand. She glanced up at him, then tore her eyes away again.

"I have clothes for you," she said.

"Oh, good," he said. He released the towel. "Which bag?"

She turned back toward him and let out a hiccupping sound. Her eyes were pinned to his crotch. To his surprise, she actually covered her eyes. He looked down and asked, "What?"

"Put that away," she scolded.

"Are you going to fix me?"

"Fix you?"

"I'm wounded," he said. He turned to show her the bullet wounds; one high on his right side, and the other in the back of his leg. "That's why I called you, remember?"

"Oh," she said. Her cheeks flushed bright red. "*Oh.*"

"What did you think I meant?"

"Nothing," she said. She murmured something under her breath, but he didn't quite make it out. After depositing her bags on the floor at the foot of the empty bed, she hurried to the bathroom and turned on the water. Under the harsh fluorescent light, he could see the feverish flush to her cheeks. She was embarrassed. Was it him?

He caught a glimpse of himself in the mirror. Being Kadirai meant frequent transformations between human and dragon form. Clothes didn't survive, so he was used to being naked both before and after the transformation. It didn't bother his kind, but something about him had Gabrielle flustered. The younger dragons under his command bragged constantly about how human women fawned over them on their trips into the city. Was he displeasing to look at by human standards? He frowned, feeling oddly self-conscious as he examined his reflection.

The door opened again, and he jumped in surprise, hoping she hadn't caught him checking himself out in the mirror. She pointedly ignored him and walked past with a stack of white towels in her arms. After dumping the towels on the empty bed, she took a box of rubber gloves from one of the bags and removed a pair. As if she'd forgotten he existed, she began looking over Ashariah.

As the doctor inspected the princess, Tarek's gaze was drawn to her. Her long dark hair was pulled into a ponytail that waved gently, revealing the graceful line of her neck. Her brown eyes were concerned, squinting under furrowed brows as she pressed a stethoscope into the princess's chest. She checked her eyelids, shining a bright light into each of her eyes. Her touch was gentle as she moved around, then pressed her thumb into the sole of Ashariah's foot. The princess twitched her toes. That seemed to satisfy Gabrielle. She rearranged the flimsy gown, then carefully covered her with the sheet again.

He could have watched her all day. With the way she worked around Ashariah, it surprised him that she had no idea who she cared for. The woman in her bed was a princess of the Stoneflight, the daughter of the renowned and feared Queen Halmerah, arguably the most powerful of the dragon queens. The position of court healer, the one who normally would have cared for the princess, was a coveted and respected position, yet Gabrielle had no idea. Though he had barely met the woman, he knew with absolute certainty that she would have given the same care to anyone she met.

"What's her name?" Gabrielle asked.

The sound of her voice after so much quiet startled Tarek. He shifted uncomfortably, biting back the pain so she wouldn't hear it in his voice. "Ashariah."

"Ashariah," she murmured. "All this time, I've been calling her Jane Doe. It's a beautiful name."

"You say it beautifully," he said, suddenly feeling bold. It sounded natural on her tongue, the way her voice lilted and clipped the r.

She looked at him strangely. Under her analytical gaze, he felt even more naked. He couldn't read her expression. Was she baffled, intrigued, or utterly uninterested? As if she'd only just remembered him, she shook herself. "Let's have a look at you."

She sidestepped him and shook out a towel on the bed. "Lay down," she said. Her arms were folded across her chest as he stood. Again, her eyes traced the lines of his body. She offered him her hand as he stood, but he gritted his teeth and managed to flop ungracefully onto the bed. There was something oddly vulnerable about lying on his belly, his entire body exposed to this strange human woman that had him so off-balance. He jumped in surprise when her hand brushed over his back. They moved dangerously close to the scars across his back.

"Did that hurt?"

"You surprised me, that's all," he said.

"Sorry."

Her fingers were gentle and feather-light, touching the tender area around the bullet wound. "With you being...uh...what you are..."

"Kadirai."

"Okay, so that completely didn't answer my question," she said.

"It's what I am," he said. "The word means *children* in my native tongue." In ceremonial settings, the dragon shifters were referred to as *kadirai dar Isina*, the children of the Skymother.

"Getting closer. You're a..." She sighed. "I cannot believe I'm saying this. You're a dragon."

"Yes," he said. She'd already seen him transform, so what was the point of trying to lie his way around it? When the situation had been dealt with, and Ashariah was safely home, then he would return and gently push Gabrielle's mind. It would be just enough that she would think she had dreamed the whole thing.

"Do you heal faster?"

"Than you, yes. But my healing is still slow here. How do you know that?"

"Her," Gabrielle said. "I took care of her from the moment she was brought in. Some of her wounds showed days' worth of healing in a couple of hours." She patted his shoulder and said, "Okay, this is gonna be cold." He braced himself, but it was merely a cold touch of metal on his shoulder blade. "Take a breath." He obliged. She moved the metal. "Again." They repeated the process several times. Whatever she was looking for, she seemed satisfied. "I have good news and bad news."

"Okay."

"The good news is that the bullet is kinda wedged between your ribs. It didn't affect your lungs at all. I can get it out."

"And the bad news?"

"Bad news is that I have needle and thread, but nothing to numb it. If you want it to not hurt, then it'll take me another few hours to go back to the hospital for supplies."

"Do what you have to," he said. "I trust you."

"I'm going to quote you on that in a few minutes."

CHAPTER TWELVE

IT TOOK GABBY a few solid deep breaths to get past the sight of Tarek naked. Her imagination hadn't even come close to doing it justice. Yes, she was a doctor, and she saw people of all shapes and sizes in various states of undress. That was detached and clinical, like this should have been. But it was safe to say she'd never seen someone like him on the table. Thankfully, she'd had the presence of mind to cover his bare ass while she inspected the bullet wound on his back, but there was plenty more for her to look at.

His skin was golden tan, and strangely smooth. His broad shoulders were thickly muscled, joining the gentle slope of his back. It took a considerable amount of willpower not to run her finger along the carved line where muscle met along his spine, as precise and smooth as if it had been worked from marble over months of chiseling and polishing. Spreading across the planes of both his shoulder blades were old scars. Slightly raised, they had the rough texture of burns, but they blended into his coppery skin.

And for a man who'd probably been sweating and marinating in adrenaline, he smelled strangely good. Maybe dragon-dudes emitted a pheromone that appealed to female doctors who worked too many hours to date.

Focus, Gabby. You're a professional.

She emptied the closest shopping bag. A soft peach terrycloth robe tumbled out in a heap. She reached over and set it neatly on Ashariah's bed for later. The rest of the bags contained first aid supplies and a sewing kit. Doctors no longer carried the iconic black bags she used to see on TV as a kid. Even so, she always kept a large toiletry bag in her car stocked with basic first aid and over the counter medications, thanks to a worrying mother who had ingrained in her from a young age that it was always better to be prepared. But Gabby was prepared for the occasional scrape or upset stomach, not stitching up a gunshot wound.

Trying not to think too hard about the naked man—*dragon*—inches from her, Gabby spread out a towel and arranged her supplies: large bottles of sterile alcohol and hydrogen peroxide, gauze pads, and a sewing kit. After taking a needle from the sewing kit, she threaded it with a double length of black thread. She added a glass from the ice bucket set and poured an inch of alcohol into it. After tearing open the blister pack, she put a pair of oversized tweezers into the alcohol. Finally, she changed gloves and regarded Tarek. He was oddly calm as he watched over his shoulder. His eyes met hers, sending a shock down her spine. God, he was gorgeous. And naked. It was kind of impossible to ignore.

With her hands trembling a little, she grabbed the bottle of alcohol. "This might sting," she said. She took a breath and doused the wound on his back.

His back arched as he sucked air through his teeth. But he was silent and stoic as she gently dabbed away the dried blood encrusting the bullet wound. The entry wound was a neat hole. Lodged against his ribs, the bullet had simply flattened and stayed put. It was an ideal situation.

"Where are you from?" she asked. She took the tweezers from the glass of alcohol and eyeballed the wound, trying to mentally plan the angle she'd use to get it out.

"It's better for you to know as little as possible."

She scowled at the back of his head and nipped her tweezers at him. "You called *me*," she said. "And I should bill in the thousands for a visit like this. You're getting off cheap. Hold on." With a deep breath to steady her hands, she used the tweezers to grab the bullet. He jumped a little in surprise. She squeezed tight on the tweezers and maneuvered the bullet out as carefully as she could. Fresh blood bubbled up from the wound.

He groaned, an insistent sound that said he wanted to shout obscenities but was too polite. She ignored him, grabbed one of the washcloths, and pressed it hard to the wound to soak up the blood. With her other hand she held the bullet in front of him. "One down. So?"

He sighed. "You are very insistent."

After a few seconds, she took the washcloth away and inspected the wound. It was relatively clean, although he'd certainly dislike what came next. She doused the open wound with hydrogen peroxide. He groaned again, and shifted his shoulder slightly like he was trying to get away from the burning sting.

"I'm sorry," she said.

"It's all right," he said, his voice strained.

Before she realized what she was doing, she peeled off her right glove and stroked the back of his shoulder, relishing the warmth of his skin underneath. His skin pebbled with goosebumps at her touch. The tension in his muscles relaxed, and he flattened onto the bed. As her fingers traced the fine lines of his back, her gaze was drawn to the curve of his neck, the way his dark hair curled slightly at the nape.

Her cheeks flushed at the thought of twining her fingers into his hair. This certainly did not fall under the umbrella of good bedside manner. She cleared her throat and put on a clean glove. "Well, now that I see it, I think you'll be all right without stitches," she said. "So that's a plus."

"Oh," he murmured. "Good."

After packing several pads of gauze tight against the wound, she taped it thoroughly. Satisfied with her work, she moved on to the second shot. It had struck him high in the thigh, and considering he was still alive, it hadn't hit the femoral artery. The movies always showed people getting hit in the chest or the throat, but the leg was every bit as dangerous, with a thick artery running down each thigh close to the groin. A wound to the femoral artery would bleed out in a matter of minutes if not treated.

"So you never answered my question," she said as she moved down to check the wound. She folded the towel up a bit, revealing the subtle curve of his glutes. Wow. Her cheeks flushed again as she realized how well-built he was.

"I come from a place called Ascavar," he said. She readied the alcohol. "Though I currently live in your—ouch!"

"Sorry," she said. "Continue." She dabbed away the fresh blood and inspected the wound. The bullet was buried in the dense muscle, and she could only see a glint of it through the glistening red. "What is Ascavar? A city?"

"A whole world," he said.

As she inspected the wound, she wished again for a local anesthetic. This was going to hurt like hell. "So you're from another planet?"

"Not precisely," he said. "Well, in a manner of speaking. It's hard to explain. I barely understand it."

"Sorry," she said. She gritted her teeth and grabbed the glint of metal. Her distraction technique wasn't going to work here. "Gotta pull." The muscles in his back shifted, coming into sharp relief as he clenched his fists. Fresh blood bubbled from the wound as she extricated the second bullet. He groaned again. "So how did you get here?"

He was silent for a long stretch. Finally, he took a hitching breath and spoke. "Through a gateway," he said. He sounded tired as he spoke. She couldn't blame him.

"So in Ascavar, everyone is like you? Are they all dragons?"

"No," he said. She readied the peroxide and waited for him to speak. "Only the most powerful are Kadirai. There are others who can change their form, but into lesser creatures. Most cannot change at all." He breathed heavily as the peroxide finished bubbling.

"People like me?"

"I'm not so sure."

She paused with a stack of gauze in her hand. "What do you mean?"

"I think you are more than you seem."

She continued bandaging, making sure to pack the wound tight. When she had finished, she realized she'd been holding her breath. "How so?"

He propped himself up on his elbow, finally turning to look at her. His amber eyes seemed to drill into her. "You have a warrior's heart."

She snorted derisively. "Not me. I'm a wuss."

"A wuss?"

"A coward," she said. "I'm not brave."

He raised an eyebrow and flipped over onto his back. The towel didn't quite make it with him, giving her an up close view of his equipment. His eyebrows perked as he followed her gaze down to his groin. With a little cough, he snagged a pillow to cover himself. Still, the glimpse had been enough to set her mind spinning. It wasn't like she wanted to jump his bones right there, but most of the time when she was sitting in bed with a naked man, it was headed somewhere.

Resting his elbows on the pillow, he shook his head. "You are certainly not a coward." He chuckled. "You were ready to fight me off to protect her."

"That's my job."

"See? Warrior's heart."

What was it about him? She still wasn't entirely convinced that they were both sane, but she liked the way he described her. The way he spoke to her wasn't flattery, the slimy insincerity so many men used in attempts to disarm her and get close. The way he spoke was matter-of-fact, as simple as if he'd told her she had brown eyes.

She cleared her throat. "Who is she to you? Not your sister, I don't think."

"She is a princess. The daughter of a queen."

She stared at Asharah for a long time then. All of it was hard, almost impossible to believe. But she'd seen him transform with her own eyes, and she couldn't deny hard evidence like that. And if she could accept that, then it wasn't so much of a reach to believe that there were other worlds, and that in one of them, this lovely, young Jane Doe was a princess.

Like she'd taken the last of her waning energy to accept what Tarek had told her, her body suddenly felt heavy and exhausted as the last of her adrenaline ran out. She slumped. "I should probably get going."

Tarek's brow furrowed. Maybe she was a silly little girl, but the look of disappointment made her heart soar. "Would you stay? In case something happens? With Ashariah, I mean."

Did she want to go? There was a part of her that wanted to sleep off the craziness of the day and wake up to a world that was orderly and predictable, just as she liked it. And yet, there was another part of her that wanted to stay in Tarek's presence, in the presence of something so foreign and utterly magical that she'd never even imagined it was possible.

She nodded, too quickly to be cool or casual. "I'll change. And you have to put on clothes."

CHAPTER THIRTEEN

WHILE GABRIELLE SHOWERED, Tarek rooted through the bags she'd brought him. Inside there were some strange, thin black pants that made a rustling sound when he shook them. There were a few t-shirts—his size, which impressed him—and two pairs of blue jeans. She'd brought a pair of rubber shoes, which wouldn't do much to replace his nice leather boots, but that was his fault for changing on the fly and not taking care of his things.

He winced in pain as he bent at the waist and flexed his injured leg to pull on a pair of boxers. Raising his arm to put on a shirt reminded him of how his attacker had nearly wrenched his shoulder out of its socket. The joint caught, and he found himself stuck with one arm overhead, a sharp pain throbbing in time with his heart. When the bathroom door opened, he was still sitting on the edge of the bed with his arm tangled in the shirt and his head halfway through the neck opening.

Gabrielle emerged, wearing a pair of form-fitting black pants and a turquoise t-shirt. Through the stretched neck of the undershirt, Tarek gazed at her appreciatively, taking in the sight of her lush curves that were thoroughly accentuated by the snug pants. It afforded him a much finer view of her body than her loose hospital clothes had. She caught his eye and burst out laughing.

Had she caught him inspecting her? His cheeks flushed as he retorted,

"What?"

"I'm sorry," she said. Her lips were still curved up in a smile as she composed herself. He realized it was the first time he'd seen the expression, and he quite liked it. There were little fine creases around her eyes, and a faint indentation on her left cheek as she smiled. He could have watched it all day. "Very unprofessional of me. Do you need help?"

"Yes. My shoulder," he muttered. She approached him, and with her came a rush of clean floral scent. He tried to maintain his composure as she got close enough to brush against him. Her hands were gentle but strong as she took his arm and pulled it up high. She gently pushed on his shoulder joint with one hand. There was an audible *pop*. A fleeting moment of pain gave way to a warm relief.

As she pulled the shirt down over his chest, her hand brushed against his stomach and grazed his groin. She didn't seem to notice, but his body certainly did. Heat surged down his spine and pooled in his groin. He shifted uncomfortably and nodded to her. "Thank you."

She nodded back. "Would you mind if I..." She gestured to Ashariah and held up a fuzzy orange robe. "I thought it would be nice for her to have something other than that ugly hospital gown."

And yet again, she surprised him.

"Help me," she ordered. She gently lifted each of Ashariah's arms, peeling away the flimsy hospital garment. Tarek averted his eyes from the princess's naked body. "It's okay. I won't tell anyone."

"I cannot," he said.

She sighed. "*Dios mio*," she muttered. "You're not a perv, or something."

"Of course not," he protested. "But she is the princess. And I certainly should not see her in this state."

"You were just walking around naked twenty minutes ago."

"Yes, and that was my choice. I cannot see her this way without her permission."

She rolled her eyes at him. "I have to give you credit for sticking to your principles. Close your eyes, then."

He complied, instead listening to the quiet rustle of fabric against skin. A few minutes later, Gabrielle tapped him on the shoulder. He peeked to see her standing over him with her arms folded. He craned his neck to see Ashariah wearing the softer robe, belted with a neat bow around her waist, with a pillow propped under her head and one under each arm.

"Is she all right?"

"That's relative," Gabrielle said. "She's stable, so there's that." She looked around, then headed for the stiff chair near the door. As she started to sit back in it, Tarek shook his head.

"You should lie down here," he said, gesturing to the bed. "I'll take the chair."

She shook her head. "You got shot. You should sleep in the bed."

"You could lie with me."

Her eyes widened. "I, uh...um..."

Her cheeks flushed high, with bright spots of red on her full cheeks. "Not like that," he said. "I would not touch you." She flinched. *Vazredakh, fool of a dragon.* He might as well insult her outright. "I only mean to say that you would be safe."

75

She looked longingly at the bed, then down at the chair. After a long hesitation, she nodded and crossed the room. "This is crazy," she said to herself more than to him. She sat cross-legged on the edge of the bed, her weight shifting slightly and bringing his legs to rest against hers.

"You asked me questions, now may I ask you a question?" Tarek asked. It had to be the chaos of the day taking its toll on him; as her body touched his, a pleasant warmth washed over him like sun breaking through the clouds.

"Sure," she said. She reached for one of the pillows and wrapped it close to her chest.

For a moment, he had the insane, utterly irrational wish to be that damned, scratchy hotel pillow that smelled like bleach and residual sweat, if it meant he would be pressed tight to her body. He shook himself. He had to focus. It had to be the blood loss that had him so out of sorts. And the irresistible smell of her.

"You said in the hospital that Ashariah showed you something. What did you mean?"

She nodded and frowned. "Before you arrived at the hospital, I checked her responses to determine what her level of brain activity might be. We test reflexes, pain response, and eye tracking. When I shined the light in her eye, I swear she looked right at me, and I saw something."

"What did you see?"

She paused, her teeth grazing her lower lip. Her brow creased as she pondered. Her eyes searched him, like she was afraid of embarrassing herself. "It's crazy."

"Crazier than anything else?"

"No," she said. She smiled reluctantly, exposing a sliver of white teeth as her lips curled up. "If she's like you...a..."

"Kadirai."

"That," Gabrielle said. "Then it makes more sense. Something was chasing her and hurt her. It knocked her out of the sky and onto the road."

Tarek sat upright, regarding her sternly. "Who was it? Did you see?"

She shook her head. "The sun was in her eyes. Everything was in silhouette."

"*Vazredakh*," he cursed. But he knew, didn't he? The blade buried in Surik's chest had been engraved with the markings of the Ironflight. The dragons of Stone and Iron had warred for many years, and had only set their differences aside in the Great War over a century earlier. The peace could not hold forever, not with two headstrong queens who would never yield to one another for the high seat of Empress. Attacking Ashariah was surely the first salvo in a full-out war on the Stoneflight.

"So what's next?" Gabrielle asked, jarring him from his thoughts of war.

"I will take her home," he said.

"Do you have doctors there?"

"Healers," he said. "And we have the *Avekh dar Isina*."

"Huh?"

He chuckled. "A very beautiful garden at the center of our home. The *al-hatari* is very powerful there."

"The huh?"

"*Al-hatari*. It's...energy. Life. It nourishes all living things."

"You said a garden," Gabrielle murmured, her voice dreamy. "Did you play with Ashariah there?"

He tilted his head. "You saw?"

"You were playing hide and seek there. I think she wanted me to know I could trust you."

"And do you?"

She narrowed her eyes. "I'm still not sure. Sorry."

He shook his head. "A warrior is always cautious. To answer your question, I will return her there as soon as sunrise comes. I should regain some of my strength by then, at least enough to take her home."

"And...you'll stay there?"

Was that a note of hope hiding in her question? And was that a note of hope hiding in his gut that she might ask? Fool of a dragon.

"I'm not sure," he said.

She flinched, then regained her mask of neutral curiosity. "I understand." She released the pillow and got up to check on Ashariah again. She repeated the examination she'd done earlier, and when she seemed satisfied, returned to the end of the bed. "I could probably use a few hours of sleep."

His breath caught in his chest as she climbed into the bed and snuggled herself down under the dingy comforter. Still damp and fragrant from her shower, her dark hair spilled in waves across the white pillowcase. She lay on her side, facing the wall so that her back was to him. He was struck suddenly with the urge to lie next to her, body pressed tight to hers so that he could feel each curve and edge of her form, the warmth of her skin pressed to his, and inhale her scent.

And as he watched her get comfortable, one arm splayed under her head while the other rested on the swell of her hip, he contemplated what it might be like to peel off her clothes, running his hands over the smooth, warm skin, and feeling the heat of her all around him. His blood surged, and he clamped down on his errant thoughts. He had been too long in the human world, stuck guarding the Gate with nothing but brash young men for entertainment. Some of them, like Shazakh, took regular trips into the city to entertain themselves with eager young women and men who were easily impressed by the big physique and uncanny eyes. That had never been Tarek's way. But he had never met someone like Gabrielle, and his resolve was put to the test as he listened to her breathing slow into the gentle rhythm of sleep.

But he had sworn that she would be safe, and he would honor his promise and her dignity. Even if she did smell divine and look like a dream come true.

As the night crept on, he periodically got out of bed quietly to check on Ashariah. He was no doctor, but he sensed no distress. Once, he sat on the edge of her bed and watched her sleeping. It was unusual for a dragon to sustain such severe injuries, and rarer still for it to take so long to recover. Surely, she'd improve immediately upon returning home. This world was not meant for their kind.

It was part of the reason he himself had been so slow to heal. The old scars on his back were the ones he'd sustained in the ambush that left Ashariah's sister Ivralah dead, and him barely clinging to life. He'd awoken in the healing gardens of Adamantine Rise weeks later, his *al-hatari* virtually obliterated. It had taken months for the wounds to close enough that they didn't constantly bleed, and only recently had they closed to puckered pink scars, barely healed over.

His eyes had barely closed when he heard the sound. It was only a gentle tap on the door, but it sent a hot rush of adrenaline rushing through him. He sat upright. Even in human form, he could smell the gathering magic in the air, that same odd smell he had caught before in the hospital.

Was he panicking and imagining it all?

He took a deep breath and listened for it again. There were footsteps outside the door, and the scent of magic was still there, not just in his imagination.

He reached over and shook Gabrielle's shoulder. She stirred, her eyes languid as she looked up at him. "She all right?" she slurred.

"She's fine. Someone's here," he said quietly.

Gabrielle sat bolt upright, rubbing at her eyes. "I'll go check," she said quietly. She started to scoot off the bed, but he grabbed her arm lightly. Her eyes were wide and confused as she looked back at him. "What?"

"Stay here," he said. A wave of dizziness washed over him as he stood up, tiptoeing silently across the room.

His heart pounded as he listened for footsteps. Silence hung thick and heavy around him. Maybe it was nothing. He crept closer to the door, curling his bare toes into the flat, scratchy carpet to ground himself. Something scraped along asphalt, sending a chill down his spine. Then it was quiet again, but the electric smell of magic thickened, as if something had burst open outside his door.

Or a Kadirai had just made the transformation into dragon form.

Adrenaline dumped into his system. He looked back at Gabrielle and said quietly, "Get your things. We have to move. Quick."

Eyes still wide, she nodded rapidly and sprang into action, stuffing the first aid supplies she'd brought into her pink bag.

How had they followed him? His affinity for the wind granted him the ability to conceal himself, and they should have never been able to follow him. The trail of magic was even dampened, at least enough that only the sharpest trackers could see it. Had they waited to follow Gabrielle?

He took a deep breath, assessing his own strength. He hadn't recovered enough for a lengthy battle. Another transformation so soon would drain him, and it wouldn't take much to drop him from the sky. But he had to do what was necessary.

"Okay," Gabrielle said. She was wiggling her feet into her sneakers and adjusting the pink bag on her shoulder. She continued to surprise him with her readiness to act. As he'd said to her earlier, she had a warrior's heart. "What do we do?"

CHAPTER FOURTEEN

"I DON'T WANT to involve you any further," Tarek said, looking down at her.

Gabby threw her hands up in frustration. "I'm involved already, get the hell over it. What do we do?"

The walls shook. They both froze, eyes wide as they stared at the ceiling. Something heavy thumped rhythmically across the ceiling. Her imagination ran wild, picturing a fire-spewing dragon crouched atop the motel waiting to devour her whole. A car alarm shrieked outside, then a second wailed in response. Glass shattered, setting off another chorus of alarms.

Tarek searched the bedside table, found a pen, and grabbed her hand. She'd always been complimented on her hands—large but graceful, the hands of a piano player or a surgeon—but they were dwarfed in his. Holding her wrist firmly with one hand, he scrawled on her palm.

Drakemont Inn

1382 Stonecrest Road

Boulder City, Nevada

"Seriously? That's almost to Vegas!"

Tarek shook his head and dropped her hand. "They're following us somehow. They either followed you here, or they followed my trail."

"So your response is to send your princess off with me?" This was a bad plan, a very bad plan. He was ignoring her, rooting through a leather satchel on the floor. He withdrew a wickedly sharp knife and held it out. "What am I supposed to do with that?"

"Hopefully nothing," he said. "Take it."

She stared down at the knife. Unfamiliar symbols were carved along the blade, which had a barbed edge. Glittering red stones decorated the handle. He made a gruff sound of irritation, grabbed her wrist, and pressed it into her hand. What looked like a hunting knife in his hand felt like a sword in hers. She reluctantly took it and looked up at him. With the weight of the knife in her palm, the surreal situation had suddenly become intensely real.

"I'm going to distract them," he said. "Possibly worse." His nostrils flared, and his strong hands clenched into fists. "I'll change, and I'll get you both to your car. Drive as fast as you can and don't look back."

"What about you?"

"I'll be fine," he said. "I'll catch up to you when I finish them off. I can smell you."

"Tarek, I just don't think...wait, you can smell me? Dude, seriously, that's just—"

"Gabrielle, this is not up for debate!" he shouted. "Take her. Ask to speak to Shazakh. Tell them Tarek *efan* Izera sent you."

"I—what?"

He gripped her shoulders, lowering himself to her eye level. Creased with concern, his eyes bored into her as he repeated his instructions slowly. "They may be suspicious, but that should be enough to get you to safety." She took a breath, but he cut her off. "Please, just listen. I need you to do this for me."

"Fine," she retorted. She stowed the knife in her bag and secured the strap over her shoulder, leaning a little to compensate for the extra weight of the first aid supplies. Maybe she should have listened to Logical Gabby last night and headed home to the safety of her four walls instead of staying here with Tarek.

Tarek sucked in a sharp breath, his hands out and already in a clawed position at his sides. He yanked the door open and rushed through. As soon as he stepped clear of the door frame, he let out a ferocious roar that could never have come from a human throat.

Gabby rushed to the doorway to see what happened. He was mid-transformation already, lighting the darkened parking lot with a display of shifting blue light. He was still between shapes when a streak of silver cut through the sky like lightning. "Tarek! Above you!"

His blue wings unfurled as he looked up. He snapped his head around like a whip. There was no light, but the air seemed to change around him, shimmering like a mirage. The shimmer coalesced in a crescent, hurtling toward the silvery white dragon. The white dragon banked sharply, but whatever he'd done still hit it. It flew backward, its body twisting awkwardly to protect its belly. Tarek finished transforming, his dark blue scales reflecting silver in the moonlight. Then his massive wings spread, lifting him high into the sky. Animal roars and screeches rose above the wailing car alarms.

Gabby peeked out, watching the frenetic activity in the skies above. Tarek flew after the white dragon, attacking with those same shimmering crescents. The other dragon dodged them, folding her wings tight and flying like a spear to dodge them.

She was so enrapt with the battle unfolding above that she never saw the second dragon land. Thunder cracked, seemingly right outside, followed by a flash of blinding white light. The side wall of the motel room imploded, and white-hot flames burst through the shattered remains.

She screamed involuntarily, moving to block Ashariah. A scaly golden head poked through the open doorway and roared. The sound scraped at her eardrums and left her ears ringing. She screamed back and waved it off like it was a pesky stray dog. Suddenly the spiked head jerked and pulled back. Gleaming white teeth were buried in its throat, jerking it away. It was Tarek.

"Come out!" he roared. The sound made her blood run cold, a shiver running down her spine. She ran to Ashariah and wrapped her arms around the princess, then lifted with her legs. She'd helped her mother move Anna many times, although the princess was considerably taller and heavier than her frail younger sister. The adrenaline certainly helped.

Gabrielle shuffled awkwardly to the doorway, where Tarek waited. As soon as she stepped clear of the door, he roared again, flinging another crescent of shimmering air over his shoulder. There was a lower roar in response. With one huge arm, Tarek wrapped her and Ashariah in a tight bundle. Gabby winced at the crushing grip. His scaly hide was rough against her bare skin, like gravel embedded in sandpaper. His chest rumbled, like a massive cat purring.

He leaped into the air, but he was jumping more than flying. Still, as they soared in an arc across the parking lot, her stomach did a sickening lurch, and she had to squeeze her eyes shut. With a crunch of metal under his clawed feet, he landed atop a red pickup truck next to her car. He lumbered down the front of the truck and landed in the grass behind the cars.

"Go!" he ordered.

"But ..."

"Go!" He suddenly sprang into the air again, the gold dragon in hot pursuit.

Gabby shook herself. Assess, decide, execute. Flames spread along the bottom floor of the motel, bursting out through windows. People scurried out of the rooms like ants from a kicked anthill. Judging by their open-mouthed stares overhead, some of them had noticed that something was going on above them. Sirens rose in the distance. It didn't take a rocket scientist to figure out that she needed to haul ass.

With a full tank of gas, a change of underwear, and a lost dragon princess in her custody, she was ready to roll. After maneuvering Ashariah into the back seat, Gabby jumped into the front seat, and backed out of the lot. As she peeled away, one of the dragons roared into the night, drowning out the shrill car alarms and distant sirens.

Something in her said *don't look*, like Lot's wife fleeing Sodom and Gomorrah, but how exactly was she *not* supposed to look at the epic dragon battle behind her? It would have taken a will of pure steel, and stubborn as she was, she didn't have it in her.

She looked over her shoulder and froze, her foot slamming on the brakes instinctively. The gold dragon was right behind her. His horned head completely filled the back window. Glass blew out of the windshield, and she heard the screeching of metal as his claws raked over the roof and dug in. Hot air blew through the car, searing her skin like she'd leaned into an open oven.

She stomped the gas, but the tires squealed uselessly like she was stuck in mud. She fumbled to get the knife out of the bag, but she had a feeling it would be like poking a T-rex with a toothpick.

Was this how she was going to die? She'd always figured it would be cancer, or maybe some freak car accident. It was safe to say that she had never once feared being burned to death by a pissed-off dragon due to her involvement in a dragon gang war. At least she'd be unique.

The golden dragon jerked suddenly, and through the open back window, she saw him receding, rolling on the ground in a knot of armored limbs and wicked claws with Tarek.

"Go, go, go," she ordered herself. She stomped the gas again, bumped up over a curb, and skidded onto the main road. There was literally nothing she could do to help Tarek fight, not when they were in their dragon form. What she could do was take away his worry for Ashariah's well-being by getting her out of immediate danger.

And that was what she did. She took care of her patient's, and no matter how weird the circumstances had gotten, Ashariah was still her patient.

Gabby floored the accelerator, heading for the interstate.

CHAPTER FIFTEEN

"IN NINE MILES, take exit on left," her GPS ordered. Gabby jumped in surprise at the voice and checked her rearview mirror for the hundredth time. The sun was rising on the horizon, casting an orange glow over the desert.

Thanks to the double shot of Five Hour Energy with a Red Bull chaser, Gabby managed to drive straight from Reno to a few miles from Las Vegas, where her GPS had directed her. The excessive dose of caffeine hadn't helped her racing heart, and she was sweating like she'd run a marathon. She'd seen no sign of dragons, but she'd also heard nothing from Tarek. And that wasn't for lack of obsessive checking of both her phone and the lightening sky.

That concerned her. Had he sacrificed himself to make sure they weren't followed? Surely, if he'd survived, he would have called to let her know he was all right. Then again, his priority was Ashariah, not her peace of mind. Still, her stomach churned a hot wave of dread through her every time she considered the thought of that beautiful blue creature, or worse, the golden-skinned man who'd refused to look at his princess undressed, lying broken and bloodied with no one to care for him.

No. That kind of thinking wasn't going to help anyone. He was a dragon and he could take care of himself. At least, she hoped he could, with a desperation that surprised her.

She followed the GPS and exited the interstate, following the side road until she reached the dingy-looking motel. She paused on the road, idling at the edge of the parking lot before turning in. Surely this was wrong.

"Arrived at destination."

She wasn't sure what she'd expected, but this definitely wasn't it. The building was a motel, and a crappy-looking one at that. A cracked plastic sign that had seen better days in the seventies read *Drakemont Inn*. Drakemont? Seriously? Wasn't that a little on the nose? The dingy marquee below said *Under Rennovations: Open for Bizness This Winter*. Whoever had done it sure couldn't spell. The parking lot was empty, but there was a light on inside the front office.

Before she drove in, Gabby called the number Tarek had called her from earlier. It rang four times, then went to the pre-recorded message that informed her that he was unable to take her call and instructed her to leave a message. She took a deep breath, tried to calm her nerves, and said, "Tarek, it's Gabby. Gabrielle," she amended, remembering the way he said her full name in his faintly accented, precise way, leaning on the *-elle*. "I'm here. We're okay. I was just wondering if you were okay. Give me a call."

She hung up and looked over her shoulder at Ashariah. The princess was still breathing, although she was still terribly pale. For a moment, she could only think *what the hell are you doing?* Twenty-four hours ago, she'd been aimlessly watching Netflix and walking on the treadmill in her living room before her shift. Now she was embroiled in a dragon turf war, entrusted with the safe passage of their princess and heir to the throne. It was so far beyond the realm of what she would have thought possible, but she couldn't deny what she'd seen with her own eyes. And if it wasn't real, that meant she was having a hell of a psychotic break, so she might as well roll with it at this point and enjoy the ride before she got the crazy medicated right out of her.

Gabby turned into the parking lot and parked sideways in the spots near the office to make it easier to get Ashariah out. She winced at the sight of her car; the back windshield was shattered, and there were deep furrows where the gold dragon's claws had dug into the roof and the trunk. Tarek or his queen officially owed her a new car.

She slung the gym bag over her shoulder and went to the glass door. Her legs were rubbery with nerves as she knocked on the door. At first there was no answer. She knocked again, more firmly this time.

Inside the office was a waist-high reception desk. It looked like any number of crappy motels on any highway across the country. Behind it was an unusually ornate wooden door that seemed rather out of place in the shabby office. After a minute or so, a tall man came from the doorway, rubbing his eyes. He yawned, approached and said "no vacancy" loud enough for her to hear through the glass. Though he wasn't quite as tall as Tarek, he was attractive in the same way, making it clear he wasn't fully human. Eerie, pale silver eyes raked over her.

"Do you know Tarek?" she asked. "Wait. I'm supposed to ask for Shazakh. Is that you?"

Narrowing his eyes, he opened the door and looked down at her. Without the layer of glass in front of him, she felt the real sense of menace from the man. "How would you know those names?"

"I'm Tarek's..." she trailed off. How odd it was that her first instinct was to say *I'm his friend.* She'd known him less than twenty-four hours, but it felt right to claim some sort of bond after what they'd been through. She shook herself. "I helped him with the princess. He told me to come ahead and tell you that Tarek...if and..." What was it again?

"Princess?" the other man said forcefully, apparently not caring that she couldn't remember Tarek's full name. "Where is she?"

"Are you Shazakh? That's who I'm supposed to talk to," she said, folding her arms across her chest.

"You will speak to me. I am his superior."

Dread gnawed at her. What if this was one of the men who'd attacked Ashariah in the first place? With a deep breath, she crossed her arms. "I'm not telling you until I can talk to Tarek and be sure."

The man looked her over, then raised his nose. He sniffed the air, taking a long, deep breath. His gaze suddenly snapped to her car. Without looking at Gabby, he brushed past her, making a beeline for the car.

"Wait!"

Suddenly, a nightmare scenario played out in her mind. The enemy dragons could have tortured Tarek to find out where she was taking the princess, then flown ahead to intercept her. How would she even know the difference in their human form?

Gritting her teeth, she unzipped the gym bag and pulled out the heavy, ornate knife. She'd cut into plenty of cadavers in med school, but she'd never stabbed a real human being. It wasn't rocket science. Thanks to anatomy class and several years working the ER, she knew half a dozen places to aim that would cripple him with one blow and a handful more that would kill in minutes.

Testing the heft of it, she stalked toward the car. The man was already trying to maneuver Ashariah's body out of the back seat. "Get away," she barked, hoping she sounded a lot more fierce than she felt. Shit, this was a terrible idea. He was huge. "One warning, *pendejo*. That's all you get."

He whipped his head around and scowled at her. "Who are you?"

"Get away from her," she ordered, lunging toward the man.

He moved lightning fast and caught her wrist, closing vise-like fingers around the fine bones. When she swung her fist on him, he caught it, then pinned both wrists in one hand so he could grasp her face with his free hand. His grip was firm, but not painful. He lowered his head to make eye contact. "Tell me your name."

A strange sensation pushed into her brain with insistent, scratching fingers. "My name is Gabrielle," she blurted. As he brought his face closer, she closed her eyes and turned away. There was something unpleasant about his gaze. It was the same sensation she'd experienced when Tarek first tried to make her release Ashariah to him.

"Look at me," he said, his voice resonating unnaturally into her chest. He was close enough to smell the faint hint of sweat from his skin. "You will stop fighting and walk into that door."

The push intensified, a pressure that seeped into her mind and made her ears and sinuses feel too-full. Something in her wanted to do it. It reminded her of college, before she'd realized her limits with tequila. Once she hit a certain point of intoxication, she'd have the sudden urge to go tell a guy how hot he was and smack him on the ass. Usually she was just aware enough to realize it was a bad idea, even though she still wanted to do it. This felt the same, a barely restrained urge that bubbled just beneath the surface. But she didn't *want* to go with him.

"Like hell I will," she spat, twisting against his tight grip and pulling her face away.

His eyes went wide and shocked. She took advantage of his surprise by kicking hard at his knee. Grunting in pain, he released her wrists. She tried to dart away, but a thick arm encircled her neck from behind, pressing in tight. Her pulse throbbed against the blockage. She beat her hands against his muscular forearm, even dug her short nails into his skin to try to hurt him. The hard, ropy muscle shifted as he maneuvered her into a chokehold. Her head pounded as her body screamed for oxygen.

She knew the science. She had less than ten seconds before unconsciousness. Her self-defense classes came back in flashes. Using one hand to try to support her weight, she dug her fingers into the wiry tendons in his elbow.

Less than five seconds now. Her vision contracted, with black slowly leaching in around the periphery. Tears of frustration pricked her eyes. She threw her elbow back, trying to catch the side of his head, but her arm sailed uselessly through open air.

The world faded.

CHAPTER SIXTEEN

THE PALE SILVER DRAGON lay motionless on the cracked ground, her soft underbelly ripped open in a long bleeding gash from Tarek's wind-blades. She hadn't died yet, or her body would have transformed back into human form. Tarek hovered a hundred feet above the ground, trembling with the effort of flight and maintaining the illusion that concealed him from sight.

It seemed that an eternity had passed since the fight had ended, though the dark sky and high full moon told him little time had passed. Finally, the silver dragon shuddered, and the pale scales melted away to reveal the still body of a woman, with the porcelain skin of her bare chest slashed open.

Under different circumstances, he would have ripped her head from her shoulders and sent it to the Ironflight as a message. Likewise, he would have flown a few miles back and made sure the gold dragon was dead. Instead, he'd left the male dragon shuddering in a stand of scraggly desert brush, his bloodied scales melting away to reveal his battered human form. Tarek had taken that as a sign that death was imminent, which had been sufficient confirmation with the silver dragon still trying her best to rip his throat open.

With his own strength failing, he had to be pragmatic. In his state, he wasn't sure he'd make it back to the Gate. He had to fly while he still could.

From high above the desert, he still had a vantage point of the burning motel. The low building was entirely consumed by fire now. The fire confirmed his suspicions; most of the dragons who pledged allegiance to the Ironflight were fire dragons.

Frightened people clustered in the grass, gawking at the blaze. Emergency vehicles clustered around the inferno, their blue and red lights strobing into the night. There would be strange stories once people started comparing their accounts. Though Tarek had drawn the battle out toward the desert, they had fought for a while above the hotel, and even the cover of night wouldn't have concealed their silhouettes entirely. So much for keeping the secret. There would be a hell of a lot of cleanup to do if they weren't engulfed in all-out war tomorrow.

With grim determination, Tarek wheeled around and began his flight to the Gate. With the battle over, his worries returned to Ashariah and Gabrielle. He had kept the attention of the Ironflight dragons long enough to let them escape, but he had no way of knowing if they had arrived safely. He could call ahead to Shazakh, but if he transformed back into his human form, he wouldn't have enough energy to take flight again.

Once, Tarek had the strength to transform between his forms at the snap of a finger, battling with equal ferocity in either form. Since the ambush that had left him barely clinging to life, he'd never completely recovered. It wasn't for lack of effort; he spent most of his free time at the Gate training himself, but it was like he was inside an invisible cell. He simply couldn't break past a barrier, and even more frustrating, he couldn't figure out the problem to solve it. It was like sword-fighting an invisible opponent who made no sound and had no scent. He sometimes feared he would never again be the dragon he once was. The queen saw him as weak and ineffectual now, and he could hardly blame her.

The flight to the Gate was grueling. He resorted to murmuring a hymn to the Skymother to keep his mind off the burning in his muscles and the ache in his chest. Between stanzas, his mind drifted to Gabrielle. At first, his concern had only been for Ashariah. He could have cared less if some human was killed in the crossfire, regardless of how pretty she was. And yet, when he'd seen Gabrielle care for the princess, then protect her, and then step up to carry her away to safety as if she was a sworn member of the Adamant Guard...something had changed. His lips might still swear that his full allegiance was to the queen and her daughter, but his heart no longer completely agreed.

The sun had barely cleared the burnt orange horizon as Tarek landed in the parking lot of the Drakemont Inn. The effort of flight caught up to him, washing over him in a wave of exhaustion. His feet tangled as he hit the ground, and he immediately lost control of his dragon form. Involuntarily, his dark cobalt scales melted away, the bones contracted, and he collapsed. Sweat poured off him in rivulets, pooling on the dry asphalt below.

Gabrielle's small black car was parked parallel to the front office. The back window was shattered out, with deep claw marks down the back where the gold dragon had attacked them. However, his relief at seeing that she had arrived was short-lived. Her pink gym bag lay on the ground next to the trunk, and the blue scrubs spilled over the open edge. A sudden fear cut through his fatigue and got him moving again.

Still stark naked, he stumbled up to the office door and entered the code on the keypad. He missed a digit the first time and swore loudly. After entering it again, he yanked the door open and bellowed, "Where is she?"

Everything seemed to be going sideways as the exhaustion took over. He planted one hand on the desk to keep himself upright, then propelled himself past the desk and down the narrow hallway and down into the subterranean chamber.

His younger subordinate, Shazakh, paced in front of the portal, a sword clutched in one hand. His dark hair was mussed, like he'd been in a fight. Tarek froze at the sight of him. "Oh, thank the Skymother. You would not believe what has happened."

"Where is she?" Tarek asked.

"Ashariah? She's safe. We carried her through the Gate, and the Adamant Guard is carrying her back to the Rise," Shazakh said.

Not her. His initial thought shocked him. Tarek had to pause for a moment to recover his expression. "That's good," he said. He hesitated. "What about the woman with her?"

Shazakh frowned. "The Vak woman? She attacked Zafar with an Ironflight blade and resisted his persuasion. We suspected foul magic."

"She's a human, you idiot," Tarek seethed. The room swayed, and his stomach lurched at the thought of Gabrielle under attack. "Where is she now?"

"Since you were not here to advise us, Zafar said it would be best to take her back to Adamantine Rise and let them handle it."

"She saved Ashariah, you idiot!" Tarek shouted. What moron thought the Ironflight would send a spy in the form of a human woman? Shazakh tentatively stepped forward to grip Tarek's arm and hold him up. The contact, overly and offensively familiar, sparked his anger again. He threw off the younger dragon's grip. "Where is she now?"

"Zafar already took her through the Gate," Shazakh said. "Tarek, you must rest."

"I'm going."

"You cannot travel like this," Shazakh said, going again to grab him.

Tarek growled and shoved the younger man in the chest. As Shazakh reeled, Tarek drew a deep breath and took a lurching step toward the Gate. As he did, black fog pressed in around his vision, and he tripped headlong to the cold stone below. His last thoughts before unconsciousness took him were of Gabrielle, and the sinking realization that he had doomed her.

CHAPTER SEVENTEEN

THE WORLD RETURNED IN FLASHES of light and sound. She vaguely remembered being tossed over a thick shoulder, her head swimming as someone roughly bound her hands. Just when she got the energy back into her limbs to fight, a blinding light enveloped her. Intense pressure surrounded her, like she was in a giant blood pressure cuff that kept tightening. Unconsciousness swept over her again.

In the next flash, she opened her eyes to see a shattered gray landscape blurring beneath her. Cold air nipped at her exposed skin. Her body was chained somehow, and when she looked up, she saw her own wrists and ankles, secured with chains that were clutched in the sharp, black claw of a dragon. Her view was nothing but the pale green underbelly that faded into sharp, emerald-colored scales. Massive wings buffeted her with cold air. Their huge span blotted out the sun.

She couldn't even draw a breath to scream. With her stomach churning and head throbbing, she squeezed her eyes shut. *This is a nightmare, it's not real.*

Her whole body tensed as the dragon swooped downward and released the chains. She gasped as freefall took her. Seconds later, she slammed into the ground and rolled awkwardly, banging her elbow against cold stone. Consciousness rushed back as the shock shot through her arm, destroying her conviction that she was dreaming. Grit ground against her cheek as she looked around. She tried to stand, but the chains weighed her down. Each wrist and ankle was secured with a heavy, dark metal manacle connected to a thick chain, all of which were connected to the thick metal ring the dragon had carried.

A man and woman in matching dark blue uniforms approached her. They both wore long-sleeved coats with tails that split from knee to hip, with a silver crest on the chest. The pale woman had black hair in an ornamental braid twisted around her head. She was easily six feet tall, with broad shoulders that made most of the human men Gabby knew look puny. Her partner was even bigger, with deeply tanned skin and thick blonde-streaked hair that swept away from a strong brow and proud nose. Like Tarek, they passed for human at first glance, but their size and bright eyes made them look strange.

The dragon that had carried her roared, sending a crawling sensation down Gabby's spine. He was perched on the corner of the rooftop, sharp talons curled around the ledge. The sound was inflected and broken, like he was speaking, but she couldn't understand the guttural syllables. The female guard responded, and a brief conversation followed. The dragon stepped down from the ledge and curled his green wings around himself. Dazzling greenish light surrounded him as the emerald scales melted away. It took no longer than a minute for the monstrous creature to transform back into a man.

Standing where the huge dragon had been was the same dark-haired man she'd encountered outside the Drakemont. "You! I told you I helped her, and—"

Throbbing pain bloomed on her left cheek as the female guard struck her in the face. Tears pricked her eyes at the sheer surprise and pain. She'd never been hit in the face, and it was shocking how much it hurt.

"*Vezhare!*" the woman snapped.

"But I—"

The woman raised her hand again, and Gabby recoiled.

The dark-haired man from the Drakemont raised a hand and said something in a mild tone to the woman. He didn't seem to be bothered that he was naked as a newborn. When he spoke again, it was in thick accented English, and directed toward Gabby. "We will find the truth of this. It would be wise for you to comply and save yourself further pain."

Further pain. The implication of what he said rang in her head like an echo. What the hell had she fallen into?

The female guard bent to grab the ring holding Gabby's chains. While she situated the metal loop in her hand, her partner grabbed Gabby roughly under the arms and hauled her to her feet. Her foot rolled painfully under her as he did, but her yelp of surprise elicited no response from him.

Tears welled up in her eyes as the strange man manhandled her. This had gone from being scary but in an exciting way to utterly terrifying. They had to listen to her. She'd saved Ashariah's life, and they were treating her like the enemy. It would be all right. Tarek would come, and he would explain it all.

But what if he didn't?

They stood on a huge flat platform atop a massive stone structure. It spread out below them like a pyramid; from what she could see, it was a fortress or a castle. Mountain peaks stretched into the distance in either direction, painted in shades of blue and gray by the hazy light. Below the fortress, the mountains sloped into a craggy valley with scraggly-looking trees. The sky overhead was a strange shade of blue, tinged with a hint of green as if the whole world was ill.

Beneath her feet was a pattern of gleaming reflective stone. A sharp contrast separated the reflective stone from the darker stone around it. As she traced the pattern with her eyes, she realized the reflective pieces formed a geometric pattern against the dark stone. Like the huge white H painted on the hospital's roof, this was a landing beacon, only for dragons.

She sure as hell wasn't in Kansas anymore. Her head spun again as she realized how far she was from anything familiar.

The woman yanked on the chains, pulling Gabby forward to a doorway. With the chains, she had to follow or fall flat on her face. The links were heavy, and her muscles soon burned with the effort of keeping herself moving.

Set into the mountain itself, the doorway led into an anteroom with several more armed guards flanking each interior door. The anteroom was rounded to a dome at the top, carved from smooth dark stone. There were no decorations, save for simple engravings over the arches of each of the three interior doors. The door guards each wore the same dark blue uniform. And each carried a spear as tall as a man, with a wickedly jagged edge that would tear at the innards of whatever it penetrated.

The naked man flanked them. As he entered the anteroom, he spoke to the nearest guard. Gesturing with his spear, the guard pointed toward the far wall. The naked man followed his gesture and disappeared into a side door.

The center door, directly opposite the outside door from which they had entered, was three times the width of the others, while the others that sat adjacent to it were close to the size of a normal door from home. Each door had a silver plate mounted at shoulder-height on the left side of its frame. When they approached, Gabby saw what the plates were for.

The woman holding her chains spoke to the guard at the right-hand door. There was a hint of movement as each of the guards eased the spears forward, like they were waiting for an attack. As if the trussed-up human woman posed a threat to a bunch of hulking dragon-men with spears.

After inspecting Gabby, the guard wrinkled his nose and put his bare palm against the silver plate. Purple light radiated from his hand, spreading out on the plate. A few seconds later, the light faded, and the guard pushed gently on the door. It swung inward, allowing the woman to pull Gabby inside.

A now-familiar voice called from behind them. The man from the Drakemont had covered himself with a rough leather loincloth, leaving his powerful chest and arms bare. He hurried toward them, taking up the last remaining space in the small room.

The room was small, no bigger than a bathroom stall. Inside, one wall housed a square array of the silver plates. The woman put her palm on the plate in the bottom right corner. It lit up, and suddenly the room moved. It was an elevator.

When Tarek had referred to his home, it hadn't seemed like a reality to her. She hadn't even been able to conceive of another entire world beyond her own, but here she was, watching two dragon-people operate an elevator seemingly by magic. If not for the insanity of the whole situation, Gabby might have enjoyed the novelty of it. As it was, she was praying that she didn't vomit up her midnight gas-station snack. Where exactly where they taking her? It couldn't have been to a penthouse suite for honored guests, not with chains snapped around her wrists like a prisoner.

There was also Tarek's notable absence. She'd have understood if he'd been a few minutes behind her, but it didn't make sense that it had been so long. She'd never been the type to wish for someone to swoop in and rescue her, but if there was an appropriate time for it, it was now.

The lift was surprisingly fast. When it finally stopped its descent, they emerged into another austere chamber. A doorway opposite the lift was dark, the space beyond a mystery. The air smelled musty, and only worsened as they got closer. She didn't know what was past the dark archway, but she didn't want to go there. Instinctively, she dug in her heels, trying to lean back and keep them from taking her beyond the door.

The man in the loincloth sighed. "Really?"

The two guards were unfazed. The woman yanked hard on the chain to pull her off balance, while her partner shoved Gabby in the back, toppling her onto her hands and knees. With her head bowed, she sucked in a sharp breath, clenched her fists, and swallowed down the panic. This was scary, but she was going to handle it like she did everything else. Assess, decide, execute.

Emotional Gabby wanted to pitch a fit and fight the whole way. Logical Gabby knew she was outnumbered and outmatched, and that resistance was going to get her hurt or worse. It would be smarter to go along with them and watch for anything that she could use to free herself. When the male guard grabbed her under the arms again, she didn't resist.

The archway opened to a larger room, walled in silver-flecked stone like the rest of the fortress she'd seen so far. The room was dim, lit only by glowing blue lamps mounted on the walls. Toward the back of the room was a rough-hewn table holding three metal mugs and a platter of bread and cheese. Her stomach growled at the sight of it, reminding her she hadn't eaten a real meal in a while.

Behind the table was a wooden door standing ajar. To the left was another dark doorway, and to the right of the table were two more hallways. Guarding each corridor was a pair of armed guards. They looked less ceremonial than the guards who were escorting her, with plainer blue tabards over scuffed, dark leather garments.

Her captors walked her toward the left doorway. The two guards parted, not even giving her a second look as she passed. The corridor beyond was lit only by a hazy glow from a series of glass orbs hanging from chains overhead. Either side of the corridor was lined in barred cells, each narrow and cramped. They passed a few empty cells, then came to one holding a huge black and white cat pacing the cell. It looked like a panther that had rolled in flour. It paused its pacing, then lunged at the bars and snarled. Gabby screamed in fright, prompting a laugh from her captors. The woman shouted at it. It growled in response, but it backed away from the bars.

Nearly at the end of the corridor, the guards stopped. The woman reached out to one of the cell doors on the left side of the hall, which was secured by one of the glowing plates she'd seen in the elevator. The door swung open, and her partner shoved Gabby inside. She stumbled, but managed to stay on her feet.

Inside, the cell was barely wide enough for her to spread her arms, and she could easily reach up to touch the ceiling. It was dingy, but not filthy. There was no bed to speak of, only an oblong cubby carved into the stone wall. A thick ring was mounted to the wall above the cubby. Moldy straw was piled in the back corner.

Her heart thumped as she inspected the cell. *Don't panic*, she scolded herself. What would she need to get out of here?

Hope rose in her as the female guard entered the cell and knelt in front of her. With a key from her belt, she unlocked the shackles around Gabby's ankles. Gabby resisted the urge to kick the woman. It might have been satisfying, but it wouldn't have accomplished much other than angering her.

The woman rose, still holding the small key, but didn't unlock her wrists. She folded her arms over her chest and regarded Gabby with her nostrils flared. "*Inan tam?*"

"I don't understand you," Gabby pleaded.

"You only speak English?" the man from the Drakemont asked.

"And Spanish," she said. "I'm not from your world."

"That much is clear," he said. He spoke to the female guard, eliciting a curt response.

"What is this about?"

He ignored her question and waited for the female guard to finish working. The woman unlocked the manacles from Gabby's left wrist, then threaded the chain through the ring on the wall. When she had finished, she backed away slowly.

The chain was heavy and cold, but she had enough length that she could let her arm rest by her side. She didn't test it, not with three pissed-off dragon people staring her down, but she estimated that she'd have enough length to get to the cell door.

The man from the Drakemont spoke to the guards. The woman exited the cell, then locked it behind herself, again by placing her palm on the metal plate. There was a metallic chime that rang in the air, and then she disappeared down the dark corridor. Crap. There was no key to steal. How was she supposed to get out?

"What is this about?" Gabby asked again.

"You tell me," the man said. "You arrived at a secret location of my people, bearing with you the badly injured body of our princess. You carry the weapon of our enemy, and you know names you should not."

"But I told you, I met Tarek and—"

"And I might have gotten the truth out of you the usual way, but that's the most interesting part. You are Vak, a human, in your language. I should be able to command you to speak the truth, and yet, you resist. That is very unusual. What are you?"

"I'm just a human doctor," she said.

"Maybe you are," he said. "And maybe you are something else." With that, he turned to walk away.

"Wait! Where are you going?"

"To give my report to the Adamant Guard. May I offer some advice?

When they return to question you, be honest. Things will be much easier for you. The queen will not take this lightly upon seeing her daughter's condition." He walked away, ignoring her protests hanging in the air.

Chilly dread settled over her, weighing on her like an icy blanket. They thought she had something to do with Ashariah's condition. A spy, maybe. It was ludicrous, but the logical side of her could understand where they'd piece it together.

When they return to question you.

A shudder skittered down her spine. She'd managed to be relatively calm and logical until now, and she wasn't going to allow herself to fall apart. But she was skirting that edge as she slowly faced the realization that she was in a very bad situation with no way out. She was utterly helpless, which made her sick to her stomach. Unless Tarek arrived to clear things up, or Ashariah miraculously woke up, then she was about to face a bunch of angry dragons with only her word. She'd never wished for a man to rescue her from anything, but she was wishing it now, with everything she had.

Please hurry, she thought as much as prayed. *Please come for me.*

CHAPTER EIGHTEEN

AWARENESS CAME SLOWLY to Tarek. First he smelled a familiar, spicy scent like burning incense. Then he heard the low hum of the portal, which snapped his attention to the present. He opened his eyes to see a low gray stone ceiling.

As his sharp eyes scanned the room, the long embroidered silver banners told him he was no longer in the human world, but instead in his home world of Ascavar. He sat upright and groaned as the headache of a lifetime pounded at his temples like a sledgehammer. A thick quilt covered his lower body, which ached like the rest of him. Dark gray curtains hung around his sickbed to create a tiny private room.

"Easy," a female voice said. One of the Ascavar Gatekeepers, Kaliyah, sat on a stool in the gap where the curtain parted, allowing her a vantage point of the portal and Tarek simultaneously. With her dark skin and unusually pale blue eyes, she was lovely. She was as deadly as she was beautiful, which was why she guarded the Gate on the Ascavar side. "You're home."

"I need to go," he said. He threw off the quilt, exposing his body to the cold air. With a violent shiver, he stood up, catching Kaliyah's eye.

She raised an eyebrow and looked him over. "It would be wise to rest instead. You've clearly had an interesting day."

He looked down. A trio of claw marks ran from beneath his left nipple to his right hip, where the silver dragon had slashed him. The wounds were smeared in a healing ointment, glistening with a faint green tinge. There were black and purple splotches of bruising across his right shoulder and hip, and his right calf was still seeping blood. The gunshots Gabrielle had patched for him no longer bled, but they remained open wounds surrounded in dark bruising. He had definitely seen better days.

"I'm fine."

"I politely disagree. You should rest," Kaliyah said. "We can maintain watch without you."

"Watch?" Tarek said incredulously. "You took an innocent woman to the dungeons. I have to go before they make a mistake."

"Who?"

Who? Did none of them care what had happened? "The woman who brought Ashariah here," he said. "Did Shazakh not tell you?"

"Shazakh said that one of the Vak had brought Ashariah here, and that they suspected her of collaborating with the Ironflight."

"*Vazredakh*," Tarek spat. "I'll kill him. I told him to speak to—"

"Calm yourself, Windstriker. After dragging your stubborn hide through the gate, he passed along your concerns and told me you insisted the Vak was an ally."

"And what are you doing about it?"

"Until approximately two minutes ago, I was watching over you to ensure you didn't bleed to death, you fool of a dragon," Kaliyah snapped, eyes narrowing into a glare. "I sent a messenger ahead to the Rise."

Tarek growled low in his throat. "If they hurt a single hair on her head, I will tear them limb from limb."

Kaliyah chuckled, one eyebrow arched in amusement. "My, Tarek. This Vak must be quite the seductress to have you so agitated. I've not seen you in such a state in many years."

The other Gatekeeper's casual tone ignited a firestorm of rage in his gut. His stomach lurched, and before he realized it, his hands were curled into fists. He took a clumsy step toward Kaliyah. Her lazy smile evaporated, and her hand went instinctively to the knife on her belt. Her blue eyes widened as she rose from the stool and stepped back into a defensive stance. The realization that he was ready to attack one of his own stopped him short.

"I'm leaving," Tarek said, forcing each word out and tempering his voice with great effort. "And you will not stand in my way."

Kaliyah regarded him sternly. Then she shrugged. "What is it to me if you die of your injuries? You won't be the first fool to die of stupidity." She stepped out of his way gesturing toward the portal, beyond which was a barred wooden door to the outside world. "By all means."

With his bare feet on the stone and gravity working against him, he realized how much the last day's efforts had taken out of him. He was exhausted, with an ache that radiated from his very bones. Each step on the hard stone sent a tremor through his body, a stinging soreness that the healing ointment did not touch.

"I'm sure it simply slipped your mind, but the princess was brought through several hours ago," Kaliyah called out, her clear voice filling him with guilt. "If you decide to vent your rage to the queen, perhaps you should start with inquiring after her daughter."

He growled under his breath and stalked toward the barred door. The nearest Gatekeeper, a young Kadirai he didn't recognize, hurried to unbar it, giving him a nod of respect as Tarek stormed past.

The Stoneflight were not known for being cruel for cruelty's sake, but neither were they known for being merciful. And if they believed Gabrielle to be responsible for Ashariah's condition, then they would err on the side of swift justice. The death of Princess Ivralah still lived fresh in the collective memory of the Stoneflight, and they would relish the chance to exact justice on the coward who ambushed the queen's only remaining child.

It took Tarek a moment to acclimate to his home world once more. Inside the small chamber of Broken Stone Keep, near the Gate, it was nearly the same as the Gate in the human realm except for the decorations adorning the walls. It had the same humming portal, around which was a large chamber built of silver-flecked stone. But beyond the heavy wooden doors, everything was different.

The Broken Stone Gate was one of a dozen that had been discovered in Ascavar. They were tears in the fabric of the world, like hidden burrows that connected their realm to the human realm. Legend told that they had been torn open by the long-extinct Duskflight, servants of the Skymother's antithesis, the Shadow King himself. As far as Tarek concerned, those were mere fairy tales. But the gates were certainly real.

Once just a novelty that allowed for a peek into the human realm they called Eldavar, the Gates had become of great strategic value when the ancient Empress Adushari had used the portals to travel their world quickly and obtain passage into hostile territories. Once, the portals had been open to all, but during the Great War, their locations had become fiercely protected secrets.

The landscape around the Broken Stone Gate was shattered, marked forever by the foul magic unleashed during the Great War. The ground was cracked and gray, with not so much as a blade of grass in sight. The sun burned high and hot in the green-tinged sky. Behind him, Broken Stone Keep appeared to be a natural rock formation, protected with an illusion built by the air dragons of the Stoneflight.

Tarek knelt on the cracked ground, passing his hands over the dry, rough surface. It wasn't warm or welcoming, but it was home. He took a deep breath and drew on the ragged threads of his energy to make his transformation. He felt a great deal better than when he'd stumbled into the Drakemont, but now he felt like a bag of bones covered in a giant bruise. Once the great bones had formed, leathery wings stretching between the fine flight bones, he let out a sigh of relief.

With a burst of force down through his scaled legs, he soared into the sky. Orienting himself by the distant swath of green forest and gray mountains, he flew toward his home. Here in Ascavar, magic was active and wild, crackling in the very air and tickling the smooth surface of his wings. It made him stronger and faster, but it also made him vulnerable. His hold on his form was more tenuous here. Paired with his weakness from the battles of the previous day, it would take just one wrong breath to lose control and fall from the sky.

No matter. He had to get to the Rise, even if he collapsed on his feet as soon as he landed. He would not allow Gabrielle to be harmed.

As he closed the distance to the citadel, his mind drifted to Gabrielle. Would she be pleased to see him? Or would she be justifiably angry that he'd sent her into an ambush? He should have known that his fellow Gatekeepers would err on the side of caution, and finding a human with an injured Ashariah in tow was strange enough for them to toss her into a cell and ask questions later.

Nestled into the craggy wall of the Azure Peaks, the huge fortress of Adamantine Rise came into sight within half an hour. The fortress filled the space between two mountains, which had given rise to many bawdy jokes among the Adamant Guard. It was integrated almost seamlessly into the mountains, with large portions of the fortress actually carved into the natural stone. Terraces and balconies dotted the sides of both mountains and the structure itself. Long, narrow walkways with curved roofs bridged the higher levels. The fortress extended away from the mountains on either side in curving walls that met at the great gates to the city below. Within the curving walls was the green expanse of the healing gardens.

Below the Rise was the bustling city of Farath, inhabited by the other shapeshifters, the Edra, and the Vak, the humans who also dwelt in Ascavar. Dragons circled the skies above and soared between the skywalks, unworried about being seen from below. The humans of Ascavar were used to the sight of winged dragons soaring above them.

The citadel rose nearly to a pinnacle, but instead of a sharp point with a wind-whipped banner, it was topped by a rounded stone room. From above, it looked like a cake that had been cut into a crescent. Most of the level was taken up by the landing platform, but along the side closest to the mountains was an enclosed anteroom where the guards kept supplies. A large statue of the Skymother, wings spread and neck arched toward the sky, perched on top of the guard's chamber.

All along the landing platform, guards in human form and dragon form stood at the ready. Four in human form held spears, with two guarding the doorway into the fortress and two patrolling the perimeter. Two dragons perched on vantage points, while a third circled the sky above.

Bright white stone was inlaid in the darker stone to create a landing beacon for the Kadirai. He turned in a wide spiral as he slowed his flight, landing neatly on one point of the seven-pointed star. As soon as his talons clacked against the stone, he lost control of his transformation. His body burned with feverish heat as he returned to human form. The guards on the platform snapped to attention, bringing their spears to the ready.

"*Dath sequa*," he said breathlessly, his chest still heaving with the effort of transformation. As he spoke, he made a fist and bowed, greeting them in the traditional way of the Adamant Guard. He didn't recognize the guards, but they seemed satisfied that he belonged there.

Beyond the guards was a crescent-shaped chamber. At the center of the back wall was a wide archway that granted access to the citadel. Off to the right was a small cabinet, a weapon rack, and a table for the guards. To the left was a smaller room with an open doorway. Tarek entered the open door and scanned the supply room. A rough-hewn trunk sat in one corner, and a rack of plain garments hung on the wall. He grabbed the first thing he saw, a smooth leather waistcloth, and tied it around his waist to cover himself. The room was intended for that very purpose—for the queen's staff to dress themselves and prepare to enter the citadel.

Without waiting for an escort, Tarek approached the larger door. He repeated his greeting, and the two guards nodded to him as they stood aside to let him enter. Beyond the archway was the central column with a winding staircase that snaked around two magic-powered lifts. The Gatekeepers had likely brought her here and headed down the lift to the dungeons, so that was where he followed.

The foul smell of fear and desperation greeted him as soon as the lift stopped in the basement of the citadel. The dungeons of Adamantine Rises were buried deep in the mountain, far from the open skies and fresh air.

When he reached the anteroom, two of the Adamant Guard sat at a table eating from a wooden platter of roasted meat and flaky bread. At his approach, they both looked up. The man, who was huge and made the blue uniform tabard look like a scarf strung around his neck, stood and looked over Tarek, looking unimpressed.

"Who are—"

"Where is she?" Tarek demanded. "The Vak?"

The female guard swallowed and put her half-eaten slice of bread on the tray. With her eyes still on him, she stood and rested her hand on the heavy sword on her belt. Her body language gave her away; she was intimidated and trying not to show it. "What business is it of yours?"

"You will release her."

"We have orders from the queen to keep her here," the woman snapped at him, her posture stiffening.

"Did you tell the queen that the Vak saved her daughter's life?"

The two guards glanced at each other, looking like they were trying to decide if he was lying. Tarek took advantage of their distraction and hurried past them down the corridor on the left. The sight of the tiny, dirty cells set off the blaze of anger in his belly again. "Gabrielle!" he bellowed.

The sound of his voice set off some of the other prisoners. A huge cat shifter threw itself at the bars, snarling at him. He ignored it, hurrying past as he called her name again and again. The deeper he went into the dungeon, the harder his heart thumped. If things had moved quickly enough, a vindictive guard might have gotten orders to question their prisoner, and the thought of them torturing her for answers she couldn't give whipped his guts into a sickening churn.

"Gabrielle!"

"Tarek?" a distant voice called from down the corridor. "Tarek!" Her voice stopped suddenly, as if someone had struck her. A rage like he'd never experienced washed through him. White spots flashed in his vision as he hurried toward the large door at the end of the hall. As he got closer, he could detect her smell; the intoxicating smell of her shampoo, but underneath, an acrid note of fear.

Voices issued through the heavy door. He raised a fist and pounded hard enough to make his joints hurt. "Open the door!" he bellowed in Kadirai. Before he could pound again, the door flew open.

The room was a small interrogation chamber, with enough sharp implements and chains hanging from the walls to intimidate the most stoic warrior. Gabrielle sat in a rough wooden chair in the middle of the room, a heavy chain wrapped around her waist and pinning her arms to her sides. A possessive, fiercely protective anger swelled up in him, followed closely by a hot wave of guilt. Her pretty face was marred with a dark, swollen knot on her cheek, but she looked otherwise untouched.

To his surprise, Zafar, one of the Gatekeepers from the Drakemont, leaned against a table. He looked up in surprise. "Tarek?"

"Oh, thank God," Gabrielle blurted. "Please, tell them—"

"Let her go. Now," Tarek said.

Another of the Adamant Guard, an older and high-ranked officer named Rezahn, stood behind Gabrielle. He remembered Rezahn from his days as a recruit guarding the dungeons. Rezahn's wiry silver hair was cropped short and combed away from his sharp features. "This is a serious matter, Tarek. This woman—"

"This woman saved the life of our princess," Tarek said. "And mine. If you do not let her go, I will gladly inform the queen of your mistreatment."

"The queen ordered that she be questioned," a hesitant female voice spoke up. A diminutive Kadirai woman stepped forward from the shadows. Her ornately embroidered blue dress, cut with angular panels over dark leg wraps, identified her as a page for one of the queen's councilors. A dark silver sash crossed her chest, pinned with a large medallion that identified her as a servant to the library. She worked for Councilor Eszen, the queen's historian and magic scholar.

"Then the queen does not know the whole story. Either get her down here, or I will go to her. Your choice."

CHAPTER NINETEEN

GABRIELLE HAD NEVER BEEN SO HAPPY to see a man in her life as when she saw Tarek barrelled into the room. He looked rough, with deep slashes across his chest and a smattering of dark bruises all over. Like the other man from the Drakemont, he wore a loincloth around his waist. He could have shown up in a tutu and she would have still have been ecstatic.

Considering all of the conversation was in their native tongue, she didn't follow it. But she didn't have to understand a single word to know that Tarek was furious. His fists clenched so tight that the thick veins stood out from wrist to shoulder. After a heated argument, the small woman who'd been observing the questioning sprinted out of the room.

She'd never been a damsel in distress, wishing for a prince to save her. You couldn't count on anyone to save you. She'd learned that from a young age, when her father took off and left her mother to care for a sick child alone. Life had only reaffirmed her philosophy as the handful of guys she'd dated throughout college had all eventually drifted away, saying she was too involved in her studies. God forbid a girl be motivated. She'd given it one last shot in med school, but when she'd let her walls down for Tyler, another medical resident, he'd broken things off, telling her she was too independent. According to Tyler, he didn't want to be with someone who didn't need him.

Well, maybe Tyler would have been pleased to see this turn of events.

For the first time in decades, maybe her entire life, Gabrielle Rojas needed someone to rescue her. She was about as damsel-in-distress as it got at the moment, and the only person who could save her was a strapping hunk of a man. Not quite a knight in shining armor, but a dragon-man in a precariously short loincloth would have to do.

"Did they hurt you?" Tarek asked.

"I'm okay," she said. "You have to explain what happened. They didn't believe me."

Tarek glowered at the man from the Drakemont. "You did this?"

"What did you expect? If you were on watch and a human showed up carrying the broken body of our princess, would you have patted her on the head and sent her on her happy way?"

"I'm not a dog," Gabby said flatly. "Can you please unlock this?"

The chains were heavy and cold, although her treatment so far hadn't been the nightmarish torture she had imagined in the hours before they came back for her. The other man, the older one with the silver hair, had grabbed her face to silence her when Tarek called, but otherwise, they'd been humane. Still, considering how frustrated they'd seemed, she was sure they were ready to escalate their methods at any moment.

"Unlock her," Tarek ordered. When the other man, her translator, just stared at him, he barked the same order in the other language. The older man sneered and retorted. Tarek bristled, taking a long stride toward the other man. The silver-haired man's hand went to his sword, fingers curling slowly around the hilt. Neither made a move. Then Tarek broke away, muttering to himself. Instead, he positioned himself next to Gabby. He looked down and spoke softly. "I'm sorry. I'll handle this. I promise you."

She nodded slowly. "I trust you."

The older man had been barking questions, which the man from the Drakemont translated. The same thing over and over. *Who are you? How do you resist? Where did you get the blade?*

One of the questions was easy, even though they were convinced that she was hiding something. The blade concerned them; they said it was from the Ironflight, which meant nothing to Gabby. It was an enemy, which was probably all she needed to know. The thing that really had them worried was her resistance to their attempts to control her mind. Both of them had tried, making that same intense eye contact and then pushing somehow from inside her head. Every time, it was the same uncomfortable sensation, but nothing more. They weren't pleased about it, demanding to know how she was immune. Telling them "I guess I'm just a special snowflake," hadn't done much for their mood.

Tarek's hand rested lightly on her shoulder. The warm, kind touch was a welcome change from her unpleasant treatment over the last few hours, though she wondered how much was for her sake and how much was to keep himself standing. He leaned on her enough that she could tell he was struggling. The weight came and went, like he couldn't quite find his balance. A faint sheen of sweat glistened on his brow and along his muscular back.

They waited in silence for what seemed like ages, all of the dragons glaring at each other. From down the corridor came a gradual crescendo of noise that resolved into individual voices as it got closer. Metal clanged in time with rhythmic footsteps. Then it was quiet.

Two uniformed guards appeared at the door. Both men were a sight to behold, standing at least six inches taller than Tarek, who was already a big man. Their muscular frames were adorned in fine dark blue uniforms, with elaborately engraved shoulder pauldrons, ornate chest plates, and wickedly jagged spears standing at their sides. They were both beyond attractive; beautiful was a more appropriate term to describe their chiseled faces and bright eyes.

At the sight of them, Tarek straightened suddenly, placing his fist to his chest and tipping his head slightly. The other two men stiffened, turning toward the door and making the same gesture. Gabby craned her neck to see what they were looking for.

A tall, regal woman stood in the open doorway. She had to be the queen.

Well over six feet tall, she wore filmy garments of blue and purple that veiled her body and left her long, muscular legs exposed. Ornate golden jewelry with glittering blue stones decorated her neck, wrists, and bare feet. In place of a crown, she wore a circlet with a glowing purple gem. Thick dark hair spilled back from the circlet and over her shoulders. Her face was beautiful, but somehow strange, with razor-sharp features that were inhuman enough to warrant a second glance. If Gabby had seen her back home, she might have thought *way too much plastic surgery.*

And her eyes, so pale blue they were almost silver, were fixed on Gabby. Her full lips were set in a grim slash as she examined Gabby. She carried no weapons, but her very presence was intimidating. It felt like she consumed all the air in the room.

The queen spoke to her, her voice rich and smoky. Raising his head slowly, Tarek responded. At first, the queen looked annoyed at his interference, but he gestured to Gabby and shook his head as he spoke again. The queen nodded slowly. She raised an eyebrow and said, "Do you understand me now?" in thickly accented English.

Gabby stared at her in surprise for a few seconds. "Yes. Yes ma'am," she amended. "Your Highness."

The queen turned to Tarek. "Highness?"

"*Su'ud redahn,*" he replied. Apparently that got lost in translation. He spoke rapidly to the queen, but she cut him off with a single word.

"Tell me what you know of my daughter. Do not lie."

"I'm a doctor," Gabby said.

"*Thodar,*" Tarek interrupted. The queen nodded in understanding, but she squinted a little, like the description he'd given didn't match up with what she saw.

"She was injured and was brought to my hospital. I took care of her," Gabby said. She resisted the urge to say *very good care of her* and waited for the queen to acknowledge it, but she maintained that stoic, stony expression. It took a concerted effort not to babble on to fill the awkward silence.

"And how did you get the knife you carried to my Gate?"

"Tarek gave it to me," she said. "To defend myself."

The queen gave Tarek a sharp look and asked him something in their language. He responded quickly. The queen looked back to her. "Tell me of the dragons who attacked you."

"One of them was silver," she said. "I think that was the woman with white hair. And the other one was a man who turned into a gold dragon."

The queen looked back at Tarek, who nodded in confirmation. She took a deep breath and closed her eyes. For a second, the mask of the imperious queen slipped, and the smooth skin around her eyes creased, her brow furrowing. That was the look of a concerned mother, of someone who feared the unknown. Gabby had seen it on a hundred human faces as they listened to her describe the tenuous situation of a patient. In that tiny lapse, the queen became the most familiar thing Gabby had encountered since meeting Tarek.

The look disappeared as quickly as it had come on, and the queen opened her bright eyes again. "How is that you resist the commands of my men?"

"I don't know," Gabby said. The queen stepped in closer. The air felt thin as the imposing woman approached, close enough that Gabby could have touched her face if her arms weren't pinned down. The woman reached out one hand. Each finger was tipped in a gold filigree claw embedded with blue stones. Her hand rested on Gabby's face, icy cold.

Her silver eyes fixed on Gabby's. "Tell me the truth. How have you resisted?"

The force of the queen's will hit her hard. Where the men had caused an unpleasant crawling sensation, the queen made her head ache with a sharp, stabbing pain, like she'd gotten the brain freeze to end all brain freezes. Her entire body went ice cold. "I don't know!" Gabby blurted, squeezing her eyes shut to escape that terrible gaze. Like someone had hit a switch, the painful cold stopped.

The queen's thumb found the other side of her face, squeezing enough to make her point. "Open your eyes and look at me." Her voice carried a resonance that vibrated into Gabby's stomach, but she still didn't open her eyes.

"I said I don't know," Gabby said. "Please stop. It hurts."

The queen spoke rapidly in their language, then leaned in close to Gabby. She inhaled sharply, her jewelry jangling. "You smell like my daughter."

"I took care of her," Gabby said, still squeezing her eyes shut.

"It's more than that," the woman said. "I smell her magic on you." Suddenly, she released her grip. Gabby risked opening one eye and saw the queen's back as she spoke to Tarek. They talked for a while, Tarek's eyes intense. Finally, they paused. The queen looked down at Gabby. "I trust Tarek's word. Therefore, I will choose to trust yours," she said. With a dismissive gesture, she gave an order to the silver-haired man. His face went slack in surprise, but he didn't argue, just knelt behind Gabby to unlock the chains. "However, if you have come here to harm my people, or if I find out that you are responsible for my daughter's attack, then I will..." She trailed off and looked at Tarek and told him something to translate.

Tarek swallowed hard and kept his eyes away from Gabby. "Then you will beg for mercy and she will not grant it. More or less." The grim tone twisted her belly into knots of dread.

"However, if what you say is true, then I thank you for protecting my daughter," the queen added, her voice lighter now, as if she hadn't threatened to torture Gabby to death. "Tarek tells me that you cared for her and

125

protected her as one of my Adamant Guard would."

Gabby looked at Tarek hesitantly. His eyes widened as he nodded. "Yes, ma'am. I tried my best, at least."

The chains loosened suddenly. She wriggled her shoulders, loosening them further until one end hit the ground. Tarek turned and unwrapped the chain quickly, leaning close to her as he did. For a moment, she rested her head against his shoulder and inhaled his warm, musky scent.

When the chains were completely loosed, he offered his hand and helped her stand. Her legs and knees ached from sitting in the low chair, but she was fine otherwise.

The queen nodded to her and gestured to her guards. In a single snappy motion, they moved their spears to clear the path. The queen hesitated before leaving. "I would offer you my...*thivedh*..."

"Hospitality," Tarek offered.

"I wish for you to speak with one of my councilors. While I trust Tarek's word, I am concerned about why you resist our commands," she said. "I must ask you to stay until we have answers."

Gabby's stomach sank. "With all due respect, it doesn't sound like you're giving me a choice."

The queen regarded her with a cool, stoic expression. "I am not. Even if your intentions are good, I still have unanswered questions whose answers may be very important."

Anger swelled up in Gabby's chest, hot and sudden. She couldn't be sure how much time had passed since she answered Tarek's call, leaving behind her normal life, but it wouldn't be much longer before her mother figured out something was wrong and began to worry. "I have a family at home. And a job. An important one."

"I will press my councilors to move quickly," the queen said.

"But—"

"Gabrielle," Tarek said coolly.

Gabby took a deep breath, giving her temper a moment to settle itself. In an even tone, she asked, "Will I have to stay down here?"

Tarek's gaze lingered on the queen. The regal woman shook her head. "Of course not. You shall be my guest until we can have you returned home," the queen said. "Come along."

Gabby had to hurry to keep up with the queen's long strides. As they walked back down the corridor, the inhabitants of the other cells were eerily silent, as if they were afraid to attract the queen's attention. Gabby couldn't blame them. The queen spoke rapidly to the guards on either side of her. She sounded furious. She'd have to make a point of asking Tarek to translate later.

The queen paused in the open area outside of the lift that Gabby had ridden down to the dungeons. She made a graceful gesture, brushing her fingers over her brow, then sweeping her hand down toward Gabby. "Thank you again," she said. "Tarek will escort you to the guest quarters, where my staff will ensure that you are cared for. We will see that you return home as quickly as possible."

"Thank you," Gabby said.

The queen nodded, her lips curving in a smile that did not meet her cold, calculating eyes. "Remember what I said. Do not violate my trust. You will not live long to regret it."

Chapter Twenty

The Queen's Guards escorted Gabby and Tarek up on the lift, though they had put away their weapons and even struck up casual conversation with Tarek. The unfamiliar language left her feeling utterly alone, and she was relieved to step out of the lift and into a long stone corridor. One side of the hall was lined in carved wooden doorways, while the other was a series of wide open window frames. They opened onto small balconies overlooking the city below. Cool, fresh air blew through the open arches. Outside the citadel, the evening sky was streaked in coral and fiery red by the setting sun.

Halfway down the hall, a pair of finely dressed attendants waited at a door. The woman, a petite brunette in a blue and silver gown waved, her face lighting up in recognition at their approach. The man immediately made the same salute of respect that the guards had shown the queen, placing his hand to his heart. The others followed suit.

When Gabby and Tarek reached the doorway, the woman began speaking rapidly in the dragon language, her face animated and smiling. Gabby stared at her helplessly, then looked to Tarek. He responded to the woman, who looked at her male companion and gave him a *shoo* gesture that was apparently universal. Without protesting, he left and headed back toward the lift. The woman looked at Tarek expectantly, then shooed him away. Tarek shook his head and gestured to Gabby.

The woman sighed and motioned for Gabby to follow her into the room. Gabby only made it a few steps before she froze, staring around in wonder. When the queen had mentioned guest quarters, she had imagined a modest room, but she stood in a room that was a cross between an obscenely extravagant penthouse and a fortuneteller's tent.

Dark-stained wooden doors opened onto a small balcony, allowing a cold breeze to blow through the room. Gleaming silver decorations adorned the stone walls. An enormous bed took up one corner of the room, with a canopy draped in shimmering blue silks. Cushions and pillows were strewn about, all glittering with embroidery and tiny silver beads. And it smelled divine. Though she knew it couldn't be, it smelled like when her mother cooked homemade cinnamon rolls for breakfast on Christmas morning.

The woman spoke rapidly, and Tarek touched her arm lightly. "This will be your quarters while you stay," he said.

Stay. Even if she had a pretty cell, she was still a prisoner. She quietly thanked the servant woman and glanced back at Tarek.

"The queen obviously appreciates your aid," he said.

"Yes, so much that she decided to keep me," Gabby murmured.

Tarek sighed and rested his hand on her shoulder. He gestured toward the balcony, then walked outside into the warm light of the setting sun. She didn't follow right away, and instead enjoyed the view. Up until now, she'd been a little preoccupied with the whole being thrown into dragon prison and waiting for something to either kill her, eat her, or both. Now she could really appreciate that Tarek was wearing little more than a loincloth, with the evening light playing off his dark golden skin. Bruises and half-healed cuts

130

marked his back, and for the first time it occurred to her that he'd been through a hell of a battle to get to her. A pang of guilt struck her as she realized how focused she'd been on herself.

"Are you coming?" he asked, startling her. One eyebrow perked in amusement. *Oh hell.* Her cheeks went hot, and she shook herself as she scurried toward him.

He gently touched her shoulder as she leaned against the waist-high wall around the balcony. The dark gray and blue of the mountain peaks stretched far beyond them, zig-zagging against the sky. Below them, the citadel's walls curved out and around, like someone wrapping stone arms around the courtyard below. A stone dome covered much of the courtyard, but the center was open, revealing a dense canopy of green speckled with bright tropical flowers. Gabby was jolted suddenly with a sense of recognition. This was the garden she'd seen in Ashariah's memories, where the princess had played as a child.

Gray pillars broke through the green canopy. Tarek leaned on the waist-high stone wall around the balcony. "Those are the *Avekh dar Isina*," he said. "It means the Bones of the Skymother, more or less. The garden is the heart of Adamantine Rise."

"Tarek, this is beautiful," she said. "But I can't stay here."

"You do not have a choice," he replied.

"Is that how you do things here?"

"If the queen orders it."

"I have a life at home," she snapped. "And people who are probably worried about me."

A sad smile tugged at his lips. "I know. I am sorry to have involved you." His eyes creased as he examined her. Hesitant at first, he extended his hand and lightly brushed his thumb along her cheek, outlining the tender, swollen welt where the guard had cuffed her. Though his touch brought a slight ache, it also sent a pleasant tingle down her spine. "Would you like me to break the hand of whoever did this?"

She laughed despite herself. "It's tempting, but you don't have to," she said. "But why are they making such a big deal out of me?"

He turned to face the mountain vista. The blaze of sunset set off coppery tones in his hair. "It's very strange that you can resist our commands."

"Yeah, what is that?"

Glancing over his shoulder, he asked, "Do you remember when I tried to tell you to release Ashariah to me? And you fought me on it?"

"Of course."

"You shouldn't have been able to do that," he said. "My kind can influence lesser minds." As soon as he said the words, his eyes widened.

"Lesser minds? I went to medical school, jerk."

"That's not what I meant," he said. "You are very intelligent for the Vak."

"Tarek!"

His cheeks flushed. "I'm saying things badly." He sighed and touched her hand lightly. "I did not mean to say you were stupid. Clearly, you are not. Your kind is not gifted with magic. Mine is. That's all I meant." She gave him a cool stare. "I apologize. I truly meant no insult to you."

After a long stretch of silence, watching him squirm, she finally nodded.

"I accept. You can influence humans." He nodded. "Who are also people who can be perfectly intelligent and capable of taking care of dragons who get themselves shot."

He rolled his eyes, though the corner of his mouth pulled into a ghost of a smile. "Yes, of course."

"Carry on."

"I cannot force you to do something that you find abhorrent. If I told you to climb onto this ledge and jump, you would be able to resist, unless you were already considering it," he said, giving her a questioning look. "But if I told you to go lie down inside and have a nap, you would immediately do it, regardless of what else you were doing. Likewise, if I commanded you to tell me the truth about something, unless you had an iron will, you would have to tell me. When you resisted me, I assumed that it was me, or that you were so devoted to protecting the princess that my persuasion didn't work. But when the others at the gate had a similar failure, I doubted that was the case. And when you resisted the queen's commands and broke eye contact with her, that confirmed it."

"Confirmed what?"

He shrugged. "There is something unusual about you. Did you feel anything?"

She nodded. "I felt this crawling sensation in my head. With the queen, it felt like my whole head was going to explode."

He nodded. "That is why she insists on you staying. If there is a way to create a resistance to our commands, then we must know. That would be a very useful magic for our enemies to possess," he said. "The queen's council will work on it. Hopefully it won't take long."

"It better not," she said. "Is there a way to make contact with my family? My mother calls me every day. If she doesn't get me, she'll start freaking out."

He folded his arms over his broad chest. "We could send word back to the Gate. One of my subordinates could go speak with her and tell her that you were called away for work."

"She wouldn't believe it if she doesn't hear from me," Gabby said.

"We can make her believe it."

Gabby stared at him in shock. "I don't want you to use your little mind tricks on her," she said. "She's a person, not a puppet."

He threw up his hands in frustration. "I cannot take you back. If you wish for her not to worry, this is my only suggestion."

She stared out over the foreign landscape. This was all too much. There was a part of her that wanted to find a blanket to curl up in and cry like a little kid, from the sheer overwhelming weirdness and helplessness of the situation. But if she hadn't broken down already, she wasn't going to do it now. She'd get through this just like always.

Okay, Rojas, think. Her mother would be distraught if Gabby was out of touch for more than a day. Even when she was on call and sleeping in the hospital for two days at a time, she always touched base with her mother via text message. Her mother's despair would reach Anna, who couldn't handle a lot of stress to her already weakened system. And when she got home, which she had to believe she would, she'd have a mess to deal with.

"Okay," she said, breaking the silence after taking a while to think. "I need a pen and paper. I have instructions."

Tarek quirked an eyebrow. "You're giving orders?"

She crossed her arms over her chest. "The way I see it, you and all your scaly friends owe me for all of this trouble. This is the least you can do."

"Your wish is my command," he said. "Give me a moment."

He turned and walked back into the room, where the servant woman was still fussing around, unloading a small basket with linens and candles. She listened intently as Tarek spoke to her, then bustled out of the room. When he returned, he had a smile on his face. "Your will is done. To be honest, I am much happier that you are staying for the time being."

The butterflies in her stomach swirled in a tornado of giddy nerves. What the hell was wrong with her? She managed to keep her voice even. "Why?"

He tilted his head. "Things may become...unpleasant as the queen investigates this issue. I would feel better knowing that you are here where you can be protected."

"What will she do?"

"She will likely send additional troops to patrol the skies near our Gate, The Drakemont, where I sent you with Ashariah. And she will almost certainly request an audience with Queen Tarim."

"Who?"

"She is the queen of the Ironflight," he said. "The dragons who attacked Ashariah were from the Ironflight. They are old enemies. We are at peace, but it has been uneasy. The knife I gave you was of Ironflight make. I found it buried to the hilt in the chest of one of Ashariah' guards in the desert."

"I'm going to ignore the part where you gave me a used knife, because that is incredibly unsanitary." Tarek grinned, etching pleasant creases around his warm eyes. Mirth was a good look on him. Well, everything was a good look on him, but the rare smile sent a thrill of delight through her. "If this other queen is attacking you, why would she come here?"

"Unless she wishes to openly declare war, she must grant an audience when requested," Tarek said. "It would be very rude and dishonorable otherwise."

Gabby snorted. "Because apparently trying to murder the princess is so polite and honorable?"

"We have our ways," Tarek said. "Halmerah will demand her presence immediately. We will have an answer one way or the other soon."

"So what do I do in the meantime?"

He shrugged. "The queen's councilors will probably wish to speak to you. Otherwise, you are free to do as you wish. If you would allow me, I would show you around. And of course, I will protect you from harm."

His eyes fell on hers. She felt trapped in his gaze, but she didn't want to be free of that trap. Gabrielle Rojas was an independent woman, dammit, but right then, she would let him protect her against anything. Without breaking her gaze, he raised her hand to his lips and kissed her fingertips lightly. A shock shot down her arm and straight to her spine. She tried not to gasp in surprise.

"Tarek," a woman said. Gabby snapped to attention to see the servant woman holding out a beautiful pendant in one hand and a roll of paper in the other. The pendant was a polished purple stone, wrapped in silver wire and hanging from a delicate chain. The stone twisted slowly on its chain as the woman held it out.

"It's for you," he said. He took the necklace in one hand, then brushed her hair over her shoulder. A shiver broke across her skin as his fingers grazed her neck and fastened the pendant. It was pleasantly warm against her chest. She turned to see Tarek giving her a curious look. "Do you understand me now?"

"Of course I understand you," she said.

"It is a great pleasure to meet you, Gabrielle," the woman said. "My name is Raszila. I serve the queen and her guests."

Gabby frowned. Was she...

"It's the amulet," Tarek said. He touched the amulet gently. "As long as you wear it, you will be able to understand the tongue of the Kadirai."

"And I'm..."

"You're speaking it," he said, his lips quirking into a smile.

She touched the amulet, stunned in wonder. "Is this...magic?"

"No more magical than your iPhone."

"And the paper you requested," Raszila said, handing it over. Tarek accepted it, then waited for the women to draw a crude pencil from her apron. "I can find a nicer pen if you'd like, but you asked for it quickly."

Tarek glanced at Gabby. "This is fine," she said. "Thank you."

Gabby took the paper, a piece of thick ivory parchment, and the pencil. After glancing around, she sat on the cool stone of the balcony and used the flat surface to write on. "Oh, Miss Gabrielle, please come in and sit where it is comfortable," Raszila said, wringing her hands.

"I'm fine, thank you," Gabby said. She took several minutes to write precise instructions. One of the neurosurgeons had a cabin in the Colorado mountains and was always offering to let the other physicians use it for vacations. That would be her story. After writing down the passcode to her phone and describing exactly what kind of charger to buy, she wrote several text messages to send to her mother, including a few key Spanish phrases that her mother would use and expect a response to. Drawing a line to divide the carefully labeled *Mama* section, she wrote the names of her key contacts at the hospital. After examining her list, she realized it seemed woefully small. She had a few friends, but no one that would be frantically worried if she didn't contact them for a few days. Work was her life, with family a close second. It was a bit sad. Finally, she looked up at Tarek. "Here are my instructions."

He scanned it over and gave her a bemused look. "You are very thorough."

"I want you to get this right," she said primly. "Will it hurt my mother at all?"

He shook his head. "It is no more than a gentle suggestion. It will simply put her worries at ease."

"Okay. Then have your guys do this," she said. "And tell them to be nice to her. If they do anything—"

He laughed and took her hand. "Gabrielle, they will not do anything to harm her. You have my word." His eyes bored into her as she considered the value of what he promised. Thus far, he had been a man of his word. Finally, she nodded.

Raszila made a clucking noise with her tongue. "Now, will you please leave us? You have your job, and I have mine. I would see that our guest is taken care of."

"I will be back to check on you," Tarek said. Raszila rolled her eyes and planted her hands on his bare back, pushing him gently toward the door. For a second, Gabby was terribly envious of the woman getting a handful of those muscles.

"Don't rush. After I take care of her, she will not need you," Raszila said. Tarek laughed as he went. She shooed him and closed the door behind him.

Gabby watched him go with regret lingering in her mind. After he had left, Raszila turned back to her. The beautiful woman was about Gabby's height, but slight of frame. She was much smaller than the Kadirai that Gabby had seen, which made her wonder if Raszila was human. "Now, where were we?"

The woman ushered her to the corner of the room, where a large silver-ornamented tub stood inside long drapes of blue silk. The pleasant warmth of steam reached Gabby even from a few feet away. As she approached the tub, she realized just how long it had been since she'd gotten a chance to relax and shower. Her gym clothes could probably stand up on their own, especially after the adrenaline-soaked flight from the Gate to the fortress and the subsequent unpleasant visit to the dungeons.

The warm touch of Raszila's hands on her hips startled her from her reverie. Gabby instinctively covered the woman's hands, keeping the hem of her shirt down. The servant looked at her, surprised. "I can do it," Gabby insisted.

"But the queen insists," Raszila said.

"She said you have to undress me?"

"She said you were to be treated as royalty," Raszila huffed. "She will be displeased."

"It's okay. I promise I won't tell her."

Raszila sighed, then waved her hand in a *go ahead* gesture. Gabby carefully peeled the sweat-sticky shirt over her head, then hesitated with the clasps of the sports bra covering her chest. She jumped a little at the warm touch of fingers on her shoulder. Raszila fingered the elastic material, pinching it and stretching it out with an expression of wonder on her face. She was unfazed by the magical amulet that translated languages, but apparently spandex was a miracle.

"Can you close your eyes?"

"Your body will not surprise me," Raszila said.

"It's not you," Gabby said. "I don't like being naked in front of people."

Raszila raised an eyebrow. "Very strange, your kind." She shrugged and made a point of closing her eyes. Gabby quickly shucked off her pants, hesitating before she sent her underwear with them. After checking that Raszila still had her eyes closed, Gabby carefully lifted one foot over the stone ledge and into the warm water. It was pleasantly warm and effervescent. She slowly crouched into the tub. When she was in the water up to her chest, she said, "I'm in."

Raszila sighed and made a clucking sound with her tongue. "Will you allow me to do nothing?" She bustled around the tub and returned with several glass jars clutched to her breast. After perusing them, she opened one and released a wave of delicious, earthy-smelling scent. "May I at least clean your hair?"

"Yes," Gabby said. Her body tensed as the woman approached, but when the first wave of warm water poured over her scalp and down her neck, she relaxed. It was like having her hair done at the salon, except instead of a hairdresser, she had someone who worked for a dragon queen. Close enough.

The other woman's fingers gently massaged her scalp. With the wonderful, tingling sensation radiating from her touch, the tension flowed out of Gabby's muscles, and she leaned back against the stone ledge. The scent of spice filled her nostrils as Raszila massaged the shampoo into her hair. Her scalp tingled with the cool sensation. As she worked, Raszila hummed a song under her breath.

"Are you a dragon?" Gabby asked.

"No," Raszila said. She poured more water over Gabby's hair, and then began combing it gently.

"What are you? I'm sorry, is that rude?"

Raszila chuckled, her hands shaking with the laughter as she combed through Gabby's hair. "I am Edra."

"What is that?"

"Oh, of course. You are an outsider," Raszila said, still combing gently. "The Kadirai are dragons. There are others who have an animal spirit. They call us Edra."

"So you're like a werewolf?"

"A..."

"Shapeshifter?"

"Shape...shifter," Raszila said. "Yes. I can change shapes. I was born with the spirit of the lark."

"So are there lots of Edra?" Gabby said.

"Oh yes," Raszila said. "Many more than the Kadirai, although there are not many here in Adamantine Rise. It is a great honor to serve the queen. Most of the Edra live in Farath, the city below."

Finally, Raszila finished combing, twisted the wet tresses, and pinned them in place on top of Gabby's head. Something pleasantly rough, like an exfoliating sponge touched Gabby's shoulder. "Do you mind?"

Gabby's inhibitions were rapidly eroding. The warm water and the luxurious smell had sapped all the tension out of her. "No," she murmured dreamily.

Raszila continued to hum quietly as she scrubbed Gabby's back and shoulders. The sponge dipped over her shoulder, brushing across the top of her breast. After a pause, she held out the sponge. "Unless you would like me to. As royalty."

"I can handle it," Gabby said. She took the sponge and finished washing herself, then handed it back.

"Sit," Raszila said, patting the edge of the tub.

Along one corner of the stone basin was a smoothly curved seat. Gabby sat on the edge, crossing her arms over her breasts.

There was a hint of warmth at the nape of her neck, and then a heat that sank from her skin into her bones. Raszila rubbed an ointment that smelled of mint and eucalyptus into her skin, working her nimble fingers into the tight muscles. Gabby groaned in pleasure as the woman massaged her shoulders. For a moment, she allowed herself the fantasy of Tarek doing this work instead, of his strong hands working down her back and caressing her warm skin. A twinge of heat bloomed at her center, and she felt herself blush furiously as she crossed her legs.

"Are you all right?" Raszila asked. "Have I hurt you?"

"Not at all," Gabby said quickly. The woman continued her massage, working down the muscles in each arm, then kneading the knots out of her back. After a few minutes that seemed way too short, Raszila brought her a light dressing gown and helped her out of the tub. The servant woman led her to a low seat with a pile of plump cushions. Once Gabby sat down, Raszila knelt at her feet. With the jar of glittering green ointment, the woman turned her attention to Gabby's feet. The pressure verged on painful, but left a pleasant tingle in its wake. She could definitely get used to the royal treatment.

Raszila glanced up at her, her eyes playful under thick lashes. "I will assume that you would not care for any further relaxation or release."

"Uh, huh?"

The woman chuckled. "Never mind," she said, laughing to herself. After she continued her massage up to the knees, she rearranged the dressing gown over Gabby's legs and stood up. "Are you hungry?"

"Very," Gabby said. She'd managed to forget about eating but just hearing the question had reminded her stomach of how empty it was.

"I will see to it. And I am certain you will be pleased."

CHAPTER TWENTY-ONE

AFTER LEAVING GABRIELLE in Raszila's capable hands, Tarek wandered the familiar stone corridors of Adamantine Rise. He'd always hated to admit to weakness, but stubbornness would not heal the damage wrought upon his body by the battles of the last few days. And a visit to the healers' pavilion among the Bones would let him check on the princess.

Little had changed in Adamantine Rise since he had left some ten years earlier, but his former home now felt distant and strange. The cool stone under his bare feet, the scent of incense in the air, and the faint tingle of magic in the air were foreign to him. He found himself longing for the familiarity of the human world: the unrelenting desert sun, the reliable morning bite of black coffee, and of all things, Gabrielle. Though he'd known her for barely a day, he felt connected to her, like he'd known her for years.

He'd been shocked at the ferocity of his rage when saw her in the stinking depths of the dungeon, and equally shocked at his pride and vindication upon seeing Queen Halmerah order her release and honor her as a guest. Those intense emotions, the warmth that stirred in him at the thought of her, reminded him of a life that was so long ago it almost seemed like a dream. He didn't dare acknowledge the thoughts that swirled in his mind, the ones that spoke of a bond more than the temporary one born out of danger and necessity. Down that road lay too much potential for loss and pain. It would be far wiser for him to keep his distance, especially with another war with the Ironflight brewing. Distance would let him focus, and she would be safer without his attention and cursed nature on her.

Tarek descended a spiraling staircase into the cool green expanse of the gardens. Just entering the powerful circle formed by the Bones brought a shift in the atmosphere. There was a weight in the air, a crackling energy that tickled his bare skin. The injuries all over his body suddenly eased, the sensation muffled to a dull ache.

Smooth stone paths cut through the gardens. Several of the Kadirai along the way greeted him, but no one lingered for a conversation. There was a quiet tension in the air, no doubt because of the news of the attack on the princess. And those who had gathered in the garden were there to meditate and find solace in the soothing energy there, not to gossip.

In the northeast corner of the garden, the stone path sloped upward to the healer's pavilion. Armed guards were posted on either side of the steps. Though he didn't speak, the guards gave him a nod of recognition and allowed him to enter.

Inside the pavilion, a ring of beds draped in pale linens surrounded one of the Bones. Silver veins ran down the stone pillar and across the floor like tree roots. At the far side of the pavilion, a crowd surrounded one of the beds. Even from far away, he immediately recognized Halmerah's tall silhouette among them.

A healer dressed in light gray clothing and plain silver jewelry approached him. Fine gray and silver gleamed within her braid, though age had only touched her kindly face with the faintest creases at the corners of her dark blue eyes. After looking him over, she said quietly, "Come with me."

"Will you tell the queen that Tarek Windstriker is here?"

"Of course," she said. Without question, Tarek followed her to an open bed. Her hands were warm as she untied the leather garment covering him. Taking a step back, she examined him with the practiced eye of a professional and paid no more attention to his nakedness than she would have a speck of dust. After briefly prodding at the worst of his injuries, she gestured for him to sit. "I'll be back," she told him before retreating to a storeroom to gather supplies. He watched her head bob as she walked down a spiraling staircase to the underground storage below the pavilion.

He had just turned back to let himself relax into the soft comfort of the bed when he heard the gentle swish of fabric on stone. As his gaze swept up from the shapely legs to the queen's haughty visage, he leapt off the bed to find a chair. The queen waved him off. "I can fetch my own chair, you fool of a dragon," she said. Her tone was an attempt at being playful, but worry drained the humor from her rich voice.

"As you wish, su'ud redahn," he said. Her dismissal was for the best, since the quick motion had set his head spinning like a tornado. He fixed his gaze on Halmerah to steady himself and plopped back onto the bed.

Halmerah raised her eyebrows at the honorific, then looked around the niche surrounding the bed. She found a low stool by the next bed and hooked it with her foot to pull it closer. With her legs neatly folded and her posture ramrod straight, she made the rough-hewn wooden stool look like a throne. She had changed out of her silken finery from earlier and into a plainer robe-like dress that crossed over her chest and tied with a wide silver sash.

The healer returned and gasped in surprise. "*Su'ud redahn,*" she breathed. "Allow me to get you something more appropriate to sit upon."

"Nonsense," Halmerah said sharply. "Please inform me if I am any hindrance to your work."

The healer gaped, her gaze flitting between Tarek and the queen for several seconds. "I—yes, of course," she said. Her gaze remained on the queen as she laid out several stoneware jars and a bundle of clean rags on a wooden tray.

The healer was silent as she opened a small blue jar and scooped out a handful of its contents. Tarek gasped in surprise at the cold, jelly-like substance she spread across his shoulder. While her touch was gentle, it was clinical and detached. He couldn't help thinking of Gabrielle and the way she had responded to his discomfort by peeling off her glove and caressing his skin, making contact and providing more comfort than she'd realized.

Halmerah ignored the healer and Tarek's sound of surprise. "My daughter has not woken despite being here among the Bones for hours," she said flatly. "What happened over there?"

"The human woman spoke the truth," he said. "I found Surik dead in the desert with an Ironflight blade in his chest."

Halmerah cursed. "He was one of my best." She pressed one hand to her brow. Her jewelry tinkled lightly with the gesture. Beneath the span of her graceful hand, her face was creased with worry. She took a deep breath, but she couldn't conceal the hitch in her breath that spoke of tears that wanted to spill over her cheeks. There was a joke among the Adamant Guard that if

Halmerah were ever to cry, she would weep chunks of pure marble. Tarek had laughed right along with them until he saw her weep for her slain elder child. Those tears, the same bitter rain as the most humble Vak, proved that the queen's heart was not made of mountain stone as they had once suspected. When Halmerah looked up again, her face was as cold and imperious as ever. "I do not understand the Ironflight. Why now?"

He shook his head. "They have long been upset at the balance of power."

"But to attack my daughter," she said. She glanced over her shoulder to look at Ashariah. Several more healers hovered over the princess, while a number of clerics in dark purple robes knelt at the end of her bed praying to the Skymother. "I would rather they had attacked me directly. She is innocent and naïve, too young to even know of the war. She knows of the struggle only from our stories. She has nothing to do with this. This was a cowardly act."

"I know," Tarek said. Speaking openly with Halmerah was the most familiar thing he'd experienced since returning home. It brought back the old days, when he was in her trusted circle, serving in Adamantine Rise instead of guarding a musty chamber with a seldom-used Gate. "Have you sent for Queen Tarim?"

Halmerah's nostril flared as her full upper lip curled. "My messengers have gone with my demand for an audience. I somehow doubt that she will..." The queen trailed off and looked over Tarek's shoulder. The soothing motion of massaging across his shoulder stopped as the healer realized Halmerah was staring at her. "I'm sure I do not have to tell you that whatever you hear is not for outside ears."

"No, *su'ud redahn*, of course," the healer said quickly. Tarek could feel the subtle vibration against his shoulder as her hands trembled. "I will not speak a word."

"Good," Halmerah said. "If Tarim is honorable, or at least pretending to be, she will answer my summons. As is proper, I will throw a feast to receive her. And then she will answer for what she has done."

"And if she doesn't?"

"Then she will learn why the Stoneflight holds the throne here at Adamantine Rise," Halmerah said forcefully. The sadness in her eyes turned to steely resolve.

"Are you preparing for war?" Tarek asked.

"The Stoneflight must always be prepared for war," Halmerah said. She shook her head and waved dismissively. "But you need not concern yourself with such things. You should rest. And I hope you will do me the honor of sitting at my side for the feast tomorrow. I wish for Tarim and her thugs to see that a warrior of the Stoneflight is not easily felled."

The sudden change stung worse than the healer's ministrations. However familiar the conversation had seemed, he was a fool to think she still trusted him as she once had. He was a guest in his own home, and the past remained between them like a stone wall.

The queen suddenly looked up. Tarek followed her gaze to see the healer holding out a steaming cup. "This will help you sleep," the healer said.

Tarek accepted it reluctantly, but did not drink from it. He stared into the amber liquid as he spoke quietly. "I would help you, if you would allow me."

Halmerah shook her head. "I know you wish to be of service. But for now, I would rather you rested and healed. Now, drink up."

He sighed and sipped the fragrant tea. It was a potent blend, almost alcoholic in its strength. He drained the cup and handed it back to the healer, hoping the sting of rejection didn't show on his face.

The queen gently touched his shoulder. "Do not trouble yourself, Tarek-ahn. All will be well."

"Thank you," he mumbled. The herbal mix was already slowing his mind, making his tongue thick and heavy. "And what of the woman?"

Halmerah raised an eyebrow. "The human?"

"Yes."

"I need time to seek counsel over today's events. I will have Councilor Eszen speak with her and attempt to understand what magic allows her to resist us. If she is under some spell, I would know of it. A Vak who can resist compulsion would be a dangerous spy in the wrong hands. She will stay here until I have answers, and then you will take her home and things will return to normal. It is not proper for a Vak to reside in my palace, no matter how altruistic their deeds."

The dismissal of Gabrielle cut through the haze in Tarek's mind like a knife. "She helped us. She helped Ashariah."

"As I said, I am grateful," Halmerah said sharply. "Have I not been gracious in her accommodations?"

"Yes, of course," he murmured.

"Now, you should rest. Everything will be back to normal soon."

"But..." he trailed off, his head spinning as the healer eased him back to the soft palette. As the heavy weight of sleep overtook him, he realized something odd. He didn't want things to go back to normal. He wanted for things to change. He wanted to be part of the queen's circle once more. He wanted to carry the sword in her name. But more than any of those things, he wanted to touch Gabrielle and to feel that connection again.

He was in trouble.

CHAPTER TWENTY-TWO

GABBY OPENED HER EYES to sunlight pouring through an open window and the smell of hot tea in her nostrils. She sat bolt upright in surprise. She'd overslept. Shit, she was supposed to be at the hospital already. Panic overwhelmed her as she looked around frantically and began the rapid mental calculations of how long it would take to get dressed and drive to work, complete with shortcuts like skipping the shower and buying coffee at work instead of making her own. As she took in her surroundings, panic was replaced by confusion and gradually, disbelief.

Instead of the beige walls and wall-mounted TV across from her bed, she was greeted by silver-flecked stone and an elaborate mosaic of a red dragon soaring over mountain peaks. The bedclothes were a textured weave of dark blue. Suddenly, it all came crashing back. Dragons. Magic. Shapeshifting.

"Holy shit," she murmured. Dizziness swept over her, and she flopped back on the huge bed. Silver veins in the stone ceiling gleamed bright in the morning sun. It was all real.

"Miss Gabrielle, are you awake?" a familiar voice said. Gabby sat up again and braced herself against a thick cushion as Raszila bustled into the room with a tray of food and drink. The servant woman's face creased in concern. "Are you all right?"

"Yes, just surprised," Gabby said.

"Did I wake you?"

"No, not at all," Gabby said. In fact, she couldn't remember the last time she'd woken up on her own, not to a shrill alarm clock or a midnight emergency call. "I just...this whole thing is strange. I almost thought it was a dream."

Raszila shrugged and placed the tray at the end of the bed. "Shall I get clothes for you while you eat?"

"That would be wonderful," Gabby said. The pretty servant woman nodded and left her to eat. Her breakfast consisted of a tray of fresh fruit and an assortment of sliced breads that were still piping hot. Small dishes of colorful sauces were arranged in the gaps between oval plates. She broke off a piece of golden flaky bread, dipped it into the yellow sauce, and popped it into her mouth. She groaned with pleasure as a mix of cinnamon, butter, and something almost like pineapple exploded on her taste buds. Each bread was different, but she didn't find a single one that wasn't delicious. She was polishing off what looked like blueberries but tasted more like grapes when Raszila returned with a bundle of red fabric laid over one arm and a small basket tucked under her other arm.

"We start," she said. "If you are finished."

"Oh, yes," Gabby said, a little sheepish as she surveyed the scattered crumbs that were all that remained of her breakfast.

Raszila nodded. "If you would like me to close my eyes?" She gestured broadly to the basket.

"Thank you," Gabby said. She pawed through the basket and found her own clothes from the day before folded neatly and tucked tight into one side.

The other garments in the basket were made of ivory linen, shot through with gold threads.

"The gold ones, if you please," Raszila said without opening her eyes.

Gabby shook them out to find a pair of loose drawstring pants and a short top. After appraising her own body, she reached for the familiar comfort of her black sports bra and put it on. She quickly put on the other garments and said, "Okay."

Raszila opened her eyes and smiled. Then she stepped closer and reached for Gabby's shoulder. She gave the strap of the bra a pop. "What is this?"

"It's a bra," Gabby said.

Raszila rolled her eyes. "You do not need this."

"I'm wearing it."

The woman threw up her hands. "Fine," she said. She shook out the pile of red fabric. The long rectangle of textured silk was trimmed in sparkling gold, with elaborately beaded designs in opposite corners. Raszila started neatly folding pleats with her thin fingers as guides. She tucked the pleats into the waistband, creating a skirt, then made a few elaborate folds and twists to bring the fabric around Gabby's torso and over her shoulder. Sure enough, Raszila pulled a twist of fabric tightly around Gabby's chest; even without a bra, it would have kept her chest supported. When she was finished, she used several long looped pins to secure the fabric to Gabby's shoulder and hip. She stepped back, adjusted a pleat here and there, then finally gave a nod of approval. "Red is very nice on your skin."

"Thank you," Gabby said. She glanced down to see her body wrapped in the sparkling red fabric. Surprisingly, it wasn't tight or uncomfortable, but was wrapped just right to let her walk and move comfortably.

"You have lovely hair," Raszila said. "May I?"

"Of course," Gabby said. She could get used to someone else taking care of her. It beat the hell out of blow-drying her own hair.

At Raszila's direction, she sat on a low chair and let the other woman style her hair. Her fingers were strong and deft as she sectioned off Gabby's hair, twisting and braiding as she hummed. After a while, she nudged Gabby's shoulder and guided her across the room to look at a mirror hanging on the wall.

Gabby froze. Though her face seemed strangely bare without any makeup, she couldn't help but be amazed at her appearance. Red fabric hugged her curves tightly, giving her an hourglass figure and setting off her golden skin. Her thick hair was arranged in an elaborate style with braids and twists wrapping around a fluffy bun atop her head. As a finishing touch, Raszila produced a gold comb with irregular red gemstones and wedged it into the hairstyle.

"Now, the queen sends instructions that you are permitted to explore the palace if you wish. However, you should probably have an escort to ensure that you don't get lost," Raszila said. She gave Gabby a knowing look in the mirror. "I'm sure you wouldn't mind if your friend Tarek came."

Gabby's cheeks heated. "Well, he is the only person I know here. Besides you."

"And I'm terribly busy today, so it will have to be him," Raszila said as she fiddled with the folded fabric on Gabby's shoulder. "However, you are to stop by the library and speak with Councilor Eszen this morning. Tarek will know where to go."

"Councilor Eszen?"

Raszila nodded. "He oversees the Great Library. He is a scholar of magic and history. What would you talk to him about?"

Gabby hesitated. How much was Raszila supposed to know? "I'm not sure. Maybe how to get me back home," she said.

The woman shrugged. She was about to speak again when a light knock sounded from the door. Raszila scurried to open it, then greeted the visitor. "Good morning, Tarek," she said, emphasizing his name. The sound sent a thrill of nervous excitement through Gabby.

Tarek was still acknowledging the servant woman with a nod as he entered the room. He turned to Gabby and stopped short, his eyebrows shooting up. "Oh," Tarek murmured. "Well."

Was he blushing? Gabby's cheeks heated as she realized he was checking her out unabashedly. She didn't mind her view either; though he'd put on loose pants and a shirt cinched with a wide leather belt, she still had a fine view of his muscular arms and narrow waist. His dark hair was swept away from his face, which looked fresh and well-rested.

"It's weird, right?"

"Not the word I'd have chosen," he said.

"Are you here to show Lady Gabrielle around?" Raszila asked pointedly.

He looked at the servant woman in surprise. "I—yes?"

"Good," she said. "You're to visit the library as well."

"Of course," he said. "Thank you." He held out his hand. "Would you allow me to show you my home?"

"I would be honored," she said. She hesitated, then placed her hand in his. As his strong hand closed around it, another tingle of excitement washed over her like an electric current. He squeezed it lightly and brought it to his lips, kissing her fingers gently. Heat rose on her cheeks as his gaze met hers over the curve of her knuckles. *Is this real life?*

Like Alice down the rabbit hole, she had fallen smack-dab into the middle of her own bizarre fairy-tale. It was beyond weird, but what was the harm in enjoying the trip?

By day, the massive castle was bustling with activity as servants and guests hurried along the corridor. Daylight poured in through the open windows lining the stone wall. But as she looked closer, she realized there was something strange about the light. It was not the warm glow of the sun she knew, but a harsh white light that seemed to wash the stone out, like bleached bone. And despite the bright light, it was cool, bordering on cold with the constant breeze. Raszila had draped a soft wine-colored shawl around her shoulders before leaving, and now Gabby understood why.

As they strolled down the gently curving corridor of the guest quarters, Gabby felt the weight of inquisitive glances that lasted too long. But she felt strangely safe and secure with Tarek at her side.

"Did you sleep well?" he asked.

"Very," she said. "I think she put something in the tea."

"I'm sure she did," Tarek said with a laugh. "Halmerah's staff is notorious for it. If the queen orders you to rest, then you will rest whether you want to or not."

"How about you?"

"I saw the healers," he said. "I'll be fine."

She paused and tilted her head. "You got shot."

He shrugged. "I told you, things are different here."

With a frown, she circled around him and touched his shoulder. It had been bruised and cut when she last saw him, not to mention the bullet hole. His upper arm was now smooth, marked with only fine white marks like light scratches.

Tarek chuckled, then pulled the bottom of his shirt up to reveal his torso. There were old scars across his back that she'd glimpsed when she took care of him back in the motel. And right where she'd pulled a bullet out of him, there was a closed pink mark, maybe the size of a nickel. It wasn't fully healed, and it was still surrounded in the purplish shadows of deep bruising. But she'd seen it with her own eyes less than twenty-four hours earlier.

She hesitated, then rested her hand against his back. His skin was warm, and he jumped a little at her touch. Then he relaxed, glancing over his shoulder as she gently ran her hand down the nearly healed plane of his shoulder blade. She was on the verge of asking *how's your ass* when she realized how inappropriate it would sound.

"Do you believe me now?"

She was startled by his voice. As she looked up, she noticed a pair of servants carrying trays of food, both staring at them. Well, to be fair, she was a human who appeared to be groping Tarek, who had his shirt pulled halfway over his head. They weren't blending in so well. "I believe you."

"So I can put this back?"

She stole another glance at his muscular chest and the smooth curve from broad chest to narrow waist. It was a shame to hide it. "I suppose."

He cocked his head, his lips quirking into a smile. Then he chuckled to himself and tucked the shirt back under his belt. "Is the doctor satisfied with the healers' work?"

"It's impressive," she said. "How?" The kind of healing he'd shown would take weeks or months in her world. She wanted to bottle up whatever they were using and take it home.

Tarek shrugged. "How does the sun come up in the morning?"

"Well, technically, it doesn't. The earth, or whatever we're on now, just rotates," she said.

He raised an eyebrow. "You are very strange."

"In a good way?"

He smiled and continued walking down the corridor. Her heart thrummed with nervous energy. She felt like she was on a first date, and instead of counting the minutes until she could go home to a bottle of wine and the couch, she wanted desperately to impress Tarek.

"In a good way," he agreed finally.

She felt such a sense of relief and pride that it nearly overwhelmed her. How ridiculous was that? There was a shelf life on their relationship, and not a generous one. Whatever was between them would be over as soon as he got her home where she belonged, and her life would go back to being painfully normal. She knew all of these things, but her heart hadn't gotten the memo. Her heart, idiot that it was, was stuck on the dreamy eyes looking up as he kissed her hand and offered a tour of the mountain castle he called home.

Screw being logical for once.

"So you still didn't answer my question about how they do it?"

"Healing magic," he said. He shrugged. "I don't understand it any more than I understand electricity in your world. It is a natural occurrence. I don't mean to frustrate you, but it's beyond my ken."

Gabby sighed. "Well, I'm at least glad you're feeling better. How was the princess?"

"Much the same as when you cared for her," he said. "They are healing her external injuries, but she still sleeps without waking. They are at a loss."

"That doesn't make any sense," Gabby murmured.

"I know," Tarek said. "Have you seen this in your work?"

"I ordered scans on Ashariah, and none of them showed any significant trauma to her brain," she said. "It's possible that she had a bleed that only presented after some time had passed."

She looked up and saw Tarek staring down at her, his eyebrows raised. "I'm don't understand."

"Sometimes an injury to the brain doesn't show up for a day or two after it has time to swell and bleed," she said. "But Ashariah didn't show any signs of that. I'd like to take a look at her."

Tarek hesitated. "We can try. They may not allow you in."

At the end of the corridor was a round chamber with lifts on either side of a spiraling staircase. Tarek paused, offering his hand to support her. Though her instinct was to resist, she rather liked the idea of the gallant man guiding her around the castle. She might as well enjoy it while she could. She placed her hand in his larger one, and he grasped it gently as he led her down the stairs. As Gabby carefully took the first stair, navigating the unfamiliar skirts, she saw Tarek's feet were bare, like Raszila's were. The servant woman had brought her a pair of soft slippers after noticing her 'delicate feet,' as she put it. If the hard stone bothered Tarek, he didn't show it.

"What about my mom?" she asked.

He nodded. "I sent strict instructions with Zafar, the Gatekeeper who brought you here." A scowl darkened his handsome features.

"I don't want him talking to her."

"I thought you might say so," Tarek said. "That is why I told him to send Shazakh. He is young and spends a great deal of time among humans. And on his phone." He rolled his eyes. "But he is good with people. He will handle it well. If he does not, I will string him up by his wings."

Gabby laughed. "Thank you."

He shrugged. "It was my pleasure."

After descending several flights, they emerged onto another floor of the fortress. This one was busier, with people chattering loudly over papers and hurrying in all directions. Beyond a heavily guarded doorway was another hallway lined in huge open windows. But instead of the garden, these windows overlooked a city that spread out from the base of the mountain. Every so often, a small balcony jutted out from the window.

The balconies seemed out of place. They were only a few feet square, hardly big enough to sit and enjoy. But her confusion was resolved when she watched a young woman step onto the closest terrace and peel off a dingy linen robe to reveal her naked body. After dropping the robe into a small basket under a bench, the woman transformed into a small red dragon as if it was no more unusual than taking off a winter coat. The red creature soared into the sky and then shot upward.

Gabby rushed out onto the terrace, clutching the railing as she stared up at the red figure spiraling upward into the sky. "Whoa," she breathed. The red dragon sailed away from the fortress and over the city below.

Tarek joined her on the balcony and gestured to the city. "This is the city of Farath," he said. "The Kadirai live here in the citadel. The Vak live down there." There was a note of disdain in his voice that she didn't like.

"The Vak. You mean, normal people. Humans. Like me."

He tilted his head. He looked confused. "Normal is relative, Gabrielle. This is normal for me."

"They're not allowed up here?"

"No," he said. "Not usually."

"So that explains why people have been looking at me funny," Gabby said. She tried to sound light-hearted, but things were starting to make more sense. The dragons were in power, ruling from their secret clubhouse up here on the mountain. As far as they were concerned, everyone else was below them, literally. "That seems kind of exclusive."

He shrugged. "It could be worse. There are places where the Vak are slaves to the Kadirai. At least they are free here. It is easier on all of us to remain separate."

"I'm guessing you don't know too much Earth history," she murmured. He tilted his head quizzically, but she decided it wasn't the time for a lecture on segregation. "So the queen allows others to have slaves?"

"It is not her choice. While she voices her displeasure when given the chance, she has no power outside our lands. Though she wishes she did," Tarek said drily. "The Kadirai are fractured into many flights. Each flight has its own lands, its own queen, and its own ways. We do not interfere with the other flights. We mind our own lands and protect them from here."

The city below them spilled over the slope of the mountain and into the valley below. Thin plumes of smoke arose from thousands of chimneys, while a thicker cloud of dark smoke hung over a dingy patch of buildings on the far edge of the city. Here and there, massive towers rose from a patch of otherwise identically colored and shaped buildings. After watching for a moment, Gabby saw a dragon spiral around one of the towers, then land on it. From another tower in the distance, she saw three large birds take off and split paths into three directions. One, a hawk with dark brown feathers, flew toward the fortress.

"What do you protect them from? The Ironflight?"

"The Ironflight, and others. Our people are conquerors. We are not peaceful by nature, so the flights have often warred with each other. Even in the rare times of peace, we are attacked by the Vak and the Edra from outside our lands. The relative calm we have known for the last decade is rare, and I fear it is at an end," he said.

"Because of the princess?"

"Indeed," he said. Tarek gently took her hand, then guided her back into the corridor. Her heart raced as his strong hand closed around hers. He was close enough that she smelled the pleasant, earthy smell of him and felt the warmth radiating from his skin. "There has always been a strong sense of distrust and anger between the Stoneflight and the Ironflight. They believe their queen should be the empress."

"Is your queen...Halmerah?" He nodded. "Is she the empress?"

"There is no empress anymore," Tarek said. "The last High Empress was assassinated during the Great War, many years ago. She had united the flights, but in the aftermath of the war, the flights fractured again. Halmerah and Tarim can both claim her lineage, but neither could convince all of the flights to unite under her. The empress used to rule from this very fortress, so many believe Halmerah should hold the title. In any case, there are many other conflicts between us; contested lands, trade disputes, but I believe it is sheer stubbornness."

"And all of that would be worth attacking Ashariah?"

"Oh yes," he said. "I imagine Queen Tarim would do anything to topple Queen Halmerah from her throne."

"What is Halmerah doing about it?"

"She has sent word to the Ironflight. She will give them a chance to admit to their crimes and to make restitution," he said. "Even if their intent was to kill her, Ashariah lives, and so they may be able to come to a peaceful agreement."

"And if they don't?"

"Then the peace will come to an end," Tarek said flatly. His eyes narrowed as he stared out at the city.

"Would you have to fight?"

His mouth twisted into a bitter expression. "I would. But the queen would not have me."

"Why?"

Just like when she questioned his ability to protect Ashariah, she saw the stone wall come up. The fine creases around his eyes smoothed suddenly, and his shoulders squared. It was as if he turned to the same cold stone that formed the citadel. "She thinks I am better suited for protecting the gate than the people," he said finally. Each word was carefully chosen.

"Why?"

He ignored her question and gestured to the end of the hall. "Come, let us meet with Councilor Eszen and be done with it." The way he dodged her questions so easily irritated her, and only intensified her curiosity.

They continued their path through the massive citadel, with Tarek pointing out various sights—a commemorative fresco depicting a great battle of some dragon empress or another, a heavily guarded sword belonging to a former royal guard—but he said little about himself. She would do her best to dutifully nod and watch, but each time, she found herself drawn to him, watching the way his eyes flicked to her warily.

And she had to admit that the grand tour was a lovely distraction. Gabby was blown away by the sheer size of the citadel. She quickly lost track of how many huge windows they'd passed, how many dragons she'd seen step onto a platform and leap into the open sky with wings unfurling as they soared. They took a long detour through a cathedral-like wing with enormous stained glass windows in cool shades of blue and purple, each of which depicted a stylized scene from a story she didn't recognize. Angular runes were painted in silvery-gray paint on certain panels of glass, but it seemed her magical amulet didn't extend to reading. It was incredible to immerse herself in someone else's world, especially one that was so wonderfully strange.

But as they continued through the busier parts of the citadel, she'd noticed more and more strange looks. A passing stranger would suddenly pause, their gaze flicking to Gabby and then looking her up and down. A faint twitch of the eyebrows, a little frown pulling at their lips; they all sent the same message. *Who are you? Why are you here? You don't belong.*

By the time they had reached the end of a winding hallway lined in sculptures of dragons who all looked the same, she had grown tired of the staring. As Tarek slipped into an unremarkable door between two of the statues, she pulled back on his hand. With one foot on the stairs, he paused and looked back. "What's wrong?"

"People are staring at me," she said quietly. "I shouldn't be here. Will you take me back upstairs?"

He frowned. "You have Halmerah's blessing. Let them stare."

"That's easy for you to say," she said. "They're not staring at you."

His mouth pulled into a lazy, crooked smile. "No, but they'll surely be discussing me later. Let them talk. I certainly don't mind." He pulled gently on her hand, and she reluctantly followed him. The door took them to a small, plain stone staircase. As before, Tarek lightly clasped her hand while she gathered up the flowing fabric around her legs. Though the red silk was beautiful, she missed the comfort and practicality of her hospital scrubs.

The next stop on her grand tour was a set of massive wooden double doors. Carvings of a large dragon with wings spread dominated the dark-stained wood. At their approach, the guards on either side moved closer to the handles and spoke to Tarek. "Your business?"

"Tarek Windstriker, with orders to escort the queen's guest to Councilor Eszen," he said authoritatively. As he spoke, his spine straightened, his face taking on a stony expression. With a nod, the guards each stepped in to push their door open.

The familiar, dry smell of old books hit her like a physical force as she walked into the Great Library. Dark stone shelves towered overhead. Some were filled with neatly organized books, while others were fitted with wooden racks that formed diamond-shaped cubbies for rolled scrolls. Small wooden work tables filled the central area, most occupied by a person in a blue uniform and silver sash. Some read, while others were writing furiously on a stack of paper. A woman near the door worked on a large blue stone mounted on a metal apparatus. She appeared to be engraving its surface with a small metal tool.

"Welcome to the library," Tarek said. As they lingered in the doorway, a diminutive woman in a blue uniform appeared from a row of shelves. The silver sash and medallion on her uniform was familiar; it was the same as the one worn by the woman who'd been in the room while they had questioned Gabby right after her arrival. Dread crept over her. What were they walking into?

"May I help you?" the woman said politely.

"We are to speak to Councilor Eszen. He is expecting us," Tarek said. The woman nodded and hurried across the central area toward a door against the back wall.

As Tarek started to follow, Gabby tugged lightly on his hand. "What is he going to do to me?"

"He will only ask you questions," Tarek said. He paused to look down at her, his brow furrowed. "Are you afraid?"

"Considering the welcome I got yesterday, yes," she said. "I recognize that uniform."

He tilted his head. "You do?"

"I pay attention," she said.

He smiled and offered his right hand to her. His eyebrows piqued as she stared at him in confusion. Finally she offered her hand, letting him clasp it above his heart. His left hand covered hers as he gazed down at her. "Upon my honor, I will not allow any harm to come to you. As long as you are here, you are mine to protect."

"Yours?"

His cheeks flushed, but he composed himself quickly. "Do you object?"

She hesitated. Independent twenty-first century women most certainly objected to a big, albeit gorgeous, man proclaiming they were *his*. "I don't," she said quietly. To hell with the twenty-first century.

"Councilor Eszen will see you," the woman said. The wooden door was open, revealing a brightly-lit room beyond.

"Very good," Tarek said, his affectionate tone gone as he regarded the woman sternly. Releasing her hand, he motioned for Gabby to follow the woman into the room.

The small room was a private study. The curved outer wall was lined in windows, like much of the fortress. The stone walls were crammed with shelves, as impeccably organized as the ones in the main library. A large desk stood in the center of the room, with a neat stack of papers on one corner and no other clutter. The man at the desk rose as they entered. He was easily as tall as Tarek, though more slender. His gray robe was split along the sides over dark trousers. The smooth fabric was embroidered with an ornate, swirling pattern, and a silver sash crossed his chest. It was a much more intricate version of what the two women had worn.

"I am Councilor Eszen," he said brusquely. He nodded politely, but there was no warmth in his expression. "You must be Gabrielle."

"Yes," she said quietly. Her heart pounded as the tall man rounded the desk and approached her. Without warning, he reached out with both hands and lightly grasped the sides of her face. She recoiled instinctively. "Excuse you."

The taller man frowned, his eyes narrowing slightly. His eyes flicked over Gabby's shoulder, where Tarek was waiting. He nodded, then spread his hands. "May I? I mean no harm."

"Fine," she said, steeling herself and drawing herself up to her full height. She was short by human standards, and next to a dragon-in-man-form that would have topped six feet at a slouch, it didn't do much for her.

Eszen gently touched her face, leaning down to peer into her eyes. His eyes were a stunning shade of green, the color of new grass in spring. "I want you to resist me. Like you did before," he said. His pupils dilated, and as before, a crawling sensation tickled at her skull. "Look at me. Go sit down. You should—" Gabby simply closed her eyes, cutting off the unpleasant situation. Eszen stopped mid-sentence and said, "Huh. Well, that's something." He released her face and said, "It's fine to open them now."

"It's all right, Gabrielle," Tarek said mildly.

When she opened her eyes, Eszen was flanking her to stick his head out the door. "Khazarin! Come write for me," he ordered. The woman who had greeted them scurried into the room and around the desk. As she arranged a stack of ivory paper and prepared a fountain pen with a small jar of ink, Eszen gestured absently to a pair of wooden stools near one of his shelves. "Uh, you—was it Marek?"

"Tarek," he corrected.

"Yes, of course. You can go."

"I will stay," Tarek said.

Eszen opened his mouth as if to protest, then shook his head. "As you wish. Gabrielle, can you describe for me how you are able to break our compulsion over you?"

"No," she said flatly. At his look of surprise, she shrugged. "I'm not doing anything on purpose."

She expected him to be irritated, but his eyebrows perked in intrigue. "So it's passive, then," Eszen said. "Tell me what you experience. Every detail."

She did her best to describe the physical sensations, and he nodded thoughtfully, occasionally checking to make sure his scribe was keeping up. "When Tarek first showed up, his was the strongest at the time. After that, no one else had that much of an effect except for the queen."

Eszen's gaze flicked to Tarek. "Is your persuasion particularly powerful?"

Tarek shrugged. "No."

"And he was the only Kadirai with whom you made contact?"

"No," she said. "Ashariah."

Eszen's eyes narrowed. "And was this before or after Tarek?"

"Both," she said. "Ashariah was unconscious while I treated her, but I think she woke up, or at least had some level of consciousness. She grabbed me, and I saw a vision of her attack. Then Tarek arrived, and shortly after, she touched me again to show me a memory of him."

"Interesting," Eszen said. "And you have never encountered the Kadirai before?"

"No," she said.

Eszen leaned over and nodded to Tarek. "Has she?"

"Why are you asking him? I just told you no."

The councilor tilted his head. "It's possible that you have crossed paths, and you were made to forget, or to believe it was a dream. This is how things are done in the human realm, yes?"

Tarek sighed. "Yes. To my knowledge, none of my men have crossed her path."

She wanted to protest, but considering she'd asked him to take advantage of that handy power to keep people from wondering where she was, she couldn't exactly criticize.

"In any case, tell me more about what you saw in the princess's vision."

Eszen was thorough to the point of being irritating as he asked her to recall each detail, particularly about the dragons she'd seen. He matched the silver and gold dragons with the ones who had attacked them at the motel, but wondered about the larger white ones. Neither Gabby nor Tarek had answers for him. Gabby's butt had started to go numb from sitting on the hard wooden seat by the time Eszen said, "I think I've got somewhere to start.

You can go."

"What are you thinking?" Tarek asked.

"Are you a scholar in the concept of psychic transference?"

"No," Tarek said.

Eszen raised his eyebrows. "Then my answer will not make sense to you. I don't think it's anything Gabrielle has done, and it seems unlikely to be an external source of magic or enchantment. I need to research more and conduct an experiment to test my theory."

"Experiment...on me?"

He shook his head. "You are already contaminated," he said. "I need a fresh subject."

"Thanks for the compliment," Gabby said.

The councilor shrugged. "Thank you for your time. I do appreciate your attention to details. Please enjoy your stay." He rounded the desk to look over his scribe's shoulder. As an afterthought he looked up and said, "It would be wise to keep our discussion quiet. If we are under attack, it would be helpful to have a Vak who cannot be compelled. The queen feared an enemy spy. We may have our own."

"You will not use her as a spy," Tarek said hotly.

"I did not suggest it. I merely said it would be wise to keep any tactical advantage a secret," Eszen said. He made a shooing gesture. "Go on. I have work to do." With that, he bent his head to speak quietly to his scribe, watching as she spread out the pages of notes she'd taken.

When they had returned to the main part of the library, Gabby paused and looked up at Tarek. "Well, that was intense."

"You handled it very well," he said. He set his jaw, his eyes narrowed in concern. "Though he was not very personable, I agreed with what he told us. I would assume the guards have already been instructed so, but you should not mention your resistance to anyone else."

She nodded. "Agreed."

"Come, let us see the sun," he said. "We have been inside for far too long."

Another few minutes of walking finally brought them outside. Gabby's senses were overwhelmed as they stepped out into the light. She had to stop and catch her breath as she absorbed what was around her. Beyond the sheer size and beauty of the garden, she was struck by the overwhelming familiarity of it. The sprawling green garden beyond her was the place she'd seen in the vision from Ashariah. But calling it a garden was insufficient; that was like calling the ocean a puddle.

The gardens were massive, with variegated shades of green as far as she could see on either side. Trees soared up toward the stark gray sky. Outlining the green was the silvery rim of the stone roof she'd seen from the balcony. It was open in the center, allowing the harsh sunlight to pour in.

Ahead of them was a massive stone pillar, the same silver-shot grey stone she'd seen all through the citadel. But instead of random veins and flecks of silver, the pillar was entwined by a neat spiral of silver, as if it had been designed that way. Finger-thick silver roots twined around the pillar from its base amidst wild ferns and bright yellow flowers and up as far as she could see.

"I've seen this," she murmured.

"Yes," he said. "The Bones. You saw them from your window this morning."

She shook her head. "No, not that." She extricated her hand from Tarek's grasp and hurried toward the pillar. It drew her in, like some sort of magnetism. Before she knew what she was doing, she pressed her hand to the stone. It thrummed, sending a vibrating current up her arm. A warm sensation washed over her. She gasped in surprise. "What are they? Are they..." Despite everything she'd seen, she couldn't bring herself to say the word and admit that her reality was no longer what she'd once imagined. He raised his eyebrows as he waited for her to finish. She took a deep breath. "Are they magic?"

"Yes." He placed his hand next to hers, leaning in close so his voice rumbled at her ear. His breath was warm on her cheek. "Some say that the very spirit of the Skymother still lives in the stone."

"Skymother?"

"She was the mother of all of the Dawnflight," Tarek said. "Of me, of everyone in this citadel. She died many centuries ago, but now her spirit watches over us."

With her hand against the stone, Gabby felt connected to something bigger. She could feel the power of the stone in her veins and all around her. She couldn't explain it with science or logic, and for once, she didn't care. There was a subtle pulse, a heartbeat so slow she'd have missed it if she didn't linger. The world was so much bigger than she'd imagined.

"I thought you were of the Stoneflight," she said.

He smiled. "I am. But long ago, there was no Stoneflight. There were the Skymother's children, the Dawnflight. And there were the others." He frowned. "The Duskflight. They served an evil force. They are no more." He waved his hand. "I don't need to bore you with our history. Come, let's walk," Tarek said. She hesitated, and he gently took her hand to guide her away. She felt suddenly empty and cold as she broke contact with the pillar. "Adamantine Rise was built around these pillars thousands of years ago. Even in the aftermath of the war, everything still grows here. Things that have long died out in the outside world thrive here."

Together they strolled along a smooth stone path into the heart of the garden. Great sprays of leaves and vines hung over the path, surrounding them with cool green and the fragrance of things new and growing. "The war?"

"Not long ago, the dragonflights came together against a common enemy. We called them *Raspolin*," he said. "They sought to destroy us, using foul magic that split open the skies and shattered the ground. It has been over a century, and our lands still haven't recovered." He paused and lifted his hand to touch a leaf. He pulled a vine down for her to look closer. "All of our lands, Vakhdahl, used to look like this. It was nothing but green forest and clear blue sky as far as you could see. This is a reminder of what it once was."

Gabby had seen some of the devastation as she'd been flown in. Though her concerns had largely been with where the hell she was going, she'd noticed the odd cast to the sky and the cracked dry ground below.

"What was the war about?" she asked.

He shook his head. "Power. Subjugation. Fear," he said, his nostrils flaring. "That's what wars are always about."

"Did you fight in the war?"

He shook his head. "It was before I was even born," he said. "But I inherited the aftermath."

"How old are you?"

"Seventy-seven," he replied.

She gaped at him. "You're seventy-seven."

"Yes," he said, giving her a quizzical look. "Why?"

"That's...well, that's old."

His brow furrowed. He actually looked offended, which made her want to laugh at the ridiculousness of it. "That is not old."

"For humans, it is. How long do you people live?"

He shrugged. "Remaining in good health, we live many centuries. My grandmother was nine hundred and thirty-seven when she died." He gestured toward the garden. "Shall we walk?"

"I'm still a little stuck on you being a senior citizen," she said. Despite the humor of it, she had to wonder at the wisdom of becoming infatuated with a man who would outlive her by centuries.

He frowned. "What?"

"An old person," she said. He certainly didn't look seventy-seven, but if it was the norm for them to live so long, he was practically a teenager by dragon standards. "You look good for your age."

His lips curved into a playful smile. "Do I?"

"You don't look a day over seventy-five," she said.

He laughed, a rich sound that warmed her like a long drink of hot chocolate on a cold day. "Come along." His hand rested on the small of her back as he led her through the garden.

The greenery enveloped them in a cool, quiet embrace, making it easy to forget that there was anything beyond it. Heavy-laden branches crossed over the path, twining around each other like braids overhead. Plump purple flowers dotted the twisting branches like huge jewels on a chain. And it was oddly quiet; there was no birdsong or even the whisper of wind, just the barely audible sound of their footsteps on the stone.

"Look," Tarek said. His voice was startling in the silence. Ahead of them, the dense curtain of green parted to reveal a large raised pavilion. At the very center of the pavilion stood another of the Bones. A gracefully curving white roof surrounded the pillar like an enormous day lily.

More of the Adamant Guard, dressed in their impeccable dark blue and silver-embellished uniforms, stood in formation on either side of the stairs up to the pavilion.

"What's this?" Gabby asked.

"The healer's pavilion," he said. "The Bones exude a healing aura. Our healers are more powerful here, and simply resting among them grants a renewed energy and well-being. That's how my wounds healed so quickly." He smiled at her. "Ashariah is here."

They approached the stairs, where Tarek nodded to one of the guards. With the help of the amulet, she finally understood the exchange. "I request permission to see the princess," he said.

"The queen has ordered that no one is to see the princess," the guard replied.

"I'm sure she wouldn't mind if her guest visited," Tarek said smoothly.

The guard looked down at her, one eyebrow arched imperiously. "She was quite clear. No one is to see the princess."

Gabby craned her neck to see. At the far end of the pavilion was another raised platform surrounded in filmy white veils. The princess had to be there. "I took care of her before she came here," Gabby said suddenly. "I'd like to see her."

"Need I repeat myself again?" the guard said. "No one—"

"Got it. Can you at least tell me how she is?" The guard was silent and stony-faced. Gabby sighed. "Well, at least you're consistent."

Tarek gently took her arm. "Come, I'll show you the everblooms on the other side."

Tarek's tour of the citadel continued for another few hours. As before, he provided extensive commentary on the fortress and its many notable features, but never disclosed anything significant about himself. After they passed an enormous kitchen that smelled of roasting meat and heavy spices, Tarek commented that he was hungry. When Gabby agreed, he walked her back toward the guest quarters.

As if someone had heard their growling stomachs, they returned to a meal already set for them. A low table near the window was set with a spread of fruit, thinly sliced meat, more bread, and a stone pitcher. Gabby looked around for Raszila, but there was an unfamiliar woman pulling at the bedclothes. When she looked up and saw them, she smiled and bowed her head politely. "I hope you enjoyed the sights of our home. Please come and eat."

Gabby didn't have to be told twice. As she sank down to the over-sized cushion on the floor, her feet ached, and she realized just how much they'd walked that day. She looked at the woman and said, "I appreciate this, but where is Raszila?"

"Oh, she was called to tend to the Ironflight guests," the woman said. "My name is Irinakh."

"Ironflight?" Tarek said. "They've arrived?"

"Yes," Irinakh said. "They arrived perhaps an hour ago. The queen was adamant that they be treated with the utmost consideration."

Tarek knelt by Gabby. "I have to go. I will check on you later."

"Oh," she said. He pressed her hand to his lips again and kissed the back, but there was no sign of affection on his face. Instead, his features were creased with worry, and she felt strangely rejected as she watched him go.

"Perhaps I could rub your feet for you?" Irinakh said. She was eager to please, but Gabby's mind was with Tarek.

"Do you know why they came? What's happening?"

Irinakh paused, then shrugged. "I don't concern myself with such things," she said. "Nor should you."

Gabby sighed. She knew that by their standards, she was an outsider. Maybe it was stupid, but she'd gone through a lot of trouble in the last few days, and felt a little like she'd earned some insider info.

"But there is to be a feast for our guests tonight," Irinakh said, her expression brightening. "The queen wishes for you to be there, so I must see that you are dressed appropriately."

CHAPTER TWENTY-THREE

THE ARRIVAL OF THE IRONFLIGHT contingent had all of Adamantine Rise in a frenzy. Tarek's attempt to visit the queen was thwarted by her cadre of attendants who told him she was preparing for the feast. Having been on the other side of the door years before, he knew there would be as many servants primping the queen as there were advisors preparing her for the delicate political dance that was to come.

Likewise, the Ironflight guests had sequestered themselves inside their guest chambers. As he passed by, Tarek didn't miss the presence of dozens of guards from both flights. There were the familiar blue and silver uniforms of the Adamant Guard, and scattered throughout the halls, the fiery red and bronze regalia of Queen Tarim's guards, the Iron Blade. Though there were far more people moving about the citadel than usual, it was oddly quiet and tense, as if the wrong word would be the spark that ignited the powder keg.

After leaving Gabrielle to eat and dress for the evening, Tarek longed for something familiar, but he realized he had nowhere that was his own to go. For nearly ten years, home had been in the human world, in a musty corner room of the Drakemont Inn. His barracks in the Adamant Guard wing of the citadel had long been reassigned, and any trace of Tarek Windstriker was no more. He felt as much an outsider as Gabrielle must have.

Ah, Gabrielle. Even with the tension of the day and the troubles that had befallen his people, there was a pleasant thought. It had been indescribably wonderful to escort her around Adamantine Rise, watching her face light up as he pointed out the sights. Her favorite had obviously been the gardens, which hadn't surprised him. And though her beauty was matched by her insatiable curiosity and sharp wit, he'd managed to dodge most of her probing questions.

He had no intention of allowing himself to get closer. He would be her protector and no more. While it wasn't precisely forbidden for him to consort with a human, it was frowned upon. In fact, it was quite unusual that a human would even be allowed into Adamantine Rise beyond a quick visit to the lower halls to handle an affair of state or trade dispute. Leaders of the Edra and the Vak down in the city sometimes met with the queen's advisors, but only in the lower levels. Edra messengers who could take a flying form often brought messages to the watchtower atop the citadel. In any case, humans were rarely welcomed as guests of the queen. There was a word for dragons who lowered themselves to the Vak—*t'haran vo'shedh*—one who rolled in the mud. They were more lenient about it in the human world, but only because there were so few options for companionship with only a dozen guards living in a small, secluded space.

But Tarek certainly didn't plan to remain in the human world forever, guarding a dusty Gate with new recruits who were only paying their dues before being promoted to a proper position. If he hoped to return to his position here in the citadel someday, there was no future for the two of them. And he would be fine with that, as he always had. Tarek had known several lovers in the decades he had lived here, though they had been more relationships of physical convenience for both of them. There was no real connection, nor desire to forge any stronger bond. His duty had been to serve the queen and her family, which had been fulfilling on its own, almost a sacred duty.

Then why the hell couldn't he stop thinking about her? Tarek tried in vain to push her pleasant glow out of his mind as he climbed the narrow servant stairs to the military wing. There was a beautiful softness to her, even as she showed her hard edges and steel spine. He wondered what it would be like to caress the gentle curve of her hip, to feel her pressed tightly to him. Sacred duty or not, it had still been more than a decade since he had been with a woman.

No.

He had to focus on the task at hand. At the moment, he was headed into the stone-enclosed barracks of the military wing. This had been home for many years, a place where he was known and greeted at each turn. Here there was none of the opulence of the guest quarters or the galleries; the walls were plain rough stone, the corridors narrow and low to maximize space.

A few heads turned as he walked through the austere halls, but most barely paid him any notice. The passage of time and his plain clothes had made him virtually invisible here. He expected the sound of raucous laughter and shouting over a game of dice, but it was quiet like the rest of the citadel. Tension hung in the air as the entire Stoneflight watched the shadow of war approaching.

Several of the narrow corridors met in an open circular area. Three wooden doors, these embellished with crude carvings of Kadirai runes, stood at even intervals along the wall. The central door led to the guard captain's chamber, while the other two belonged to his immediate subordinates. At one time, Tarek had imagined himself living in one of these rooms, spacious and well-appointed. That was a long-dead dream.

Tarek's stomach twisted into a knot as he approached the center door. Not long after Tarek had been reassigned to the Gate, the previous captain had stepped down to serve on the queen's council, leaving the position open. A capable young Kadirai named Navan had taken the mantle, surprising many who expected a much older, more experienced soldier to take over. Tarek had known Navan for decades and had trained alongside him. In fact, they'd discussed their designs on the two rooms flanking the captain's quarters over too many drinks on more than one occasion. The disparity in their current positions did not escape him.

With a deep breath for courage, Tarek rapped on the door. A young woman in the plain clothes of a servant opened the door a few moments later. She looked a bit frazzled, with a familiar black cape draped over her shoulder waiting to find its place on the captain's shoulders. "Yes?"

"Hello, miss," he said. "I've come to visit with Captain Navan."

She held up her hand in a *wait* gesture, then retreated into the room. After a moment of quiet conversation, Navan himself came to the door to greet him. The other man was barely older than him, with dark skin that gleamed under the candlelight and close-cropped dark hair. He was still dressing, with one ceremonial bracer strapped on and his other arm bare. As he walked to the door, a young male servant was chasing him with the other bracer, looking harried as he tried to catch Navan's hand to put on the armor.

"Tarek Windstriker," he said, his voice deep and booming. "It has been a while." The servant boy tried to get the armor over his hand, but Navan waved him off and gestured for Tarek to follow into his room. "Come in."

The captain's quarters were considerably larger than the regular guard lodgings, although it looked like a hovel in comparison to Gabrielle's guest quarters. A large open window overlooked the city, allowing a chilly wind to pass through. A polished wooden desk took up part of the far wall, with a row of neatly arranged leather-bound ledgers and a stack of papers in one corner. There was a sitting area, a low table surrounded in thick cushions and a dense fur rug for warmth. His bed was covered in a rough spun quilt and several thick knitted blankets. At the foot of the bed was a large basket holding various small armor pieces, leather ties, and polishing compounds.

"I had a hard time finding you," Tarek said. "I didn't know I had to ask for *Captain* Navan."

Navan grinned, his white teeth brilliant. "I've moved up in the world. I told you this chamber would eventually be mine, though I didn't think it would be so soon," he said. He gestured to Tarek. "And you? How has the human world treated you?"

"As if I was never there," Tarek said. "Which is as it should be."

"Sir," the male servant finally interjected. "Your hand."

Navan rolled his eyes and held out his bare arm for the servant boy. He waited patiently while the young man slipped the bracer over his hand and began the work of lacing it. With a pointed look at Tarek, he said, "Despite my position, they still think I can't dress myself."

"Sir..." the young man protested.

"I'm joking," Navan interrupted. "You're a very good armor polisher, lad. Keep up the good work. And as for you, Windstriker, you belong here to teach my recruits how to do more than flap their wings like some idiot bird. When will you return?"

Tarek sighed. "The queen will not have me."

"Have you asked?"

"I can't."

"Bah," Navan said. He waved dismissively, then looked at his servant sheepishly. The boy scowled and waited for Navan to be still before continuing to buff the shining decorative bracer with a cloth. "What happened to Ivralah was not your fault. It was the cowardice and dishonor of the Silverflight. It could have happened to any of us."

"I know," Tarek said automatically. How many times over the years had he heard those words? But the face of the princess, her mutilated body; those were the first things he saw upon waking in the morning and the last things he saw before going to sleep. She had trusted him, as had her mother, and he had let them down. It was so easy for the others to dismiss it, but they didn't have to carry the shame of failure upon their shoulders as he did. "I am not quite the dragon I was."

Navan hesitated, not quite meeting his eyes. There was truth and agreement there. "I wish you would return."

"Maybe someday," Tarek said.

Navan nodded. He took a breath, then plastered a smile onto his face, obviously eager to change the subject. "What brings you here?"

"I came to ask if I could borrow clothing for the feast," he said. "I came

185

here somewhat unexpectedly, and I have nothing."

"You don't even need to ask," Navan said. He gestured to the servants. "Alora, see that my friend has whatever he needs. Khizek, the armor is more than shiny enough. Take a break and bring us wine. A great deal of it."

They passed the next hour laughing over glasses of wine, carefully dodging the uncomfortable topic of the past. Navan told him the stories of his promotion and how he'd been keeping an eye on the shapely scholar Ohldana. Tarek told his old friend of the sights and sounds of the human world, including the neon glitz of Vegas. There was nothing that compared in their world, and he knew his words didn't do it justice.

"I should like very much to see this Vegas," Navan said.

"It would be my pleasure to introduce you," Tarek said, though he knew that it would be nothing short of a miracle for the captain of the Adamant Guard to leave the citadel for such a frivolous journey. As the guard captain, he served with the sword as needed, but primarily acted as an overseer and administrator to all of the guards and soldiers who served the queen.

Alora tapped Navan's shoulder and waited patiently for him to acknowledge her. "Sir, it's time."

"Oh, just another glass," Navan said.

Alora raised her eyebrow. "Sir," she said emphatically. "You will be late. Again. And then Raszila will be angry with me for not helping you properly."

Navan gave a long-suffering sigh, drained the last of his glass, and rose to his full height. He glanced over his shoulder, then crouched so that he was on eye-level with the petite woman. Despite Navan's position, it was clear who was really in charge. Navan raised his eyebrow. "You should tell Raszila to scold me next time," he said.

"Sir, I am certain she would be happy to scold you," Alora said. With a practiced gesture, she swept the heavy cloak around Navan's massive shoulders and used several long, sharp pins to connect it to his ornate chest armor. After fiddling with the minute pleats and gathers, she finally left Navan alone and brought Tarek a decorative chest plate and a plain, dark cloak. The chest armor was polished silver with the queen's crest in a raised pattern across the sternum. With the efficiency of a soldier, Alora ordered him to turn and crouch so she could fix the straps. If she thought anything of being so close to him, she didn't show it. He was no more interesting to her than a bare patch of wall that needed to be decorated. Even when she had to adjust his trousers to lay properly under the plate, she didn't bat an eyelash. He wasn't sure whether to be insulted or not. When she was satisfied with her work, she nodded her approval and patted Tarek's armored chest.

"You may go," Alora said with the same imperious air of the queen.

Navan smiled indulgently at her. "I guarantee we will be the best dressed of the Stoneflight."

"Flattery gets you nowhere, sir," Alora said. But Tarek saw the way her mouth quirked up as she turned away to gather Navan's discarded clothing.

"Well, my old friend, I should like very much to continue this conversation, but I have to wrangle this bunch of fools into shape before the feast. Please, stop by again before you leave," Navan said.

"I will," Tarek said. He felt strange, dressed in the clothes of the Adamant Guard once more. Technically as a Gatekeeper, he was still part of the guard, but it was a distant branch, with little of the responsibility that lay upon those who protected the royal family. Still, there was something familiar and comforting about it. For many years, he had worn the heavy cloak about his shoulders, the hammered breastplate and decorative bracers on his strong arms. They spoke of his sacrifice and loyalty; they were the symbols of his competence, the signs that told enemies not to make the mistake of attacking him.

His stomach lurched as he thought again of Ivralah and Ashariah. It had been so long since he was around his former comrades in any number. Did they think of him as an abject failure, a cautionary tale?

He needed more wine. It would be a long night ahead.

The grand ballroom of the citadel was like nothing he'd seen in the human world. Tarek had reluctantly gone along with some of the other Gatekeepers into Vegas, into the dazzling casinos and nightclubs. They were impressive, to be sure, but he had still never seen anything as wondrous as the queen's ballroom at its finest.

The ballroom jutted out from the core of the citadel, with large windows that overlooked the city of Farath. Stone archways along the perimeter led to small balconies, each furnished with a plush settee and draped with decadent silks in blue and silver. Inside the ballroom, glass everlights cast a diffuse glow in soft blue, purple, and pink, twinkling like stars. The everlights were delicate glass globes filled with tiny motes of everbloom, the glowding seed pods of a flower that grew only within the queen's gardens. The pods were rare and expensive, used only for special occasions. More silks and sheer drapes hung from the ceiling, many emblazoned with the crest of the Stoneflight. Long tables were arranged in rows that angled gently toward the dais at the far end of the room, where the queen and her entourage would sit.

Huge sprays of blue and purple flowers decorated the tables, which were also draped in dark blue silks. More everlights lit each table. The queen was clearly making a statement to impress and even intimidate her guests with her wealth. Guests in traditional Stoneflight garb milled about the grand ballroom, but the dais was noticeably empty. The queen and her honored guests would arrive last.

There were, however, dozens of the Adamant Guard in official regalia casually walking about the room. In addition to their longswords, they wore their ceremonial uniforms with horned silver shoulder pauldrons and ornate jointed plates down the spine, evoking the impressive silhouette of their dragon forms. And while a civilian wouldn't have noticed, Tarek also knew there were twice as many guards in plain clothes. He recognized their faces as they filled glasses with deep red wine and saw the constant movement of their eyes even as they chatted casually with the other guests.

Tarek accepted a glass of wine from a passing servant and positioned himself near the entrance. As he watched the familiar scene, he took a drink of his wine. He hadn't tasted the traditional berry wine, the *vris m'hiri*, in over a decade. The sweet taste and strong alcoholic brew struck him with a wave of nostalgia so strong that it was hard to get a full breath. He could remember a hundred such feasts, standing on the dais behind the princess and thanking the Skymother that he had been entrusted with such an important duty even at such a young age.

That was a long time ago, a distant memory.

His heart thumped as the musicians played a flourish. A herald in a sharply pressed uniform stood at the edge of the dais to announce guests. First came the queen's trusted councilors. "Lord Eszen *efana* Shundilzin, personal advisor to the queen and curator of the great Library." Eszen had changed into a far fancier robe, though he looked annoyed to be at the feast instead of in his study. Each councilor was announced in turn, and Tarek tuned them out in favor of his wine. When a murmur rippled across the gathered guests, he looked up from his glass and nearly dropped it in surprise.

"The queen honors a friend to the Stoneflight, one who has exemplified the honor and cleverness of her kind. Lady Gabrielle *efana* Maria of...Reno," the herald said. He looked a little puzzled, then gathered himself.

Tarek hadn't expected Gabrielle to be present. And he certainly hadn't expected the sight that awaited when the human woman stepped into the room.

She was dressed in an ornately jeweled and embroidered dress of purple fabric, wrapped carefully so that it hugged her hips and breasts, leaving one shoulder and most of her back bare. The queen's servants had dusted her coppery skin with a powder that left it glittering like scales. Her eyes were heavy-lidded and darkened with makeup, her lips stained a red that made him think of strawberries and wine. And her hair was arranged around a metal crown of some sort, elongating her features and making her look like a queen in her own right. He hadn't even seen her yet, but he had the traitorous thought that Queen Halmerah would look like a potato in a paper sack next to Gabrielle.

Tarek forgot how to breathe as a surge of heat rushed down his spine and into his groin. As his cheeks flushed, he gulped down half his wine and relished the sting of alcohol in his throat. He barely heard the next few announcements, walking without thinking toward Gabrielle. A pair of servants had guided her from the entrance toward the elevated dais. He found himself trailing after them. "Gabrielle?"

She paused and turned to see him. Her heavily shadowed eyes widened and she hurried toward him. "Oh, thank goodness," she said. "I thought I was going to have to sit here by myself."

She was utterly unaware of the effect she had on him. And judging by the way a handful of the other guests were staring, not just on him. Of course, it was not only her beauty, but the fact that she was human. To their eyes, she was Vak, ungifted by the Skymother and more suited to a life of servitude in the city below, or perhaps in the fields. There would be plenty of gossip that night.

"The queen has requested Lady Gabrielle's presence at her table," one of the servants said. "You may join her. Miss?"

"Oh!" Gabrielle said. "Let's go."

Tarek took her hand and waited patiently as she gathered up her skirt to climb the stairs to the dais. On the raised platform stood a pair of long, narrow tables that had been arranged at an angle, allowing the queen to sit at its point and look down either table to see her guests. More of the everlights stood on pedestals behind the tables, casting their twinkling glow over the entire dais.

A waiting servant with a decanter of wine stood at the fourth seat down from the queen's right. He bowed politely to Gabrielle, gave Tarek an inquisitive look, then gestured to the empty seat next to hers.

As Gabrielle settled into her seat, Tarek waited patiently and scanned the room. There were dozens of eyes on them, and all of them looked curious. Some looked downright disdainful, and a few didn't bother to hide their disgust at the human woman's presence. He did not enjoy being the subject of attention one bit, but he disliked even more that people were so open in their disapproval. Instead, he ignored them and turned to Gabrielle. "You look lovely."

She looked nervous, looking down at her clothes and turning over one hand, the borrowed jewelry catching the light. "I feel ridiculous."

Ridiculous was not the word he would have used. The everlight closest to her seat held pale pink and lavender pods that cast a rosy flush over her skin. The thoughts that swirled through his mind were most inappropriate for a diplomatic feast.

"You look like a queen yourself," he said, hoping he didn't sound like a blithering idiot. It wasn't like he'd never been around a beautiful woman. "Not ridiculous at all."

"Thank you," she said. She looked him over. "You look very nice, too. You kind of have a Conan thing going on."

He tilted his head. "A what?"

"Never mind. You look very masculine. Grr." She fanned herself. "I need a drink."

Tarek gestured to the closest servant, who hurried over to fill her wine glass. Gabrielle drained it in two swallows, earning her a raised eyebrow from the servant. Without a word, he filled it again.

"I don't know what your rules are about forks and stuff," Gabrielle said.

"Just wait for the queen before you do anything," Tarek said, relieved for something to focus on besides the stunning creature at his side. She froze with the glass at her lips. He laughed. "You're allowed to drink. But once food is served, you must wait for her to give a greeting and welcome everyone."

A loud crash of cymbals and a flourish of horns sounded, then faded to silence as all eyes turned toward the ballroom's arched entrance. "May I present to you the High Queen of the Stoneflight, the anointed keeper of Vakhdahl and esteemed monarch of Adamantine Rise, protector of the great city of Farath, granddaughter of High Empress Rezharani, Halmerah Silverstone."

CHAPTER TWENTY-FOUR

IF SOMEONE HAD TOLD GABRIELLE Rojas a week ago that tonight she'd be an honored guest at a diplomatic feast hosted by a dragon queen in another world, she'd have asked them to share whatever they were smoking.

And yet, here she was, standing on nervous jelly-legs, her hands trembling under the weight of borrowed silver jewelry as she watched the queen's arrival. An enormous doorway framed in stone carved to look like twisted tree branches stood along the back wall, where most of the guests, including Gabby, had entered. High above that doorway was a smaller archway framed in silver and glittering gems, veiled in heavy midnight blue curtains. The platform was guarded by a pair of immaculately dressed guards who flanked either side of a gently sloped stairway that wrapped around the side of the ballroom and ended at the center of the dais where the queen's guests awaited.

After the herald's announcement, the guards pulled back the curtains for the queen to enter. Halmerah emerged, walking with deliberate and measured steps around the curved stairway. A murmur rippled over the crowd at the sight of her. The musicians kept a steady, slow beat, and Gabby knew they were waiting for her, and not the other way around. The universe itself seemed to keep time with her steps.

Gabby had thought her own borrowed attire was luxurious and ornate, but she was wearing a burlap sack compared to Halmerah. The dragon queen wore an asymmetrical gown in a thousand shades of gray and silver, as if someone had broken open one of the nearby mountains to reveal a hidden vein of diamonds. The gown left one shoulder bare, but a huge purple stone set in a twisted silver setting was placed on her shoulder like a piece of armor, with thin chains dripping in more stones attaching it to the gown and trickling down her arm like water. The dress reflected the light from the glass lanterns in tiny pinpoints, making her look as if she was glowing.

As she passed, guests bowed their heads politely, though they did not kneel. It took her a while to make her way around the room. When she passed behind the dais, Gabby followed the lead of the crowd and bowed her head. Before her eyes dropped, she caught a faint hint of a smile on Halmerah's red-stained lips. The woman finally cleared the steps and allowed a servant to take her hand, while another gathered up the train of her gown and pinned it into place like a bustle on her hips. When they had finished, she stepped up to the elevated seat at the center of the dais. Like the rest of the room, her seat was covered in blue and silver silk, just a step shy of being a throne.

"Thank you, esteemed friends and guests," Halmerah said after a long pause. One of the servants hurried to her side and offered her a glass of red wine. She raised it, and the other guests followed suit. Gabby quickly lifted her own glass. As Halmerah continued her greeting, Gabby noticed that there was an empty place setting next to the queen's seat. It must have been held for the Ironflight queen. "Now, allow me the honor of welcoming our honored guests, the reason for our feast."

The herald at the edge of the stage gestured to the door where Gabby had entered. "The queen extends her welcome to Prince Zayir Moltenheart of the Ironflight," he said.

A murmur rippled across the room. The queen's eyes widened as the tall, handsome prince entered the ballroom, his mouth set in a playful smile. He wore a simple, tailored bronze tunic over snug dark trousers and a thin, hammered gold crown set with a bright orange stone.

"Son of a bitch," Tarek murmured, his eyes narrowing. Gabby followed his gaze to the queen. Her lips remained in a polite smile, but her eyes had gone cold and predatory as she watched the prince saunter in.

"We also extend honor to Kaldir Dawnblaze, royal protector and esteemed leader of Queen Tarim's formidable forces," the herald said. Even he was nervous as he said it, his eyes flitting back and forth to Halmerah. Kaldir was a mountain of a man, with shoulders she doubted would fit through a normal door. He wore a dark copper knee-length garment with ornamental bronze armor that reminded her of an ancient Roman soldier. While the prince was unarmed, Kaldir carried a sword on a wide leather belt. And with his massive arms and muscular legs, there was no doubt he could handle himself unarmed. Behind him, a formation of four guards in red and gold uniforms followed, their faces stony as they stared straight ahead.

As if the musicians sensed the queen's discomfort, the music accelerated. All eyes were on the prince and his guard as they proceeded up to the raised dais. A few seconds later, a small cluster of blue-clad Adamant Guard entered, taking their positions around the room.

Once the Ironflight guests had taken their seats, the queen raised her glass again. This time, the two men joined her. Like the queen, their faces bore smiles, but their eyes were sharp, watching her carefully. There was an invisible dance going on.

"Let us greet our guests and treat them with all the kindness they deserve," Halmerah said, her inflection heavy and leaving no question as to what she thought. "As is tradition, let us drink of the *vris m'hiri* to show our mutual trust and respect. And let us not forget to beseech the Skymother for her divine blessing upon my daughter, your princess Ashariah." Halmerah turned to the prince at her left and nodded. His eyes never left her as he took a sip of his wine. All around the room, guests took a sip of their wine. Gabby followed suit, glad for the warm bite of the sweet wine. It was much stronger than she expected, but the syrupy sweetness of it softened the kick.

Tarek watched her with an amused smile. The Ironflight might have looked stylish, but Tarek put them to shame. The soft glowing lanterns set his dark golden skin gleaming, bringing the defined muscles on his arms into sharp relief. "That wine will sneak up on you. Be careful."

"It's very good," she said. And between him looking good enough to eat and the queen looking like she could breathe fire at any moment, she needed something to take the edge off.

He raised his own glass and swirled it, watching the deep scarlet liquid coat the frosted glass. "This is the *vris m'hiri*," he said. "I haven't had it in many years. It's very old-fashioned."

"It tastes like...maybe raspberries?"

"Blackberries. Or our version of them, at least," he said. "It's served at any affair of state where the dragonflights come together." He took a long drink, his smooth jaw working. Maybe it was the wine talking, but she could have watched him drink wine all night.

Definitely the wine talking.

"What makes it so special?" she asked.

"The story goes that the berries grew from the Skymother's tears, and the Raspolin had such evil souls that they could not even taste the fruit without becoming violently ill."

"The enemy you spoke of before?"

He nodded. "It was served to ensure that they had not infiltrated our strongholds. But they are long gone," he said. "An old enemy, now just a fairy tale told to young, mischievous dragons who don't mind their elders. The wine is a tradition, a symbol more than a necessity."

"Are you boring your guest with ancient history, Windstriker?" a deep voice asked. "It's a crime of etiquette, if not of the law."

Gabby jumped in surprise and turned to see a handsome man looking her over, a look of amusement pulling at his full lips. He had a brilliant white smile set against gorgeous dark skin and eerie amber eyes. A heavy dark cloak hung from his shoulders, pinned to his chest armor on either side with fist-sized silver emblems of a snarling dragon with blue stone eyes.

"Not so ancient that one should forget," Tarek said mildly.

The other man rolled his eyes and raised his glass to Gabby. "I had no idea the Vak could be so lovely," he said. Despite his undeniable beauty and seemingly jovial expression, his tone was condescending. It wasn't insincere; he probably thought he was being complimentary, but it was a backhanded compliment, like *you're really pretty for a Hispanic girl*, which she'd heard enough times to piss her off.

Her face flushed under the shimmery powder Irinakh had dusted her with. "I had no idea capes were in vogue here."

The man tilted his head in confusion. "In vogue?"

Lost in translation, jerk. She was preparing to tell him where he could stick his compliment when Tarek squeezed her arm lightly. When her eyes flitted to him, he gave her an almost imperceptible shake of his head. "Gabrielle, this is Captain Navan of the queen's guard."

For a moment, the notion that Tarek would dare tell her to keep quiet made her even madder than Navan's comments. She had plenty of ammo to unload both barrels on them and go back for seconds. But the sheer strangeness of her situation kept her tongue in check. She was a stranger in a strange land here, and while it might have felt good for just a moment to unleash her temper, it would be beyond stupid to anger a dragon under any circumstances, regardless of whether he deserved it. They'd tossed her into a dungeon over a misunderstanding once already; how much worse might they do if she insulted a high-ranking dragon like Navan?

She forced her expression into a smile. "Thank you for the lovely compliment," she said, hoping her irritation didn't seep through the fake sweetness like hospital stink through disinfectant.

"Tarek, you neglected to mention your beautiful companion when we spoke earlier," Navan said. Interesting. Who was this guy to Tarek?

"Did I?" Tarek said mildly. He took a sip of his wine, then glanced down the table. "Do you see what I see?"

Gabby followed his gaze. Halmerah spoke quietly to the prince, her mouth set in a tight smile. Despite the expression, her eyes were creased with anger, and in the time Gabby watched, she saw the queen flinch several times, as if she'd remembered she was supposed to look interested. "The queen is not pleased," she said quietly.

"She's doing much better at hiding it than I'd expect," Tarek said in her ear, his breath warm and wine-scented. It was definitely the wine talking at this point, but she was overcome with the urge to turn and nuzzle into his strong neck.

Instead she kept her tone measured and said, "Why is she so angry?"

"She called for an audience with the Ironflight queen," Tarek said. "They sent the queen's brother instead. It's an insult, as if Halmerah is not worthy of Queen Tarim's attention." He leaned closer, his lips brushing her ear. A shiver burst across her skin. "What else do you see?"

She turned to him for a moment, her face inches from his. His eyes went wide in surprise, his lips parting. It would take nothing at all to close the distance and kiss his wine-stained lips. No more wine for her. With her cheeks burning, she turned back quickly before she did something that would cause even more of a scene than a human showing up at the dragon party.

Looking back toward Halmerah, she noticed something for the first time. The seats along the two angled tables were all occupied by well-dressed, beautiful people, all with the bright eyes and sharp, exotic features that made the Kadirai look otherworldly. Except for one. The seat immediately to Halmerah's right was empty, but the place had been set with dishes and silverware. Even the glass had been filled halfway with dark wine, but it stood untouched.

"There's an empty seat," Gabby said. "But it's on her side, so whoever sits there should have already been here before the queen."

Tarek chuckled. "Clever girl. It's for Ashariah."

"She's making a statement to the Prince," Gabby said. "She wants to draw as much attention as she can to the princess."

He glanced at her, his eyebrows arched in surprise. "Very good."

"Don't look so surprised. I watch TV," she said. The servants brought out the first course, long oval dishes of thin flatbread and an array of colorful sauces and pastes that reminded her of hummus. Gabby waited nervously for someone else to take food from the dish. Navan took two pieces of bread and dipped them directly into the pastes. The germaphobe in her was happy to see that he only dipped once—even dragons didn't double-dip, it seemed.

She followed his lead and dipped a triangular piece of bread into a pale green paste. *Please don't be brains or intestines,* she prayed. Her apprehension must have showed on her face, because Tarek leaned over and helped himself to a piece, then showed it to her. "It's *dashal,*" he said. "Ground-up *erfadh* with oil and spices. It's a kind of bean. Completely safe."

She breathed a sigh of relief and took a bite. Sure enough, the consistency reminded her of hummus, though the flavor was both sweet and smoky at the same time. It was quite good, and she helped herself to another piece of bread slathered with it. Between bites, she leaned back to Tarek. "Is there a king?" She'd been so swept up with her unpleasant arrival and then the flurry of preparations that it hadn't occurred to her that she'd only heard mention of the queen and her daughter.

"No," Tarek said. "Some queens marry, some do not. There are

201

sometimes political marriages, but the Stoneflight tradition has always been for the queen to take a royal consort. He or she has no power, but may sit on the queen's council if she so chooses. Halmerah has never named an official consort, but the princesses were both fathered by a highly-ranked officer in the Adamant Guard."

"Wow...and she doesn't keep him around?"

"He still serves in the Guard. He commands an outpost protecting another Gate in the southern reaches of Vakhdahl," Tarek said. "If the queen wishes for his company, he grants it. It was not a relationship of love; she wished for a very powerful mate to father equally powerful children."

"Isn't that weird for him?" She could only imagine how people would react if the President kept a couple of concubines around.

Tarek shrugged. "He did not seem to mind. Halmerah is quite lovely."

"Wait, you knew him?"

"They don't proclaim it from the throne, but it was not so secret either," Tarek said. "Particularly among the Guard."

Gabby raised her eyebrows. "Does the princess know him at all?"

"She does," Tarek said. He glanced down the table, then turned back to her. "Just a moment." He stood and raised his glass, looking down the table at the Ironflight guests. The motion set the ornamental armored bracers on his wrists gleaming in the light. In a loud, powerful voice, he said, "*Nalak halar!*"

Halmerah looked up from her glass of wine, her expression stoic as she watched Tarek. Her gaze slowly drifted to the prince. Scanning the crowd, Gabby realized most of the gathered guests had turned their attention to the prince, waiting expectantly for a response. This was some tricky step in their dance of diplomacy, and she had no idea what to expect.

After a few heart-pounding seconds, Prince Zayir grinned, flashing perfect white teeth. "*Nalak halar anan*," he replied. "Well spoken, my friend." He raised his glass high, then pointedly took a long drink of his wine. "Your wine is very good, Halmerah. It has a sweetness that reminds me of a time long past."

"Your taste is quite apt," Halmerah replied as she held up her own glass and examined the liquid. "This particular cask was produced several hundred years ago, long before our lands were broken. I had hoped to honor your sister with this wine, but I trust you'll carry my regards to her."

"But of course," Zayir said. "She, of course, regrets that she was unable to attend such a fine feast. When I tell her of your wine and your musicians' fine playing, she will surely be angry that I came in her stead."

Having gotten a glimpse at the intrigue behind the veil made the entire exchange fascinating for Gabby. Halmerah was making passive-aggressive jabs, and Zayir knew it. Gabby's heart thumped as the queen gave him a predatory smile and took another long drink of her wine.

The prince's guard, Kaldir, wrinkled his nose. He had raised his glass in response to Tarek's toast, but he didn't speak or drink. "Is it a Stoneflight tradition to invite the Vak to your feasts and dress them in your clothes?" Kaldir asked, his eyes falling on Gabby. She instantly disliked him. He was certainly pleasant to look at, in a *hot damn he's huge* sort of way. But he made no attempt to hide the cruel cast to his gaze.

"It is a Stoneflight tradition to honor those who show respect and concern for their princess," Halmerah replied sharply. "I'm sure you're aware that my daughter was attacked. A cowardly act, to be certain." She glowered at Kaldir. "These *t'haran dan keth* have made a grave mistake. It would have been wiser to attack me openly than to ambush my child."

Several of the guests gasped at her words. Gabby had realized over the course of her tour with Tarek that the amulet couldn't translate certain phrases, most likely because they didn't have a direct equivalent. But she didn't need a translation to know that *t'haran dan keth* was a serious insult.

Halmerah gestured to Gabby, directing more attention to her. "This woman saved my daughter's life and protected her until one of my Gatekeepers arrived. Together, they saw that she was returned home safely."

Had the queen really invited her to show her gratitude or to rub it in the Ironflight's face that their attempt to kill Ashariah had failed because of a human's interference? She didn't care for being a political token, even if it involved pretty dresses and excellent wine.

Prince Zayir tilted his head, his jaw dropping. Gabby watched him, trying to figure out if his confusion was genuine or forced. If he was faking, he was damn good at it. "I had no idea," he said. "I'm terribly sorry to hear of her misfortune."

Halmerah simply stared at him for a moment. "And may I ask, where is your sister? I had truly hoped to honor her presence and ask to join me in prayer to the Skymother for my daughter's health."

Kaldir shifted uncomfortably in his seat, his eyes narrowing. Prince Zayir put up one hand, effectively dismissing his guard as he leaned over to talk to Halmerah. "My dear sister Tarim finds herself utterly overwhelmed with pressing matters of state, as your Excellency will no doubt understand and empathize. We currently find ourselves at odds with a rogue element of Edra who fancy themselves a sovereign nation. They have continually harried us, attempting to breach Ironhold."

"I am surprised Tarim has not already put an end to them," Halmerah said mildly.

"A hundred years ago, perhaps. Given their considerable numbers and impressive organization, we seek a peaceful understanding rather than plunging ourselves into an unnecessary war. In any case, my dear sister regrets that she could not attend herself, and apologizes for my obvious inadequacy," Zayir said. "Anything you wish to discuss, you may communicate to me, and I will relay it to her with the utmost accuracy. And to be certain, she will share in seeking the Skymother's favor upon your daughter."

"Very well," Halmerah said. "Tell me of your travails into Eldavar."

"My sister has not traveled there for some time. Nor have I. I mean no offense to your esteemed guest, but I find little of interest in the human realm," Zayir said. He held up his wine glass and waited patiently for a servant to approach and fill it. When the servant had finished filling it, he turned slightly in his seat and gave the woman a smile that would melt panties and inhibitions in a split second. The servant woman blushed and hurried away. He watched the woman retreat, then slowly turned back to Halmerah.

The queen's mouth was set in a firm line as she watched him eyeballing the servant woman. When she had the prince's attention again, she raised her eyebrows. "And your soldiers?"

"What of them?"

"Have they recently visited the human realm?" Halmerah said, looking past the prince to glare at Kaldir.

"Most esteemed highness, it seems there is something weighing upon your noble heart," Zayir said, his tone as smooth as sun-melted butter. "We have known each other for many years. This game is unnecessary between us. You may speak plainly. If we cannot converse freely, then..."

"Very well," Halmerah said. Her tone was still cool, a marked contrast to Zayir's slimy, used-car salesman tone. She set her glass down. The icy expression on her face was familiar; it was the one she had worn when she'd first arrived in the dungeon cells and stared Gabby down. It was the same one she'd worn when she promised that if Gabby was lying, she would see that Gabby begged for the mercy she would not grant. Halmerah was as hard as the stone of her mountain citadel. "Did your soldiers attack my daughter and her guards?"

Zayir choked on his wine. After dabbing a droplet from his lip, he pasted on a smile. "My dear Halmerah, however could you think such a thing? We have the greatest respect for you and your house."

"Your smile will win you no favors here," Captain Navan said, his expression grim.

"May I suggest that we have this conversation privately? Your guests seem quite interested in your private affairs," Zayir said.

"An assault upon Stoneflight royalty is no private affair. It is an act of war that concerns all of my people," Halmerah said. "Could it be that you prefer privacy so you do not have to perform for such a large audience?"

Zayir burst out laughing. The room had quieted. Though the musicians continued to play, most of the conversations around the room had stopped.

Many of the guests were attempting to look as if they weren't paying attention, but Gabby caught a few looking up over the edge of a wine glass at the unraveling situation.

"*Su'ud redahn,* I apologize for my rudeness. I believe your grief has affected your mind," Zayir said. "The thought that I or any of my kind would lay so much as a finger upon your precious daughter is ludicrous. Surely you cannot believe that my sister would order such a thing."

Halmerah simply stared at him without responding, her brow furrowed like she was starting to believe him. One of the queen's councilors snapped his fingers and gestured toward the herald. He took a noisy breath and stepped up to speak. "Queen Halmerah, the musicians are prepared for the *vizaran.* Shall I have them wait?"

Halmerah snapped her head up and gave the herald a baleful stare. He shrank back, looking as if he was regretting his line of work. Her gaze flicked back and forth between him and Zayir, then she finally took a breath and nodded. "There is no need to wait. I would show my guests the great hospitality of the Stoneflight," she said. Looking relieved, the herald signaled to the musicians, and the music suddenly shifted to a light but rhythmic drumbeat.

As if the tense argument had never taken place, Prince Zayir rose from his seat and held out his hand to Halmerah. "Allow me to offer my hand in peace," he said. "Neither my sister nor I wish any harm to befall your great house. And I speak on behalf of the Ironflight when I say that our resources are at your disposal to find the one who has grieved you."

Halmerah stared at him. The tension in her face remained, but she stood slowly and held her hand out to the side for Zayir to grasp. He lightly kissed the back of her hand, bowing his head in respect, then led her down the front of the dais.

Gabby looked to Tarek. "Oh my God, I thought she was going to kill him."

Tarek's gaze followed the queen as she bowed politely to Zayir. "She may yet. I don't believe what he's saying. And neither does she."

"He's slimy," Gabby said.

"That's an understatement," Tarek said. "Now we have to dance."

The thought of dancing with Tarek made her heart beat faster. She held out her hand, but he shook his head. The sting of rejection set a flush in her cheeks. "Oh. I thought..."

His jaw dropped. "No, no," he said. "Believe me, I would much rather dance with you. But you're the next female guest. If Ashariah was here, it would fall to her, but she's not. So you have to dance with him." Tarek gestured with a nod of his head.

Gabby turned to see Kaldir hovering a few feet away, looking as if he'd just smelled a fresh turd. "No," she murmured. "He obviously hates me."

"It'll be fine. He wouldn't dare be rude."

She sighed and pasted on a smile. This could be fun. Royal intrigue and hidden agendas; it was like a TV show. But her optimism faded as the Ironflight guard approached. He was enormous, standing a full foot taller than her. Her hand was dwarfed in his as he guided her down from the dais and into a position near the queen. But despite his scowl, his touch was oddly delicate, as if he was afraid he would break her hand by squeezing too hard.

Gabby felt strangely jealous as Tarek crossed the tables to greet one of the guests from the opposite side of the table and led her down to the floor. She took her place next to Gabby, continuing to form a line with the queen. The woman was obviously one of the Kadirai, with her exotic silver eyes and impressive height.

I bet she didn't go to medical school. She couldn't blame that on the wine. That was nothing more than petty jealousy.

Her heart pounded as she looked up at Kaldir. His bronze skin gleamed in the candlelight. He was made of delicious muscles, and had that perfect dusting of scruff along a sharp jawline that made him look rugged but not unkempt. His thick dark hair had been barely tamed, smoothed away from his face with some sort of oil, but a few pieces sprang loose to fall toward his face. He may have been unpleasant, but he was easy to look at.

The music continued, and all of the men stood in a straight line. They gave a series of bows and hand gestures, each sharp and almost military precise. Gabby tried to follow the women as they did a similar series of moves in response, theirs more graceful and flowing. This wasn't so bad. She managed to fumble along and make her way back to the line before tripping anyone.

After another musical flourish, the two lines met in the center, with the men taking their partners by the waist. Kaldir's large hand rested on the small of her back, and he kept his gaze fixed over her shoulder. It was awkward, to say the least. The peacemaker in her wanted to say *sorry you got stuck with me*, but he'd been way too much of a jerk to deserve an apology.

Still, despite his obvious dislike at the situation, he was a skilled dancer.

He was a little stiff; his precise, sharp movements reminded her more of a martial arts sequence than a dance. But there was still unmistakable grace and skill in the way he moved. And he guided her perfectly. Her family had all been avid dancers, and she'd always enjoyed a partner who could lead well.

There was a build in the music, a thrumming on a loose-sounding drum, and Kaldir murmured, "I will not let you go." The statement sounded strange, though it sounded as if it was meant to be reassuring. Suddenly, he took her right hand and spun her quickly, setting her jewelry jangling and her skirt swirling around her legs. Her heart raced, and a giddy excitement rose in her belly. Then, just as quickly, he wrapped her in close, pressing her tightly to his body. And what a body it was. He looked down, his eyes raking over her. "Trust me," he ordered.

Then he spun her again, letting her drape over his arm. She tensed at first, then leaned in into the dip and let herself arch backward his strong arm. He scooped her around in an arc, then pulled her up tightly to himself.

"You surprise me," he said, breathing a little heavier than before.

"How's that?"

"You are graceful."

"For the Vak, you mean."

"No," he said flatly. "You are graceful. You move with beauty."

"Was that a compliment?"

"If you interpret facts so," he said dismissively.

The music abruptly stopped as the crowd began to murmur. The quiet chattering rose into a chorus of shouts. Kaldir's grip on her hand tightened painfully as he spun her around, nearly wrenching her elbow out of joint. She started to protest, but she realized his violent reaction was to get in front of her. With his broad frame, he blocked her entirely from whatever was happening.

She peeked around his shoulder to see a naked young man stumbling down the center of the ballroom. Servants and guards alike trailed after him, as horrified guests stared.

The young man was bloodied and bruised, nearly all of his skin marked in some way. The worst of it that Gabby could see was a twisted rune scorched into the skin across his muscular chest. He left bloody footprints on the cold stone as he limped toward the front of the room, where the queen was frozen in Zayir's arms, staring in horror. The prince looked equally horrified, but Gabby couldn't tell if it was the same shocked surprise or the look of *oh shit I got caught*.

"Hold!" Captain Navan screeched. The queen's guards had leaped into action, leaving overturned glasses and holding their weapons ready as they approached the newcomer in a tightening circle.

The queen stared at Prince Zayir, then looked closer at the newcomer. "Dakhar?" she murmured. Her eyes widened as she stared at him.

The man—Dakhar—was babbling, virtually incoherent. "The Ironflight, my lady, they are coming. I must...I must..." He collapsed on his knees. As he hit the ground, the hazy bluish light struck his back, which was carved with a string of twisted symbols down his spine. On all fours, he moaned in pain, then fell unconscious. The room was eerily silent as everyone stared.

A terrible scream of rage broke the silence. Halmerah gasped for air, staring down at the wounded man. Her fingers twitched and twisted into a claw-like shape. Her smooth skin split across her spine and shoulders, revealing dark amethyst scales. Her eyes swelled, with lightning strikes in their icy depths. The stony façade was obliterated by her wrath.

As the queen transformed, the Ironflight prince twisted away from her. His charming smile melted as he frantically scanned the room for an exit. The room erupted into chaos again as the Adamant Guard swarmed toward them.

Kaldir shoved Gabby away hard and bolted toward the prince. Her feet caught in the long gown, and she hit the ground hard. She had barely made contact when Tarek dashed toward her and scooped her off the ground like she weighed nothing. He carried her effortlessly up to the dais and left her there. "Go up there," he said, pointing to the staircase that Halmerah had descended in her grand entrance.

"But—"

"Please, Gabrielle," he said. "Just go!"

She nodded and gathered up her skirt in handfuls, then hurried up the staircase. Another pair of guards rushed past her as she climbed. Down below, Tarek shouted to the guards as he hurried toward the wounded man.

Meanwhile, Kaldir had drawn the ceremonial sword from his belt and waved it in threatening flourishes as he protected Zayir. They had started to retreat, but they were cut off by Captain Navan and a handful of the queen's guards. All around the room, the queen's guards skirmished with the Ironflight guards.

"*T'haran dan keth!*" Halmerah bellowed as her face elongated and darkened. She had not fully transformed, and it was a terrible sight to see her halfway between human form and dragon form. Her legs were still human, but her heavy upper body had weighed her down so she was supporting her halfway transformed body on thick, muscular purple limbs. She threw her head back and roared, so loud that it left Gabby's ears ringing.

A handful of the Ironflight guards had broken away to surround the prince. Halmerah snapped her head around and swiped her claws toward them. Though they were well out of range of her razor-sharp talons, a wave of energy broke away from her, toppling tables, chairs, and people alike as it went. The three guards were swept off their feet and slammed hard into the stone wall across the room.

"Take them!" Navan shouted.

Kaldir was doing his best to fight, swinging the sword in powerful arcs. As he fought, he always had one arm back, blocking Zayir from harm. But there were too many of the Stoneflight guards, and they overpowered him. One knocked the sword from his hand, while another kicked the back of his knee and forced him to the ground. He started to fight back again, but one of the other guards punched him across the face, leaving him dazed on the ground. It surprised Gabby that she felt a little bad for him.

When Kaldir fell, Zayir put up his hands in a sign of submission. The queen's guards still brandished their swords, but it was to hold him at bay rather than to wound him. He didn't resist as they forced him to his knees, twisting his arms behind him. The beguiling smile and warm eyes were gone, filled with anger as he shouted, "My sister will hear of this! A clever gambit, Halmerah, more than I would expect from you."

Halmerah roared again, this time throwing another of those great waves toward them. The sheer force of it pushed Zayir and the guards holding him back until they all slammed into the heavy wood doors. "Tell her to come!" she roared, her voice terrible and deafening. Through the amulet, Gabby not only understood the language, but felt the sheer rage and anguish that saturated Halmerah's words.

A hand fell on her shoulder. Gabby shrieked in surprise and looked up to see Tarek crouched on the stairs next to her. "I'm getting you away from here. The queen is dangerous like this. Come with me."

CHAPTER TWENTY-FIVE

THE LAST TIME Tarek had seen the queen lose control, allowing the terrible dragon to emerge, was when her daughter Ivralah had died. Not long after, the ill-fated Silverflight, who had coordinated the ambush, had been wiped from the face of Ascavar. They were literally only a memory now, leaving only shattered ruins and whispered stories.

His heart had not slowed from its breakneck pace, even now that he had gotten Gabrielle away from the grand ballroom and back to the safety of her quarters. She had been remarkably calm, keeping her voice even and her pace measured, but he saw fear written in her tight jaw and creases around her eyes.

All through their retreat, as they bumped through the noisy crowd, he'd heard *Ironflight attack* constantly. There was a nervous buzz in the air, and many of the Kadirai had already exchanged their fripperies and jewels for lightweight clothing that would allow for a quick transformation should the occasion arise. Though only a small number of the Kadirai served in the Adamant Guard, every single one underwent combat training at a young age and were expected to defend the queen and the city in the event of an attack.

And to think, he'd actually believed Zayir's smooth words, right up until he saw Dakhar stumble in bearing the marks of the Ironflight. Now, it seemed that their long-held peace was in its final days. Dakhar had been among Ashariah's guards on her visit to the human realm. After finding her guard Surik dead, Tarek had assumed the others were dead.

When they emerged from the crowded stairs into the guest wing, there was finally a break in the noise and the pressing energy of the crowd. Servants hurried up and down the corridor, some carrying linens and trays laden with tea as if nothing was amiss, while others paced back and forth between open doorways and the windows overlooking the garden.

Tarek paused and looked back at Gabrielle. She had her long skirt balled up in one hand as she followed him. "Are you all right?"

"I'm not sure I know how to answer that right now," she said. She managed to curve her lips in the semblance of a smile, but her eyes were still wide and fearful.

He waited for her to catch up, then rested one hand on her back and gently guided her up the hallway. Her breathing was heavy and labored with fright, and he suddenly felt guilty for bringing her into this mess. And yet, he knew that if the alternative was to have never crossed paths with her, he wouldn't have chosen otherwise. Maybe it was selfishness, maybe it was attraction; maybe they were the same.

When they reached her quarters, Tarek opened the door for her. Her shoulders hunched slightly as she entered the safety of the room. He started to close the door behind her, but she turned, her lips parted and a strangely hopeful look in her eyes. "Will you be all right?" he asked.

She hesitated. Fear still lingered in her eyes. "If you have to go, I understand."

He should. He wanted to know what was going on. If an Ironflight attack was coming, he would be needed. But he could spare a moment to see that she was all right. When he stepped into her room, the tension in her face suddenly eased. A warm thrill of pride rushed over him.

Priorities, Windstriker. She was lovely indeed, but there were more important matters. And while his mind understood that, his heart and his body only wanted to stay here with her and pretend the chaos around them was nothing but a dream. A nervous thrill washed over him as he felt himself edging toward a precipice. His dogged insistence on not letting himself get attached was rapidly eroding.

"I can stay for a moment," he said. A genuine smile curved her lips, and he felt like he was plummeting from the skies. He hesitated at the door, then closed it quietly behind him to shut out the chaos outside.

"What's going to happen?"

He bolstered his courage and walked toward her. She looked up at him, her eyes searching him. "I'm not sure," he said. As he looked down at her, he noticed she was trembling faintly. She was doing her best to look stoic and steady, but he knew the telltale signs of the adrenaline rush fading. "Come, sit with me."

He crouched in the sitting area near the window, folding his legs under him. He patted a deep red cushion next to him and offered his hand to help her sit. As she fussed with the draped dress, he caught a glimpse of her tan leg, nearly to the hip. He swallowed hard and looked up at her face instead, helping her sit next to him.

"The guy who showed up...the naked one," Gabrielle said. "Who was he?"

"He was one of Ashariah's guards," Tarek said. "When I first thought something was wrong, I followed their trails and found one of her guards dead. She had at least two more guards, but I assumed they were dead. It seems the Ironflight had captured Dakhar, and perhaps the other. We will find out soon enough."

"He looked awful," Gabrielle said.

Tarek nodded. "I'm sure they tortured him."

"For what?"

"The location of the Gate," Tarek said.

"You mean where I took Ashariah? Why?"

Tarek hesitated. It really wasn't for her to know, but considering she'd been sucked right into the heart of the storm, it was only fair. "Our world has been...broken. I told you before of the war that shattered our lands." Gabrielle nodded in understanding. "Because of the Raspolin and their foul magic, huge swaths of our lands are uninhabitable now. The Gates around our world can provide safe passage to distant locations. Their locations are fiercely protected, as they grant access to the domains of the other dragonflights."

"And that would be worth torturing someone for?"

"Oh yes," Tarek said. "As it stands, the Ironflight's safest passage to our lands is a narrow path through the mountains, past several heavily fortified outposts. However, if they were to learn the location of our Gate on your side, they could launch a surprise attack by moving their forces through your world and crossing over. By the time we saw them, it would be too late to mount a successful defense. Rumors abound of a Gate that enters directly into Adamantine Rise, but it is truly only a rumor."

In the human realm, the Gates were protected with powerful warding spells that concealed their location, much like Tarek and the other wind dragons concealed themselves. Even a keen tracker would be hard-pressed to follow a trail back to the Gate, instead finding that the trail suddenly died off miles away.

"So everyone here is in danger?" Gabrielle said.

Tarek hesitated. "You'll be safe here. The citadel has never been breached." There had been many attempts, resulting in a sort of patchwork effect of repairs to the stone walls around the perimeter, but that wouldn't do much to assure her.

"But will you be safe? You're going to get involved, aren't you?" The way she asked wasn't accusatory, but the resigned sound of someone who knew it wasn't worth arguing. How long had it been since someone had been concerned for him?

"I have to," Tarek said. He took a deep breath and took Gabrielle's hand. She slowly raised her eyes to his. After brushing a kiss across the warm skin, he said "I'm sorry to have brought you into this." And while he was sorry, he wasn't sorry to have met her.

"Is it weird that I don't really mind anymore?"

She gently extricated her hand from his, leaving him bereft and wondering if he had made a misstep. But instead of retreating to herself, she brushed her fingers against his cheek. Her touch left blazing trails along his jaw. Without thinking, he leaned in. Her lips parted. He had never wanted something so much as he wanted to kiss her in that moment, to unwrap the bothersome silk covering her body.

He leaned in and murmured, "May I—"

She cut him off with a kiss that took his breath away. Her lips were on his, warm and tasting of fine wine. He wasted no time, curling his arm around her waist and pulling her tight to his body. Her touch was fire on his skin. With her chest pressed to him, he felt her racing heart against his.

She broke away for a second, breathing heavily, eyes wild as she searched him. The sight of her lips, plump and pink from his kiss nearly drove him mad. The part of him that stupidly thought he could resist the temptation was losing the battle.

"Shall we?" he said. Her mouth quirked in a smile as she pressed closer to him, reaching back to pull the constricting silk dress up around her legs. He groaned and pulled her into his lap, her shapely legs squeezing either side of him. Her mouth found his, tongue lightly playing across his lips. Lust overwhelmed him, and he forgot all about his resolve to keep his distance. To hell with distance and detachment.

Dizzy and breathless, he ran his hands from her hips and traced the graceful curve of her body. Through the textured fabric, he cupped her breasts. As his fingers grazed the tender peaks, her breath hitched, and her hips twitched against his groin. A wave of heat rolled over him as he stiffened.

"Miss Gabrielle? I've brought you some—oh!"

Tarek gasped in surprise and looked over Gabrielle's shoulder to see a young servant woman standing at the door with flushed cheeks. She looked back and forth and finally said, "Should I come back?"

"I—uh," Gabrielle stammered. Her hair was messy around her face. She bit her lip, her head hunched as if she was trying to hide.

Outside, a long horn sounded three times. Along with the handmaiden's arrival, the sound of it jolted him out of his lustful reverie. They were on the brink of war, and here he was letting his lust do the thinking. He squeezed Gabrielle's shoulder lightly and spoke quietly. "It pains me greatly to leave, but I should go."

She started to speak, then closed her mouth and nodded. "You should go."

He carefully rearranged his clothing and hoped the evidence of his indiscretion wasn't too obvious. The handmaiden was pointedly looking away as he got to his feet and composed himself. "I'd appreciate your discretion," he said.

"Of course," she said.

He gave Gabrielle a lingering glance. With loose strands of hair falling around her face, her lips and cheeks flushed, she looked even more beautiful than ever. And now that he had tasted her kiss, touched the swell and curve of her body, it took all of his willpower to look away.

Damn the Ironflight.

The barracks were swarming with the Adamant Guard. Narrow wooden doors stood open as the guards hurried to don uniforms. Shouts echoed in the stone corridor as they yelled back and forth with rumors and orders. Tarek found himself at the back of the crowd, and yet again, he was reminded of how his position had changed.

There was no breaking through the tight crowd, and even if he'd been able to get to Navan, he probably would have been told to simply be on alert like any other civilian. Instead, Tarek took advantage of his decades of service to the queen and took a side hallway that spiraled around to a side entrance to the gardens. The citadel was full of narrow passages and obscured doors that allowed guards and servants to move quickly.

As much as he wanted to see someone pay for what had happened to Ashariah, the thought of going to war with the Ironflight filled Tarek with dread. He had been barely old enough to fight during the Great War, and had lived the vast majority of his life in its aftermath. Furthermore, it was only by the Skymother's blessing that Halmerah hadn't attacked Prince Zayir. Silver tongued and calm, he was the balance to his sister Tarim's fiery temper. If Halmerah so much as singed a hair on his head, Tarim would order her armies into Adamantine Rise and promise all of the hidden wealth of Vakhdahl as a bounty for Halmerah's head. It would be an ugly fight, and one Tarek wasn't certain the Stoneflight would win.

The gardens were empty as far as he could see. Glass lanterns cast a hazy yellow glow across the path. The quiet was calming after the nervous tension in the citadel, but his mind drifted upstairs.

Focus, he thought.

Sure enough, his instincts had led him well. In the heart of the gardens, at the absolute center of the circle of pillars was a raised platform called the *farhenh dar Isina,* or the Skymother's Heart. It was austere, just a flat stone clearing with two arches that crossed overhead to keep the overgrowth from covering it. Beneath the arches, four guards were stationed at compass points while the queen sat in the middle, now in her human form. Captain Navan waited at the perimeter, along with several of the queen's councilors. Navan looked up and tilted his head quizzically at the sight of Tarek on the opposite edge of the clearing.

Though Halmerah's back was to him, she spoke up. "Old habits die hard, don't they, Tarek-ahn?"

He froze as the rest of the guards turned to face him. Several put hands to their swords out of instinct. "I came to see if you were…" He fished for the word.

"Myself?" Halmerah said. She turned and looked over her shoulder at him, her eyes heavy and tired. "In control?"

"*Su'ud redahn*, I meant no offense."

"I understand," she said. She braced one hand on the stone and started to get to her feet. One of the guards and Councilor Eszen rushed forward, but she waved them off as she stood and straightened her clothes. Her silver dress had no doubt been ruined by her unplanned transformation, and she now wore a plain dark gray dressing gown that was still finer than any formal dress he'd seen in the human world. Her dark hair hung loose down her back, with part of it pulled away from her face and caught in a silver comb. Though she remained still, he could see the change as she composed herself and took on the stoic persona of queen once more. "And I know you, Tarek-ahn. You did not come here to check on me. You want to be involved with whatever lies ahead."

"I—yes," he said. There was no point in lying to her.

"Majesty, I understand your sentiment, but…" Eszen protested.

Halmerah snapped her head around, silencing the councilor with a look.

"Tarek Windstriker was my protector long before you took your seat on the council."

Eszen glared at Tarek, but closed his mouth and remained silent.

"Furthermore, Tarek saw the evidence of the Ironflight attack firsthand," Halmerah said. "And protected my daughter against their continued attempts to kill her. He has a right to be here."

"Thank you, *su'ud redahn*," Tarek said.

"If I may speak, my queen?" Captain Navan said. "The Prince and his entourage have been secured. Would you care to be present for the interrogation?"

Halmerah shook her head. "I do not trust myself with the Prince. You, Councilor Eszen, and Tarek will go. I trust you to get information."

"You wish for me to go?" Tarek asked. Did she actually trust him with something so important?

Her cool eyes searched him. "You observed the aftermath of their treachery first hand. It makes sense, does it not?" Her expression was probing.

"Of course," he said quickly. Pride swelled in him, but he pushed it back, not wanting to let his hope get ahead of him.

Navan nodded his agreement. "By what means do you wish us to obtain this information?"

"The Ironflight are cowards for attacking my daughter when they wished to hurt me," Halmerah said. "I will not resort to such tactics. You will treat the Prince with the utmost respect."

"And his guards?"

Halmerah simply shrugged. "My hospitality has its limits, and the Iron

Blade is beyond my concern. Do what you must."

Dread gripped Tarek's stomach. He knew what that would mean. The excessive courtesy and smooth diplomacy had ended when they saw Dakhar and what had been done to him. "Has Dakhar spoken?" he asked.

Halmerah raised her eyes to him, then looked to Eszen. "Councilor?"

Eszen snapped to attention. "I will send a messenger for information immediately," he said.

"I wish to know as soon as he is able to speak of what happened," Halmerah said.

Eszen nodded. "It will be done."

Halmerah paused, then gestured to the other councilor next to Eszen. The woman was new to the council and must have been seated after he'd been moved to the Gate. "Netha, see that the Vak are notified to be on guard. They are to report anything strange to us immediately."

"How much shall I tell them?"

"They need not know details," Halmerah said. She gestured to Navan. "See that Lieutenant L'hash speaks with the City Guard. Double all posts, and send word immediately to our outposts. And send word to the Circle of Edra."

Navan exchanged a look with Eszen. "Yes, my queen," he said. "It will be done."

While most of the guest quarters in Adamantine Rise featured the huge open windows that allowed for the Kadirai to take to the skies, there were several smaller rooms with no windows. They were reserved for guests for whom protocol dictated a cell was inappropriate, but could not be allowed to roam freely throughout the citadel.

Prince Zayir had been forcibly escorted to one of these rooms. As Tarek followed Navan and a trio of guards down the corridor, his eyes lingered on Gabrielle's door. It had been at least an hour, but the mere sight of the door reawakened the fire in him. His mind drifted to the memory of her lips, of her body pressed to his.

"Are you all right?" Navan asked.

Tarek snapped to attention. "Just thinking."

"About your Vak friend?"

"She is not Vak," Tarek said. "She is from the human world."

"The words are irrelevant. She is not Kadirai," Navan said sharply. "Perhaps you have been too long at the Gate."

"Perhaps you should mind the task at hand," Tarek replied as anger bloomed in his chest, wrapping a hot vise around his heart.

Navan simply raised an eyebrow at him, then stopped at a door toward the end of the corridor. Two heavily armed guards stood outside with spears held at their sides. Navan nodded, and one of the guards removed a key from his belt and opened the door.

Navan entered first, with Tarek and Eszen close behind. As soon as they entered the room, Zayir began speaking. "I will remind you that I am the prince of the Ironflight, second only to the esteemed and divinely blessed Tarim, who traces her bloodline to—"

"Save your breath, Prince," Navan interrupted. He gestured to a small table in the corner of the room. Spread on the table were plates of fruit and bread, along with a pitcher of wine and several cups. The dishes were plainer than the fine pieces used at the feast, but still far nicer than anything Tarek had seen in his years away.

The guest quarters themselves were richly appointed; not quite as lavish as Gabrielle's room, but they were more than adequate. A bed large enough for two stood against one wall, draped with dark gray silks and an excessive number of cushions. A servant had even brought several changes of clothes, including a gray dressing gown, a pair of dark trousers, and a pair of slippers to protect a prince's feet against the cold stone floor.

"Have you complaints about the hospitality?" Navan said.

"I have complaints that I did not ask for your hospitality," Zayir said. "I came in good faith at your queen's whim. Had I known that her invitation was merely a formality to accuse my people of a horrific crime with no evidence, and that your queen had no intention of listening to reason, I would not have come."

Navan pulled the sword from his belt, and for the first time since the Prince had arrived, Tarek saw fear cross his face. Navan simply placed the sword on the table, then sat on the stool next to it as he helped himself to a piece of bread. "Do you mind? My dinner was rather rudely interrupted," he said.

Zayir folded his arms across his chest and sat on the edge of the bed. "You know this will not bode well for the peace between our people."

"Perhaps you should have considered that before attacking our princess," Navan said, taking a messy bite of the bread.

Zayir scowled. "I cannot say it any more plainly. There was no such attack."

Navan gestured to one of the other guards, who produced a small cloth-wrapped bundle and set it on the table. Zayir's eyes followed it, his brow furrowing as he waited for Navan to touch it. But Navan took his time to finish chewing his bread, brush imaginary crumbs from his chestplate, and pour a cup of wine before touching it. The prince's expression had turned to a scowl by the time Navan finally unwrapped the bundle.

Inside the linen fabric was the jagged knife Tarek had found on Surik's body. There was still dried blood along the gleaming blade. Navan held it up and made a show of looking it over. "This is of Ironflight make, is it not?"

"I'm hardly a blacksmith," Zayir replied. "It looks familiar, yes."

Navan squinted and held the blade closer to his face. "*Nalak halar*," he said pointedly. "Chosen by flame." He wrinkled his nose. "The gemstones are a bit gaudy, don't you think?"

"As I said, I'm not the maker. Can I ask why you're so intent on showing me your little knife? If it's a threat, it's not terribly effective."

Tarek watched him closely. The Ironflight prince was renowned for his silver tongue. Though he paid lip service to his sister's authority, virtually anyone who dealt with the Ironflight knew that Zayir was the puppetmaster operating the throne. It was his cunning that kept the Ironflight queen out of trouble. Zayir didn't show any of the telltale signs of lying, but Tarek had a feeling that the prince could have promised that it was indeed daylight outside and made Tarek check to be sure.

"This was buried in one of the princess's guards," Navan said. "Explain yourself, or I'll be forced to draw my own conclusions."

Zayir sighed. "Several weeks ago, one of our outposts was attacked. We believed it likely to be the work of the Edra separatists, or perhaps the Shadowflight. They left the guards slain and cleared out all of the supplies, including the armory."

"This is the first I've heard of such an incident," Navan said.

"Why would a minor larceny in Mardahl come to your attention? If there is a tradition of reporting our daily trivia to each other, I'm rather behind. If you're interested, I spent last night in the company of two lovely..."

Navan slammed the blade down into the table, rattling the plates with the impact. The prince stopped short, but his expression was amused rather than frightened. "I tire of your tongue."

"Your explanation is rather convenient," Tarek said.

"The truth cares little for convenience," Zayir said, scowling at Tarek. "May I assume that the queen will levy her accusations with equal intensity at the Shadowflight?"

Navan ignored the jab and crossed his arms over his chest. "Will your guards verify your story? We both know you are the face and the voice of the Ironflight. And you would never get your royal hands dirty with such nasty business."

Zayir threw up his hands. "There is nothing I can say that will convince you of our innocence. That much is obvious."

"The truth would be an excellent start," Navan said.

With a sigh, Zayir sat at the table directly across from Navan. Despite the guard captain's superior size and advantage in numbers, the prince looked unruffled. Neatly avoiding the knife buried in the wooden table, he topped off Navan's cup of wine, and poured himself a cup. He looked back to Tarek and the other guards, making an offering gesture. Tarek scowled in response, which only made the prince smile.

"You are not interested in the truth, or this conversation would have been over hours ago," Zayir said after taking a sip of his wine. "Halmerah craves vengeance. She always has. Your kind belittle my sister for her fits of passion, but at least my sister has never slain an entire flight for the actions of their queen."

"You will show respect," Tarek said, his temper flaring.

"And you," Zayir sneered. "Perhaps this is your way of soothing your wounded soul over the death of Ivralah. Your failures are your own, Windstriker. Do not lay them at the feet of the Ironflight. We did not kill Ivralah, and we certainly did not attempt to kill Ashariah."

Tarek felt as if the prince had slammed the knife into his belly. His tongue was dry and thick as he managed to say, "We'll see."

"One can only hope for a moment of clarity," Zayir said. "Instead, let me leave you with an intelligent thought, since they seem to be in such short supply in Adamantine Rise as of late. If we wished to bring war to your doorstep, we would not be so circumspect. We would not leave our weapons about, nor would we carve our symbols into a prisoner and let him go free. I assure you that if the Ironflight was to move against you, you would know instantly by the blade in your belly and the heat of our flames upon your face." He leaned casually against the table, staring at Navan with an unctuous smile. "You have a much greater concern. Someone has taken up arms against you, and the Skymother only knows what else they're planning while you are pressing me for answers I do not have. I hope you find them before it's too late."

CHAPTER TWENTY-SIX

GABRIELLE ROJAS HAD NEVER been kissed like that in her life. It had been worth the wait and then some. She could have strangled Irinakh for interrupting them. Then again, things had certainly escalated quickly. It wasn't like Gabby to fall into bed with a man she'd met only...oh hell, had it only been two days? And even so, she knew that she wanted Tarek more than she had ever wanted another person. It was irrational, pure primal lizard brain, and she knew it.

After Tarek's departure, Irinakh had fussed around the room for a while, politely avoiding the topic of the scene she'd interrupted. Instead, she'd busied herself with unpinning Gabby's hair, bringing her a dressing gown and a pair of thin slippers. As she tended to Gabby, she passed along the gossip she'd heard about the ball, though it was nothing of substance that Gabby hadn't seen for herself. The only new thing she learned was that the prince had been locked in one of the guest rooms; a politer imprisonment than the dungeons, but a cell no less.

By the time Irinakh had brought her a pot of tea, Gabby's mind had finally turned from Tarek to the excitement of the evening. Well, to be fair, every few minutes, her mind wandered back because *damn*, but she had mostly regained her senses. "Irinakh," Gabby said absently. "Could I go visit the gardens?"

"Oh, Miss Gabrielle, it's very late," Irinakh said. "You should rest."

"Is it not safe?"

"Oh, it's very safe," Irinakh said. "But with everything going on tonight, and the Ironflight....you should really stay in."

"But if I wanted to go, I could?"

Irinakh sighed. "You're supposed to drink your tea and rest. Raszila was very specific. I am to take care of you and see that you are treated with the utmost respect."

Judging by last night and Tarek's comment about the servants making sure guests rested when the queen wanted them to, she had a feeling there was more than tea in that pot. "Well, it would make me feel like royalty if I could go to the garden," Gabby said. "Just to clear my head for a while."

Irinakh hesitated, biting at her lower lip as she frowned. "I suppose I can't stop you. But the guards may send you back."

"If they do, I'll come right back, I promise," she said.

The handmaiden's shoulders slumped. "All right, but not like that." She rummaged in the basket of clothing she'd brought and produced a long-sleeved gray robe. After pulling it on, Gabby stood still to let her tie the white sash in a perfectly symmetrical knot, and then waited patiently for the woman to twist the top section of her hair into an elegant knot pinned with several long metal pins. "You look decent now."

"Thank you," Gabby said. "I won't be long, I promise."

Once she was out of the guest quarters, Gabby darted down the hallway toward the central staircase. As she hurried down the stairs, she kept her expression neutral and her shoulders thrown back, trying to look as if she was right where she belonged.

It had occurred to her while Irinakh was carefully removing all the many pins and decorations from her hair that Ashariah had shown her visions of what had happened in her past to make her trust Tarek. Though they hadn't allowed her into the infirmary before, the situation had clearly changed. If they would let her close, she might be able to spark another vision from Ashariah that could grant them some insight into what had happened to her.

Tarek and the others had seemed convinced all along that this was an Ironflight attack. But something didn't sit right with Gabby. The weapons left behind, and then the symbols literally carved onto Dakhar's back? It seemed too obvious, especially for someone as smooth and subtle as Prince Zayir. If they'd really done it, they wouldn't have walked into the feast and let themselves be captured.

Though nighttime had painted the gardens in shades of gray and darkest green, it was still beautiful. Thin chains connected the trees like metal vines twisting overhead, with glowing yellow lanterns illuminating the path. They cast warm globes of light on the surrounding foliage, creating a dreamy nightscape. As before, she felt the calming energy seeping into her bones, bringing a warmth and contentment all over.

Her feet carried her without conscious thought. How exactly had they approached the pavilion before? She hesitated at a fork, then took a path that seemed to go straight ahead.

Two dark-clad guards blocked the path, halting her progress. Beyond was an open clearing, lit by more of the glass lanterns. The queen stood alone at the center of the clearing, a smooth stone circle amidst the greenery.

"What are you doing here?" one of the guards barked.

"I came to see the princess," Gabby stammered, her stomach flip-flopping as she watched his hand go to his sword. "I think I might be able to help."

"You have no business here," the guard said. "Return to the guest quarters."

"Who is it?" Halmerah asked.

"The Vak woman," the guard said, giving Gabby a disdainful look.

"You know, the way you say that is very disrespectful," Gabby said. "You should really—"

"Let her pass," Halmerah said. The unexpected invitation stopped Gabby mid-admonishment, which was probably for the best. She turned, pinning Gabby with her stony gaze. "What is it?"

With the queen's fierce gaze on her, Gabby suddenly forgot how to speak. This was a woman who had Hulked out into a dragon that probably would eat her as soon as look at her. She hesitated at the edge of the stone circle. "Ma'am—uh, your Majesty. When we talked before, things were a bit tense." If Halmerah was apologetic over the whole dungeon thing, she didn't let it show on her face. "When I was caring for your daughter, she showed me things."

"She showed you things. Was she awake?"

"No," Gabby said. "When I was checking on her vital signs..." The queen gave her a confused look. Maybe that hadn't translated well. "Her heartbeat, her breathing?" The queen nodded. "I touched her, and I got this vision of when she was attacked."

"A vision..." Halmerah murmured.

"She did it again when Tarek came to find her. It was like she knew he was there and was trying to tell me I could trust him. She showed me this place, actually. She remembered watching you landing from the sky while he carried her."

Halmerah flinched then, raw anguish seeping into her eyes. "I don't understand. If you are lying..."

"Miss—queen," Gabby stuttered. "I wouldn't, I swear. I'm a healer in my world. I know how much you're hurting right now, and I wouldn't do anything to make it harder, I promise." Halmerah's expression softened finally. Gabby took it as a cue that she at least had her attention. "Is that something Ashariah could do before? The visions, I mean?"

Halmerah shook her head. "I don't think so. She never mentioned such a thing."

Gabby took a deep breath. "I know your people don't think much of humans. But I thought maybe I could see her. Maybe if we tell her what's going on, she could show me something else that would help. Maybe she knows who attacked her."

Halmerah nodded. "Let us walk together." She snapped her fingers, and the guards on the opposite side of the stone clearing parted for her. Gabby trailed behind her at first, but Halmerah slowed her pace so they walked side-by-side. "You are a healer in your world?"

"A doctor," Gabby said. "Basically, yes. I don't have magic, so we use technology instead."

236

"And you are called to this?"

"Called?"

"By your gods," Halmerah said.

"Um," Gabby said. "Not exactly. I mean, I believe it's what I'm supposed to do. And I guess I'm pretty good at it."

Halmerah fixed her with a stare. "Do you think highly of yourself?"

"I didn't mean to sound boastful," Gabby said.

"I appreciate that," Halmerah interrupted. "There is no shame in taking pride in your gifts, Gabrielle. Do not diminish your flame to make others more comfortable in your shadow."

Gabby nodded slowly. Life advice from a dragon queen. Her life was getting weirder by the minute.

They walked the rest of the way in relative quiet. The only sound was the soft rustle and occasional metallic sound of armor from the guards following them. When they reached the healers' pavilion, Halmerah ordered her guards to wait at the steps, then gestured for Gabby to follow.

The gentle aura of the garden was stronger here. As Gabby walked across the silver-inlaid floor, she actually felt the energy moving around her, like standing in the ocean as the waves crashed and receded around her legs. The healers gathered around the white-veiled bed parted as the queen approached. They bowed their heads but did not speak.

"Come," Halmerah said, holding out her hand to Gabby. She moved aside to allow Gabby to stand close to the bed, then stood just over her shoulder.

The princess lay on a nest of soft pillows. Her dark hair had been washed, and now streamed over the white linens in thick glossy waves. Her skin was rosier than it had been, and she appeared to breathe normally. Miraculously, the worst of her injuries had healed, leaving faint pink scars. There were still blotches of yellowish-green from the deep bruises that hadn't fully faded, but the amount of healing she'd done would have taken months back in Gabby's world.

"May I?" Gabby asked, pushing up the sleeves of her robe and extending one hand toward the princess. One of the healers tending her gave Halmerah a skeptical look, but the queen made a dismissive wave and nodded.

Gabby sat on a low stool next to the bed. With trembling fingers, she took Ashariah's hand and pressed her fingers into the fine bones at her wrist. Her pulse was steady and strong. Gabby pinched the fleshy mound at the base of her thumb between her fingernails. The princess's hand twitched, pulling away from the stimulus. She wished for a flashlight to check her eyes, but the reaction to pain told her that the princess' brain was intact.

"Has she woken up at all?" Gabby asked.

One of the healers shook her head. "She only sleeps."

"Ashariah, do you remember me? Dr. Rojas? I took care of you for a while," Gabby said. For the first time since she'd arrived in this strange world, she felt comfortable. She gently traced the back of Ashariah's hand. "We're trying to figure out what happened to you. Can you show me anything like you did before?"

"Was it the Ironflight who attacked you?" Halmerah asked, suddenly moving to her daughter's other side and taking her hand. "Show us, child. Show us."

Suddenly Ashariah's hand clamped down tight enough to make Gabby's fingers grind together. Like before, Gabby felt a snapping sensation in her head like she'd closed a circuit and made a connection. Her instinct was to pull away, but Ashariah's grip was tight as a vise.

The vision was disjointed and confusing, coming in dizzying flashes of movement, like fast forwarding through a movie. Gabby tried to concentrate, willing it to slow down.

She was flying high above the orange and red expanse of the desert, her heart racing with joy at the beauty below. The first of her guards to fall was Halcin, who plunged from the sky behind her. She only heard him cry out, didn't even see the attack. When she turned to look for him, one of his wings dangled uselessly, shorn nearly in half as if by a sharp blade. Her wings beat as fast as she could go, but she was still young and small, with a fraction of the wingspan of their attackers.

There were four dragons behind them, one silver, one gold and two pure white. The silver and gold dragons spiraled away to attack Dakhar and Surik while the two enormous white dragons focused their attention on her. They were bigger than any dragon she'd ever seen, easily three times the size of her mother. Their eyes were a terrible, unnatural blue and glowing like lightning caged within glass. Surik, the eldest and strongest of her guards split away, flinging a powerful stream of magic their way. The wind buffeted the two white dragons, and dark blood streamed from one of their sides, falling like crimson rain.

While Surik harried one of them, distracting it from her, the other wheeled up high and stared down at her. She tried to fly away, but it didn't approach to attack, instead, staring at her with that terrible gaze. Her eyes locked on the white dragon's, and something happened to her. Something heavy slammed into her from all directions, even though they were still some distance away. Icy numbness spread from her skull and down her spine. Her wings faltered first, and she plummeted toward the ground with the wind rushing all around her. Dakhar fought bravely, but he was far away.

Surik twisted his body, using his wind magic to lift her and let her get her wings moving again, but her body was useless. As she fell, that awful numbness pressed in tighter, squeezing her until she couldn't breathe. Whispering voices filled her mind. Most of it was unintelligible, but she caught the occasional shouted word.

Fall.

Burn.

Die.

It was something in those brilliant blue eyes. She couldn't tear her gaze away, falling ungracefully from the sky until she bounced off a crag of rock, plunging her into a world of agony.

As Ashariah fell, Gabby felt herself tearing away, floating alongside the princess and watching her hit the ground. They both looked up to the white dragon, looming like a cloud overhead. All around her, the wind howled. Under that terrible sound was a female voice wailing *no no no*, and though she'd never heard her voice, Gabby knew it was Ashariah.

"It's okay," Gabby said. "It's only a memory."

But her words were silenced in the terrible howling. Her heart pounded, her stomach lurching with dread as the sound rose. All around her, the brilliant red and orange of the Nevada desert blackened and fractured beneath her feet. Color leached out of the sky, and the sun was obscured by a huge shadow with two glowing blue orbs in its depths. As she stood there, watching in horror, an inexorable weight pulled down on her, sucking her deeper into the nightmare.

She had to break the connection and get out of Ashariah's head.

It's all in her head, Gabby thought. *Just wake up. Open your eyes and get out.*

But nothing happened. Gabby looked around frantically. Ashariah lay on the ground at her feet. Her dragon form was dissipating. But instead of the broken, bruised body, her body was intact. Bloody tears trickled out of her pale blue eyes as she stared without blinking.

"Ashariah! You have to wake up!" Gabby said. She knelt by the princess and grabbed her arms. The young woman suddenly snapped her gaze to Gabby, but there was nothing behind her eyes, just pupils dilated almost to the edge of her pale irises. Her hands moved lightning quick as the princess grabbed Gabby, digging claw-like nails into her forearms. She tried to pull away, but the princess held her tight. Rivulets of blood ran down Gabby's arms as she watched in horror.

"Help me," Ashariah murmured.

"You have to let me go," Gabby said. "I'm trying to help you now."

Gabby tried again to pull away, but Ashariah's grasp was tighter than ever. As she sat there, the white dragon circled overhead, casting a massive shadow on the ground below. The sound of wings beating filled her ears, echoing and overlapping itself until it crawled like tiny insects in her ears. And the shadow was terribly wrong; its edges squirmed and swirled as if there were crawling, writhing things barely contained within the body.

"Now we are both lost," Ashariah moaned. "There is no escape. We are lost."

CHAPTER TWENTY-SEVEN

THE ENTRANCE TO THE DUNGEON was shadowy and dark in a way that the lanterns couldn't quite dispel. The air was stagnant and bitterly cold. They had just reached the yawning arch into the cells when Navan stopped suddenly and turned to face Tarek and Eszen. His mouth was set in a grim line as he regarded them. "Allow me to speak first. I will press him for information."

"The queen has given you permission to do more than press," Eszen said, arching his eyebrow.

Navan scowled at the councilor. "And tell me, councilor, would you lift one of your well-manicured hands to attack the Ironflight queen's personal guard? Would you dare?"

Eszen bristled visibly and threw back his shoulders. He was younger than most of the queen's advisors, maybe twenty years older than Tarek. As far as Tarek knew, he had never served in the Guard. But the beaded cuffs of his robe skimmed muscular forearms that appeared every bit as strong as Tarek's. "If you hesitate to show the strength and resolve of the Stoneflight, then I will happily raise my manicured hands to attack all comers."

"Gentlemen," Tarek said mildly.

Two heavily armed guards were posted on either side of the heavy wooden door. As Navan approached, one of the guards nodded without speaking and opened the latch for him.

Tarek shuddered involuntarily as they stepped into the narrow hallway. The ceiling was low, just a few feet overhead. The still air stank of unwashed bodies and stale piss. Though he'd never had the misfortune of staying in one of the cells, he had done his time guarding prisoners here in his early days as a young recruit.

The tiny cells had low ceilings, not quite high enough for a large man to stand up. They were so narrow on all sides that even Tarek, who wasn't huge by Kadirai standards, couldn't fully extend his arms. A full-grown Kadirai would crush his own wings trying to transform inside the cells. And even if they somehow managed, the thick chains inside would prevent them from doing much.

At the end of the hall, two more armed guards stood watch over a single cell. One of them sported a purple knot on his cheek, and his partner looked disheveled, his dark brown hair sticking up in the back and his tabard hanging slightly crooked. Kaldir had given them trouble, it seemed.

As they approached, Navan snapped his fingers. The guard with the bruised cheek looked up and regarded him nervously, his eyes skating away from the captain's gaze. "Bring him to the chamber."

The guard looked resigned, but he nodded and gestured to his partner. The other guard's shoulders slumped. He took a deep breath as he put his palm on the locking plate next to the door. As soon as he made contact, the wooden door flew open on its own. There was a blur as Kaldir lunged out of the cell. Then he let out a choked sound as the chain around his neck snapped taut. His bare legs kicked out wildly, catching one of the guards at

244

the knee and sending him to the ground. He managed another few good blows before Navan took a flying leap, landed halfway in the cell, and kicked him squarely in the ribs. Kaldir doubled on himself, curling into a fetal position as he wheezed for air.

"*Vazredakh,*" Navan cursed. "Secure him." The two guards eyed their prisoner warily, making no movement toward him. Navan scowled. "If I must repeat myself, you will be scrubbing cells for the next year."

The guard with the bruised cheek jumped and scurried back down the narrow hall. He returned with a set of shackles. Navan took advantage of Kaldir's incapacitated state and knelt on his back while the other guards snapped the shackles around his wrists. As they worked, Kaldir's jaw clenched, his eyes squeezing shut. Still, he didn't make a sound to let Navan know that he was in any discomfort.

The two guards hauled Kaldir to his feet, then pulled up on the connecting chain, forcing his arms up at a painful angle. He had no choice but to walk hunched over, with his shoulders threatening to pop out of their sockets as he stumbled forward. The guards marched him into a larger room further up the hall, one that Tarek didn't care to see.

Though Halmerah would not call it such, it was a torture chamber, much like the one where he'd found Gabrielle when he first arrived in Adamantine Rise. Sharp implements were arrayed on a side table, while various hooks and chains dangled from the ceiling. To Tarek's knowledge, it had been rarely used since the Great War ended. The nasty-looking blades and hooks were left out more for theatrics.

In the years he had been posted down here, he'd only seen half a dozen prisoners brought here, and most of them had spilled their secrets within a few minutes. Tarek had no love for Kaldir, but he hoped that he would follow tradition. If the man was guilty of attacking Ashariah, then he deserved death, to be certain, but it should be a swift one that allowed the Stoneflight to maintain their honor.

The two guards dragged Kaldir in, unhooked one wrist from the manacles, and transferred the chain to a hook high overhead. When they had latched his wrist back in, the Ironflight guard's arms were pulled taut above his head, his toes barely skimming the rough stone below.

There were no built-in safeguards to prevent Kaldir from transforming, but he would be a fool to attempt a change under his circumstances. He was certainly a powerful Kadirai; to be trusted with protecting the royal family, he had to be. But even the most extraordinarily powerful of the dragons took time to transform, and the transition made them vulnerable. More than a few dragons had been slain trying to change during battle. During the Great War, the Raspolin cursed a number of dragons with evil magic that forced a transformation, then killing them while their bodies were in transition.

Though he had been stripped of all his clothing, leaving him naked as the day he was born, Kaldir was furious and scowling at them. When the door closed behind Eszen, Kaldir began ranting.

"You have made a grave mistake, *t'haran dan keth*," he spat. Well, that wasn't a good start to a diplomatic conversation. His amber eyes followed Navan's approach. He was considerably larger than Navan, and even in his vulnerable position, he managed to look intimidating.

Navan was unfazed. "The Prince already told us of your plot to attack

Princess Ashariah. Halmerah will show forgiveness to your people if you tell us of the impending attack."

Kaldir barked a laugh at him. "Idiots. There is no such plot, and you are not half the liar you imagine yourself to be. You should—*urkh...*" He trailed off as Navan swung a bladed hand toward his throat, cutting off his air. His eyes bulged as he choked, gasping frantically for air.

"Let me try restating this in a way that you will understand," Navan said. "I chose not to harm your Prince, in an attempt to preserve diplomacy between our peoples. Your hide is not nearly so valuable. And if I need to, I will flay it from your bones and send it back to your queen in a sack. Do not tempt me."

Kaldir wheezed and sucked in a rasping breath. He raised his head and glared at Navan. "I told you. There is no plot. The Ironflight has held the peace with your people for many years. I would not—"

Navan cut him off again with a fist to the belly. When Kaldir started to protest again, Navan sank his fist into the delicate ribs high under his armpit. Kaldir let out a groan of pain and lost his precarious footing as one leg buckled. Spinning slowly on the chains, he coughed violently as he tried to get his feet under him. Right as he got his left leg balanced, planting the ball of his dirt-streaked foot on the stone, Navan kicked the back of his muscular thigh with his armored boot. The Ironflight dragon slumped, his leg dangling uselessly.

"What is your plot?" Navan asked again, casually adjusting the leather bracer on his left arm.

"I told you, there is no such plot," Kaldir breathed. He coughed, then spat on the ground. Tarek watched in detached horror as a droplet of blood landed on his own foot.

Even when he had served as the queen's personal guard, they had known peace within Adamantine Rise. He had been called away occasionally to help defend their outposts against attacks from beyond their borders, but those had been skirmishes at best. The nasty business with the Silverflight after they ambushed the elder princess had been the only major conflict he had known, and he had been mortally wounded for most of the time, hearing most of it through gossip and hearsay. It had never fallen to him to bring the full force of Halmerah's wrath down upon an enemy.

It surprised him to find that he was sickened by it, perhaps because of what had happened at the hands of the Silverflight. It was easy to see himself in Kaldir. He disliked the man, and always had, but he was duty-bound and loyal to his queen, just as Tarek was. Worse, beyond the immediate discomfort of seeing Kaldir interrogated, dread prickled at him. Were they on the brink of war? Was there some way to resolve this before one of their queens threw down the gauntlet and let nearly one hundred years of resentment explode?

Kaldir's voice had lost some of its booming command as he spoke again. "I say this as one soldier to another. If you truly believe an attack is coming, then you waste your time with me. Were it my choice to make, I would spend my time ensuring that my soldiers and my people were ready."

His eyes fell on Tarek then, and they were so full of disapproval and accusation that Tarek took an involuntary step back. A knock came at the door behind them, and Kaldir's amber eyes lifted to look at the door.

"Councilor," a female voice said. A young woman in the uniform of the Library scribes approached Eszen. Her cool gray gaze fell on Kaldir, her eyes widening in horror. Then she turned away, squaring her shoulders as she spoke to Eszen. Rising to her toes, she whispered into his ear.

As she spoke, the councilor's eyes widened slightly, then found Tarek's. His brow creased in concern. "Thank you. You will stay here to return word to the queen."

"She is not permitted to be here," Navan said.

"The queen has sent word of Dakhar," Eszen said, ignoring the captain's protest, "and the Vak woman."

Tarek's stomach plunged. He tried to appear detached as he asked, "What happened?"

"She is with the healers now," Eszen said. "They say she visited Ashariah, then fell unconscious and would not wake."

Tarek was suddenly rooted to the ground. His heart raced as he thought of beautiful, fierce Gabrielle in such a state. His poor attempt at stoicism failed. "I have to go."

Eszen raised an eyebrow at him. "Is your lust for the forbidden more important than the queen's orders to you?"

He made the mistake of looking back at Kaldir. The Ironflight dragon's split lip curled into a bloody sneer. "By all means, go see to your woman. She is quite lovely, for the Vak." His expression turned Tarek's stomach, as he remembered the sight of Gabrielle in his arms during the feast.

Tarek suddenly felt his dread turn to rage. "Did you do this? If you've hurt her, I'll—"

"You'll what? She is Vak," he said. "Do not pretend her life is of any value to your queen."

Tarek's fist tightened as he took a long stride toward Kaldir. The other man flinched slightly as if he was preparing for a blow. But Tarek instead grabbed his chin. "If I find out that you did something to her, I will return and carve you to pieces myself."

Kaldir twisted his head to break Tarek's grasp. "Run along, *t'haran vo'shedh*. Let the men handle this."

Navan had protested his leaving, but Tarek would face the queen's anger himself if necessary. A muffled cry of pain from Kaldir echoed, following him as he ran up the corridor toward the central stair. He had given Gabrielle his oath, as he had sworn to the queen to protect her and her daughters. And yet again, he had failed on such a fundamental level to protect someone who needed him. He was doubly cursed.

As he ran through the halls, his mind painted a lurid picture of Gabrielle, lying pale and unconscious as the princess had done. He couldn't bear to think of her, the light gone out of her warm, kind eyes. If this was the work of the Ironflight, he would keep his promise and peel the flesh from Kaldir's bones.

His mind was so distracted that he nearly missed the egress to the gardens. He skidded to a halt, then twisted on his heel to run into the healing gardens. Voices and murmurs rose as he bolted past, heading for the healer's pavilion. The posted guards acknowledged him and let him pass.

The healer's pavilion was quiet and still. Plumes of fragrant smoke drifted up from hammered silver censers hanging from the arches of the pavilion's roof. At the far end, the queen and her guards were gathered around the princess's veiled bed. And strangely, one of the healers was crouched on the floor, tending to a still figure.

"Where is she?" he blurted as he approached.

The gray-clad healer kneeling on the ground looked up and shushed him. "Quiet," she murmured.

"I will not be silenced," he said, his tone heating.

"Tarek!" Halmerah said sharply, looking up from her daughter. "Quiet."

The queen's disapproving tone cut through his panic like a knife, and he flushed with embarrassment. He slowed, lingering at the edge of the circle of attendants around Ashariah. Halmerah stood at her daughter's bedside, but her eyes were downcast to the figure on the floor.

Gabrielle lay on the cold stone floor, one hand stretched up to Ashariah's. Their hands were entwined. The sleeve of Gabrielle's robe slipped down to expose her slender forearm. Deep red furrows marred one arm, though they did not bleed. Her body was twisted awkwardly, her hips cocked. Her dark hair was spread around her in a halo on the floor.

"Why is she on the floor?" Tarek asked quietly. He felt as though his belly was filled with ice, an odd chill washing over him. *Why is she so still?*

"That was where she fell," the healer replied.

Tarek knelt and reached for her, but was greeted with a chorus of "No!" from the attendants. The kneeling healer grabbed his wrist, her grip surprisingly firm as she pulled his hand away. He froze and stared at her in surprise. "What?"

251

"She touched the princess, and now she does not wake. We do not know what has happened."

He stared at the healer in horror. "So you just let her lie there?"

"This is the work of the Ironflight," Halmerah said. "They have gone too far."

"Fuck the Ironflight," Tarek spat. The gathered attendants stared at him, and he realized he'd spoken in English. As descriptive as the Kadirai tongue was, there was no word in the language that was as viscerally effective at expressing one's rage.

Halmerah ignored his outburst, though she was familiar with the epithet. "Dakhar has woken, but he is incoherent. He will be of no help."

But his queen was far away as Tarek stared down at Gabrielle. He had brought her into this mess. It was chance that she had been the one to care for Ashariah, and arguably it was chance that had brought her face to face with their attackers the first time. But it was none other than Tarek Windstriker who called her, asking for her help after she should have been clear of all this. He'd known if he asked for help, she would come. And this was where her warm, caring spirit had gotten her. Because of him.

Gabrielle murmured, jarring him out of his reverie. As they watched, another deep furrow appeared across her chest. Tarek cringed, feeling the pain twisting in his gut as he watched her helplessly. Her face creased, but she did not move.

"Can't you separate them somehow?"

"It's possible that it would ensnare us too," the healer said.

He stared helplessly at her. The logical soldier in him wanted to believe that this was an inevitable casualty, that anyone was expendable in the service of the Stoneflight. His life only held meaning in his service to the queen, and if he died protecting her or the princess, then it would be the greatest honor of all. The same would go for Gabrielle.

But as he stared down at this fierce, independent woman, he realized that she had softened a part of him that had been cold, hard stone for longer than he could remember. He dared not even entertain the notion of *love*, but he would have been a liar to deny that he longed for a connection. To be on the receiving end of that smile, to feel worthy in that warm gaze; that was greater than any honor the queen could bestow on him.

And here she lay, her eyes closed, her lips pale and unmoving.

He could not stand by, not again. He heard "no!" as he grabbed her hand. Darkness fell, and the world went utterly silent.

CHAPTER TWENTY-EIGHT

THOUGH HE FELL THROUGH dark, endless space, it was oddly quiet. Time stretched out as he fell, heart pounding and limbs flailing. Without warning, he crashed into something solid, but there was no pain. On contact, light exploded around him and Tarek found himself on all fours on a shattered gray expanse. The sun was a harsh white orb burning through gray haze overhead. The smell was oddly familiar; it was the dry dirt smell of the desert, though the faint reek of decay seeped through the dusty aroma.

He brushed off his knees and stood, looking around. "Gabrielle?" he asked. His voice was flat and dead.

Distant thunder rumbled as a shadow slithered across the ground. His heart raced as he looked up. A massive white dragon, bigger than any he'd ever seen, circled the skies. Instinctively, he reached for a weapon, but he was unarmed. He reached deep for the spark to ignite the transformation into his dragon form, but he was empty. It wasn't weakness; there was simply nothing there. Dread gripped his guts as he realized he was defenseless. He looked around frantically for somewhere to hide, but the surrounding landscape was a flat expanse of shattered ground as far as he could see.

"Gabrielle!" he called again. The white dragon continued its wide circle. If it noticed him, it showed no sign.

Tarek began to walk. The ground was uneven and shaky under his feet, but he kept moving. As he moved, his mind started to chase its own tail in a spiral of worry. Was he stuck here? Was he lying unconscious next to Gabrielle, useless as a dulled blade as the Ironflight prepared for war on his people? He'd been a fool to do this, but he wasn't sure he was wrong.

Sweat beaded on his forehead and trickled down his neck. He didn't know how long he had been walking when he finally paused and surveyed the gray desert again. He might have moved a mile or not at all. There were still no signs of anything on the horizon. After a pause, he shouted, "Gabrielle! Where are you?"

"Tarek," a voice whispered. Lips brushed against his ear. He whirled on his heel, but there was no one in sight.

"Who's there?"

"It's me," the voice said, now decidedly feminine. When he turned again, a figure shimmered ahead of him like a mirage in the desert.

"Gabrielle?"

The figure materialized fully into a face he had not seen since seeing her body given back to the flames over a decade ago. As she stepped toward him, it felt as if someone stabbed him in the chest. "I-Ivralah?"

"Hello. Have you come to give penance?"

Tarek was rooted to the ground, his tongue paralyzed in his gaping mouth. She was flawless, her body draped in shimmering lilac silk and silver jewelry. From the piercing blue eyes to the haughty stare, she was the mirror image of her mother.

"I...what is this?"

"Didn't you come to see me?"

"I came for Gabrielle," he murmured.

Ivralah's face distorted into an expression of anger. "You would protect her over me?"

"You're not real," he said. "You died."

She jolted a little, as if he had slapped her. Then she looked down. A wide seam opened across her throat, spilling blood down her smooth chest and onto her fine clothes. Crimson tears streamed from her eyes, staining her smooth cheeks. "Because of you."

"No," he said, though he knew it was true. "You're not real."

"Tarek," the voice whispered again. There was a strange lilt to the voice. It didn't belong to Ivralah, but he recognized that little flip on the *r*.

"Gabrielle!" he shouted. He whirled on his heel and called for her again. As he was about to shout her name again, a sharp pain blossomed in his chest. He looked down to see Ivralah's hand buried to the wrist in his chest.

"You will not leave me again," she hissed, her eyes narrowing to slits.

The shadow passed over them again, and he looked up to see the white dragon circling high overhead. There was an eerie blue glow in its eyes. "You're not real," he said again. He grabbed her wrist and pulled her away. If it wasn't real, it certainly felt real as her nails raked against his insides. Retching from the pain, he yanked her hand free of his chest. "Gabrielle! I'm here!"

"Tarek!" Her voice was louder now, with a resonance that felt more real than anything since he'd fallen into this dream place. He imagined her face, her high cheekbones and those warm eyes that said *you're home, you are mine,* and made him believe it. He imagined her shape, the full swell of her hips and the proud nose and the cascading dark hair over her shoulders, the coarse feel of it between his fingers. "Tarek!"

He spun around to see her behind him. He whipped his head around again only to find that Ivralah had disappeared. When he turned back to Gabrielle, she was still there. *Thank the Skymother.*

His relief was short-lived. Gabrielle was pale and ashen, and she was not alone. Ashariah was with her, her hands clamped on the human woman's wrists as she stared up at the endlessly circling dragon.

"How are you here? Is this real?" Gabrielle asked.

"I'm real," Tarek said. "This isn't, but I am."

Gabrielle nodded. "We have to get out of here."

"I think that Ashariah has trapped us here with her. We have to get her to wake up," Tarek said.

"It's that dragon," Gabrielle said. "I've seen it in her visions more than once."

Tarek nodded in agreement. He faced the princess, placing his hands on her shoulders and shaking her lightly. "Princess, you must return to us."

"Trapped," Ashariah murmured. "No escape." Her eyes were milky white as she stared without blinking up at the sky.

"No," Tarek said. "You just have to wake up. That dragon isn't here. It's only in your head."

"It's here," Ashariah said. "Don't you see it?"

Tarek sighed and grabbed her wrist, trying to pull it away from Gabrielle. But the princess tightened her grip, digging her long nails into the woman's wrist. Gabrielle yelped in surprise as blood trickled down her hand. "Let go,"

Tarek ordered.

"I know you're afraid, Ashariah," Gabrielle said, gritting her teeth. "But we're here. You're safe at home. Your mother is watching over you. She needs you to come back."

"Home," Ashariah murmured.

Tarek nodded rapidly. The doctor was onto something. "You are in the heart of Adamantine Rise, under the Skymother's gaze in the gardens. Nothing can hurt you there. Do you remember how I played chase among the Bones with you? And you brought me the finest stones you could find?"

Her eyes slowly dropped, searching Tarek. "Home."

He nodded. "Home."

Ashariah looked down at Gabrielle's hands, then raised her eyes slowly. "Promise me."

"I promise," Tarek said. "I will protect you."

"So will I," Gabrielle said.

Then Ashariah closed her eyes and the world around them shattered.

Reality returned like a slap in the face. First a chestful of cold, dry air, then the hard ache of stone under his body. Tarek sat up and gasped violently. He patted himself down, and yelped in pain when his hand touched the tender spot on his chest where Ivralah had plunged her hand into him. Plucking the linen shirt away from his chest revealed a fist-sized purple welt. The illusion was powerful enough to wound him in reality. That was nothing he had ever seen.

As soon as he realized he was awake, he looked over to see Gabrielle slowly sit up, blinking slowly as she looked around. "What happened?"

He didn't answer, just threw his arms around her and crushed her to his chest. He breathed deeply, inhaling the sweet scent of her skin and feeling for the steady pulse against his chest.

"Ashariah?" The queen's voice, vulnerable in a way he had never heard, broke his intense embrace. "Ashariah!"

Gabrielle pulled away from him, but her hand found his as they both rose to a crouch to peer over the edge of the princess's sickbed. The princess had opened her eyes. Her fingers fluttered like she was playing the piano, and one foot started to move. "Mother?"

"Oh, praise the Skymother. My sweet child." Without regard for her regal appearance, the queen laid over her daughter, pressing her cheek to Ashariah's.

Pride swelled in Tarek's chest as he watched the reunion. Ashariah was weak, and could barely move her head, but Halmerah was overjoyed. The reunion was short-lived as the burst of energy turned to anger. "My child, who did this?"

Ashariah shook her head. "I don't know," she said. "There were four of them. One silver, one gold, and two white dragons that were...monstrous. They had awful green eyes, and..." she trailed off, her eyes widening.

"The white dragons had some sort of magic that I have never seen," Tarek interrupted. "I believe they cast a spell that kept Ashariah in its grasp. It showed me a nightmare. Did it show you something?" He turned to Gabrielle.

She nodded. "It was seeing the dragon in her memories that triggered it for me," she said. "At least I think it was. I don't really know anything about magic, so I'm kind of guessing."

"It was powerful enough that it affected us both by contact, long after Ashariah encountered them," Tarek said.

"Like a disease," Gabrielle mused.

"This is nothing I have ever seen," Halmerah said, her expression going stony once more. She stood suddenly and rearranged her dress, mussed by her enthusiastic embrace. Her features hardened to imperious stone. "I must tend to a matter of extreme importance. Do not worry, my child. The ones who did this to you will pay dearly."

"I don't understand," Ashariah said. She started to sit up, but winced at the movement. As she sat up, her gaze found Gabby. Her eyebrows lifted in recognition. "You. Doctor Rojas?"

"How did you know that?"

"I heard you," she murmured. "And you got my message."

"Your message?"

"I couldn't talk," she said. "But I knew you were trying to understand what happened. So I showed you."

"The visions," Gabby said. "And you wanted me to trust Tarek."

The princess gave a slow nod that clearly took a great deal of effort. Her gaze flicked to him, and she smiled faintly.

The queen followed their exchange with interest, but waved her hand dismissively. "Daughter, if you can remain awake, I will send Councilor Eszen to speak to you." She turned to Gabby and Tarek. "Have the healers examine her to ensure there are no lasting ill effects, then be in the war room. We have much to discuss."

CHAPTER TWENTY-NINE

AFTER ONE OF THE HEALERS proclaimed Gabby free to leave, pressing a cup of hot tea into her hands as she went, they immediately walked up the winding stairs to the chamber in the upper levels of the fortress. A hushed excitement buzzed through the halls. There were far more weapons than she'd seen previously. By now, she should have known better than to think *it can't get any stranger.* Yet here she was, following Tarek into a stone chamber filled with the queen's advisors.

A brisk breeze blew in through the open windows along the war room's perimeter. The windows overlooked the lower levels of Adamantine Rise and the city beyond. A stone table in the middle of the room displayed a detailed three-dimensional map, painted carefully to represent the city below and the surrounding land. Plain wooden chairs surrounded the table, with one blue-cushioned chair at the end where Halmerah stood.

Though the queen had ordered Gabby's presence, her councilors made no effort to hide their disdain, which only added to her discomfort. The one exception was Councilor Eszen, who gave her a nod of acknowledgement before finding his seat. She had a pounding headache from her trip into Ashariah's fear-addled mind. After the sheer strangeness of the whole evening, her mind drifted to thoughts of her normal life out of reflex. But she found herself resisting the idea. And that resistance had an irresistible form: it was Tarek. A day ago, all she'd wanted was to wake up in her bed, but now that pull seemed to go both ways. The relief of being home, where things were familiar and safe, meant she wasn't here with Tarek.

Ugh, she was in trouble. Logical Gabby had left the building, apparently.

"How come the preparations?" Halmerah asked, jarring Gabby out of her thoughts. The queen took her seat, and the standing councilors all followed.

One of the councilors, a pale man with dark hair that shone blue-black like a crow's feather, spoke up. "We have spoken to the Circle of Edra and the city guard. They are mustering at the gates of the city and clearing the common areas as much as possible. We are preparing one of the underground shelters for the Vak if things become untenable."

"And the Adamant Guard have positioned themselves throughout Adamantine Rise. Every able body is armed and ready, my queen," Captain Navan said. He sat immediately to the queen's right. "I have dispatched scouts to the Splintered Pass, as well as to the Talons to watch for Ironflight movement."

"Very well," Halmerah said. "I also wished to speak to you of what happened to my daughter."

"Our condolences," a woman in red robes murmured.

Halmerah ignored her, apparently unimpressed with her sympathy. "I spoke with you previously of the attack. Councilor Eszen has spoken with Ashariah and Lady Gabrielle in an attempt to understand our enemy." The weight of inquisitive eyes fell on Gabby as the queen mentioned her. "Eszen?"

The chesnut-haired man rose from his seat. "My research is not yet complete. Upon speaking to the princess briefly and comparing her story with the visions reported by Lady Gabrielle, I believe the source of Ashariah's affliction to be the large white dragons she saw. She insists that she never made physical contact, and that her mind was affected simply by making eye contact with these creatures. We have no precedent for this in our history."

Everything was painfully still and quiet as the council stared at Eszen. He seemed unperturbed as he spoke matter-of-factly. "The fact that Lady Gabrielle was afflicted by making physical contact, as was Tarek Windstriker, tells us that whatever this psychic effect is, it is transferable."

"It's contagious," Gabby murmured.

"What?" Halmerah asked.

Her cheeks flushed. "I'm sorry, I didn't mean—"

"Please share," the queen said. Her expression was open and encouraging, not angry.

"I said it's contagious," Gabby said with more confidence. "Like a disease."

"But you touched the princess to help her before," Eszen said. "When you cared for her in your world."

Gabby sat in silence for a long stretch to think. "What if it wasn't active yet? Diseases in the human world often have an incubation period. There may have been a window where she was unconscious due to her injuries, but the full effects of the magic hadn't really hit her yet."

"Then how did you see her visions?"

"She made me," Gabby said, the realization hitting her as she said it. "That wasn't the magic at all. She just made me listen to her in whatever way she could."

"She compelled you," Eszen murmured. His eyebrows arched as if something had just struck him. "If she compelled you prior to Tarek's arrival, then—"

"Councilor?" the queen said. Her tone was indulgent, but firm. "Is this germane to our discussion of dealing with this enemy?"

"Uh...no," he admitted. "I believe I may know why Lady Gabrielle was unaffected by the attempts to compel her, though. I'd like to conduct a few more experiments to confirm."

"Will you need her any further?" Tarek asked.

Eszen tilted his head. "I-I don't know."

"*Su'ud redahn*, if it pleases you, I would take her home in the morning," he said.

Tarek's words hit her like a blow to the stomach. With his jaw set and eyes cold, he didn't even spare her a glance. Home was what she wanted, wasn't it? Home meant her normal life. But home also meant no more Tarek, and it surprised her how much that hurt.

"Why the urgency?"

"If we face a battle, I would prefer that she be spared. As a friend to the Stoneflight, I cannot ask her to risk her life for our wars," he said.

The queen's eyes narrowed. "Very well. Carry her home, then return here immediately."

His eyes went wide. "Return?"

"You are needed here," the queen said. "Captain Navan has already sent an additional patrol of forces to help guard the gate. Your expertise is better served here at the moment."

He stared at her, his jaw hanging. Then he shook himself and nodded. "Yes, of course. Thank you."

Her ears rang as she watched him. He was looking out for her. That was what she had to believe. And she didn't belong here. But for as scary as all of it had been, she couldn't deny that part of her wanted to be here. And *here* was a relative concept; it seemed to be tied to one particularly handsome dragon.

"If we are finished discussing the very pressing issue of the Vak woman..." one of the councilors said archly.

"Mind your tongue, Thiven," the queen said sharply. "I will conduct my business as I see fit, and your insipid attempts to curry favor do you no favors. Let us continue to the preparations. Captain Navan, prepare an armed envoy to Ironhold. Though she has behaved with dishonor, I will still observe our ancient ways and give Tarim a final chance to make peace before I rain down war."

"Yes, *su'ud redahn*," Navan said.

"Are you sure?" Tarek said quietly.

"Should I send word of your prisoners?" Navan said, as if Tarek hadn't spoken.

Gabby glanced at Tarek. His teeth tugged at his lower lip, and he was tense, leaning toward the table as if he was going to lunge. Tension creased his warm eyes. It was nice to think he might be at least a bit forlorn about her leaving, but she knew it was more than that. She tapped his hand lightly. "What's wrong?" she asked.

"I can't shake this feeling that there's more going on."

"Say something."

He shook his head. "It's not my place. I'm surprised they even brought us here."

"Tarek is concerned," Gabby blurted. The room fell silent as the entire gathering turned to look at her, all of them oozing disapproval.

"The Vak woman speaks for you now?" Thiven asked. "Is it not enough that—"

"Tell them," Gabby said, ignoring Thiven's glare. They figured she was inferior anyway, so what did she care if they thought she was rude? She knew the feeling of being ignored and talked over, and had learned from college onward to speak up and apologize later if necessary.

To her surprise, Halmerah didn't look angry. In the ring of glares, she was the single person who looked receptive, her face smooth and her eyebrows raised. "Well?"

Tarek took a deep breath. "I accompanied Captain Navan to speak with both the Prince and his guard. They both swore there was no plot to attack us."

"And you believe the Ironflight to be honest?" Eszen asked. "Since when?"

"Not necessarily," Tarek said. "It just..." He glanced at Gabby. She nodded at him. "When have we known the Ironflight to be so indirect? Their methods in this situation are erratic, at best. They attacked the princess, but let her live. They left behind weapons, of obvious make. They literally carved their symbols into Surik and Dakhar's bodies. And yet they send the Prince to attend your feast as if nothing happened?"

"Prince Zayir is renowned for his cunning," Netha said.

"I know this," Tarek said. His hand clenched into a fist as he spoke. "But this is not the way of the Ironflight, cunning or not. If this was their plan, Zayir would be the decoy while hundreds of the Iron Blade infiltrated the city."

Navan's eyes widened. "Perhaps that is exactly what has happened."

Tarek shook his head. "I don't think it is. Consider the flames."

"The flames?" Eszen said skeptically.

"There were none. Most of the Ironflight are fire dragons, yes?" Tarek paused, looking around at the table. There were a few reluctant nods, and more than a few puzzled expressions. "Then why were none of Ashariah's guards, nor Ashariah herself burned?"

"She was attacked in the human world," one of the councilors said. "My understanding is that our affinities are far weaker there."

"They're weaker, but any of them would be a fool not to use it as a weapon," he said, unbothered by the attempted explanation. As he spoke, his shoulders slowly rose and his voice took on strength. It filled Gabby with an odd sort of pride to see him being bold. "Then there's the psychic attack. Which we've already discussed, but you can't dismiss it as something for Eszen to read about when it's convenient. In Ashariah's visions, there was a monstrous dragon, bigger than anything I've ever seen. There is something unnatural in this, but I'm not sure it's the Ironflight. No. I'm certain that it's not the Ironflight."

There were murmurs as several of the councilors spoke to each other.

They started arguing across the table. Finally, Halmerah raised a hand. She stared at Tarek, as if to say *we will talk about this more*, and spoke loudly. "Tarek, I trust your observations and your insights, I do. But how does this affect what we must do to prepare ourselves?"

Tarek was silent for a long stretch. Gabby's heart pounded as she took a breath. "Well, forgive me for interrupting, but it does matter. If it's not the Ironflight, then someone really wants you to think it is."

"And why would they do such a thing?" Halmerah asked. She didn't look quite as receptive as she had when Tarek spoke, but Gabby didn't care.

"For distraction," she said. "You're so busy watching for the Ironflight that someone could easily sneak up on you from the opposite direction."

"Then who? The Shadowflight? The Stormflight?" one of the councilors blurted. As soon as he spoke, the rest of them burst into a flurry of heated arguments.

Captain Navan raised his voice above the din. "Does it really matter? We will guard the gates and the citadel, as we have always done. Whether it is the Ironflight or some other upstart, we will face them and we will defeat them. Simple."

Halmerah hesitated then nodded. "Lady Gabrielle, I do appreciate your insight, and it gives me much to think about. But at the moment, we must focus on the battle ahead."

"A corpse is a corpse," Navan said by way of agreement.

Tarek nodded to Gabby, his eyes warm and appreciative. "What can I do? I wish to fight."

"You have the queen's orders," Navan said. "When you return from your task, return to my office and I will see that you find a place." He looked up at the queen. "*Su'ud redahn,* with your permission, I wish to reduce patrols and activate the City Guard under emergency protocol. My men should rest for a few hours to prepare for battle."

"You intend to send your men home for a nap at a time like this?" a councilor asked.

Navan scowled. "Many of my men have been awake and alert since before the Prince arrived yesterday. They are exhausted, and exhausted men make mistakes in battle. We have many reserve soldiers who are guarding the citadel, and many more men in the city keeping watch. The City Guard and the Circle of Edra are all on high alert. They will raise the alarm if anything happens between now and sunrise."

"Very well," Halmerah said. "Permission granted, Captain Navan. You are dismissed. Gather here at sunrise."

The councilors looked around, then slowly departed from the table. Some headed straight for the door, while others lingered near the windows to talk quietly.

Halmerah gestured to Gabby. "Lady Gabrielle, I thank you again for your assistance and your devotion to my daughter. I wish you safe travels home."

"Oh," Gabby said. She looked up at Tarek, who was pointedly not meeting her eyes. "Thank you. Thank you for your hospitality." It seemed a bit anti-climactic, but she supposed staying in the citadel and being invited to the ill-fated party had been Halmerah's way of showing her appreciation.

The queen nodded, then turned to speak to Eszen quietly. Tarek stood and gestured for Gabby to follow. His face was unreadable, smooth and hard as granite. The gathered councilors didn't even spare them a glance as they walked out of the war room and toward the winding staircase.

When they had cleared the room and gotten past the clusters of messengers and guards lingering outside the main chamber, Tarek paused and looked down at her. He hesitated, then rested his hand on the side of her face. "Thank you."

"For?"

"For speaking up," he said.

"Sometimes we need a push," she said.

His eyes creased as he stared at her. "Would you think me foolish if I said I wished you could stay?"

Her heart pounded. "No," she said. "Not at all."

His lips quirked into a faint smile. "Good."

"To be fair, you did ask to take me back," she said. "She might have forgotten me otherwise."

He shook his head. "She might have. And if war comes upon us and finds you here, I would not forgive myself. You have been through enough difficulty already."

She sighed. "I feel crazy for saying it, but I don't really want to go."

He took her hand, clasping her smaller hands in his. Not for the first time, she marveled at his size. She was not a small woman, but he was certainly a big man. His hands dwarfed hers, and standing this close, she had to look straight up to see his eyes. "I have to do my duty," he said. "And I swore to you that you were mine to protect."

"I know."

"But we have a little time. Sunrise won't be for a few hours," he said, his lips quirking into the ghost of a smile. "Shall I take you to your room?"

CHAPTER THIRTY

FOR ONCE, Raszila and Irinakh were nowhere to be seen. It was just as well. The handmaidens were lovely and thorough, but if Gabby had walked into her room to see a woman fussing with the pillows, she would have thrown her out the window.

Her heart raced as Tarek gestured for her to enter the room. Irinakh had left several lamps burning, casting a warm glow. The night air kept the room chilly, but there was a pile of thick blankets piled on the end of the bed for her.

As Gabby moved past him, her arm brushed against his chest. She hesitated. There were no clocks in the room, but she knew sunrise wasn't far off. Tarek must have sensed her hesitation. He looked down at her, then his shoulders slumped. If he'd been hinting at something more with his offer to walk her back, he'd lost his nerve. "I should leave you to rest."

Nervous anticipation tried to take over. She almost said *that would be best,* but she caught her tongue and held her breath for a moment. The last few days had been like a bizarre dream, and it was about to end. Tarek had his orders, and she had a life to return to. There was a place she belonged, and it certainly wasn't here. And when she got there, what would become of them?

Stupid girl. There was no *them*.

But couldn't there be? Just for one night? She had played it safe her whole life, and it hadn't gotten her anywhere.

"Please don't," she blurted. The words seemed to hang in the air as she waited for his response. He didn't speak right away, but his expression changed ever so slightly. It reminded her of a time lapse photo of a sunrise over the desert, the way the shadows moved to reveal an entirely new landscape. Though he was still the tall, powerful warrior, his face looked open and hopeful, even shy.

"You would have me?"

"I would have you," Gabby said. "If you would have me."

His lips curled into a genuine smile then, and his gaze raked over her. He stepped closer to her, near enough that she could smell the warm scent of him. He tentatively kissed her. She leaned in and felt him smile against her lips. His hands rested on her shoulders for a moment, then slipped around her waist. One strong arm pulled her tighter to him while the other slipped between them, pressed between their bodies. Her heart quickened as his fingers moved against her belly and untied the sash holding her gown closed. There was a cool touch of air as the robe opened. Then his hand was burning hot against her skin, resting first on her hip, then moving upward with fire in its wake. Her breath caught as his large hand cupped her bare breast, thumb circling maddeningly slow. He broke away from the kiss, bending lower to kiss into the curve of her neck. Tingling electricity radiated from each slow kiss, her skin practically jumping at his touch.

This is really happening.

Both hands went around her waist then, his arms against her bare skin.

274

She felt naked and vulnerable, and yet she had never felt quite so safe. She threw her arms up and around his muscular shoulders, and he lifted her effortlessly, pressing her tightly to his body. Their mouths met again, teasing at each other, as he walked her backwards. Her legs bumped against the soft cushion of the bed, and he slowly leaned down to let her rest. As his body pressed against hers, she felt the firm evidence of his arousal press against her.

He braced himself on either side of her, darting in for a nip of a kiss here and there. "You are so very beautiful," he murmured. "I wish we had all the time in the world."

"Then we should make the best of what we have," Gabby said.

His smile changed then, a wolfish, hungry look. He leaned back for a moment and deftly pulled his loose tunic over his head to reveal the smooth planes of chiseled muscle. Then he sank back down to her, bracing himself with one hand to kiss her neck while his other traced down her breast, then down her side. She shivered at his touch and caressed the hard muscle of his shoulders, then the graceful curve of his back. He tensed slightly as her fingers brushed the rough ridge of scar tissue.

She held his gaze. "Is this all right?" He nodded silently. She slowly traced the edge of the scarring, exploring the history written on his back. There was a story there she wanted to know, but it was the wrong time to ask.

As if he'd sensed her thoughts, he made up his mind to distract her by teasing his fingers along her inner thigh. He pressed his hand against her, sending a delicious shiver breaking over her like a wave at high tide.

"May I?" he murmured into her ear, his lips hot as he nuzzled at her.

"You better," she growled. And he did. His fingers danced nimbly across her entrance, teasing gently until she moaned with pleasure. A mindless wave of sheer sensation washed over her, her back arching as his fingers slipped inside to stoke the embers into a full-on inferno.

How long had it been since she felt so connected? So absolutely safe and valued?

Never, she realized.

His kiss was ravenous, his hands deft and practiced, leaving her breathless as white-hot pleasure gathered in her core, almost agonizing in the tension. She let out a wordless cry as the tension finally broke, leaving her gasping for breath. When she opened her eyes again, Tarek was close, brushing her hair away from her face with warm, gentle fingers.

"You are so beautiful," he said.

"I want you," she replied. "Now."

With his powerful arms on either side of her, eyes locked on hers, she had never wanted a man so badly. Dipping his head to capture her mouth with his own, he pushed himself fully into her. She gasped in surprise at first, then relaxed to allow him deeper. Then he moved in her, and she couldn't hold back a moan of pleasure as he found a slow, agonizingly sweet rhythm.

As he moved, she moved her hips to meet him, tracing his beautiful body with her hands. The world drifted away, and with it, the logical part of her brain. All she cared about was this moment, the way his skin burned against her touch, the strength of him as he moved in her, surrounding her like a stone fortress, and the blazing heat at her core.

Gabby had never liked to lose control, but she did then, gasping in pleasure as the molten hot center exploded, sending shockwaves of pleasure throughout her body. A moment later, Tarek groaned. His back arched, the solid muscle shifting under her hands as he climaxed. They were silent and still for a moment, the only sound their breathing.

Finally, he met her eyes, searching her. He smiled, then languidly kissed her. First her forehead, then her cheeks, then a lingering kiss on her lips. His lips tasted faintly of salt, a pleasant bite on her tongue.

He murmured something quietly. "*Marta keth uran d'Isina.*"

"I don't understand," she said.

He smiled. "It doesn't translate. It's a blessing, you might say. An honorable man thanks the Skymother when he is given the honor of making love to a woman of such beauty and honor."

"Beauty and honor, huh?"

He rolled over to lay on his back, breaking the warm connection between them. Seconds later, he looked at her expectantly, and she eased over so she could rest her head on his chest. His golden skin still gleamed with a fine sheen of sweat. She traced the lines of his chest with one finger. He laughed a little, the rumbling sound into her body as it vibrated. "Beauty and honor, indeed," he said. "I do not deserve such a queen."

A shadow flitted across his face as he said those words.

"What happened?"

He tilted his head. "What do you mean?"

"Something happened. Maybe a long time ago," she said. "You wear it like a scar."

His eyes flitted to his chest, as if he was looking for the physical evidence. "I don't know what you mean."

"Tarek."

He sighed. "It seems that you care for me, though I certainly am not worthy."

"I do," Gabby said. And it no longer surprised her.

"But you would not if you knew of my shame."

"Tell me," she said.

He rolled onto his side, propping his head on his arm. He did not bother to cover himself, leaving the long, finely cut lines of his body exposed. And it was certainly a sight to see. But his face no longer wore the easy smile, the satisfied expression of a sated lion. He looked grim. "Why?"

"If it's too hard, you don't have to," she said. "But there is something in you. A tender spot. And not in a good way." He winced at that. "I don't mean it as an insult. But it's obvious that you're carrying something very heavy."

"Well, I'm rather strong."

"Tarek."

He sighed. As he searched her with his eyes, she realized she was pressing too hard. What right did she have to pry? And if he was about to take her home, what did it matter?

It mattered. Because somewhere in her mind, whether it was silly or not, she envisioned something beyond the sunrise. It couldn't be that fate would bring this strange, beautiful soul into her life only to snatch it away after a few days.

But he was clearly uneasy. She shook her head. "I'm sorry," she said. "I didn't mean to press." She rested her hand on his arm, tracing the firm line of his triceps with one finger. "Let's just enjoy the moment."

278

He breathed a sigh of obvious relief, then smirked a bit. "How much would you like to enjoy it?"

"How long is it until sunrise?"

CHAPTER THIRTY-ONE

As Tarek watched Gabrielle sleep, he marveled at how lucky he had been, even if it was short-lived. He had fallen under the dreamy haze of sleep, still holding her in his arms. But when the first servants began walking past the door talking quietly, he'd jolted awake. He'd thought to wake her up, but she slept soundly. Long lashes fanned against her flushed cheeks, her lips curved in a faint smile as if she dreamed of beautiful things. He did not dare wake her, and instead watched the steady rise and fall of her chest.

His joy was tinged with sadness. The sky was still dark, but the first hints of pale blue clung to the mountain peaks like mist. *Just wait*, he thought. Were it in his power, he would have stopped the sun where it hung in the sky, holding back the dawn to make this moment last forever.

He had known lovers over his decades, but this was different. Though he still knew relatively little about Gabrielle, he somehow felt as if he had known her for many years. He didn't know where she lived, or what her family was like, but he had seen her stand in the face of danger. He had seen her face down those who would harm Ashariah—even *him* before he'd convinced her that he was an ally—without faltering. She had managed to charm the queen, and even earned the hint of a smile from the notoriously sullen and moody Kaldir. He had watched as the Ironflight guard danced with her, with no small amount of jealousy boiling in his veins. And without consideration for the danger, she had risked herself to save Ashariah once more, breaking the hold of magic that even the skilled Stoneflight healers could not solve.

She was extraordinary, which made their impending farewell all the more painful to consider. She had a life of her own, and it didn't include him. *Shouldn't* include him. She was safer without the presence of the Kadirai and their wars. She was better off without him.

Something touched his shoulder, tracing down his arm and leaving a crackling electricity in its wake. He turned to see Gabrielle looking at him, her eyes still sleepy and heavy. "Have you slept?"

"For a while," he said.

The bedclothes whispered against skin as she sat up and touched his shoulder. "Is it time?"

He sighed. "It will be soon. We should prepare."

The sun had climbed above the horizon by the time Gabrielle finished dressing. The queen's servants had laundered her old clothes, and it made Tarek oddly wistful to see her dress again. She was every bit as lovely in her normal clothes, but they only reminded him of the distance, that she was a stranger in his world.

After fussing with her hair for a few minutes, she threw up her hands and said, "This is as good as it gets. Apparently hair-ties aren't a thing here." Her dark hair hung in loose waves around her rosy-cheeked face.

He eyed her. "One could not ask for better."

"Stop it," she said, though her lips quirked up into a smile.

"Are you ready to go home?" he asked. The words felt like bitter ashes on his tongue.

She hesitated, then gave a perfunctory nod. "I guess I am. It feels like it's been forever, but it's only been a few days."

Tarek felt a sense of heaviness, like he was barely holding something back. Gabrielle seemed unaware of his discomfort, busying herself with straightening the bedclothes and looking around for anything she had missed. He wanted to say something, but he wasn't sure what it was, only that it was important and his chance was slipping away.

Gabrielle looked up suddenly. "What about this?"

Her voice startled him. Her hand rested on the *hanassa* amulet lying on her chest. "We have to return it to the queen," Tarek said. He crossed the room quickly to help her. Sweeping her hair away from her neck, he unfastened the chain.

Gabrielle turned to look up at him, fixing her warm gaze on him. "This was like a dream," she said.

He hesitated. Looking down at her sparked his desire again, and he was overcome with the need to lift her off her feet and take her to bed again. But that would only make what was to come more difficult. Instead, he kissed her delicately on the forehead. "A beautiful dream. But—"

"Don't," she said, looking pained suddenly. "I know." She pulled away from him, leaving him feeling cold and empty. With a soft breath, she squared her shoulders, fiddled with the hair around her face again, then looked back at him. Her expression was mild, but it was not the wide-open warmth he had seen before. It was a guarded look, one that made him feel like they were already separated.

He took a deep breath, and gestured for her to follow him into the corridor. Several servants were carrying linens and trays from the lift. He stopped one and gave her the amulet with a request to return it to the queen. When he had finished, he rejoined Gabrielle.

With dawn still on the horizon, it was quiet and peaceful for their passage down the empty corridor. Tarek stopped at the first great open balcony and stepped outside, looking out over the city. There was so much he wished she could still see, but her home was in another world. This was not where she belonged.

He took a deep breath to bolster his resolve, then slipped his trousers down over his hips. This time, he felt no shyness about his naked body in front of her. Closing his eyes, he began the transformation. It was a subtle heat at first, then a searing explosion in his chest as the dragon broke free. His bones cracked, his skin splitting as massive muscle swelled. A maddening itch rolled over him as thousands of gleaming blue scales emerged along his limbs.

It took a moment to regain his center, his sense of who he was, as the dragon took over. He was still Tarek, but he was also more. Through his enhanced eyes, Gabrielle was even lovelier than she had been. He could see the fine threads of coppery-gold in her dark hair, a faint bronze sheen to her skin. In the growing light of dawn, she glowed.

She hesitated, then put out one hand toward him as if she was going to touch him. His dragon instincts had him more tense than usual, but he controlled himself, instead leaning his head toward her. Her fingers grazed the smooth row of scales along his jaw. A pleasant warmth, a campfire on a cold night, ignited under her delicate touch. He let out an appreciative sound that rumbled in his chest. She jumped back in fright, but he remained steady.

"Is it all right?" she asked.

He rumbled a *yes* in Kadirai, and she tilted her head in confusion. With a little growl, he managed to say it in English for her. Speech was difficult, but she seemed to understand. She smiled in recognition and touched him again, tracing the long tapered snout, then following his neck to the row of spines on his back and to the root of the great wings. When her fingers came upon the scars of the Silverflight, where their liquid fire had nearly melted him, he winced. She recoiled and said, "I'm sorry!"

He shook himself a little. Now the sun was fully over the mountains, throwing its pink-orange veil over the sky. With the sun glowing behind her like a halo, all Tarek wanted to do was scoop Gabrielle into his arms, fly her far away, and hide her away like a treasure. But he knew what he had to do, even if it broke his heart.

He shifted his weight onto his powerful back legs and gestured with his front claws for her to approach. She approached him tentatively. The smell of her reached his powerful nose and nearly made him growl. He smelled himself on her skin, the earthy smell of their bodies pressed together.

The Kadirai were not dragons to be tamed by humans, and they certainly did not make a habit of allowing riders. They had harnesses and other contraptions to allow for carrying loads over a distance, but none of them would have been comfortable for Gabrielle.

"I'm not sure what to do," she said.

If she had simply been a prisoner of war, he would have grabbed her around the waist and flown off with her hanging from his claws like a sack of flour. But that seemed too undignified for her. Instead, he gestured with his head in an arc, toward his back. She followed his gesture, walking around him and touching his back. Then her weight shifted onto him as she swung a leg over his spine. Her instincts were good; she positioned herself high on his back, above the strong joints where his wings joined his body. Her hands felt for purchase and finally rested without grasping on either side of his neck. "Is this all right?"

He chuffed a response and nodded. Her legs squeezed lightly on either side of him. He growled quietly, beat his wings several times to catch the air, then launched himself upward. The extra weight made him shaky at first, but he instinctively reached out for the filaments of the wind's magic, focusing his mind on the currents and twisting them to his advantage.

Navan and the rest of the Council would certainly have something to say if they saw him, a proud Kadirai, in the sky with a human woman riding him like some pack animal. But he would not dishonor Gabrielle by carrying her like worthless cargo. To hell with their sneers.

He wheeled to the east. As he leaned into the wind, Gabrielle's body pressed tighter to him. With a little grin to himself, he growled, a long, satisfied sound that vibrated his entire chest and throat. He felt her legs clamp down tighter on him, her hips twitching forward ever so slightly in response. Oh, what he could do to make this trip entertaining. But it occurred to him that it might be a rather cruel prank to distract her while flying high above the shattered earth.

Vakhdahl lay under him like a picturesque tapestry through the golden-orange filter of sunrise. Beyond the valley surrounding the city of Farath, the land was wild and dangerous. The Azure Peaks stretched on behind them, while the Iveron Forest spread beyond like wild grass. Slashed gray streaks broke the dense green of the forest, as if some great beast had clawed through them. Nothing dared to grow on the wide swaths of bare stone.

Only a tiny piece of the forest lay in Vakhdahl. From there, the Iveron spread like a wedge out into the other lands. Instead, the Stoneflight claimed dominion over the vast, ruined gray expanse. It had the dry, jagged landscape of the deserts in the human world, but the color was leached out of the very ground. Even the sunrise took on a harsher cast, the healthy pink-orange a glaring, washed-out orange shade.

Broken Stone Keep was barely discernible from the craggy stone around it. The camouflaging structure had been built over years, with dragons flying at all angles to ensure that it was invisible from the sky. Huge blocks of stone had been chipped away from the mountains and carried across the shattered landscape, dropped haphazardly to help the keep blend in.

With the keep in sight, Tarek began a slow spiraling descent; if it were only him, he would have plummeted like an arrow from a bow and pulled up at the last second, but he was sure Gabrielle wouldn't appreciate it. Instead, he flew in a wide circle.

As he looked down at the well-concealed Gate, he noticed something strange. A young man stood outside, watching the sky. And despite being positioned here in Ascavar, he wore street clothes from the human world.

Dread gripped his belly. Focusing his will, Tarek pulled the air around him like a dense curtain. He would appear as no more than a mirage if the young man even looked his way. Tarek spiraled down closer to get a better look. He could not sense if he was Kadirai.

That didn't matter, because closer to the ground, he smelled blood. He smelled death.

He growled instinctively and tensed enough that Gabrielle shifted her weight in response, her hands suddenly pressed against his neck to steady herself. He turned abruptly, flying a hundred yards or so away from the Gate to another rocky outcropping. After landing quietly, he shook his body lightly to send Gabrielle the signal to get off. There was a shift in her weight, then a gentle scrape down his side as she slid off. She looked at him quizzically. "What's going on?"

He growled again. Her brow creased, her eyes flitting over him in worry. He prodded her as gently as he could manage with his head, leading her behind the rocky formation. He tried to form the word *wait*, though it came out low and growling.

"Wait?" she said.

He nodded, then wrapped his wings around himself as he knit together the illusion. He heard her gasp in surprise as he disappeared from sight. Then he took flight, barely skimming the ground.

As he landed just outside the Gate chamber, he poured more energy into the mirage. Then he quieted, sitting still to listen. The stench of death—of metal and excrement and burnt flesh—was strong here, strong enough to make his stomach churn. Inside, there were a number of voices speaking English. There was chatter about bodies.

The voices grew louder. Someone called, "Manit!" The young man standing outside snapped to attention and ran inside. Tarek crept away from the building, watching from a few yards away as three men emerged. Between them, they dragged a body with a shock of familiar chestnut hair.

Kaliyah.

A spark of anger flared to life in him. His recognition turned quickly to rage as the men dragged her naked body out of the Gate and left it sprawled on the ground. Her dragging feet left faint grooves in the loose gravel and grit. Angular symbols had been carved into her coppery skin.

His body trembled with anger as they left her there for the world to see, her eyes wide and unseeing as they stared up at the morning sun. It took all of his control to stay still, to not run to her and tear them to pieces where they stood. One of the men fiddled with her body, adjusting one of her arms, then tilting her head, as if he was trying to get the perfect angle to be as disrespectful as possible to the dead. The other two walked inside, then came out a moment later with another body. Tarek didn't recognize this one, but he knew it was one of the Stoneflight. He was already tensing his muscles, about to take to the sky, when they did something strange.

It was obvious that both of the Gatekeepers had been dead for some time, but two of the men took daggers from their belts and plunged them down into the bodies. Then they left them there, dark handles protruding like spines. When they had finished, they simply walked inside and did not return.

From this distance, he couldn't see the details of the blade, but he recognized the dark metal and the curved hilt. They were similar to the one he'd recovered from Surik's body in the human world and given to Gabrielle to protect herself.

What was he to do? He was a proud man, but he knew he could not fight all of them. As he listened, he made out at least five different voices. If they were all Vak, and all of them came out to face him, he might have a chance. But if he was to go on the attack, he would have to assume the worst case scenario: that they were all Kadirai. And he could not face five full-grown dragons and survive, not even at his best.

Instead he spun away, flicked his wings to carry him upward, and skidded to an ungraceful stop near Gabrielle. He bumped her with his head and flipped his head dramatically toward his back.

"Get back on?" she said incredulously.

"Yes," he said, hoping the word was clear.

"Why?"

He growled impatiently.

"Fine," she muttered. She threw her leg over his back again. As soon as she had leaned forward, settling her weight, he crouched, then shot straight upward. She let out a yelp of surprise and wrapped her arms around his neck tight enough to crunch the scales together. He desperately hoped they hadn't heard.

He released his illusion and pulled the currents tight around him, propelling himself as quickly as he could toward the west. His wings stretched and burned with exertion. The ground zipped away below them at a dizzying rate, so he kept his eyes to the sky, searching for home. Gabrielle's grasp on him tightened, and he felt the warm pressure and contact as she pressed the length of her upper body to him, holding on for dear life.

What did this mean? Whoever had attacked their Gate likely controlled both sides. And since the city had not heard of it yet, they had killed everyone, preventing a messenger from escaping. It could be a prelude to war, allowing the Ironflight or some unknown enemy to move their forces through the human world and into Vakhdahl via the Gate. With no warning, the city would never see it coming from the Gate.

The Ironflight was the obvious culprit, but as he'd argued to Halmerah, it was almost too obvious. Regardless of who was responsible, the attack was imminent. It didn't matter who was behind it; he had to warn the city.

Tarek caught the wind, pressed forward, and hoped to the Skymother he would be fast enough.

CHAPTER THIRTY-TWO

THE FLIGHT AWAY FROM THE CITY had been beautiful, though a bit wistful, like flying away from a dreamy vacation. Then Tarek had left her behind a rock, disappeared, and reappeared five minutes later growling. He was practically dancing in place and gesturing with his scaled head for her to climb on again. With his wings twitching and tail swishing like a perturbed cat, it was clear that something was very wrong. She climbed on as quick as she could and had barely gotten herself righted on his back when he took off. Whatever he'd seen had been enough to defy the queen's orders to take her home, so it couldn't have been good.

When she made the mistake of looking down at the blurring ground below, it almost made her sick. Where their initial flight had been sort of leisurely, with Tarek gliding through the air gently, this was an intense, breakneck race. Each stroke of his huge wings jolted them forward. Powerful muscle and sinew shifted under her, and she felt as if she was constantly on the verge of falling.

With the wind rushing in her ears and her heart beating painfully hard, she pressed herself close to him and clung to his neck. The hard spines dug into her cheeks, but they at least gave her something to hold onto.

The cracked gray landscape melted into forest, and soon back into the small villages dotting the landscape beyond the city. It could have been five minutes or two hours before he finally began to descend toward the edge of Farath. Over the city, the sleek outlines of dragons circled in wide, slow spirals. Along the peaks that framed the mighty citadel, the early morning light bounced off the reflective scales of dragons standing guard. There were dozens in the mountains and more still perched on the ledges and terraces of Adamantine Rise.

Tarek growled, a sound that rumbled all the way into her guts like a subwoofer. Then he hurtled downward. Her stomach crawled into her throat, and she held on so tight that she might be choking him but didn't particularly care. A stone plaza rushed up to them, with a massive archway carved in angular dragon runes. Why was he landing here instead of going straight to the queen?

She didn't have time to think about it. Tarek landed hard, sending a hard jolt up into her body and rattling her jaws. He grunted with effort, crouching so she could climb off. Her legs were weak and shaky, and she had to brace herself with one hand on his side to steady herself.

Flanking the archway were clusters of guards. Several wore the dark uniforms that she now recognized as the Adamant Guard, while the others wore plainer, rough-spun gray uniforms. The ones in gray were smaller than the ones in blue; they had to be the Vak City Guard.

Tarek spoke, and while it sounded to her like unintelligible growling, one of the Adamant Guards nodded in understanding. He relayed the message to the guards around him. If Gabby had known they'd be coming back to the city, she'd have held on to the queen's amulet a little longer. Maybe he was warning them since they'd be the first line of defense against whatever Tarek had seen. Surely they would head up to the citadel to warn the queen next.

One of the guards looked up suddenly, his eyes going wide. It was the most basic human response; when someone looked shocked, it was only natural to turn and see what they were looking at. When Gabby turned and saw the huge creatures in the sky, the world fell away. The guards' voices behind her sounded like they were far away, underwater, even.

Closing on the city in a wide triangular formation were three massive white dragons. As if they'd been waiting for someone to notice them, one of them let out a long, ear-splitting cry. It was the sound of a roar mixed with the long air horn of a barge and a freight train combined. It was so loud and low that she could hear the individual waves of the sound shaking its mighty vocal cords. That sound went into her ears and down into her guts, making her legs go rubbery and weak as she shuddered involuntarily.

"What is that?" she breathed. But she knew, didn't she? She'd seen it before. Not in person, but she recognized these dragons from Ashariah's nightmare. She'd thought maybe the nightmare had exaggerated their size, but they were even bigger and more terrible to look upon in real life. As she watched them, her head swam. Their outlines shimmered like a desert mirage. Focusing her gaze on them made her head throb.

A choked sound came from behind her. She whirled around to see one of the Adamant Guards with a knife to his partner's throat. Without warning, he drew the blade across delicate skin, spraying blood everywhere. Flinging the shuddering guard aside, he lunged for Gabby.

Tarek lashed his tail, propelling the man backward. But he was undeterred as he stumbled and hit his knees. Instead, he crossed his arms over his chest, bellowed in rage, and transformed in mere seconds into a pale green dragon. The guard uniform fell around him in dark shreds. Instead of taking to the sky, he skittered up the wall like a lizard and then did a graceful loop around to land on Tarek's back. He clawed at Tarek's spread wings, worrying at him as Tarek tried to shake him loose.

Tarek twisted and maneuvered his front leg around to slash at the smaller dragon. It leaped away from his swipe, leaving bleeding furrows down Tarek's wing. The green dragon tried to fly away from him, but Tarek lunged and caught his slender tail in his powerful jaws. Whipping his head around, he smashed the smaller dragon onto the cobblestones. The green dragon said something, his voice burbling and choking. Tarek growled back and waited for a response. When the green dragon choked something back, Tarek roared and slashed his long claws across the other dragon's throat, pinning the smaller creature's head to the ground until it quit fighting.

Gabby gasped involuntarily as the green dragon twitched one last time and fell limp. The surviving guards were all shouting at each other, at her, and she didn't understand a word of it. One of the white dragons roared again.

She sank to her knees, covering her ears in fright. Forget her second thoughts. With chaos erupting around her, she wanted nothing more than to wake up in her normal, boring bed. *There's no place like home,* she thought crazily. Didn't work. *Damn.*

A heavy hand touched her shoulder. She gasped and looked up to see Tarek. He had turned back to his human form, but he was sweating and trembling. There were long, deep scratches on his back where the green dragon had torn his wing.

"Are you all right?" she asked.

"I'm fine," he said between heaving breaths. "We have to get back to the citadel. It's not the Ironflight. We have to tell them."

"What? What do you mean?"

"I can't explain right now, but I know for sure that I'm right," he said. "I'm going to carry you to the Rise. If something happens to me—"

"Tarek, don't..."

He silenced her by lightly pressing his hands to her face, then kissing her forehead. "Be practical, Gabrielle. I would very much like to live, but we cannot stand on sentiment. If something happens to me, you have to tell them. Try to get the amulet. The word is *hanassa*."

"*Hanassa*," she repeated. Her voice shook as her brain helpfully supplied an image of Tarek broken and bloodied like the green dragon, laying lifeless on the cold ground.

"If they're too slow or they can't get it, you have to tell them this. *Ordahnar ira'nan arvedh. Oberzhan koth.*"

"I can't."

"Gabrielle, you must," he interrupted. "Say it, please."

"*Ordahnar. Ira'nan. Arvedh. Oberzhan. Koth,*" she said, trembling with each word. He smiled and pulled her forward to kiss her. There was a hunger, a fervor to him that reminded him of when he made love to her the night before. It was a kiss that said he imagined it might be the last.

"Now we have to go," he said. He hunched again, and the glistening golden skin on his back split again to reveal the growing shape of the dragon. When he had finished transforming, he took a graceful little jump into the air and hooked his talons around her shoulders, digging painfully into her collarbones. She clutched the scaly claws, praying that his grasp was more secure than it felt. As he soared into the sky, she got a dragons-eye view of the city below. Dragons of all hues exploded upward like steam geysers. They skirmished in pairs over the city, tangling and slashing at each other mid-air, while screams and shouts rose from the streets below.

Suddenly Tarek dipped in the sky. He roared, a sound so loud it left her ears ringing. He canted dangerously to one side, spinning several times as he fell. The world spun around her, and she screamed in panic. One of his wings was shredded and smoking. He released her suddenly, tossing her away like a piece of garbage.

She squealed and braced herself for the inevitable agony of broken bones, but she crashed into a giant pile of rugs. There was still a terrible jolt, and her vision flashed white as she made impact, but she remained conscious and still felt her toes. Slowly, she opened her eyes to see a cart and bright green awning hanging overhead. Piled on a nearby workbench were piles of yarn in tight skeins and a loom draped with a half-finished project. She tested her limbs and managed to get to her feet.

Tarek stood in the middle of the wide bazaar, growling at a silver-scaled dragon circling him overhead. Tarek reared back his head like a snake going to strike, then lunged toward the other dragon. Though she saw nothing, the other dragon screeched in pain and rolled out of the way. Whatever Tarek had done left a long slash on its belly, spattering blood to the stone below.

She looked around for a useful weapon, but it was as if Tarek sensed her trying to help. He turned and roared at her. The sounds were hard to understand, but she made it out. "Run!"

Biting back on her protest, she took a deep breath and turned on her heel to run. *Hanassa,* she chanted to herself. She needed the amulet. *Hanassa, hanassa, hanassa,* she murmured until it barely made sense. Get to the citadel. Find the amulet. Warn the queen. Save the city. No big deal.

The white dragons sounded that terrible call again, and she froze in mid-run. All around her in the bazaar, metal tools clattered and glass shook in its panes. The very stone under her feet vibrated, shaking up into her spine. She was overcome with the desire to lie down and curl into a ball, shoving her fingers in her ears to block out the awful sound.

A shadow passed over her, darkening the entire city street. Gabby stared up at the beast's silvery white belly, passing slowly overhead. It wasn't looking down at her, but rather up at the citadel. She sucked in a deep breath and held it, willing her heart to slow its frantic rush. Then she ran again.

As she approached the citadel, she merged into a procession of hundreds fleeing for the safety of the mountain-bound fortress. The people surrounding her were her size, probably the Vak that made up most of the city's population. There were women clutching babies to their chests, and men carrying children on their backs. The queen had spoken of making arrangements for shelter if needed. Well, it was clearly needed.

A row of ornamental gardens and a wide stone-walled chasm separated the citadel from the rest of the city. Dotted throughout the crowd were the familiar, finely cut blue uniforms of the Adamant Guard. They looked like they were trying to direct the stampeding crowd, but to no avail. Things had reached a tipping point where the guards' shouts only blended with the rest of the noise.

A piercing scream sounded, cutting through the roar of the crowd. As if they'd been waiting for the cue, everything went still and quiet as a thousand pairs of eyes looked skyward. One of the white dragons circled directly overhead.

No, no, no, Gabby thought. "Don't look at it!" she yelled. "Don't look!" A woman near her turned at the sound of her voice, staring at her quizzically. "Don't. Look!" she repeated emphatically, as if saying it louder and slower would suddenly make the other woman understand English. She shook her head, pointed to her eye, then pointed up to the dragon, and shook her head again. Then she covered her eyes. The woman tilted her head, then looked up again as the dragon roared. *No, dammit.*

A massive beam of white light exploded from its body, a solid stream of white energy like a lightning strike hammered straight. The light struck the closest cluster of people directly, flattening them immediately. Dozens more were thrown back by a shockwave, rippling outward. But worse than that, people were still staring up at it. It was a natural reaction, but it was going to get them killed.

Gabby watched as a young girl tugged on the hand of an older woman that had to be her mother, or maybe her grandmother. The little girl's face contorted with fear as she pleaded, pulling as hard as she could. Frozen and stiff like a mannequin, the woman simply toppled to the ground, her eyes wide and unseeing.

Gabby dashed forward and grabbed the girl's hand. "Keep going!"

The girl stared at her, still crying pitifully for her mother.

Gabby crouched and hooked her arms under the woman's armpits, hoping that making contact through her clothes wouldn't have the same effect as touching Ashariah. She hauled the woman up, then awkwardly maneuvered herself so that she had one arm slung over her shoulder. After a few lumbering steps, the woman's weight shifted. A dark-haired man had joined her to support the woman from the other side. The little girl was cradled in his free arm, sobbing into his shoulder. He spoke rapidly in Kadirai, but she shook her head. "I don't understand. But thank you."

He kept chattering away. He started to look up, but Gabby paused and used her free hand to snap her fingers in his face. She repeated her pantomime to tell him not to look at the dragon. She added a dramatic face with her eyes rolling and her tongue hanging out, hoping it conveyed *it'll melt your brain right out of your skull* effectively enough.

Screams erupted behind her as the white dragon released another bolt of energy. She and her companion nearly lost the woman they were helping, but they managed to keep her upright. The screams and shouts changed tone, more like shouts of victory and encouragement than abject terror. Gabby spared a glance above her. The white dragon flailed in the sky, with half a dozen smaller dragons attacking it. Two of them had latched onto one wing, ripping at it with sharp talons. As she watched, another one did the snake-striking maneuver that Tarek had done, and the wing split nearly in half. With another roar, the white dragon beat its wings and sent the smaller ones on a temporary retreat.

The man shook her, still speaking rapidly in the same language that she still didn't understand. Maybe he had the same idea she had; if he repeated himself enough times, she'd magically understand. Apparently that was universal.

They were on the drawbridge now, shuffling along with the crowd. Thick chains on either side of the bridge were their only protection from falling into the deep stone chasm. Fear gripped her as she looked over the edge.

Up ahead, the ground entrance into Adamantine Rise was a massive archway. Long blue banners decorated with the silver crest of the Stoneflight hung from the dark stone on either side. Guards lined the bridge and ushered the crowd inside, while four dragons guarded the airspace above them. Two perched on stone pillars, surveying the crowds, while the other two circled in tight spirals over the mass of people. All around her was the hot press of a terrified crowd. The noise and the cramped space made her head spin.

Guards shouted as they crossed the threshold from the bridge through the gate. Another soldier in the now-familiar dark uniform appeared in her path, shouting at her. His voice was clipped, his expression stern. Language and matters of magic aside, she recognized his demeanor. It was the necessary harshness of a crisis; she'd been the same way many times in her emergency room and didn't take it personally.

The guard pointed to the unconscious woman and repeated himself. Gabby just shook her head. "I don't understand you. I have to see—Oh! *Hanassa!* I need... *hanassa!*" She patted her chest. The guard shook his head incredulously and turned to the man who'd been assisting her. After a brief conversation, the guard hoisted the catatonic woman into his arms like a child. The little girl screeched, and the man made a soothing noise and stroked her hair as he hurried after the guard.

Like getting sucked into an undertow, Gabby was pulled along with the crowd into a wide, low hallway. The noise echoed in here, and it was atrociously hot with so many people pressed close together. There was a mildewy, wet-dog smell in the air. One side of the long hallway was lined in identical arches that all opened into one huge common room. Inside were hundreds, if not thousands of people already. Once she went in there, she wouldn't get back out easily.

She tried to fight the flow, but there were too many people, and without being able to speak the language, she couldn't insist on the importance of her task.

Outside, one of the white dragons roared again. The sound shook the very walls of the citadel. It went eerily quiet inside for a moment, then the shouts of fear started, louder than ever. One of the guards shouted over the crowd, his voice booming like thunder in the enclosed space. The crowd quieted, some looking sheepish while others scowled. But the noise didn't rise again, remaining instead at a dull roar.

Along the opposite side of the corridor were closed wooden doors. As she passed one of them, a guard stepped out with a pile of neatly folded white cloth stacked high in his arms. She zig-zagged around a woman with a wailing baby and planted herself in the guard's path. "*Hanassa*," she said. "I need the *hanassa*."

He frowned at her and tried to go around.

"No!" she said, sidestepping to match his movement. She sighed and pointed upward. "I need the *hanassa*," she said. "To talk to Halmerah. Tarek sent me. I'm uh...the Vak who saved Ashariah." She watched him for any sign of recognition. He seemed to follow the names at least. She took a breath. "He said *ordahnar ira'nan arvedh.* Uh...and *oberzhan koth.*"

"*Oberzhan koth,*" the guard murmured. He narrowed his eyes as if he was remembering something. "*Na Halmerah sequa so-Vak thiv?*"

"Um...yes?" She nodded.

His eyes widened suddenly in recognition as he grabbed her arm. Her heart thumped and she started to cry out, until she realized he was guiding her through the crowd and farther down the hall. Past the last entrance to the great hall was the huge spiraling staircase that formed the spine connecting the many levels of Adamantine Rise. He cupped his free hand to his mouth and called toward the guards on the stairs.

One of them jogged to her and gave a little bow. After listening to his fellow guard, he nodded, took Gabby's arm and started guiding her up the stairs. The noise died away quickly as they rose above the first floor. He moved quickly ahead of her, bounding up the stairs two at a time. "Wait," she panted. Her legs were heavy and exhausted after her sprint through the city.

She took a deep breath, held it, then exhaled heavily as she hurried after him. They hurried up three flights of stairs, her mind racing as quickly as her feet. Was Tarek all right? Was the whole city burning around him?

Shouts broke into her worrying. She looked up to see a trio wearing sapphire blue uniforms. They had fanned out to block the way up. A woman stood at the center of the formation, gesturing angrily to Gabby as she spat orders. Gabby's guards turned and looked at her quizzically.

Dread washed over her like a hot cloud of steam. They were going to turn her away. One of the guards went to grab her arm. She held up her hand. "Wait! I need to see the queen!" she insisted. The guard took her arm, though he didn't look particularly happy about it.

"Halmerah! Tarek said *ordahnar ira'nan ahrvahl. Oberzhan koth.*"

The female guard froze. The guard who had met her at the stairs said, "*Halmerah sequa so-Vak thiv. Taure efa hanassa.*"

The woman nodded in recognition. She stepped out of formation and reached for Gabby. Her hand was open, but Gabby just stared for a moment. The woman shook it, and Gabby finally accepted it. Her armored glove closed gently, and then she pulled Gabby toward her. "*Takh n'adan!*" When she took off running up the stairs, Gabby had to sprint to keep up.

The woman guided her up another flight of stairs. When they emerged into a tapestry-lined hallway, Gabby recognized the ornate woven art and the double doors at the end of the hall. The wooden doors to the library stood open with a single uniformed guard pacing with his spear.

The female guard shouted at im. "*Ordahnar ira'nan arvedh! Oberzhan koth.*" She shook Gabby's arm roughly, though it seemed more from excitement than trying to scare her. "*Taure efa hanassa! En fara Eszen!*"

The guard didn't respond, but he moved his spear and gestured for them to pass. The female guard yanked Gabby along, toward the office in the back of the library. Councilor Eszen stood inside, shaking his head rapidly as he flipped through a stack of notes. If the battle raging outside bothered him, he didn't show it.

"*Taure efa hanassa!*" the guard shouted at him. Eszen's eyes widened in shock, but he didn't hesitate. Spinning on his heel, he lunged for a shelf and took down a lacquered box. His robe swirled around his legs as he rushed to Gabby and held out the open box to display the familiar purple stone wrapped in silver wire.

She seized the amulet and fumbled to fasten it around her neck. The dreamy, slightly pressurized feeling of its magic settled around her. "Do you understand me?"

Eszen nodded. "You said the Ironflight is not our enemy, but the Gate is lost. Is that what you meant to say?"

"*Ordahnar ira'nan ahrvahl,*" she murmured. "Is that what I said?"

"Yes," he said. "How do you know?"

"Tarek said so."

"He's sure? How?"

"Tarek took me to the Gate, but something had happened there and he turned back. I don't know, but he said it was important. He said I had to make sure the queen knew."

"No," Eszen murmured. "How can this be?"

"I don't know, but he took off quick and in a hurry," she said.

Eszen shook his head. "He was wise to send you here. We must tell Halmerah before she does something rash. War with an unknown enemy is bad enough; if we provoke a war with the Ironflight on top of it, we will surely be lost. We must go."

CHAPTER THIRTY-THREE

BATTLE WAS NOT THE GLORIOUS DANCE spoken of in the great stories. Maybe years later, the survivors could forget the horror of it; its edges softened by time and overcast by a haze of hard-won victory. But the reality of battle was blood and teeth and death, and Tarek had already had more than enough of all three.

With one wing in tatters, barely functional, he launched himself into the sky. He had to get back to the citadel, not for his own protection, but to prevent the queen from doing something that would make this battle look like an argument between squabbling children. They were certainly under attack, but his hunch had been correct; it was not by the Ironflight. And he knew Halmerah all too well. Once she heard the first reports, she would do something drastic, like kill Zayir to strike at the Ironflight queen. And once she did that, there would be no chance at diplomacy. He had to hope that Gabrielle would make it to the citadel and deliver his message in time.

Tarek gritted his teeth and growled through the pain searing his injured wing. It was one of many injuries he'd already taken, but he'd survived worse. He caught the current and used it to propel himself upward. One of those awful cries came from the white dragons. The sound was bad enough, but it washed over him, making him feel as if tiny insects crawled under his scales and through his skin. Whatever they were, they were evil and unnatural.

The sound at his back made him fly even faster. He instinctively headed for one of the side terraces of the citadel for easy access, but the iron bars had been dropped at all of the windows to protect the inner levels of the fortress. It left him only the upper landing, which would be heavily guarded. He forced his wings to carry him higher, fighting against the fatigue until he cleared the edge of the stone. He tried to call out *dath sequa*, a greeting of honor between the Adamant Guard, but his lungs wouldn't comply. As it was, his landing was more of a stumble and concession of defeat to gravity.

Barely on his feet, he released his already tenuous hold on his dragon form. There were a dozen guards on the platform, all armed to the teeth, but they recognized him and put away their swords.

"Do you have news?" one of them said.

"I need to see Halmerah immediately," he said.

The guard looked as if he wanted to give Tarek a hard time, but instead he sheathed his weapon and hurried toward the locked door leading down into the citadel. On the way, Tarek grabbed one of the leather kilts, wrapping it around himself as he took the stairs three at a time. "She is in the gardens," the guard said.

"The gardens," he murmured. "Why?"

"So she can join the battle if she pleases," the guard said politely.

Oh, that would not do. The gardens were open to the sky, with a chain net that could be pulled over the open ceiling in such an event. It could be retracted just as quickly to allow a furious queen to join the fight. And when she heard of the ambush on Broken Stone Keep, she would surely be out for blood.

Tarek quickened his pace. He was so focused on moving ahead that he plowed into a familiar blue-robed figure on the stairs. "Eszen," he blurted. "I'm sorry."

"Tarek?"

The sound of Gabrielle's voice was a balm to his wounds, a warmth that instantly lifted the ache from his muscles. She was disheveled and looked terrified, but she was alive. She hurried toward him with open arms, and he embraced her, ignoring the inquisitive expression on the councilor's face. "Mr...Councilor Eszen was taking me to see the queen."

"I'll go," he said. He turned on his heel and snapped at the retinue following Eszen. "I want you to escort her to the dungeons."

"I am not going down there again!" Gabby spluttered.

Tarek glared at her. Her stubbornness had its drawbacks. "It's standard protocol for guests, Gabrielle," he snapped. "It's one of the safest places in the entire citadel." Tarek made eye contact with one of Eszen's messengers. "Please see that she is comfortable, but ensure that she arrives."

"Tarek—"

He ignored her. "Councilor Eszen, you must see that the prince is released before Halmerah harms him."

"Wait, I am not giving that order without her permission," Eszen said.

"But I just told you," Gabrielle protested.

"I believe you," Eszen said. "And I will help plead the case to the queen."

"Then let us ask her together," Tarek said. "But we have to act now."

Eszen hesitated, then nodded in agreement. He snapped his fingers at the messengers behind him. "Take her to safety." One of the men nodded and took Gabrielle's arm lightly. She scowled, but followed him down the corridor with an angry look thrown back at Tarek. He winced, but did not call back for her. She could be angry from the safety of the mountain's depths, where the chaos of battle would not reach her. "The rest of you, with me."

Halmerah paced the length of the *farhenh*, the heart of the gardens. Her eyes flicked from her councilors up to the open sky and back. There was a nervous energy about her as she moved. This was the first time the city had been attacked in over a century, when her grandmother was the Empress during the Great War.

Her councilors were posted around the perimeter of the *farhenh*. Several of them wore heavy purple amulets like Gabrielle's. Rather than translation, these allowed for long-distance communication with a paired amulet. Each of the councilors had messengers or spies posted through the citadel and the city below, sending reports back to the queen.

As Tarek approached, Councilor Netha suddenly lifted the amulet over her head and covered her mouth. Her face was pale, and it didn't take much to realize what had happened. The connection through the amulets was telepathic, and something unpleasant had happened on the other end. Halmerah didn't flinch, but she wasn't particularly calm either. Though her face was as stoic as ever, her fingers fluttered against her legs as she paced. Her feet were bare, and she only wore a light robe belted with a silver sash, as if she was simply waiting for the signal to transform and take on the attacking force herself. During the Great War, she had fought as fiercely as the

Adamant Guard in her grandmother's name.

"Majesty, I have news," Tarek said. He hurried toward the platform and sank into a kneeling position. His tired muscles protested as he crouched.

"Get up," she snapped. "What is it?"

"*Su'ud redahn*, our enemy is not the Ironflight," Tarek said. "I flew Gabrielle back to the Gate, and I found everyone slain."

"On both sides?"

"I wasn't able to find out," he said. "I think we have to assume so."

"How did they find it?"

"Dakhar," Tarek said quietly. "Did he talk to them?"

"He swears he didn't," Councilor Thiven answered.

"Is that your news?" Halmerah snapped. "I'm not sure how you feel that exonerates the Ironflight."

Tarek winced at her sharp tone. "I was attacked several times coming here. Each time, my attacker said *ordahnar ikh valahn*." *Long live the Ironflight.*

"So?"

"So, the Ironflight never refer to themselves that way," Tarek said. "I even spoke to one of them and gave the traditional greeting *nalak halar*, and they didn't respond appropriately."

"Get him out of here," Halmerah said. "I don't have time to debate language with you, Tarek. You sound as foolish as Thiven and his etiquette rules."

Two of her guards rushed forward and grabbed his arms. Tarek struggled against them and shouted back at her. "Wait! You have to listen!"

"You waste my time in the heat of battle," Halmerah said, her temper slipping through her tenuous grasp. Light flashed behind her eyes, as if the dragon was about to overwhelm her. Her eyes narrowed. "And for what? A discussion of the manners of those who attack my city with dishonor?"

"That's what I'm trying to tell you," Tarek said. "It's like we've been saying. These people want us to think they're the Ironflight, but they're not. The Ironflight find it offensive to be referred to as *Ordahnar*. You know that. Don't you remember? When the girls were very young, you had to pay Tarim a tribute to make up for them using *ordahnar* at a state dinner. They would never refer to themselves that way, especially not as a battle cry." *Nalak halar* was the traditional Ironflight greeting; the word *nalak* actually meant chosen. They used it to mean that they were chosen by the flames.

Halmerah stared at him. "Why does it matter?"

"Because you—we—are not ready for what's out there," he said. "There are two white dragons that are unlike anything I have seen, except for in your daughter's nightmares. They are not of the Ironflight. There were three, but one of them was felled, at the cost of many of our own."

"Then I will face them myself," Halmerah said. She pulled the silver crown from her head and threw it aside. One of her attendants cringed and hurried to pick it up, surreptitiously brushing it clean. "Pull back the chain. They will soon see who they call to battle."

CHAPTER THIRTY-FOUR

AS SHE DESCENDED into the reeking depths of the dungeons, Gabby was seething at Tarek. It wasn't like she had much to offer in battle, but she didn't want to be tucked away in some corner of the dungeon.

She'd thought Tarek was spinning a tale to get her down here and far away from the battle, but sure enough, there were half a dozen other guests looking frightened as armed guards ushered them into the dark, musty corridors. Eszen's messenger led her toward the right corridor, on the opposite side of where she'd first visited. She shuddered involuntarily as she recalled her unpleasant welcome and subsequent trip through the leftmost doorway.

Along the right corridor, half the cells stood open. In the first cell they passed, a worried-looking man stood in the doorway, craning his neck as if he could see the action if he looked up. He flinched suddenly as a shout of fear and rage came from the cell across the hall. Though the cells were windowless and the noise of battle was far away, it was like the prisoners could smell the tension and the blood in the air. They were noisy, their half-crazed cries echoing off the stone.

The messenger took her to a cell halfway down the corridor and gestured for her to sit. It was similar to the cell they'd brought her to before, with a cubby carved into the stone and metal rings on the wall. Someone had brought a rough-hewn wooden chair inside in an attempt to make it a fraction more inviting. "It's not terribly comfortable, but it is safe," the messenger said apologetically. "I must return to Councilor Eszen."

He bowed politely, then left Gabby alone in the cell. She waited a moment, then walked to the door and looked up and down the hallway. A guard with a stack of linens up to his chin waddled down the hall. He stopped at each open door in turn and handed a blanket to its occupant. When he reached Gabby, he tilted his head in surprise. "Weren't you..."

"I've been here before," she said drily. She took the scratchy blanket from him and set it inside the stone cubby, then folded her arms over her chest.

"Well...let me know if you require something," the guard said. He cleared his throat and hurried out of the cell.

When he had left, she waited in the doorway, listening carefully for any sign of the battle outside. But she heard nothing; the dungeons were deep in the citadel. Nervous energy took over, and she tiptoed out into the hall to wander. She didn't go all the way back to the entrance, but slowly walked up and down, casually inspecting each cell. There were seven other cells that had open doors and guests inside. Two cells were entirely empty, and the rest were locked. With each lap up and down the hall, she peeked into the round antechamber. Several of the guards gathered around the table, talking quietly. Nothing interesting.

She lost track of how many times she had walked the hall when a pair of armed guards came down the hall with swords drawn. With a quick step back to clear their path, she watched as they prepared to open a locked cell a few doors down. When the female guard placed her palm on the door, the other stood with his sword ready to strike. They nodded to each other as if they were preparing for an ambush. A flash of hot anger burned in Gabby's chest as she recognized the woman. It was the same guard who'd taunted her and dragged her down into the dungeon upon her arrival here.

The door swung open, and the guard with the sword jumped a little. The woman stepped into the cell, and emerged a minute later leading a prisoner. With his wrists shackled in front of him and connected by a heavy chain, Kaldir emerged from the dark cell. As soon as she saw him, her heart sank. He was naked and covered in bruises and welts. He'd had a rough night by the looks of it. The woman led him, the chain dangling from her hand, while the male guard followed close behind with his sword still in hand.

"We ought to do it ourselves," the male guard said. "Save the queen some trouble."

Kaldir's eyes went wide. "What's happened?"

The woman scowled and threw an elbow back into his ribs. "Don't play stupid."

Kaldir took the blow silently and doubled over, then straightened with an imperious scowl. "If you touch the prince—"

"You'll what?" the woman responded. "The queen plans to send your head on a platter back to your bitch queen in Ironhold. Maybe with some flowers to make it pretty."

They hadn't gotten Tarek's message to the queen, or if they had, she hadn't cared. Gabby swallowed the lump in her throat. She stared at Kaldir, her heart pounding as she contemplated his fate. As if he felt the weight of her eyes, he looked up suddenly, his amber eyes locking on hers. He looked calm, but not entirely resigned.

He was like Tarek, only with different allegiances. And if they killed him, they would probably do the same to the prince.

Led by the guards, Kaldir shuffled closer, the links of the chains clanking together and scraping against the floor. Her heart pounded as she pondered what to do. If Tarek was right, and she had to believe he was, then that would start a war. Thousands of innocents would die in the city, and while she didn't know them, that mattered. If Tarek was wrong, then releasing the prince and his bodyguard still wouldn't hurt anyone.

"Excuse me," she said, her voice small and shaky. "Guards."

The woman looked up and frowned. "What?" She tilted her head. "Wait, what are you doing here?"

"I'm one of the queen's honored guests," Gabby retorted. "And you're about to make your second huge mistake in a week."

"What are you talking about?"

"It's not the Ironflight," she said. "We saw it ourselves."

The woman ignored her and kept walking until she was within arm's reach of Gabby's door. With a deep breath, Gabby stepped into the middle of the narrow hall. Even with her smaller size, they wouldn't be able to pass her. "Move," the woman said.

Kaldir tilted his head quizzically. She set her jaw and planted her hands on her hips to make herself as big of a presence as possible, hoping she channeled the renowned Rojas stare the nurses talked about. "He doesn't have anything to do with this. If you kill him, you're only going to piss off his queen and have twice the problem you have now."

"You should listen to the Vak woman," Kaldir said mildly.

"I've been to the Gate," she said, emboldened by Kaldir's endorsement. "And I saw what's going on in the city. Unless the Ironflight suddenly have white dragons the size of tractor trailers, then it's not them."

The woman frowned. "Tractor..." Damn amulet. Her confusion evaporated into a scowl. She made a growling sound of annoyance and threw out her arm to push Gabby out of the way. As soon as the woman moved, Kaldir fixed his gaze on Gabby and said, "Move."

She crouched and flattened herself against the wall as Kaldir brought his chained wrists around like a club. The female was distracted with trying to move Gabby. Reacting to the clank of metal, she turned just in time to catch Kaldir's balled fists directly in the nose. She yelped in surprise and brought one hand to her bloodied face, and Kaldir took advantage of her distraction to strike another vicious blow to the back of her head. Like someone had flipped a switch, she flopped to the ground in a tangle of limbs.

Without even looking, Kaldir whirled and threw his elbow back into the male guard's face. A graceful spin brought him face-to-face with the guard. Kaldir body-slammed the other man into the stone wall, pressing his thick forearm to his throat and leaning in hard. "Drop the sword."

"*Vazredakh*," the guard spat. With the tight quarters and Kaldir pinning him, he couldn't do much, but he still managed to strike at Kaldir's back and side with the hilt of the sword. The bigger man winced, but kept his grip. Kaldir hiked his shoulder up and lifted the guard clear off the ground. His face reddened as he tried to get a breath.

"Drop it," Kaldir said. The guard was persistent; even with his eyes rolling back from lack of air, he continued swinging at Kaldir with his sword.

Gabby lunged around them and grabbed the guard's elbow, digging her fingers deep into his sleeve and feeling for the wiry tendons in his elbow. She pinched as hard as she could, prompting a choked yelp as his fingers opened. The sword clattered to the floor.

Kaldir looked down at her, his jaw slack in surprise. "Get his keys."

She found the ring on his belt quickly and pulled it free. There was a noisy *thud* as Kaldir released the guard and let him fall. As soon as he hit the ground, Kaldir kicked him hard in the face. His head snapped back, and a spray of blood spattered the stone. It was a surprisingly savage move, but judging by Kaldir's state, it might have been justified.

"Did you kill him?"

"He's unconscious," Kaldir said. "Though they were going to kill me."

"It was a misunderstanding," she said.

"Which would have been of great comfort when my head was on a platter," he said drily. He held out his chained wrists. "Release me."

"Would a please kill you?"

He stepped toward her, his face set in a dark, grim expression. She swallowed hard. She sure hoped she hadn't just bet on the wrong horse. "This is not the time for wit."

"Are you going to hurt me if I release you?"

"I have no reason to hurt you," he said simply.

She fumbled through the keys to find one that would fit the odd hexagonal keyhole on his manacles. It was distracting to be so close, with six

316

and a half feet of glorious Ironflight muscle in her face. His chest and sides were marked with dark welts, and she could picture the clenched fist that had left each one. He was still handsome, but he smelled pretty rough. She tried not to think too hard about the details of the last twelve hours of Kaldir's life.

Finally, she found a key that worked, and released the manacles. As soon as she had unlocked the second chain, he crouched to grab the guard he'd pinned to the wall. With a groan of effort, he hauled the guard into the empty cell he'd vacated. He returned for the other, and closed the door behind him. A subtle smile pulled at his lips as he turned away from the door.

With the distance between them, she couldn't help but notice that he was naked as a newborn.. *Good Lord.*

He caught her inspecting him and gave her a wry smile. "Are you impressed?"

Her cheeks flushed hot. "Should I be?" His smile widened. "Besides, I was noticing your leg. You're limping."

He looked down and flexed his right knee with a wince. "The hospitality of your friends."

"If you want me to fix it, I will," she said.

"I do not need your help."

"And that changed when? Because two minutes ago you sure did."

He scowled at her. She raised her eyebrows and stared back, hoping he couldn't do some crazy dragon thing and spit fire at her from down the hall.

"Will you help me?" he finally said.

"It would be my pleasure," she said in an overly sweet tone. He rolled his eyes and approached. "Go sit in there."

After using the guard's sword to start a few strips, she left Kaldir shredding her blanket while she peeked out into the antechamber to see if the guards had noticed anything amiss. One of the guards sat at the table, absently shuffling through a deck of cards while the other rattled about in the storeroom. Whatever noise Kaldir had made in the scuffle with the guards hadn't caught their attention.

She returned to her cell and found him sitting on her chair with his legs splayed.

"Oh good God," she muttered. She pointedly looked away.

"You seem very uncomfortable," he said.

"You dragons are way too comfortable being naked. Just because you've got it doesn't mean everyone wants to see it," she replied. She knelt in front of him, then looked up. "Don't you say a word or so help me..."

His lips quirked. "I would not dream of it."

"This may hurt," she said. She gingerly touched his knee, and sure enough, it was completely out of place. With one hand supporting the inner part of his knee, she gently straightened his leg and moved the kneecap back into place. He grunted in pain, his muscles tensing. "Give me those." He handed her the strips of linen, which she wrapped carefully in a makeshift brace. After tying them off, she looked up. "Any better?"

"Much," he said, though his face was still etched with pain. She stood up and handed him the ragged remains of the blanket. "What's this?"

"You wanna go get your prince? Then suit up and let's go."

"Tell me first why you interfered," he said. "You could very well be leading me right to Halmerah so she can take my head off."

Gabby shook her head. "You think they staged those two coming to get you so I could save you and then trick you? That's about the dumbest thing I've ever heard."

He stared at her coolly. "Then why are you doing it?"

"Because I know you didn't hurt Ashariah," she said. "We figured it out yesterday, and Tarek confirmed it."

"That's still not an answer," he said. "Why risk yourself?"

"Because that's what the good guy has to do," she said. "I'm not going to let them make a mistake and kill you."

"And if you get hurt?"

"You'll protect me."

He stood suddenly, and she became keenly aware of how big he was. He had to hunch slightly to even fit in the room, and he had a solid foot of height on her. "Will I? I think you presume too much."

Her heart thumped. Had she misjudged him? "You already did once." He tilted his head. "At the feast. When everything went to shit, your first instinct was to protect me. And then, I was just an inferior human to you."

"You say that as if you're no longer just an inferior human," he said.

"Has anyone ever told you that you're kind of a jerk?" He cocked his head in confusion. "Whatever the dragon word is for asshole. You are one. A simple thank you would suffice." She threw up her hands. "Do what you want. I'm going to see if your prince is a little more grateful."

She stepped out of the cell and headed down the hall. Kaldir's hand closed around her arm. With the same gentle, yet unyielding lead as when they had danced at the feast, he pressed her against the wall and went ahead. As an afterthought, he looked back. "Stay behind me. Your skills lie in healing. Mine lie in protecting." It was strangely comforting, though he was the very opposite of warm and fuzzy. He continued forward, and she had to hustle to keep up with his long strides.

Pressing tight to the wall, he peeked around the doorway at the guards. He looked back to her. "Will you distract them?"

She nodded and slipped past him to approach the table. Both guards were sitting there now, talking quietly. They looked up, hands going to their weapons as she scuffed one foot against the gritty floor. At the sight of her, they relaxed, though their expressions were skeptical. She sat at the far end of their table so they had to look away from the doorway to see her.

"I was wondering if you had something to eat," she said, her heart thumping with apprehension. "I was supposed to go back home this morning, and I didn't want to eat before traveling, cause, you know, flying and all that, and now it's been...well, I don't know how long, and I'm starving." They looked like they would have prepared her a seven course meal if it would make her stop talking. "If you have some of that flaky bread I had yesterday, that was amazing." As she chatted about all the food she'd tried on her visit, Kaldir poked his head out, scanned the room, then bolted through the small chamber and toward the central stair. Tension flowed out of her shoulders as he disappeared from sight.

"We haven't sent up for anything yet," the older of the two guards said, cutting her off in the middle of enthusing about the wine from the feast. "We'll be getting some provisions down here soon for all of you."

"Yeah, but I'm hungry right now. And I have this blood sugar thing. Do you guys know what blood sugar is? You know, like when you don't eat for a while and you get all dizzy," she said. The younger guard rolled his eyes. Now it was getting fun. "You know what, I remember where the kitchen is. Could I help out and go get something?"

The older guard looked pained. "You really should stay put."

"It'll only take me a few minutes," she said. "Do you want something? What about some of that crazy good cheese? You know the spicy one that they served warm? God, that was so good I woke up this morning thinking about it."

The younger guard flicked his eyes to his partner. The mention of cheese had piqued his interest. "You should stay."

"But cheese, right? Just wait, I'll be right back. I'll bring you some too. And some beer or whatever you like," she said. "Oh, this is going to be great." She jumped up from the table and hurried toward the stairs.

"Miss—" the older guard called.

"I'll come right back, I swear! You guys just hang out, let me do my part for the cause," she said. When she glanced back, the guards hadn't made a move other than standing up from the table. She gave them a wave, then headed for the stairs.

The round stairwell was empty and eerily quiet. Had Kaldir left her? As she looked around, he rose from a crouched position along the wall. She gasped in surprise and waited for him to join her.

"Where is he?"

"He's on the guest floor," she said. "It's up about four levels, I think."

"I know where it is," he said mildly. "I have been here many times. Let's go." Gabby had to take the stairs two at a time to keep up with him. The injured knee wasn't slowing him down one bit.

They were on the second floor above ground when she paused to speak. "Kaldir?"

"Hm?" She sprinted up half a dozen stairs to catch up with him. He clearly heard her approach, held out an arm to bar the way, and looked over his shoulder with irritation on his handsome face. "Stay back."

"Can I ask a question?"

"If you must," he said. "But stay behind me as you do."

"Why would someone pretend to be the Ironflight?"

"To provoke war," Kaldir said, as if it was the most obvious thing in the world.

They reached the first level above ground. As soon as they crossed the threshold, emerging from the dampening depths of the stone, the noise rose dramatically. There were panicked shouts, the metallic clanging of bells, and the occasional screech of a dragon engaged in battle.

"But why?"

He paused and surreptitiously rubbed the back of his knee. "I don't know. Strategy is the prince's domain. But I do know that a war between us and the Stoneflight would be hard-fought and disastrous for both sides."

They continued plowing up the stairs. As they ran, Gabby tried to stay focused in the moment. Fear was an ever-present companion that kept her head spinning and her stomach churning. *What would happen? Would she survive? Would Tarek survive? Would she ever get home?* But she knew that there

322

was nothing she could control except this moment, right here and now. She could climb these damn stairs and get Kaldir to his prince. And when that was done, she'd worry about the next thing.

They had rounded another spiral of the stairs, passing a familiar archway when she realized where they were. She lunged forward to grab Kaldir's muscular forearm. He tensed and looked back at her. "It's here," she blurted, breathing hard. He'd been about to run past it, which confirmed that even dragon men wouldn't ask for directions.

He nodded and brushed past her into the hallway. Things up here looked calmer than they had downstairs. The signs of the raging battle were subtle here. All along the corridors, the open windows were barred. A pair of Stoneflight guardians paced the hallways with jagged spears at the ready. The sounds of battle were different here, too; it was far away and muffled by their height over the city. Here and there was a clear screech or roar, but the shouting of the human crowd was far away.

As they rushed down the hallway, the two patrolling guards suddenly snapped to attention, pulling their spears up at the ready. "Stop!" they ordered.

Kaldir hesitated for a second. The muscles in his back twitched, then he flew into motion. With a quick lunge forward, he grabbed the spear of the closer guard, just below the sharp head. He yanked it back, then slammed it forward so it struck the man right in the forehead. The guard's head snapped back, and he slumped to the ground like someone had taken the skeleton right out of him.

The second guard whipped his own spear around and went for a vicious lunge.

"Stop!" Gabby shouted. "We're on the same side! Quit fighting!"

But the two men were too busy showing off their battle prowess. Their spears clanged together noisily. Kaldir was strong, swinging with powerful strikes that would have laid any normal man flat on his back. While he moved with efficiency and great skill, he didn't have the same natural grace that Tarek did. Instead, he used his huge size to his advantage. He eventually managed to knock the other man's spear away, then slammed his own spear into the man's chin, butt first. Like his partner, the guard hit the ground hard, unconscious before he even hit the ground.

"We could have talked to them," Gabby said.

"Fighting is much faster," Kaldir said. A shallow cut marked his cheek, a trickle of blood running down his jaw. He didn't seem to notice. "Which door?"

She pointed to the end of the hall. "Last one."

He nodded and handed her the spear. "Can you use that?"

She accepted it and nearly dropped it. The way he'd flipped it around, she'd expected it to be no heavier than a broom. It weighed easily twenty pounds, if not more. She recovered and leaned it over one shoulder. "Enemy gets the sharp end, right?"

"Good enough."

Kaldir charged toward the door. He didn't even stop when he reached it, just let out a shout of effort and barreled into it with his shoulder. The wooden door shuddered in its frame. He backed up and hit it again. The door splintered away around the lock. He put out one hand and simply shoved it. It swung open, with a crescent torn out of one side as if something had bitten through it.

Well, that was impressive.

Upon walking through the doorway, he immediately bowed at the waist. "My prince."

The prince had been treated far better than his bodyguard. The room was well-furnished, though not quite as nice as her own room. It was light years better than the cell Kaldir had been locked in. Zayir had changed clothes into some plain, linen-looking garments like what Tarek had worn to show her around the fortress. The dark circles under his eyes said he hadn't slept, but he looked unharmed. "Interesting," the prince said. "Not who I had expected."

"My prince, we must go," Kaldir said.

The prince regarded him. "You've had a shit time of it, haven't you?"

"I'm fine. Come along."

Zayir instantly reached to pull his shirt off over his head.

"What the..." Gabby murmured.

"My prince, really? Now is not the time for your vanity."

"My vanity knows no schedule," Zayir said. He tossed the shirt onto the bed and raked his fingers through his glossy hair like he was fluffing it up for a picture. Like Kaldir, he was easy to look at. He was considerably smaller, but was still lean and muscular. His fancy clothing might have evoked a foppish noble, but the chiseled muscle and smattering of scars across his chest spoke of someone who had both fought and survived a number of battles.

What had she stumbled into? This was not at all how she'd seen this situation going. Kaldir's shoulders slumped. The prince looked up and caught her staring. What was it with the Ironflight dragons? "I know, this is truly a work of art, my dear woman," he said wryly. "I can hardly blame you for looking."

"I didn't mean to—I swear—I mean—"

Zayir laughed, a rich sound that broke the tension of the situation. He crossed the room quickly and picked up a bundle of fabric. Upon shaking it out, she saw that it was the gorgeous copper tunic that he'd worn to the feast. He threw it over his shoulders, leaving it open over his bare chest. With the smirk he gave her, there was no doubt that he did it on purpose. "I will not make my exit looking like some common Stoneflight peasant."

He placed the hammered bronze circlet on his head, then slung a crescent-shaped leather satchel over one shoulder, like the one Tarek had carried to keep his belongings when he transformed.

As if he'd just realized who Gabby was, he stared at her quizzically. "Why exactly...never mind. I'm sure there's an explanation, and I'll be happy to learn it from the safety of Ironhold."

"Now can we leave?" Kaldir asked, with the air of the long-suffering.

"Now we can leave," Zayir said. He eyeballed Gabby and said, "A lady has no business with such an ugly weapon."

"You're much prettier than I am," Gabby said. "I'm keeping it."

Kaldir snorted a laugh as he brushed past her and into the corridor. As before, he led the way, but Zayir took a place between them. It was clear who took the highest priority for protection.

But to her surprise, Kaldir started down the stairs, instead of up toward the roof. She wasn't the only one to notice. "Kaldir, while I always trust your judgment, at least insofar as wine is not involved. But shouldn't we be heading upward?" Zayir said.

"I would take our friend here to safety below ground again," Kaldir said.

"Which will have us pass directly by Halmerah and her retinue, along with every guard in the palace who may still wish to remove your head from your shoulders." Zayir arched an eyebrow. "Besides which, I'm sure you're quite lovely by Vak standards, but I would hardly call you a friend to the Ironflight."

Kaldir paused and looked back at his prince. "Yes, my lord. Friend. She knows that we are not the enemy, and she helped free me and cared for my wounds. That is worthy of such a title."

"Oh, would that the Flame Lords would strike me dead," Zayir groaned. "You and your bloody honor." He rolled his eyes, although the whole exchange seemed jovial, the banter borne out of a long friendship. He looked back at Gabby, then nodded politely. "We will escort you as far as the gardens. Count yourself lucky to be escorted by not one, but two dashing gentlemen of the Ironflight."

"My lucky day," Gabby said.

"Quite," Zayir said. "And I'll thank you to remember it when your queen asks about the events of today."

Despite his previous behavior, the prince was quiet and nimble as they moved through the citadel. He followed Kaldir's lead, often pausing to duck out of the way while his bodyguard checked the way ahead for safety. If Kaldir gestured for him to stop or move, the prince did it without question.

They were descending the last spiral stairs into the garden when Zayir paused. "This is it," he said. "Kaldir, I must insist that we leave now."

Kaldir paused, then gestured for Gabby to come down the stairs. As she passed him, he took her hand. His callused hands were huge compared to hers. He raised it to his lips and kissed the back lightly. Then he released it, pressed his closed fist over his heart, and bowed slightly. "Go safely," he said. "*Na keth uran halar.*"

"What does that mean?"

The prince made a chuffing noise. "He requests the blessing of the flames upon you," Zayir said. "It's a compliment. If it's all the same, I'll pass on the hand-kissing and all that. Thank you for your assistance, though I'm rather sure Kaldir could have handled the door-kicking without you."

"You're welcome," Gabby said drily.

Zayir eyed the spear. "Don't think you'll be needing that now." The way he said it was light, but had a clear command.

She hesitated, then handed it over. "Don't work up a sweat. You might mess up your hair."

Kaldir's eyes widened a little, and she wondered if she might have made a misstep. Instead, Zayir laughed. "That would indeed be a tragedy of epic proportions. Thank you very much for your concern, Lady Gabrielle."

With that, he turned to follow Kaldir back up the spiraling stairs, leaving her alone. Gabby hurried through the archway and into the garden. She followed the spiraling paths until she came upon the central clearing. Strange shadows criss-crossed the stone floor. Overhead, the open roof had been covered in a net of chains. The sky was still visible, but it was marked into a grid through the heavy links.

Tarek, still in his human form, turned and walked toward her. "What are you doing here?" he spluttered. "I told you—"

"I just broke Kaldir and the prince out," she said quietly. "Either the queen didn't buy your story, or the message didn't get to them, because they were bringing Kaldir up to her."

Tarek rubbed his forehead. "Are you all right?"

"I'm fine."

He nodded. "Then I need you to go back down. Things are getting bad."

In the center of the pavilion, Halmerah paced with her councilors all talking seemingly at once. The low, shuddering call came again. As it echoed, a shadow fell over the garden. The councilors quieted suddenly, all of them slowly looking up. The sky was obscured by the white dragon's monstrous form. There was a thunderous sound as it seized the chain net and shook it.

"Enough," Halmerah spat. "I will do this myself."

"*Su'ud redahn*," Tarek protested. He squeezed Gabby's shoulders. "You have to go back down where it's safe."

The chains shook again, followed by two distinct percussive sounds as the white dragon planted its two front feet on either edge of the open roof. Then it let out a deafening roar and fixed its gaze on the gardens below.

White light exploded downward in a blinding column. Gabby had only a split second to react as it struck the ground, liquefying the stone. Lightning bolts exploded out of it. She could only watch, stupefied, as a bolt arced out of it and struck her. It felt as though a fist the size of a watermelon slammed into her chest, throwing her off her feet and into the air. The aftershock rolled over her, her muscles contracting painfully as her back arched until she thought her spine would snap. The world went white, and all she could think was *not like this.*

CHAPTER THIRTY-FIVE

TAREK'S SCREAM OF ANGUISH surprised everyone around him, himself most of all. Like lightning woven into a net, the white energy rolled over Gabrielle and blasted her off her feet. Her beautiful face contorted as she flew through the air and landed in a tangle of limbs at the base of one of the pillars. She was too still, and the image of Princess Ivralah, dead on a funeral pyre, flashed before him.

"No!" he shouted. He clenched his fists and stared up at the hulking shadow. High above, the white dragon had been joined by two smaller dragons. They flitted around the chains, circling its head. The white dragon roared again, curling its claws into the chain. Then it yanked upward.

For the first time, Halmerah's fear showed. "It can't break through," she murmured, her eyes wide. It was a question as much as a statement.

Tarek threw his hand out in a sweeping gesture. "Get the queen somewhere safe!" If the white dragon managed to destroy the chains, the rest of the attacking force would pour into the fortress, not to mention what it could do with its terrible gaze. He ran to Eszen, who was still staggering from the aftershock of the terrible blast. "Get as many of our forces here as you can. We need everyone. And get the queen away."

"What will you do?"

"Whatever I can," he said.

The chains gave a terrible metallic screech as they snapped at the huge bolts holding them at one corner. The white dragon pulled the chain net back, leaving a small opening. The two smaller dragons climbed through and hurtled downward like spears. One of them was a sleek red-scaled dragon, and the other was terribly familiar, a scarred dragon with a gleaming golden hide.

He spared a glance at Gabrielle. If it was within his power, Tarek would have stopped time, stopped the spinning of the world itself to save her. But this was what he had to do.

"I'm sorry," he murmured. He looked up at the descending dragons. With the spark of rage building deep in his soul, he let the dragon take over him. He did not control the transformation or think about how it would burn through him; the man simply imploded as the dragon took form.

He leaped into the sky instantly, targeting the red dragon. It reared its head back to unleash an elemental attack, but Tarek beat him to it. He channeled the air and slung energy out like a sharp blade. The sheer effort left him breathless. The bolt caught the red dragon squarely in the belly, slicing it open from sternum to the base of its tail. Before the red dragon realized what had happened, it twisted its body to whip its tail around at Tarek. The twisting motion opened the deep gash, exposing muscle and bone beneath as blood poured from the wound and splattered the stone below.

Tarek showed more mercy than it deserved. He bore the red dragon to the ground, pinned its head with one claw, and drove one sharp front talon into the base of its skull. The body twitched, then went limp as the fire went out of the red dragon's eyes.

He looked over his shoulder to see Councilor Netha ushering Halmerah away. The queen bellowed in protest, but Netha ignored her and dragged her toward the healers' pavilion. Beyond the underground healers' storage was a secret passageway that led to the inner sanctum of the fortress, a series of secret chambers below the dungeon with a hidden passageway out through the mountains. They would gather Ashariah on the way and ensure that the royal line was protected regardless of the outcome.

As Tarek watched Halmerah's retreat, something landed hard on his back, crushing him between its weight and the spiny corpse of the red dragon. Tarek roared as claws tore into the side of his neck and raked down his flanks. He whipped his tail around, striking something solid as he propelled himself upward. He spun in the air, freeing himself from the gold dragon's grasp. There was no question that it was the same one he'd fought before.

The gold dragon roared and came for him again. They tussled in the air, a flurry of claws and swiping tails. Tarek managed to get another air blade off on him, but it left him tired, trying to regain his flagging energy. The deep gouges in his side sent a searing, throbbing pain through him with each ragged breath.

Metal twanged as another bolt snapped overhead. The white dragon roared, and another bolt of light shot down through the net. It wasn't elemental energy in the way that Tarek knew it; it was not flame, nor lightning, nor air. It was something altogether different. He felt it crawling on his skin and whispering along his eardrums. It made him want to find the nearest corner and curl up to hide.

The bolt struck the empty stone just as the gold dragon recovered and made a lunge for Tarek. The aftershock caught him, tangling his wings and sending him flying. The gold dragon landed hard on the stone a few yards from Gabrielle and lay twitching, one wing crushed under him. As the net of lightning surrounded him, his dragon form melted away to reveal the dark-haired man who had attacked him in the hospital. Through the crackling light, the man convulsed violently.

Tarek's instinct told him to kill, to tear out his sorry throat, but a logical part of him answered. A prisoner would be more useful, and there were bigger dragons still to slay. He looked up to see the white dragon starting to push its head through. The opening wasn't yet big enough for it, but it wouldn't be long.

Tarek looked around at the gardens. The beautiful tranquility had been shattered. Blood had been spilled in the healing gardens, one of the holiest of places in Vakhdahl. The woman he dared to love lay unmoving, maybe already dead, and his queen was out of sight, beyond his protection. This was all he could do, even if it killed him.

With a deep breath to connect him to the wind, Tarek shot into the sky. As he rose, his heavy wings beating against the wind as hard as they could, he prayed. *Let me do this. Let me redeem my shame. Let me die with the honor of saving my love.*

The white dragon was monstrous. Up close, it was like nothing he had ever seen. It was not just an oversized version of the Kadirai; it was something else entirely. An eerie shifting light glowed from between its scales, which oozed a sticky greenish substance. It was not the sleek, muscular form of his kind, but a weirdly proportioned body, with odd bulges instead of the beautiful lines of the Kadirai. Sharp spurs of bone protruded from its arm and leg joints. Up close, he could see three eyes; two set in its skull like any normal dragon, but with a smaller third eye that burned above them, forming a glowing triangle. The magical energy pouring off it smelled wrong, rotten somehow. It burned Tarek's nose to breathe it in.

As he got close enough to feel the hot wind from its nostrils, the white dragon began growling again. Its massive roar began as a growl that expanded to a deafening sound. Its huge size made it slow, and by the time it managed to snap its jaws at Tarek, he was already out of the way. He watched it closely for a moment, then had an idea.

Taking care to avoid direct eye contact, Tarek cut through the sky up and around. Hovering a hundred feet above the roof of the healing gardens, he saw the carnage the attack had wrought on his beautiful home. Smoke rose in plumes all over the city. The sounds of wails and clashing swords drifted to his sharp ears, even this high up.

Everything had changed. The peace he had known was broken. He could not unburn the city, or rescue Gabrielle from her fate. He could stop this monster before it did worse, and maybe that would be his redemption.

Tarek called upon the wind. *Serve me well, this last time,* he thought. He pulled the air around him tightly, concealing himself from sight. Sure enough, he heard the white dragon make an odd sound. It looked up, then to its right for him. He spiraled around, then dive-bombed its skull. With his eyes squeezed shut, he felt for the landing. His back legs landed on the hard, spiny scales. A peek through one slitted eye brought the gleaming blue surface of the bigger dragon's eye into view. Just looking at it made his head swim, and he felt a strange gravity pulling at him.

Fall. Die. You are lost, an insistent voice murmured in his head.

Not yet, he thought.

With his sharp front talons, he slashed the dragon's eye. His claws plunged through the tough membrane, burying deep into the hot jelly-like substance inside. The dragon roared again, taking on a high-pitched edge of agony. He tore his claws out and did it again, and again.

The dragon twitched its head and rolled it against the stone, throwing Tarek free. One eye was ruined, with gouts of black fluid streaming down its face. Tarek went in for the final blow. Instead of striking its other eye, he wrapped his limbs around the dragon's face. As he did, he came face-to-face with the third eye burning pure white in the middle of its forehead.

The world froze. He felt as if something ignited inside his brain, shooting fire from his skull, down his spine, and into his limbs. The eye expanded from a tiny orb to a sun to a supernova in his mind. A chorus of voices invaded his mind, shouting, *die fall burn.*

You have to do this. You have to save her.

Tarek gritted his teeth and slashed his claws across the eye. As he did, a shockwave burst from the dragon's skull, blowing him backward. His whole body burned as he fell. He tried to extend his wings to catch the wind, but they were shredded, hanging useless by his sides. As the fire burned through him, taking over, all he could think was *I did it.*

Chapter Thirty-Six

It HAD BEEN THREE DAYS since Tarek fell from the sky. It had been two days since Gabby woke up with a contact burn on her chest and a monstrous headache. And it had been an hour since the last time she checked on Tarek.

Nothing had changed.

It was only by Ashariah's insistence that she had been allowed to stay. Halmerah was overwhelmed with the chaos, and Gabby hadn't seen her since the battle. But her daughter had emerged from their hidden sanctuary to come visit the wounded warriors in the healer's pavilion. And when some of the queen's councilors insisted that Gabby be taken home, hinting that she had overstayed her welcome, Ashariah had wielded her royal influence to insist otherwise. The princess had kept her informed with what she knew, and Gabby picked up the rest simply by being quiet and listening when others spoke.

The city was in an uproar. With two of their three strange white dragons killed, the attacking force had scattered. The Adamant Guard had been on high alert for the third, but there had been no sign of it. The battle had left more than fifty of the Stoneflight dead, and hundreds more of the Vak were dead in the lower city. Many more lay injured, some of them trapped in the catatonic state caused by the white dragon's gaze.

Their attackers had fled, but the Stoneflight had captured two prisoners.

One she didn't recognize, but the second was the golden-scaled dragon, the man who had first attacked her in the hospital. Upon hearing that particular bit of gossip, Gabby had told Ashariah to have her guards be on the lookout for his white-haired companion. The two seemed to bring trouble wherever they went, and if he was close, then she would likely be as well.

The massive corpses of the two white dragons still lay in the streets; the first had been felled by the persistent attacks of the Stoneflight guard. The second had been felled by Tarek alone. Under better circumstances, she might have been proud of him. She'd already heard whispers of *hero, legend* as she walked the halls of the citadel. But his victory had come at a terrible cost.

Tarek lay in one of the healer's beds, his beautiful golden skin gone ashen and his cheeks gaunt. His body was bruised and battered, though it was already far better than what it had been a few days earlier. When she first saw him, his ribs were shattered, protruding from the skin. The healers told her quietly that it was his wings; to take such terrible injuries in dragon form would be infinitely worse upon returning to his human form.

But worse than his physical injuries, Tarek did not wake, just as Ashariah had not woken. If Ashariah had ended up in her state by simply making eye contact, how much worse would it be for Tarek actually fighting the monster up close?

It bothered Gabby to sit and watch him, unable to help. She had tried taking his hand, to enter his thoughts like she had Ashariah's, but there was no sense of connection. If Tarek was there, he was so deep that even she couldn't reach him, and she couldn't help wondering if he was simply gone. He might have magic pumping through his veins, but he couldn't defy all the laws of nature. His injuries might have been so severe that the essence of him had simply died when he hit the unyielding stone. She didn't know about magic, but she'd seen the aftermath of nasty accidents that had left patients brain-dead. Could magic bring him back from such a blow?

In the days that she had watched, it had occurred to her several times that she had been gone from home for over a week now. And yet, it seemed like a distant concern, literally worlds away. Where she had once been desperate to return home, now she only wanted to see Tarek wake.

It was on the fifth day after he fell that something changed. As she had done each day since the fighting ended, Gabby ate a small breakfast in her room. The queen had allowed her to stay in her old room, although she suspected that the gesture was less about hospitality and more that she was too busy trying to care for her battle-scarred city to even notice that Gabby was still around. She allowed Raszila to braid her hair and help her into a comfortable dress. Her eyes lingered on the bed, which had seemed too large for the last few days.

As Gabby headed down the corridor, the windows looking out over the city were still barred, showing that while things were quiet, they were far from normal. The beautiful landscape of Farath was marred with charred buildings and shattered stone, protruding from the cityscape like broken teeth. Though she couldn't see the activity down on the streets from on high, she could see the patrols of dragons circling the skies. Smaller formations of birds of prey flew at angles to the patrols.

Councilor Eszen had sent a messenger to request her presence, so Gabby went to the library first. The room was packed with Kadirai working intently to research the nature of their attackers. The bookshelves were in disarray, with towering stacks of books strewn across worktables.

As soon as she entered his office, Eszen set aside the enormous white dragon scale he was examining and ushered her in to explain his findings. His studies had been interrupted by the attack, but as soon as it was appropriate, he got back to work. He had determined that Gabby's resistance to their compulsion had come from Ashariah. The princess had pushed her memories into Gabby's head with such force, that it had been like an infection that prevented other compulsion from taking effect. He'd been confused at first, but when Gabby explained an immune response to a disease, he'd enthusiastically agreed. However, the effect seemed to have worn off over time, and she'd made a mental note to be cautious about making eye contact with dragons she didn't know. Eszen had still been musing enthusiastically about how to best take advantage of that effect, and she'd left him to his books.

Gabby hurried down to the healing gardens. Each day, the healer's ward was less crowded, which she supposed was a good sign so long as the patients had been leaving on their own feet and not wrapped in death shrouds.

She settled herself on the low stool next to Tarek's bed. "Hey," she said. She gently touched his cheek, then kissed his forehead, as she had done every day since she had awoken to find out what happened to him. "You should wake up. You're missing all the excitement."

She told him about the messenger from the Ironflight and his provocative message. The words had been carefully crafted to thank Halmerah for her wisdom and mercy in setting the Prince free, while carrying a very clear insult and threat of swift vengeance should such an offense be repeated. The message had pointed out that there were unexpected lights of wisdom and mercy in the Stoneflight, where one might least expect it. Gabby had no doubt that the message had been written by Zayir and signed by his sister. According to Ashariah, Halmerah was furious but begrudgingly accepted that the thinly veiled insult was better than the bloody war some of her councilors had expected.

Gabrielle told Tarek about the efforts to remove the giant dragon corpses, and the way Halmerah's councilors had argued over burning them as opposed to studying them. As the arguments raged, the smell of rotting flesh filled the city, and the complaints from the Vak increased.

She was telling him about the odd substance Councilor Eszen's scholars had collected from one of the white dragon's scales when Tarek's finger twitched. If she hadn't been watching so closely, she would have missed it. "Are you listening to me?"

His finger twitched again. She took a deep breath and grasped his hand. She didn't dare let her flicker of hope grow stronger. She had to be logical and practical. It could have been an involuntary twitch. Happened all the time even in critical patients.

Screw it.

She squeezed his hand. "Please come back to me. I'm right here waiting for you."

A current tingled between their palms as she entwined her fingers in his.

Then the sensation intensified, and she felt the same gravity pulling at her as when she had helped Ashariah. Fear bubbled up in her, but she gritted her teeth and squeezed his hand even harder. He had to come back to her. She would drag him out of the dark all by herself if that's what she had to do.

Her body went cold, and the lights went out.

Falling.

Crashing.

When she crashed into the ground, the world exploded around her. She was in the same bleached gray landscape she had seen before. There was no pain on impact, but it sent a shock through her as the ground formed from nothingness around her, spreading rapidly like ripples through the darkness.

She turned in place slowly for a moment, looking for any sign of life. The sun blazed white-hot in the sky above, with the shimmer of a mirage on the horizon in all directions.

"Tarek, where are you?" she shouted. "Tarek!"

Her voice didn't even echo. It was as flat and dead as the dry gray expanse.

"Just show me," she said. "I know you're here." Time inched by as she waited for any sign of him. It was eerily silent here. She'd lived in Nevada for most of her life and had spent her fair share of time in the desert. Even in the seemingly empty expanse, there was noise; the occasional whistle and *shush* of wind, the mournful call of a distant crow, and the gritty crunch of rocks and sand underfoot.

Here there was nothing. Not even the sound of her own breathing or the thump of her heart. It was dead silent.

"Tarek!" she called again. She pictured him in her mind, and was surprised to realize that she imagined both forms interposed. She saw his tall, muscular human form, the golden skin smooth and gleaming in the harsh light. In the same space, flickering around him, was the huge dragon form, blue scales glittering like gems. They were both him, both there in her mind.

She had lost track of how many times she called his name when she heard the faintest whisper, like a breeze caressing her ear. Turning toward the source of the sound, she started walking. It could have been inches or miles that she walked before she saw the figure, thrown into silhouette by the blazing light.

A male figure knelt on the ground with his hands pressed to his face. With his body bent and shoulders hunched, he looked so small. She hurried toward him, but physics was a funny thing here. Long strides barely moved her any closer, as if the ground was pushing her back as much as she pushed forward. Gabrielle fixed her eyes on the hunched man and gritted her teeth. *I will get to him,* she thought. *Whatever this is, you're not keeping me away.*

Like moving through deep snow, she inched toward him. All the while, there was a resistance, like water currents pushing her away, pulling her in any direction but toward him. As she approached, the whispering grew louder, though she didn't recognize any of the words. Even without understanding the words, she understood the tone; it was angry and intimidating, occasionally shouting in her ear as if to scare her away. Though it was unsettling, she ignored it. She wasn't going to leave him behind because of some creepy disembodied voices.

When she was close enough to see his face, she saw what had his attention. A woman in a regal white dress lay on the ground. Dark hair streamed around her face, but her eyes were wide and dim, staring sightlessly at the harsh gray sky. The white silk was stained with dirt and blood. Crimson soaked through the fabric and spread in a puddle around Tarek.

Tarek stared down at her, his lips moving silently.

"Tarek?" she asked.

He didn't look up.

The woman looked familiar, though Gabby knew she'd never seen her.

She knelt next to the woman, putting herself on Tarek's eye level. "Tarek, do you hear me?"

He was still staring down at her. His hands were bloody, gloved in red up to the elbow. He wore the ceremonial Adamant Guard uniform, but the silver emblem on the chest was stained in red.

Gabby hesitated, then reached out to take one of his bloodied hands. "Tarek, it's me. I'm here to help you."

He jerked his hands away from her, still not looking up to meet her eyes. Anguish, hot and heavy washed over her as he ignored her. Was he so far gone that he didn't know her? Or worse...that he didn't want her here?

"Tarek, who is she?" she asked.

"I failed her," he said, speaking aloud for the first time since she had arrived. His voice was unusually small and timid.

"Who?"

"The princess," he said.

Gabrielle looked down at her. The woman was not Ashariah, but the resemblance was certainly there. Her older sister, then? "Is this the princess?"

"I was supposed to protect her. I was supposed to protect them. And they all fell. All of them. Except for me."

Gabby leaned in and gently touched his arm. He shuddered away from her touch, but she reached out anyway with grim determination to touch his face. "Show me."

With her hand touching his cheek, the vision came in rapid bursts. There was Tarek, walking in the gardens with the older princess in a pristine white dress. Then he was soaring through the sky, at the head of a formation with a small, purple-scaled dragon at its center. Still in dragon form, the princess and her retinue rested in a sunny grove. Tarek watched from the bank of a narrow stream while several others circled the sky above. The princess drank her fill and splashed water down her slender neck to cool herself. There was a clipped cry of warning from above as the ambush came.

They took to the skies, Tarek shielding the princess with his body. Gabby felt the intense heat and pressure of his fear, his determination as he flew away with her in his shielding cover. Then the fire came, melting his wing away from his body like candle wax and piercing through him like a spear. The princess screamed, and he watched in horror as the glittering purple gem fell from the sky with useless, burnt wings. Tarek flew after her, but their attackers surrounded him, slashing and tearing with tooth and claw. The last thing he saw before darkness took him was the princess losing her dragon form and shifting back into a human body. Then he woke weeks later in the same healer's ward in which his body now lay, looking around frantically for the princess. A grim faced healer in gray linen shaking her

345

head. And the heavy weight of guilt and shame for his failure. The queen's rage as she mourned her daughter. And eventually, his exile, flying away from his home to a position where he could not fail so spectacularly again.

As the city of Farath receded behind him, the vision seemed to cycle. Suddenly, he was flying through the air with the purple dragon behind him again. He was reliving it, over and over.

"Enough," Gabby murmured. She took his hands. He tried to pull away again, but she held him fast. "Is this what holds you here?"

He finally raised his head to look at her. His eyes were bloodshot, as if he had been weeping for days. From one eye, a single bloody tear traced down his cheek. "I failed her. I failed all of them. I failed you."

"You didn't fail me," Gabby said. She squeezed his hands. "I'm here."

"I saw you die, just like the rest," he said. "Never prepared. Always a second too late. It's my curse."

"Tarek, I didn't die," she said. "And whatever this was, it wasn't your fault. You didn't kill her. Come with me. Let go of this and come back to me. I'm waiting for you."

He shook his head. "It's not real."

"I'm real," she said. "I'm more real than any of this." But she could practically see the guilt and shame consuming him, passing over his face like shadows. "Tarek, I don't know everything about you, but I know about my life. You know I'm a doctor."

He was silent.

"I work in the emergency room, which means I take care of people who are very badly injured and very sick. We lose a lot of patients. Sometimes

346

they're just too sick, or we made the wrong call on what was going on. Sometimes we have to take risks, like recommending surgery for someone who's vulnerable, or giving a medication that can cause complications. Most of the time things work out, but not always. Every time a patient dies, it eats me up. I mourn them like they were my own family, just like you're mourning for her."

"Ivralah."

"Ivralah," Gabrielle said. "But when I started out, one of my mentors told me that I had to detach. That didn't help, because I couldn't, and I think caring about my patients is part of what makes me good at what I do. That reminds me of you. You cared about her, just like you care about Ashariah." Gabby shook her head. "What helped me was when another doctor told me this. He said 'keep your nose to the grindstone. When you get a patient, you ask every question, run every test, and when you think you've got it, you gotta trust yourself. And a lot of the time, you win. Sometimes you don't, and when you get it together, you go back and find out what happened, what went wrong. It usually won't be you, but sometimes you'll realize you could have done something better. But as long as every single day you can say *I brought everything I had to the table*, then you're gonna be okay. No doctor's perfect. And neither are you."

"But it was my duty," he murmured.

"So if you had died protecting her, would you feel like you'd fulfilled your duty?"

He tilted his head. "Yes."

"Is that what you want?"

He was silent. "No. And it is my shame."

"Tarek," Gabby murmured. She released one hand and rested it on the side of his face. He still didn't look up at her, but there was a gentle pressure as he leaned into her touch. "I know that you would have traded your life for hers if it was in your power. There are things in this life that happen out of our control, no matter how smart or strong or good we are."

"But..."

"But you should be different?" Gabby said. She chuckled. "Tarek, come back to me. I know it's crazy, and it's all been so fast, but I love you. And I need you here. You haven't failed me yet, and you won't fail me in the future. I trust you."

At the word *trust*, his head shot up. His warm gaze locked on hers, his mouth hanging open as if he were afraid to speak. Then his eyes closed, and she felt him slip away from her, like sand through her fingers. He disappeared, leaving her alone in that gray wasteland.

"No!" she exclaimed. Thunder rolled, and the stark landscape shattered around her. She squeezed her eyes shut as a nearly unbearable pressured surrounded her.

There was a sudden cool breeze on her face as she was slammed back into her own body. Her head spun as she returned to reality, and found herself draped across the torso of an unconscious man. She shook herself and sat up, bracing herself for balance on the edge of his bed.

Tarek's eyelashes fluttered, and he slowly opened his eyes. The warm amber gaze was like seeing the sun after an endless streak of rain. He simply stared at her for a long while. He winced as he raised his arm. She couldn't help herself; she reached out to help him, holding his arm with both hands as he rested his hand on the side of her face. His muscles trembled with the effort. "You do?" he said, his voice hoarse from disuse.

"I do what?"

"Trust me," he said quietly. She nodded. "And love me?"

"I do," she said. It wasn't a question; it was an understanding, a fundamental truth that seemed so obvious that she wondered how it had taken so long. The sky was blue, the sun was warm, and she loved him. "I love you."

CHAPTER THIRTY-SEVEN

AFTER WAKING, it took nearly a week of lying flat on his back in bed for the worst of his injuries to heal. The healers poured as much of their sleeping brew as they could down his throat, so the time passed in a sort of dreamy haze. It was just as well, considering the few times he was completely lucid, he could barely keep from screaming from the agony of his shattered back and chest. It would not do for Gabrielle to hear him mewling like a baby, so he slept with the image of her face to soothe him, knowing that she was always near.

On the thirteenth day after the ambush on his city, Tarek sat up straight in his bed for the first time. His whole body ached, but it was finally whole. The healers warned him that it might be months before his wings fully healed, but he had already healed much faster than expected. It was not the painfully slow process he had experienced after the death of Princess Ivralah.

With one of healers patiently guiding him, he walked a slow, limping circuit of the healers' pavilion. His torso was still wrapped in thick white bandages, and the cloying smell of healing ointments overpowered his sense of smell. His legs were shaky as he walked, as much from injury as from disuse for nearly a fortnight. There were another half dozen Kadirai visiting the pavilion at the moment. Two were dressed, allowing the healers to check on their progress. The other four still lay in bed, resting as they recovered.

He was ready to see Gabrielle. She would be pleased to see him up and about, and it would do him more good than she could realize to simply feel her arms around him.

As Tarek and his escort finished their route and turned back toward his cot, a familiar silhouette crossed the threshold, accompanied by a hushed murmur.

The queen's long shadow stretched across the smooth gray stone, preceding her entrance into the pavilion. "*Su'ud redahn*," the healers and nurses murmured as she crossed. The queen nodded to them in turn, but her gaze fell on Tarek, making it clear who she had come for.

Her lips curved into a smile. "It is good to see you out of that bed," she said. She was dressed plainly, in a dark gray robe and her plainest crown.

"If it pleases you, he should lie back down," the healer said.

"Of course," Halmerah said. She waited patiently for the healer to help him sit and lean against a fluffy pillow. Once he was settled, she sat on the wooden stool by the bed. Though her expression was neutral, tension pulled at her pale blue eyes. "How are you feeling?"

"As if I fell from the skies," he said drily.

Halmerah simply smiled. "I am pleased that you are recovering. Verihn tells me that you should be able to fly again."

He nodded silently. "How do you fare? If I may speak plainly, you look troubled."

Her smile faltered. "An unknown enemy attacked my city and my gate. They nearly killed my daughter. If I were not troubled, I would not be worthy of the crown." She bowed her head. "I have sought guidance from the

Skymother, but my thoughts are much too muddled. Councilor Eszen has been holed up in his office for days, but so far he can only determine that the white dragons are unnatural. They are not born Kadirai, which I could have told him upon first glimpse." She waved her hand. "I wanted to speak to you about other matters."

"Of course."

"Your...friend," Halmerah said. She used the word *far-serahl,* which was a bosom companion, a friend of the heart that was more than a platonic relationship. Had Gabrielle told her about them? "Lady Gabrielle."

Just the mention of her made his heart beat faster. "What of her?"

"You are very fond of her," the queen said, a statement more than a question. "She is a woman of honor and courage. Would you agree?"

He tilted his head. This was not a turn of conversation he would have expected from the queen. All at once, it felt as if he was drawn into a delicate dance of diplomacy. With his hands neatly folded on the blanket covering his legs, he nodded and said, "I would agree, yes."

"Very well," she said, nodding solemnly. "Do you love her?"

The air rushed out of his lungs. His mouth opened and closed silently as he tried to decide what he would say to his queen. His hesitation came from not knowing how to respond; the answer to her question had come so quickly he didn't even have to think about it. "Yes," he said. "I know it is not accepted, but– "

"I did not ask about that. I only wished to confirm what I suspected." She sighed and leaned forward. "I came for another reason, Tarek-ahn. Though I feel your answer to my question has already confirmed what I suspected."

"What do you wish to ask?"

"Do you wish to return to Adamantine Rise? To stay?"

His jaw dropped. "Why?"

"Why? You belong here."

"But you sent me away," he said. "I am happy to serve, but I did not think you wanted me here any longer."

Her eyes creased as she stared at him in disbelief. "Why would you think such a thing?"

The guilt that washed over him was not as strong as it had once been, not since Gabrielle had drawn him out of the darkness and back into her light. But it was still there, a phantom pain from an old scar that ached when the winds changed. "You sent me to the gate. As far from this place as one could go. Because I failed you."

Before he could react, the queen leaned over and pressed her hands to either side of his head, drawing him forward to press her warm lips to his forehead. "Tarek-ahn," she murmured, using the affectionate term for him. "I sent you away because you seemed so haunted here. You healed slowly, and I knew you would hurt yourself trying to prove that you were whole again. I thought overseeing the gate would give you time to rest and heal. I did not realize it would cause you such pain."

Something swelled within his chest. He could not raise his eyes to meet her gaze. "Then you have forgiven me?"

She drew away from him, staring into his eyes as her thumb stroked his cheek. "There was nothing to forgive. I saw you lying in this very place, a breath away from death. There was nothing more I could have asked of you."

The intense pressure in his chest broke suddenly, and a sense of hot relief washed through him, all of his muscles going loose. He managed to keep the tears from springing to his eyes, but his throat clenched from the overwhelming emotion.

"Ashariah would be very pleased if you returned to protect her," she said. She tilted her head. "And of course, I would be pleased for you to return here."

In his wildest dreams, he could not have predicted that the queen would have requested his return, granting him in one fell swoop the two things he wanted most. At least, that he had wanted until circumstance brought him into Gabrielle's path.

"Is this a request or an order?" he asked evenly.

"A request," the queen said mildly.

His heart pounded. "Then I must respectfully decline. Would you allow me to return at a later date?"

Her lips quirked. "You wish to go back and be close to her."

There was no point in lying. "Yes. I know that it is frowned upon, but—"

"Then your service will be most valuable at the gate. Rebuilding will take time, and I will need a capable commander to develop a more effective defensive strategy in the human realm, as well as to carry out our attempts to investigate the source of this attack." She nodded to him. "Would that suit you?"

"You aren't angry?"

"I have known you for quite a while, Tarek-ahn. And in the nearly forty years I have known you, you have never smiled the way you do when that Vak woman is in your sight."

"But she is Vak."

The queen simply shrugged. "Who is queen?"

"You are."

"Then do not concern yourself with the gossip of my inferiors," she said. "Do you accept my offer to oversee Broken Stone Keep?"

"Yes, of course."

"Good," she said. "Then all will be well."

CHAPTER THIRTY-EIGHT

GABBY'S WHOLE BODY thrummed with anticipation. When she'd made her daily trip to visit Tarek, the queen's guards had turned her away. Disappointed, she'd returned to her room only to find Raszila had been waiting and buzzing with excitement.

"There's to be a party," she said. "This is wonderful."

"Why is it so wonderful?"

"That means things are getting back to normal," Raszila said. "Now, let me do something with that hair."

But Gabby wasn't certain things were going back to normal. The number of armed guards in the citadel had doubled since before the ambush, and there were constant patrols of dragons circling the skies. It didn't seem that things would return to normal until the Stoneflight had more solid answers on who had attacked them.

Nonetheless, she allowed Raszila to throw caution to the wind and carry out her master plan of hair, makeup, and clothing for another feast. The servant woman wouldn't tell her what the occasion was, but insisted that she had to look her very best.

After what seemed like hours of pampering and primping, Gabby was dressed in a sparkling gown in a dozen shades of blue. Raszila had dusted every inch Gabby would let her get to with fine, shimmering powder. With her hair elaborately braided and woven through a silver headpiece, she looked like a queen herself.

When one of the queen's attendants came to escort Gabby to the grand ballroom, Raszila kissed the air on either side of her cheeks, careful not to smudge her handiwork. "Good luck."

"Why do I need luck?" Gabby asked, nerves fluttering in her stomach.

Raszila shrugged. "You'll be fine."

Her nerves hadn't calmed any by the time she reached the grand ballroom, standing before the heavy curtains with shaky legs. The last time she'd been here, a naked man interrupted the party, the queen lost it, and both the guests of honor got arrested. When it came to parties here, she was zero for one.

The uniformed guards at the door nodded to her, even giving her a faint smile. She frowned at the unexpected expression, a marked change from the usual cool or even disdainful reception she'd come to expect from the guards. Then she realized she probably looked ungrateful, so she smiled back and gave them her best regal nod.

After a polite smattering of applause, one of the guards pulled back the heavy blue curtain for her.

"The queen graciously welcomes Lady Gabrielle *efana* Maria, friend to the Stoneflight," the herald announced.

Friend to the Stoneflight?

She entered, walking down the central aisle. With hundreds of eyes watching her, she suddenly knew she was going to fall. *Don't trip,* she thought.

Her gaze went to the queen's table, where several guests already waited, including the one she'd been wanting to see.

Tarek stood behind his seat, chest puffed out and arms locked behind his back in a stern position. His golden skin was paler than normal, and his cheeks looked too hollow. But the sight of his smile felt like a warm spotlight tracking her as she walked down the central aisle. A servant helped her up to the dais, where she took the empty seat next to Tarek. "You look lovely," he murmured. Though he kept his tall posture, he took a step closer to her, so his arm pressed against her back and anchored her.

Unlike the first feast, Ashariah was announced next. Wearing a filmy purple gown and a thin silver crown, she looked like an entirely different person than the battered Jane Doe Gabby had cared for. As she made a graceful procession around the spiraling stair, she gave Gabby a subtle smile, then nodded to the gathered guests. She took the seat directly to her mother's right. Finally, the queen entered, wearing a stunning gown of pure white. The music rose to a flourish as she arrived at her plush seat at the center of the dais. She did not sit, but instead raised her glass of dark wine.

"May we all remember and honor those who have fought bravely for our great city," she said, her powerful voice ringing through the stone ballroom. "We shall beseech the Skymother's blessing on those who are wounded. May those who fell in defense of our people be carried swiftly to her side, where they will soar through endless skies." She raised her glass. "*T'oldar!*"

The gathered guests raised their glasses in turned and echoed her in unison. "*T'oldar!*"

"Please, sit," the queen said, though she remained standing. "I wish to

358

honor several who exhibited particular bravery in the ambush upon my city. Varazh, Immila, Nalmarah, and Sharukh, please rise and come forth."

Two men and two women in dress uniforms, their armor polished to a mirror shine, rose from the table nearest the dais. They approached the dais in a neat formation. At the queen's gesture, they turned to face the gathered crowd.

"Given the responsibility of guarding the gates, these brave souls faced the wrath of the abominations head-on. Despite injury and exhaustion, they worked tirelessly to bring the Vak and the Edra from the city into the shelters below the citadel. Thousands live because of their actions."

Two servants approached from either side of the dais, carrying small leather bands with silver medallions. In turn, each of the soldiers presented their left arm, allowing the servant to affix the band over their bare arm.

"I also ask Commander Alverin of the City Guard and his lieutenants to come forward," the queen said. Judging by the wide eyes among the guests, Gabby wasn't the only one surprised to see a trio of humans come forward. "At our command, Commander Alverin mobilized his forces to minimize casualties among the people of Farath. In the initial assault, he lost many soldiers, and we mourn them along with our own."

The human man's eyes narrowed slightly, but he bowed politely to the queen. The two men flanking him bowed in turn. Like the Kadirai soldiers, they were each presented with an armband.

"Finally, I would recognize one who has been a friend to the Stoneflight," the queen said. "Her devotion to protecting my daughter equaled that of my trained soldiers, and her keen mind helped us better understand the nature of the enemy as well as to pursue diplomacy. Lady Gabrielle *efana* Maria is *kadizhan*, with the respect and honor that accompanies it."

There was no medal, but it was probably for the best. Gabby's entire body trembled as the entirety of the queen's guests turned toward her and clapped. Some looked skeptical, but others looked impressed.

"Now, please eat," the queen said. "It is right to mourn, but it is also right to celebrate those who live. It is right to celebrate that our great city stands and will not be conquered."

The music began, and the queen finally took her seat. A happy buzz of conversation filled the room as servants brought out the first course and refilled wine glasses.

Gabby's face burned as she turned to Tarek. "What the hell was that?"

"She made you *kadizhan*," he said. His eyes were wide and surprised, which made two of them.

"That doesn't mean anything to me."

"It means...it sort of means a little cousin. She has made you equal to a dragon," he said. He suddenly shook his head, smiling to himself. "She has given you the greatest honor she could possibly give."

"Why?"

"Because you are worthy of it," he said. He leaned over and kissed her forehead, then let his hand rest on her thigh, caressing gently. "I knew it. Now they do too."

Thankfully, the feast was not interrupted by a naked man. As before, they danced, though Tarek politely declined. It was clear that his injuries still caused him a great deal of pain, so he entrusted her to a younger guard who bowed politely and held her hand as if he was afraid he would break it. It was a nice change after being treated like a pariah for the last two weeks.

When the music ended, most of the dancers returned to their seats to enjoy the dessert that had been brought to their tables. The queen caught Gabby's arm as she retreated to her seat.

"Your ma—" Gabby paused, forming the syllables carefully. With a lot of time to kill, she'd been listening and questioning people on bits of language with every chance she got. "*Su'ud redahn.*"

The queen's red lips curved into a genuine smile as she nodded in acknowledgement. "Beautifully said. I rather hope I did not embarrass you with my presentation."

"Not at all. Thank you. It's an honor."

"Of course," the queen said. "I have requested an honor guard to take you home. Should you wish to return in the future, you will be welcome. I hope that the next time you come, you will find my city under more peaceful circumstances."

"I hope so too," Gabby said. "Thank you."

The queen gave her a slow nod, then headed toward the stairs to retire for the evening. Many guests still lingered, with dozens dancing and singing loudly with the musicians. But some had begun to trickle out the double doors, and Gabby was ready to join them. As she looked up at the dais, Tarek stood slowly. A faint wince gave away the pain. "Are you ready?"

"I am very tired," she said, giving him a chance to save face. "We should go."

He nodded gratefully. "I will escort you back. I wouldn't mind a bit of rest myself." Despite his exhaustion, he offered his arm, and she rested her hand lightly on it.

"The queen said you could take me home," Gabby said as they strolled out of the ballroom and up the moonlight corridor.

He shook his head. "I will not accompany you right away. I cannot fly just yet."

She frowned. "Then who?"

"Several of the Adamant Guard will accompany you," he said. "They will be much kinder than on your first trip. They have since secured both sides of the gate, and will ensure that you arrive home safely."

"And what about you?"

"The queen offered to let me return here permanently," he said.

She was silent, her body going cold as they walked in uncomfortable silence. "Well, that's good, right?"

"Is it?"

She paused and looked up at him. His face was unreadable. "Are you messing with me?"

"No," he said mildly. "She made the offer."

They reached her door, and she pushed it open to find candles already burning courtesy of Raszila. A hot bath had been drawn, filling the room with a pleasant heat. Tarek lingered in the doorway. "Well, what did you tell her?"

"I told her no," he said.

Warmth spread in her chest. "Why?"

He eased the door shut behind him. "Well, quite a few reasons," he said. With one hand, he pulled her tight to him, forcing her to look up at him. "There was..." He kissed her, his lips hungry on hers. He broke away for a second. "And I mustn't forget this." He kissed her again, his tongue searching and dancing against hers.

She broke away from him. "You're coming back for me?"

He frowned. "Does this displease you?"

She laughed. "It pleases me very much," she said.

"Good," he said. "I enjoy pleasing you."

"Do you?"

In one single deft motion, he unpinned the carefully arranged fold of fabric over her shoulder and let it fall to the floor. "Indeed," he said as he plucked the fabric away from her and let his hands roam across her breasts. As a pleasant heat crackled across her skin, she reached for the wide belt and unfastened it, tugging at the fine linen shirt. Her hands brushed across the thick bandages across his back, and he sucked a breath sharply through his teeth.

"Sorry," she said, looking up at him.

"*Vazredakh,*" he cursed. He gingerly reached to pull his shirt over his head, but winced at the motion.

"You're still hurt," she murmured.

"Yes," he said. He sighed heavily. "I am afraid I will be of no use."

"Well," she said, pushing him back gently. Limiting her touch to his shoulders, she nudged him back gently until his legs bumped against the edge of her bed. He eased himself down, putting himself on eye level with her. With her heart thumping, she untied the laces on the front of his trousers and slipped her hand downward. "Does this hurt you?" she asked, stroking him gently.

His eyelashes fluttered. "Not at all."

She tugged the snug fabric away to free him, still caressing the delicate skin slowly. This had never been her favorite thing, but Tarek was different. She knelt in front of him, looking at him pointedly. "Then let me take care of you."

CHAPTER THIRTY-NINE

One Month Later

SHE WOULDN'T HAVE THOUGHT it possible, but in the weeks that passed, Gabby found herself missing the breezy stone citadel and the delicious bread Raszila used to bring her in the morning. And it went without saying that she missed the presence of one certain dragon who had warmed her bed and stolen her heart.

As promised, the Adamant Guard had carried her home through the gate. Upon their arrival, the guards on the human world side had taken over and escorted her all the way back to Reno. One of them was a younger man named Shazakh, who looked uncomfortable at the prospect of driving but was pleased to ride in the passenger seat. He was the one who had taken over the responsibility of texting her mother to maintain the illusion of her vacation, and was very proud to show off the Spanish he had learned in the process. Pale-faced, he told her about being sent out for a short leave, only to return and find the posted watch slain. He and one other guard were the only survivors of the attack.

Shazakh and a female guard named Khazelya had alternated checking in on her once each day. As ordered, they'd left her a phone number to call if she saw or sensed anything suspicious.

When she returned to work, it was as if nothing had happened. The nurses asked her about her trip to the cabin, then filled her in on their own trip to the beach. In the aftermath of the attack on the hospital, much of the regular staff had taken vacation time to clear their heads. No one seemed to think much of her absence.

And whatever Shazakh had told her mother, it had worked. When Gabby called her upon returning home, her mother had been bubbling over with excitement to actually hear her voice. Maria had wanted to call, but she knew Gabby wanted some time away and was happy to get her nightly text confirming that she was well. After visiting home and letting her mother cook everything she felt Gabby needed to fatten up, all was well in the Rojas family.

Things had returned to factory settings, which meant she was alone again. Each evening, Shazakh or Khazelya knocked politely on the door, wearing the oversized bathrobe she now kept on her back patio for them. If she'd ordered dinner out, Khazelya was always ready to eat, but as soon as the Kadirai woman had polished off two-thirds of the food and filled her in on the progress of the rebuilding at the gates, she said her goodbyes and returned to her post. Each night, Gabby found herself sitting on the patio, looking up at the sky for Tarek's graceful silhouette.

She worried that he had changed his mind, deciding instead to stay home in Ascavar. And she could hardly blame him. That was where he'd lived most of his life, and his people were there. But that didn't mean she had to like it. It had meant something that he chose her, and she fervently hoped she wasn't being a fool by hoping he would still want her.

She started to wonder if the whole thing was a vivid dream, until an incident about two weeks after her return. Still half-asleep, she knocked a coffee cup out of the cabinet and onto her foot, where it shattered. After unleashing a string of profanity in English, Spanish, and what was probably badly mangled Kadirai, she bent over to find a puddle of blood on the floor and a shard of patterned ceramic sticking out of her badly bruised foot. After cleaning it thoroughly, she took some ibuprofen and headed to work. The rush of the day distracted her, and she didn't check it again until coming home. But when she peeled off the white gauze, the cut was closed. The skin around it was the healthy pink of a cleanly healed wound. The dark bruise was almost gone. It was impossible, but she had just come from the land of impossible.

When Shazakh arrived to check on her that evening, she showed him her foot and asked what it meant. His amber eyes narrowed as he inspected it. "This is strange," he said.

"You think? What does it mean?"

He shrugged. "I don't know. I would think this would be a good thing. Why are you concerned?"

"Because this isn't what humans do," she said. "Is this because I was in Ascavar? Is there something in the water?"

He threw his hands up. "Miss Gabrielle, I assure you that I am not hiding anything. I do not know. I would simply be thankful that you are much more durable than before."

Her mind didn't want to let go of it that easily. Her scientific side wanted to know the long-term implications. But neither of her guardians knew the answers, and the one person who might was nowhere to be found.

Nearly a month after returning home, she was reviewing patient charts at the end of her shift when her pocket buzzed. Signing the top chart with her right hand, she took out the phone with her left and scanned it.

Come outside and see me.

Her heart leaped into her throat. With a smile pulling at her lips, she quickly finished her paperwork, then scanned it again for errors. Satisfied with her work, she handed it off and hurried out the main doors to the hospital.

It was already evening, with deep blue spreading across the sky like the tide darkening sand. Cool air nipped at her face as she tugged the lab coat tighter around herself.

"I'm looking for a doctor," a familiar voice rumbled.

She turned to see Tarek step out from behind a pillar. Judging by the shirt tails hanging out of his pants and the unlaced shoes, he'd just changed back into his human form and yanked on clothes to keep from being seen naked. She ignored his disarray and ran toward him. He caught her midway, circling strong arms around her waist and lifting her up to eye level. "You're in luck. I'm a doctor. And I'm available."

"I have this terrible pain," he said.

"Is it here?" she asked, kissing his lips hungrily. His grasp tightened, pressing her tight to his broad chest as he deepened the kiss, stealing her breath.

"That's much better," he said when he finally broke away. "But I'm afraid it's much more serious than that."

"Perhaps we should go back to my home office and take a look."

The evening left her pleasantly exhausted as Tarek insisted on making up for lost time. When she woke from a dreamy sleep, the sun was coming up, painting long stripes across her bedroom. Tarek still slept, his chest rising gently as he dozed. His injuries had healed, leaving a number of thin white scars across his chest and back.

She carefully slipped out of bed, put on a robe, and crept downstairs to the kitchen to make breakfast. Though she was quiet, footsteps creaked overhead a few minutes after she started the coffee. The slow rhythm quickened as he thundered down the stairs.

She turned with a bagel in hand as Tarek rushed into the kitchen, his eyes wide. "You must be hungry."

"You were gone when I woke up," he said. "I was worried."

She laughed. "I was hungry." She handed him the bagel and put another in the toaster. After examining it, he split it and handed half back to her.

"It would not be proper for me to eat while you are hungry," he said. He waited for her to take a bite before he ate anything.

"Tarek, something strange happened while you were gone," she said, once he finally began to eat. He looked over the edge of the bagel, his dark eyebrows arched. He nodded to her. "I cut my foot, but it healed almost overnight." Leaning on the counter for balance, she held up her foot. A pleasant tingle arced up her leg as he set aside his breakfast and held her foot lightly.

He hesitated. "A number of the Vak in Farath were struck by the white dragon, just like you were. Before I left, Counselor Eszen told me that some of them had experienced strange symptoms. He told me he would be very interested to find out what effect it had on you," he said, raising his gaze to meet hers. "Particularly since you spent so much time by my side in the healing gardens."

"What effect it had on me? What does that mean?"

He released her foot and shrugged slightly. "Pure magic flows among the Bones. You cannot have stayed there so long with no effect."

"I'm not a dragon now, am I?"

He laughed. "No, I'm afraid not, *kadizhan*. But I am not sure you are entirely human anymore, either," he said. "Time will tell. I rather like the idea of you not being so delicate."

"I wasn't delicate to begin with, buddy," she said, pointing at him. "And how are you so casual about me not being human? This is a big deal."

"Time will tell," he said again. "I am not human, either. You seem to like me just fine."

"I do," she admitted.

He grinned and lightly grabbed her wrist, pulling her toward him. With her hips resting against his, he leaned back so he could look down at her with amusement glinting in his eyes. "Whatever you may be, there is no magic in this universe that would alter who you are. And that is the woman I love."

"Well, when you put it like that..." she said. He tipped up her chin and kissed her lips lightly. When he broke away, she said "So are you staying?"

"Here?"

"Well, in this world," she said. "When you didn't come back, I wondered if you changed your mind."

"Halmerah did try to convince me again, but I told her I was pleased with my decision. It was only in the last few days I was finally able to transform again and maintain it. Now that I am whole, I am taking over command at the Drakemont tomorrow."

"So what happens to us?"

He hesitated, resting his large hands on her shoulders. "Gabrielle, you are proof that the universe is good, and that the Skymother still bestows her blessings on us. I am undeserving, but it would be the greatest honor of my life to be yours. If you would have me."

Her stomach danced with nerves. The what-ifs crowded her mind, but for once Logical Gabby took a backseat and said *go for it*. She didn't know what it would mean to be in love with a dragon, especially one whose world was at war. She didn't know if they would ever have a normal life, but she knew this. She loved him, and that was all the certainty she needed. "I would have you," she said. "And I would be yours."

"Always?"

"Always."

KADIRAI GLOSSARY

NAMING

MATRONYMICS

In some cultures, children are given names that designate them as the son or daughter of one of their parents. The Stoneflight, which is Tarek's flight, names their children in relation to the mother. For instance, Tarek's given name is Tarek *efan* Izera, which means "Tarek, son of Izera." (Izera being his mother.)

- *(n)efan(a)* – "son/daughter of"

- Based on the ending sounds of the child's name and the beginning sounds of the mother's name, you will modify *efan*. If your name ends in a vowel such as "Lara," you will add the *n* at the beginning. If your mother's name starts with a consonant, you will add an *a*. This is to make the words flow more naturally.

- Councilor Eszen, one of the queen's advisors, has the name "Eszen *efana* Shundilzin." His mother's name begins with a consonant sound, so he would use *efana* to flow.

HONORIFICS/SUFFIXES

- *-(t)ahn*: an affectionate suffix; used with someone you know well and are familiar with. For instance, someone who is a dear friend, or a child. You would never use this to someone considered to be of a higher social ranking unless you had a very close relationship with them already. As with the matronymic, the beginning sound can change depending on the last sound of the name. Ashariah, the princess, would be "Ashariah-tahn," but Tarek would be "Tarek-ahn."

- *Su'ud redahn*: a Stoneflight title that refers to royalty; does not translate exactly, but it is the Kadirai equivalent of saying "Your Majesty" to the queen

FLIGHTS AND LOCATIONS

The Kadirai of Ascavar are divided into different "flights," or clans. Each has its own lands and traditions, although they do speak a common language with small variations.

LANDS

- *Ascavar:* the world of the dragonflights; is a parallel world to ours connected by portals
- *Eldavar:* refers to the human world
- *–dahl:* refers to the land or country ruled by a flight
- *Vakhdahl:* the lands of the Stoneflight
- *Mardahl:* the lands of the Ironflight

FLIGHTS

- *Zheranar:* the Stoneflight
- *Ordahnar:* the Ironflight

PEOPLE

Though the first few books concentrate on the Kadirai, there are other groups in Ascavar.

- *Edra:* a race of shapeshifters who can appear in human form or an animal form. They refer to themselves as "having the spirit of ___" whatever their other form is. They are not as powerful as the Kadirai, but they are numerous in Ascavar.
- *Vak:* the nonmagical people of Ascavar. Some use the term to refer to humans in either world, but the term technically refers to those in Ascavar.

- *kuthra:* mother
- *far-serahl:* a deep, abiding relationship; not necessarily lovers but one that is more meaningful than regular friendship
- *om-serahl:* a platonic friend
- *kadizhan:* "little cousin" – a title that grants honorary status as a dragon, given to outsiders who have earned respect and honor
- *thodar:* healer

PHRASES

Take caution! Some of these phrases are very rude, so don't say them to a dragon you just met!

GENERAL

- *kaare:* look! (an order/command)
- *inan tam?:* who are you?
- *harekh vahl:* we're done
- *takh n'adan:* let's go!
- *dath sequa:* an honorable greeting, used among the Stoneflight when soldiers greet each other
- *Nalak halar! (Nalak halar anan!)* a proclamation among the Ironflight, a sign of respect. *Nalak halar* roughly means "We are chosen by the flame." The appropriate response is *nalak halar anan!* which is an agreement and approval. Often used in diplomatic settings as a way to start conversation politely.

NAUGHTIER WORDS

- *Vezhare:* shut up (very rude)
- *t'haran vo shedh:* doesn't translate; roughly means "people who roll in the mud." It refers to Kadirai who choose to consort with the Vak. Very derogatory.

- *t'haran dan keth:* people with no honor, undeserving of respect; this is very insulting. One should not use this in polite conversation.
- *Vazredakh:* a fairly mild curse, roughly equivalent to "son of a bitch." Somewhat rude, but won't start a fight at dinner.

MISCELLANEOUS

- *al-hatari:* life energy; a concept sort of like qi in which energy flows through and around all living things
- *hanassa:* a magical amulet with the power of translation between different languages

WHAT NOW?

I hope you enjoyed your adventure into the world of Ascavar. If you did, here's some next steps!

- Write a quick review and tell folks you loved this book! Reviews help other readers find books they'll love!

- If you haven't read it yet, download the free prequel novella, *Midnight Flight*. This short tells the story of young Shazakh, and why he's so tired when keeping watch at the Gate. You can find it by heading over to my website!

- Subscribe to my mailing list to receive updates about new releases, giveaways, and other awesome news!

You can find the novella and my mailing list information on my website at

WWW.JDMONROE.COM

Of course, I'd love to hear from you on social media! You can find me on Facebook, Twitter, Instagram, Pinterest, and my website.

Facebook: www.facebook.com/writerjdmonroe
Twitter: @writerjdmonroe
Instagram: @writermonroe
Pinterest: @writermonroe
Website: www.jdmonroe.com

ACKNOWLEDGEMENTS

Writing may seem like a lonely business, but it takes more of a community than most people realize.

Thanks to…

The Tuesday Sushi Club – Hildie and Olivia, my writer BFFs – for encouragement, tough love, a never-ending wellspring of wisdom, and stickers, because we all need a sticker once in a while.

Tera Cuskaden – for great editing and encouragement.

Gayla – for incredible attention to detail and encouragement to shape this story up!

Nadine – for taking a chance at something new and knocking it out of the park.

Tambra – for being a cheerleader.

Dad – for always believing that I can, and making sure I believe it too.

Mom – for always being my biggest fan.

ABOUT THE AUTHOR

J.D. Monroe is a Georgia-based author with a love for all things paranormal, magical, and downright fantastical. She has not given up on the dream of riding a dragon someday. She has written a number of paranormal and fantasy novels for both young adults and adults.

Printed in Poland
by Amazon Fulfillment
Poland Sp. z o.o., Wrocław